THE SKY PEOPLE

THE SKY PEOPLE

S. M. Stirling

 A Tom Doherty Associates Book
New York

THE SKY PEOPLE

Copyright © 2006 by S. M. Stirling

This book is printed on acid-free paper.

A Tor Book
Published by Tom Doherty Associates, LLC
175 Fifth Avenue
New York, NY 10010

www.tor.com

Tor® is a registered trademark of Tom Doherty Associates, LLC.

Library of Congress Cataloging-in-Publication Data

Stirling, S. M.
    The sky people / S. M. Stirling.—1st ed.
      p. cm.
    ISBN-13: 978-0-765-31488-8
    ISBN-10: 0-765-31488-6 (acid-free paper)
    "A Tom Doherty Associates Book."
    1. Space colonies—Fiction. 2. Life on other planets—Fiction. 3. Space warfare—
Fiction. 4. Venus (Planet)—Fiction. I. Title.
PS3569.T543S59 2006
813'.54—dc22

                                                                    2006005727

Printed in the United States of America

0 9 8 7 6 5 4 3 2

TO JANET, FOREVER

ACKNOWLEDGMENTS

To Melinda Snodgrass, Daniel Abraham, Sally Gwylan, Emily Mah, Yvonne Coats, Terry England, George R. R. Martin, Walter Jon Williams, Yvonne Coats, and Ian Tregellis of Critical Mass for help and advice.

To Steve Brady for more help, on entomology this time.

Thanks to Edgar Rice Burroughs, Leigh Brackett, Otis Adelbert Kline, Leinster, Heinlein, and all the other great pulpsters for gracing my childhood with John Carter, Northwest Smith, "Wrong Way" Carson of Venus, and all the heroes gifted with a better solar system than the one we turned out to inhabit. From the jungles of Venus and the Grand Canal of Marsopolis, I salute you!

All mistakes, infelicities, and errors are of course my own.

PROLOGUE

Venus
June 14, 1962

The sun rose in the west.

Deera of the Cloud Mountain People ran as she had through the short hours of darkness, without hope and without much fear. The mild, warm air of the midlands made the sweat on her face and flanks feel almost cool as it dried, and the tall grass beat against her thighs as her long legs scissored endlessly. The morning sun was still low, casting the seven runners' shadows before them and turning the clouds to the color of raw gold. They had trotted through the short, bright summer night and would run on into the long span of daylight, until the great yellow globe of Kru sank in the east . . . if they lived that long, which was unlikely.

She would run until she could run no more. Then the Wergu would catch them, and they would fight, and they would die. If they were fortunate, they would die quickly; her warriors had orders to make sure of that for her. There had been some slight chance that they would reach the foothills before the beastmen caught up with them, being longer-limbed, but their foes had gained too quickly for that to seem likely. The Cloud Mountain party had been tired from a long journey when the ambush struck, and those who broke away had not had time to snatch up more than their weapons, nor had they been able to build enough of a lead to hide their trail. Now hunger gnawed at them as well as weariness, and they had had no time to do anything but scoop up water in their hands as they forded pools or creeks. The Wergu were fresh, with gourds of water at their belts and dried meat in their pouches to eat as they pursued.

Then her mate, Jaran, broke the deep rhythm of his breath, sniffing deeply.

"What is it, my love?" Deera said. "What do you scent?"

Before he could answer, she smelled it herself, and spoke: "Fire!"

The land before the dozen-strong war party was gently rolling, covered in long green grass starred with flowers crimson and white, with copses of trees along the occasional small streams. They passed small herds of *tharg* and *churr*, but luckily nothing bigger, and most animals-of-fur avoided men. Not longtooths or great-wolves or crescent-horns, but there weren't any of those in sight, either. Then they saw the thread of smoke rising skyward, and saw animals and fliers heading away. Men and beastmen used fire . . . or it might be wildfire from a lightning strike, deadly in grassland country if it spread.

"We go there," Deera said, pointing; the sunlight broke off the bright bronze of her spearhead.

She alone of their party carried metal weapons, the spear and the knife at her belt; their trading mission to the coastal cities hadn't reached its goal before the Wergu found them.

"That is where the streak-of-light pointed," her mate said doubtfully. "A bad omen."

"It is a new-thing. If we go on with no new-thing, the beastmen will crack our bones for marrow before the sun sets. If it is not a new-thing we can use, we cannot be killed any more surely."

Their bare callused feet splashed through the creek, and they eeled through the brush and trees on either side. Fliers exploded from the boughs, *eeeking* indignantly, and a hawk pounced from the sky to harvest them, its wings as broad as a man's spread arms.

Then the tribesmen stopped. A few moaned aloud in fear.

Deera's eyes went wide in wonder. For a long moment the thing in the broad meadow ahead was so strange that her eyes slid away from its shape, unable to comprehend.

Then there was a feeling like a *click* behind her brow, and she saw. It was twice the height of a tall man, and stood on three long, spidery legs amid a circle of burnt grass. The fire beneath was still working its way outward, slow and sullen in the wet growth of spring. The body above was a cone in shape, the bottom blackened and with a smaller cone protruding from it; even at two hundred yards she could feel the heat. Holes like little caves or the windows of a hut opened in the upper body, and movement there brought a gasp from her people. The scent of burning was rank, and she coughed a little at the smoke. Slowly, mastering the fear that made her skin glisten with fresh sweat—was she not the heir to the Cave Master, initiate of the Mystery?—she approached and prodded the skin of the . . . thing with the tip of her spear. There was a hollow *clunk*.

"It is metal!" she said. "But not bronze or copper or tin or gold or silver!"

Suddenly her mate pushed her between the shoulder blades. She looked around in surprise.

"Go!" Jaran said with fierce hope in his eyes. "The Wergu will fear this thing of magic. We will fight them here. If we kill many, they will not pursue beyond it. Go! Run for the mountains!"

Agony spiked through her despair as he grounded the butt of his spear and took his blowgun from the sling across his back, reaching for a dart from his belt.

"I cannot leave you!"

"You are our people's hope, and there is no time for talk. Go. Go *now*!"

Weeping, Deera obeyed.

Baikonur Cosmodrome, Kazakhstan, USSR
June 14, 1962

"*Bozhemoi!*" the technician whispered.

The grainy image flickered on the video monitors. It was in

color, for no expense had been spared. The smoke of landing had cleared, and the scientists behind him exclaimed sharply as the camera deployed and panned across a meadow scarred by fire. The audio pickups were functioning as well; there was a crackling of burning grass, the hiss of the wind, unintelligible cheeps and croaks.

"That is *grass*," one of the biologists said, slurping at a glass of hot, sweet tea from the samovar in the corner. The scent of it was strong in the room, along with the scorched-insulation-and-metal smell of tube-driven electronics. "And I would swear some sort of field-poppy."

"Parallel development under environmental influence," another, older academician said, as the recording reels whirred. "Perhaps Comrade Lysenko was right after all!"

Both fell silent as something flicked by the video pickup. The technician kept his hands off the controls. The long feedback cycle to the probe's robot mothercraft orbiting around Venus and from there to the surface and back made it impossible to track moving objects. A beaked head filled the pickup, a beak with fangs, blurred by the close-up. A tongue flicked within as the whatever-it-was gnawed at the lens and then fluttered off. It had teeth and feathered wings with claws on the forward edge. . . . Then sky showed again, white with only a tint of blue, and full of flying creatures too distant to identify. The technician looked at some trees for reference, and his eyes widened again as he realized how large some of the fliers must be.

"Are the *Yanki* getting any of this?" a KGB bigwig asked unhappily.

"I'm afraid so, Comrade General," the chief academician said. "There's no way to narrowcast a beam over interplanetary distances. Just as we will intercept their Martian probe's broadcasts when it lands next month. That is why it was decided to rebroadcast internally as well."

The security officer opened his mouth to respond, then closed it again. This time *he* whispered a curse: "*Chto za chert?*" Even the most ideologically vigilant could be forgiven a *What the devil!* at what they saw next as a half-dozen figures pushed through the brush and stood staring at the probe.

They were men—human males, tall and fair. The one who approached and tentatively prodded at the lander with the point of her spear was a woman. Oh, it was no race that Earth had ever born; that combination of umber skin, white-blond hair, tilted, light eyes, snub nose, and full lips . . . perhaps somewhere in the Urals you might find a similar mix, but the overall impression was exotic. So was the garb: loincloths and halter of scaly leather, jewelry of raw gold nuggets and carved fangs. The head of the woman's spear looked like bronze; those of her five male companions were obsidian, pressure-flaked to an almost metallic finish. All were tall and rangy, moving with a loose economy of motion like hunting wolves.

Utter silence fell. It lasted through the woman's flight, and the brief, savage battle with a larger band of newcomers that followed—brutish thickset figures who seemed almost a different species. When that was over one of the victors approached the camera, his squat, massive naked body painted in crude patterns and splashed with blood, some of it his own; more blood and brains dripped from the knobkerrie he carried in one hand.

At last the face filled the pickup. It was covered in what was either hair or a sparse beard, the prognathous, thin-lipped mouth thrusting forward underneath a huge blobby nose, the forehead slanting back from brow ridges like a shelf of bone, the long skull ending in a bun at the rear. Feathers stood in a topknot of reddish-brown hair. Suddenly the brutish figure screamed, a long snarling wail that showed a gaping mouth full of square tombstone teeth. The ball-headed club swung and the video signal vanished in static; the microphones picked up crashing and rending sounds for an instant more.

"A Neanderthal," one of the scientists said. "*Nu ni huy sebe!* What the *fuck?*"

CHAPTER ONE

Encyclopedia Britannica, 16th Edition
University of Chicago Press, 1988

VENUS: Parameters

ORBIT: 0.723 AU

ORBITAL PERIOD: 224.7 days

ROTATION: 30hrs. 6mins. (retrograde)

MASS: 0.815 × Earth

AVERAGE DENSITY: 5.2 g/cc

SURFACE GRAVITY: 0.91 × Earth

DIAMETER: 7,520 miles (equatorial; 94.7% × Earth)

SURFACE: land 20%, water 80%

ATMOSPHERIC COMPOSITION:

NITROGEN	76.2%
OXYGEN	22.7%
CARBON DIOXIDE	0.088%

TRACE ELEMENTS: Argon, Neon, Helium, Krypton, Hydrogen

ATMOSPHERIC PRESSURE: 17.7 psi average at sea level

Venus differs from Earth, its sister planet, primarily in its slightly smaller size and slightly lower average density, as well as the lack of a moon or satellite, and its retrograde (clockwise) rotation. The composition of the atmosphere is closely similar to that of Earth, the main differences being the higher percentage of oxygen and the somewhat greater mass and density of the atmosphere as a whole.

Average temperatures on Venus are roughly 10 degrees Celsius higher than those on Earth, due to greater solar energy input, moderated by the reflective properties of the high cloud layer; isotope analysis suggests that these temperatures are similar to those on Earth in the Upper Cretaceous period, at which time Earth, like Venus today, had no polar ice caps.

Most of Venus' land area of approximately 40,000,000 sq. miles is concentrated in the Arctic supercontinent of Gagarin, roughly the size of Eurasia, and the Antarctic continent of Lobachevsky, approximately the size of Africa. Chains of islands constitute most of the remaining land surface, ranging in size from tiny atolls to nearly half a million square miles . . .

Venus, Gagarin Continent—Jamestown Extraterritorial Zone 1988

Unnnngg-OOOK!

One of the ceratopsians in the spaceport draught team raised its beaked, bony head and bellowed, stunningly loud, as the team was led around to be hitched to the newly arrived rocket-plane. The supersonic *crack* of the upper stage's first pass over the dirt runways at high altitude had spooked them a little, but they were used to the size and heat of the orbiters by now.

Some of the new arrivals from Earth filing carefully down the gangway from the rocket-plane's passenger door started at the cry. When one of the giant reptiles cut loose it sounded a little like the world's largest parrot; the beasts were massive six-ton quadrupeds with columnar legs, eight feet at the shoulder and higher at their hips, twenty-five feet long from snout to the tip of the thick tail, and they had lungs and vocal cords to match their size. The long purple tongue within the beak worked as the beast called, and it shook its shield—the massive bony plate that sheathed its head and flared out behind to cover the neck. The shield was a deep bluish-gray, the pebbled hide green-brown above, with a stripe of yellow along each flank marking off the finer cream-colored skin of the belly.

Then it added the rank, musky scent of a massive dinosaurian dung-dump to the scorched ceramic odor of the orbital lander's heat-shield.

Welcome to Venus, Marc Vitrac thought, as the score or so of new base personnel and the six spaceship crew gathered at the foot of the ladder. *I'm glad it waited until the harness was hitched. That could have landed on my feet if it had happened while we were getting things fastened.*

He switched his heavy rifle so that it rested in the crook of his left arm—it was a scope-sighted bolt-action piece with a thumbhole stock and chambered for a heavy big-game round, 9×70 mm Magnum. Then he waved his right arm forward and called:

"Take it away, Sally!"

"Get going, you brainless lumps!" the slender ash-blond woman shouted from her seat in a saddle high on the shoulders of the left-hand beast.

That was purely to relieve her feelings. Nobody really liked the dim-witted, bad-tempered dinosaurs, useful though they were. The joystick in her hand was the real control; she shoved it forward, and the unit relayed its signals to the receivers on each beast's forehead, hidden under hemispheres of tough plastic. That triggered current through the implants running down through skulls and into the motor ganglions and pleasure-pain centers of their tiny brains. The two ceratopsians leaned into their harness, and the yard-thick hauling cable of braided dinosaur hide came taut with a snap. After a moment's motionless straining, the rocket stage lurched into motion and trundled down the long strip of reddish dirt towards the hangars and cranes where it would be mated with the big dart-shaped booster and made ready for its next lift to orbit.

It was a *lot* cheaper to ship electronic controller units from Earth than tractors and bulldozers, not to mention the non-existent infrastructure of fuel and spare parts. All you needed to collect ceratopsians was a heavy-duty trank gun; they'd eat anything that grew, including the trunks of oak trees, and they lived indefinitely unless something killed them.

Marc wiped his face on the sleeve of his jacket as the rocket-plane left, trailing dust, taking with it the radiant heat still throbbing out of its ceramic underbelly and a stink of burnt kerosene. The coastal air of Gagarin flowed in instead, the iodine scent of the sea half a mile northward, and smells of vegetation and animals not quite Earthly. The sun was a little bigger in the sky than it would be on the third rock from the sun, partly because they *were* closer to it, and partly from the light white haze that never really cleared from the blue arch above. Otherwise, apart from the weird fauna—and the size of the bugs—it might have been a spring day in California, temperature in the seventies and air fairly dry, yellow flowers studding a rolling plain of waist-high grass around them, just turning from rainy-season green to champagne color. Already some of the birds and fliers scared off by the rocket-plane's descent were winging back in. Something with iridescent blue-and-yellow feathers, a twelve-foot wingspan, and a beak full of teeth screeched at him as it passed, snapping at dragonflies six inches across.

Okay.

Most of the *Carson*'s six-person crew were here as well, looking a little more relieved than usual: There had been some sort of problem with the main fission reactor this time, just after the final insertion burn. The Aerospace Force kept two nuclear-boost ships on the run between Venus and Earth, the *Carson* and the *Susan Constant*.

The little clump of new fish in their blue Aerospace Force overalls stood at the base of the wheeled gangway, woozy even in Venus' ninety-percent gravity after three months of zero-G despite all that exercise *en route* could do. At least they were used to the denser air and higher oxygen, since the passenger ships adjusted their own gradually on the trip. Some of them were looking a little stunned; others were grinning ear to ear. He knew exactly what they were thinking, and his lips turned up as well—the thrill wasn't gone for him yet, not by a long shot:

Yeah, I've finally made it! All the tests and psych tests and physical tests and trials and qualifications and all the millions who started out on the selections and I was the one who made it!

One young black woman with civilian-specialist shoulder-flashes—she looked to be a couple of years short of Marc's twenty-five—bent down and gently touched the Venusian soil; when she straightened, a look of astonished delight was on her face. He met her eye and winked; on *his* first day he'd gone down flat and kissed the dirt.

"Welcome to Venus in general and the Jamestown Extraterritorial Zone in particular, folks! I'm Lieutenant Marc Vitrac, USASF, and one of the Ranger squad here, which means specimen-collector, liaison with the locals, and general dogsbody. We've got a howdah laid on. I know three months in zero-G makes you feel like a boiled noodle when you get back dirtside."

A murmur of "no problem, feeling fine" and shaking of heads: You had to be nearly Olympic caliber physically as well as qualified in two or three degree-equivalents even to get onto the short list for Venus. All of them were probably proud of it, and they were all aggressive self-starters by definition. He shrugged mentally; he'd done exactly the same thing when he arrived, and had been puffing by the time he made it to the reception hall. The plain fact of the matter was that it took weeks to months of carefully phased acclimatizing before you got full function back. That was why they used the more expensive nuclear-rocket craft for shipping people between planets, instead of the cheap but slow solar-sail freighters. A big nuclear booster could get you here in a hundred and twenty days, give or take, depending on orbital positions—the robot freighters took three or four times that long, and nobody could stand a year and a half without gravity, not to mention the risk of solar flares *en route*.

Instead of arguing, he turned to the four spaceport laborers. "*ImiTaWok s'wee, tob*," he said in the tongue of Kartahown: *Get it back to the building, guys.*

The locals grabbed the shamboo-framed wheeled staircase and began dragging it off after the rocket-plane. The newcomers spared a few startled glances at them: You had to look fairly closely to see that they weren't common garden-variety Caucasoid Earthlings. People around here tended to medium-tall height, olive coloring, and mostly brown or black hair, with a minority of blonds and a smaller one of redheads; only the sharply triangular faces and hooked noses were even a little out of the ordinary. The four workers were shaved and barbered Terran-style and dressed in ordinary-for-Jamestown pants and shirts of parachute cloth; they couldn't be told from Earthlings until they spoke. Put Marc Vitrac into an off-the-right-shoulder tunic, grow his hair long and tie it in a knot on the left side of his head, and give him a bronze sword, and he'd fit right in on this coast.

"Yeah, those guys are from Kartahown," he said, pointing east along the coast. The Bronze Age city-state, which was Venus' highest civilization, was about forty miles thataway. "Some of them have picked up English, too, since they moved up this way looking for work."

Including some escaped slaves we're sheltering from people who'd like to beat them to death with bronze-tipped scourges, but let's not get into that right now.

"That's quick," said the oldest of the newcomers, in his midthirties and with a bird colonel's insignia. "We've only been here six years, and the base was pretty small for most of that period."

"Well, we're even more exotic and interesting to them than they are to us, sir," Vitrac said. "And by local standards, we're wizards and richer than God. A steel knife or a couple of yards of parachute fabric is real money here."

Plus we don't *beat people to death with bronze-tipped scourges.*

"And if you'll all follow me . . ."

He led them off, slowly, across the cropped grass near the landing strip; there were two in an X-shaped combination, each several thousand yards long. Another ceratopsian stood waiting patiently; in fact, it was blissed out by a trickle charge to the pleasure center, drooling slightly onto the grass. On its back rested a twenty-foot howdah made of laminated shamboo, with a shaped and padded underside and two broad leather girths running under the dinosaur's belly to hold it on. The seats were stepped like those in a movie theater to accommodate the slope of the animal's back from the high point over its hips. Marc stood by the short folding ladder at the right foreleg, once or twice discreetly helping a passenger with his free hand.

More than one gave the bigger-than-elephantine beast a dubious look; its steady breathing was a machinelike *whoosh* . . . *whoosh* . . . and the heavy reptile stink was strong, like a neglected cage full of iguanas at a pet shop. The massive columnar legs were taller than a big man, too.

When everyone was settled Marc folded up the ladder, put his foot on the ceratopsian's knee, grabbed the edge of the bony shield, and vaulted into the front seat to take up the controls. Once you got your muscle tone back, the combination of lower gravity and extra oxygen made you hell on wheels physically—and they'd all been distinctly above-average specimens to begin with.

"Fasten your seat belts, please," he said.

And keep your barf-bags handy. This thing sways like a sonofabitch.

Unlike many, he didn't bother to say *git* or the equivalent, just pushed the control forward a notch and rotated the joystick. The beast gave a low coughing grunt and then a wince-inducing screech of complaint as it came out of a daze of quasi-reptilian ecstasy and turned in place before pacing forward; the weight of howdah and passengers wasn't really noticeable to something that weighed about as much as a big dump truck, and everyone clutched the grab-bars. The strings of silver bells around the edges of the howdah chimed in chorus at the first lurch, then settled down into a *ting-ting-ting-ting* beneath the heavy thud of footfalls as the animal paced along. It wasn't doing more than walk, but each stride covered a lot of ground.

Marc did start a little as the black woman slid into the front seat beside him. He didn't think it was his own overwhelming attractiveness; he was a slim, wiry man of medium height for Jamestown—five-ten—built like a gymnast or track-and-field star, which he'd been, with a pleasant open face, olive skin, and dark green eyes. His black hair was cropped short. She just seemed exuberantly happy to be on Venus, and less returning-gravity-whipped by the voyage than most of the newcomers. And of course she was less constrained than someone in the Aerospace Force, although military formality was distinctly low-key here. For one thing, there was scarcely anyone below commissioned rank. A lieutenant was on the bottom of the heap.

She touched the plank of the seat as if seeking reassurance in the rough, slightly splintery surface.

"I like the bells," she said.

"Me too," he replied. "It's mostly to warn people out of the way. These things aren't what you'd call maneuverable, even Iced."

"Iced?"

"Ah, Jamestown slang. Internal Control Device: I-C-D, and so-Iced."

"You've been here awhile, right, Lieutenant?" she asked.

"*Weh,*" he agreed cheerfully in the dialect of his childhood.

He was no more immune than most young men to attention from a good-looking woman, and on Venus you had the added pleasure of knowing she was in the top of the bell curve for brains and general ability, too. He went on:

"More than a year now, Venus year, that is. Mostly in construction, maintenance, supply, but just recently we've had more time for real exploring and research—fascinating stuff. What we're learning is going to shake the Earth. And a lieutenant is small potatoes here, ah, Miss . . ."

"Cynthia Whitlock, Lieutenant," she said, and held out a hand. "Sorry, I didn't catch your name—I was paying more attention to the surroundings than the spiel!"

"Marc Vitrac. Ethnology and linguistics, power systems and lighter-than-air pilot."

"Geology, minors in paleontology and information systems. And . . . *imiKartahownai 'n dus-jas?*" she asked.

She had a pretty good accent for someone working from recordings rather than talking to native speakers. The hand that gripped his was firm and strong and dry, slender and long-fingered; shaking it meant he had to juggle the rifle he was holding in the crook of his other arm.

"Yeah, I've picked up a fair amount of Kartahownian. It's damned useful here; a lot of people along the coast speak it, sort of a lingua franca. Some of them have acquired a bit of English over in the town, too. They've got some very smart people there—it doesn't pay to underestimate them."

She tilted her head to one side. "Louisiana?" she said.

"Evangeline, eh, she was my *mawmaw,*" he said, exaggerating the Cajun lilt for a moment. "Bayou born and bred. Grand Isle."

"*Harlem* born and bred," she replied, with only a trace of it in her General American.

Then her brows went up slightly as he took a quick glance skyward and started to raise the rifle. "Nope," he said, lowering the weapon. "He's not going for us. Guess we look too much like a 'saur."

When he'd relaxed, she went on, indicating the rifle with a glance, "That *cannon* is a bird-gun?"

"*Mais*, for those things, *weh*, certainly," he said, turning a thumb upward.

He was unsurprised she knew her way around firearms, even though she was a civilian. The selection program tended to pick intellectuals who were also outdoors types or vice versa. Then he raised his voice a little so the rest of the score of passengers could hear, and it took on a slight tour-guide tone. One that he realized was based on something he'd heard an uncle use when he conducted tours of the bayous in his swamp boat, throwing marshmallows to the quasi-tame gators for the tourists.

"Y'all might want to take a gander skyward. First big Quetza of the season, and they're quite a sight."

Most of the passengers did look up. He heard gasps. It was one thing to watch a video of a flying creature with a wingspan of eighty feet, but another to see one with your naked eye. Even back in the Cretaceous, nothing that size could have flown on Earth, but the gravity was a bit lower here, and the air wasn't just thicker but also had more oxygen per unit to power flight muscles. This Quetza was coming in low, coasting down from the inland cliffs where they nested, banking to avoid the built-up area of Jamestown, and then sweeping back seaward.

The thin long-headed body was bigger than a man's and roughly the same shape, but it was tiny between the vast leathery expanses of wing that caught the thermals; the eyes in its long, narrow-beaked head were huge and yellow and it turned one of them towards the wagon as it went by overhead. Then the wings half-folded, and the great beast came down on the other side of the runways like an arching thunderbolt of brown hide and white-and-scarlet body-fuzz and yellow jaws. Those were slender, like a great pickaxe beak, balanced by a bony crest behind, and full of jagged teeth.

"Ah, shit, it's going for that herd of *churr*, probably after a *bebette*. Sorry, people—I'm going to have to take a shot. Fire in the hole!"

It was the claws on the ends of the long legs that struck first, in a puff of dust. More dust fountained into the air as the giant wings flogged the air, and something struggled beneath them as the thirty-odd adults and younglings in the herd spattered like water on a waxed floor, bawling and shrieking in terror. The week-old *churr* colt was the size of a medium pig except for the longer legs, and it squealed like one. *Churr* were what the locals used instead of horses; Venus didn't have any equivalent of equines, as far as they knew. The shaggy, social omnivores were actually more like bears, and still more like horse-sized dogs with the digestive systems of hogs.

The pterodactyl worked for height, looked down at the animal thrashing in its claws, and dropped him from two hundred feet. The squeal ran all the way down as the falling beast thrashed his legs, then cut off abruptly at the meaty *thud* of impact. The winged reptile turned in a circling gyre as it descended and then settled to the ground like a flying avalanche, mantling its wings over the dead animal as it fed. After an instant, the long head came up with a dripping chunk in its jaws. It bolted the food whole, and you could see the lump traveling down the throat.

Marc brought the ceratopsian around and pressed the *bliss-out* button to freeze it in place before he came up with one knee on the bench, taking a hitch of the rifle sling around his left elbow to give a three-point rest and working the bolt to chamber one of the heavy rounds. Cynthia slid down and went flat to peer over the edge of the howdah, her thumbs on her ears and mouth open. The pterodactyl's huge eye with its star-shaped pupil leaped into view through the sight: about nine hundred yards. Now shift a little for the wind, *stroke* the trigger . . .

CRACK!

Recoil punched into his shoulder despite the rubber pad and the weapon's muzzle brake and the fourteen-pound mass of the heavy rifle. Through the scope he had a brief glimpse of the predator's brain splashing away from the hollow-point bullet. When he took the scope from his eye, the forty-foot wings were thrashing the soil in a last frenzy. As they stilled to twitching, the *churr* herd closed back in, standing in a circle for a moment before settling in to feed amid ripping and crunching sounds; the shaggy animals liked meat more than acorns or grass, though they'd eat anything in a pinch. They'd have it down to tatters and a skeleton by sundown, with the corpse beetles making sure not enough was left to smell by tomorrow.

This planet had an *active* ecosystem.

Marc worked the action and caught the empty shell as it ejected. That was one hundred and seventy-five dollars of the tax payers' money in shipping costs, right there, and they had their own reloading shop now. The sharp, acrid chemical stink of nitro powder hung in the air for a moment, then drifted away into the flowers-hay-hot-dirt-and-ocean smells.

"Jesus, Lieutenant!" the bird colonel said reverently.

"Yeah, sir. You've got to watch out for the Quetzas, take a glance skyward every so often; the older ones like that can lift a grown man into the air with a high-speed snatch. They can't carry that much weight for long . . . but they don't have to. And you *don't* let kids go out without an armed escort! The First Fleet people shot a half-dozen daily around the town for a while and that seems to have taught them to avoid it. Lucky there aren't all that many of the really huge ones."

"They can learn?" the colonel asked. "The reports say they're not very big brained."

"About like a smart bird, say a parrot or a bald eagle—some of the smaller dinosaurian land predators are like that, too. The herbivores like this one"—he kicked the ceratopsian's shield—"are dumb as geckos. The big Quetzas migrate to the southern hemisphere in the winter, right down to the Antarctic continent, so you only have to worry about them from this time of year to the start of the fall rains. It's a good thing there aren't more of the thunder-lizards this far north, or it'd be impossible to live outside a cave."

The colonel nodded as Marc got their mount back into motion and headed into town. "What's that over there?" he said, pointing left and southward.

Everyone looked. *There* was a fifty-acre field densely planted with a reedlike crop about twelve feet high waving in the light breeze, each stem as thick as a woman's wrist. The stems were deep, poplin green and the clusters of flowers on top were pink with white cores. They attracted clusters of palm-sized insects colored like monarch butterflies, orange, black, and yellow. There were millions of them, and they made a dense twirling blanket like a translucent Persian carpet over the blossoms. A strong scent half like cloves and half like cut grass came with the breeze, together with an occasional fluttering winged drift of the insects.

"That's our shamboo crop—the local name for it has this goddamned click sound in the middle, so we don't use it. When its shoots are just showing aboveground, it tastes like asparagus crossed with candy. Harvest it when it's four feet tall, and you can crush this sweet juice out of it and make sugar or a pretty good rum, and the Topsies—"

"Topsies?" the colonel asked.

"Ceratopsians." He slapped the shield of their mount to show what he meant "They eat it like bonbons. That's what we use most of it for. At eight feet, it's too tough even for the big critters to like much, but you can get fiber out of it that makes dandy rope and burlap and canvas, and just recently we've made some paper from it. When it's mature, the seeds taste a lot like sesame and give good oil for cooking and soap, and the stems are like bamboo only a lot stronger and tougher; that's what the howdah is made of."

He cleared his throat, sat, and got their mount going again. "Jamestown proper is, as you know, closer to the water."

That was because the first cargoes and personnel had come down in one-way capsules that had landed on the shallow bay with its half-moon curve of blinding white beach; it had taken years to get the runway and orbital boosters ready for two-way traffic. The cargo pods brought by the automated solar-sail craft that shuttled between the planets and Earth orbit on their long, leisurely arcs still did splash down there, floating the last few thousand feet on parachutes whose cloth itself had a dozen uses here. There was a long wooden dock stretching out into the clear green water of the bay now; the low solar-only tides made things easier around a port.

A native ship was tied up to the dock, a tubby fifty-footer with a mast and single square sail and twin steering oars. A Grand Banks–style schooner rested on the other side of the wharf. White sails showed farther out, where the water was purple-blue, with small whitecaps.

Marc pointed out the other features of the settlement: the helium-cooled pebble-bed reactor and generator emitting a plume of steam beneath its mound of dirt, a miniature version of the mass-produced types that generated most electricity back home these days; the airship mooring tower, built of shamboo and local woods (both the flying craft were out right now); and the semi-experimental fields growing crops from Earth alongside the Venusian plants domesticated by Kartahown. The town proper was made up of low adobe buildings lining the three dirt streets. All were whitewashed and most had roofs that were curves of green synthetic, each made of half a cargo pod; a few used reddish homemade tile or brown wooden shingles instead. Workshops and laboratories vied with warehouses and residences. The houses had acre-sized walled gardens, and there was a small park and a fair number of big trees that looked a lot like live oaks and had been standing here before the Terrans came.

Hitching posts and watering troughs stood at intervals along the streets, and there were board sidewalks on the main drag, with a proud but lonely stretch of brick in front of the town-hall-cum-commandant's-office. Riders on *churr*-back and pedestrians and carts drawn by *churr* or *tharg*-oxen made room for the ceratopsian. There were a couple of engine-powered ground vehicles in town, but they were carefully mothballed for emergencies.

Many of the people waved and called greetings, and Marc waved back. This *was* a small town. Only one hundred thirty-two Earthlings were here, not counting the score of newcomers. And counting the twenty or so who'd been born here, and the nine who'd died. Nobody here was old, and everyone was a top physical specimen, but there was a whole planet of unfamiliar perils around them. About twice as many Kartahownians and tribesfolk lived around the base, and there was a floating population of visitors from there and elsewhere, traders and pilgrims and the sheerly curious.

"Sort of an *acadaemogorsk* combined with frontier Deadwood," an English voice said from among the passengers.

Marc nodded, chuckling. He'd been a little surprised himself when the final training courses had put so much emphasis on things like blacksmithing and carpentry, but it made sense when you remembered how far away Earth was and how much it cost to ship anything this far. Every ounce counted, and every ounce acquired on Venus meant spaceship cargo freed up for something that couldn't possibly be made here, like scientific instruments.

Marc went on, "And that's the chapel; the denominations use it on a rotating basis. And here's HQ," he concluded.

That was the largest of the buildings—three stories of adobe with the viga-beams that supported the floors poking through the whitewash, in an E-shape around courtyards, with a fountain and an arcade of tree trunks at the front. People bustled in and out, and traders squatted by blankets bearing their goods, everything from jewelry to colorful dyed cloth and cooking spices.

Marc pulled the joystick back to the neutral position and pressed the *park* button that stimulated the animal's pleasure center; it put its head down and began to drool again. Ceratopsians were too invincibly stupid to learn much, but they would stand still if it made them feel very good. That let him jump down from the driver's seat and put the ladder in place. A Hispanic woman in her early thirties appeared in the main doorway, waving a clipboard.

Marc gestured towards her. "Dr. Maria Feldman will give you all the standard familiarization lecture and assign quarters. I'm afraid we're very shorthanded here, so I'll be leaving you in her capable hands."

"This way, people! This way!" she called.

The passengers began to file down. As they did, Marc noticed one of them had slipped out and was handing Cynthia down from the foremost seat; he was a man of about Marc's own age, but two inches taller, blond, blue-eyed, and handsome in a way both rugged and somehow smooth at the edges. He gave a toothy smile and squeezed hard as he shook hands. His eyes went a little wider as the Cajun squeezed back with carefully calculated force.

"Wing Commander Christopher Blair, RAF," the blond man said in an excruciatingly Etonian voice; he was the one who'd compared the place to an EastBloc research settlement crossed with a frontier town. "Anthropology and linguistics, lighter-than-air pilot as well . . . as are you, I understand? Pleased to meet you, Lieutenant."

"The pleasure's mutual," Marc said through slightly gritted teeth, surprised at the intensity of his sudden dislike.

Oh, well, they've all been together on the Carson *for a quarter of a year,* he thought as he climbed back into the howdah and watched the two of them walk side by side into HQ, chatting easily. *I just liked her on first acquaintance. . . .*

In theory half the personnel here were supposed to be female. In practice it was hard to be precise about it with such a small population, and there was a slight but noticeable surplus of males, particularly among the younger, unmarried residents. It was annoying as hell and it meant that the single men among the Old Bulls had a built-in advantage.

He headed the ceratopsian down towards the docks, shouting reminders to get out of the way occasionally when it looked as if the bells weren't enough. Most of the traffic was pedestrians, including the odd kid, and once a Kartahownian noble in a fancy, gold-trimmed shamboo chariot, gawking around in his saffron tunic and gaudy barbaric jewelry, and gawking hardest of all at a 'saur doing what people told it to. He nearly gawked too long. A ceratopsian just didn't stop, start, or turn quickly.

It was a relief to turn right, eastward, towards the stables, storage, and workshops out on the eastern edge of town; that was usually far enough for the stenches to not bother people. The prevailing winds blew south to north here in the summer, and in from the ocean in winter. Iced ceratopsians didn't need much stabling; when you pressed the right button, a ceratopsian felt increasingly bad if it walked away from the fixed broadcaster. That kept them quiet even when their instincts said they should be migrating to the highlands for the summer. There were ditches and fences made of a lattice of two-foot-thick tree trunks as backup, but privately Marc doubted they'd hold the beasts if the signal ever failed.

Real split-rail corrals confined the domestic *tharg* and *churr* they'd bought from the locals, and beyond them were tilled fields. Marc noted where a bustle of construction work was adding to the barns and storage sheds, and caught a strong whiff from the steeping vats where mammal and dinosaur hide was being tanned. They could have bought everything from the Kartahownians, of course, but sacred Policy said otherwise.

Okay, it's a fairly smart *policy,* he thought. Relations with Kartahown's kings were good, but with the city as a whole were at best . . . "fraught" was the word he'd heard General Clarke use. *I'd be less grudging if it all didn't take up so much research time.*

He turned draught-beast and howdah over to the staff, slung his rifle across his back, and walked over to the slaughterhouse that also served as a processing point for specimens. It was cool inside, cool enough to dry his sweat and even raise a few goose bumps, courtesy of a wind-vent system. It didn't even smell too bad, since the blood-beetles took care of scraps—and of the meat, unless you took elaborate precautions. Dr. Samuel Feldman, doctor of paleontology and ethnology, was watching while a crew disassembled the hung-up carcasses of six *tharg* Marc and the other Rangers had shot for tonight's Welcome-to-Venus barbeque, the giant wild variety that could weigh in at a ton and a half.

Feldman looked as much like a rumpled, absentminded professor as it was possible for anyone who made the Jamestown selection to do. Mostly that meant he forgot to shave sometimes and never quite got around to growing a beard. His pants and pocketed shirt jacket were the same as those of nearly everyone else and he had twenty-thirty vision, but somehow the lab coat and glasses were there as an intangible spiritual essence; for the rest, he was a short, fairly stocky thirty-something man with dark, curling hair, brown eyes, and a round, big-nosed face, and the body of a wickedly effective soccer goalie, which was exactly what he was in his off-hours.

"You know, dis ting is *definitely* a bovine," he said in purest Brooklyn, an accent that hadn't disappeared even while he was earning his first degree from New York University and after the time he'd spent at Stanford.

"Certainly tastes like beef. But come on, Doc. Billions of years of separate evolution here!"

It wasn't the first time they'd had this discussion; *tharg* was the commonest type of meat in the local diet after pork. Feldman prodded a finger towards the big animal whose flayed body hung head-down from a wooden hook over a big tub of oat-hulls.

"The anatomy is just too damned similar for a doubt."

"*Mais,* I think it looks a lot like a buffalo, me. Call it a bovinoid?"

"Or a tall, mean wisent," Feldman said, smiling. "But no, it's not 'bovinoid.' Clade *bovidae,* genus *bos.* This thing is descended from the same ancestors as the ones we make brisket out of back home. It's even kosher—it divideth its hooves and cheweth the fucking cud!"

"It's a buffalo that can fly interplanetary distances? I know they're pretty flatulent when they've been eating those breadnut things, but not to escape velocity, I think."

Feldman's smile turned into a grin, then died "Dammit, Marc, this is driving me nuts. What we need is a way to directly compare DNA . . . they're working on it, but it's going to be a while. Maybe we shouldn't have put all our R and D money into rocket science for the past thirty years. The serum immunology reactions, though . . . dammit . . ."

Marc nodded; he didn't have the older man's terrier obsession, but it *was* something to worry at, and they'd come here for knowledge—officially.

And to make sure the EastBloc don't snaffle off a whole planet, and to taunt the Euros once again for following de Gaulle into a blind alley. Everyone had expected wonders on Mars and Venus. Nobody had expected what they found. He ventured, "Panspermia? Microbes on meteors?"

The scientist shook his head. "Not a prayer. Okay, say life gets its start from complex molecules from space. We've *found* complex molecules in space that look like amino acids. That could get you something that's *generally* similar, starting with single-celled organisms in primordial oceans. Bugs on rocks, yeah, that would make things a bit *more* generally similar, say in the structure of genes and chromosomes. But evolution's a chaotic process; you get general similarities, but not identities. Hell, even on Earth, dolphins aren't fish and seals aren't dolphins and birds aren't bats. No *way* a couple of billion years of random evolution could reproduce, oh—"

He paused and caught a buzzing fly on the wing with the same smooth snap that he used to stop a soccer ball, then held it out in a cage of fingers, reciting in a singsong tone:

"Two-winged flying insects with distinctive wing venation: *spu-*

rious vein usually present between R and M; cells R5 and M1 closed, resulting in a vein that runs *parallel to posterior* margin of the wing; anal cell closed near wing margin. Hoverflies, to you. The only difference between this and Syrphid hoverflies on Earth is that it's as big as your little finger—and *that's* because the air here has a higher partial pressure of oxygen. You could get bugs here the size of Chihuahuas and I suspect that in the warmer areas you do."

He released the insect and stopped the butchering of the *tharg* for a second to pry things open.

"Look at *that* and *that*. Look at the structure of the shoulder joint! And the digestive tract's not just *grossly* similar; it's similar in *detail*. It's not a different structure developed to do roughly the same thing; it's the same structure doing exactly the same thing; with only very minor differences. It's no more different from a Jersey cow than the cow is from a water buffalo. It's a *ruminant*, fer Chrissakes!"

"There's grass here, too," Marc pointed out.

Feldman began to run his hands through his hair, then noticed the blood on them and poured a dipperful of water over them, wiping down on a coarse burlap sack hanging from a peg.

"Yeah. And that's way too similar to our grass."

"*Mais*, then the evidence would suggest that our theories of evolution are wrong," Marc argued. "Maybe separate evolutionary paths *can* reproduce fine details, at least when they get the same initial conditions. Remember, evidence first, theory second."

Feldman glared at him balefully. "But the facts are supposed to make *sense*. We've got to get started on a good survey of the geological strata and fossil record for this planet. Bovines date back about twenty million years on Earth. If we could compare the fossils—"

"Collected by all one hundred and forty-six of us?" Marc asked reasonably, and grinned inwardly as the paleontologist kicked the hanging carcass with concentrated venom. "Of course, maybe the God-did-it crowd is right—"

"*Them!*"

Feldman started swearing; when he switched to Yiddish, Marc had to fight to keep the grin inward.

He's a good boss, him, but sometimes I just can't resist.

Venus, EastBloc Station Kusnetsov—Low Venus Orbit

The upper stage of the EastBloc shuttle *Riga* was an elongated wedge with two vertical stabilizers at the rear. Its rocket engines were strictly for the ascent to orbit, when its first stage carried it to twenty-five thousand meters and Mach 3. It was designed to dead-stick to a landing, using its belly as the heat-shield and lifting body. Captain and pilot Franziskus Binkis floated in through the docking tunnel that clamped to the lower spindle of the wheel-and-axle configuration of the station and sighed in relief as he deftly dogged the hatch and then pushed himself down to strap into the central pilot's station. There wasn't really any difference in the stale, recycled taste of the dry air with its tang of ozone, since the *Riga* had been docked here for three days, but his lungs and nose insisted it felt more alive.

His glance skipped over gauges and readouts. Most were old-fashioned analogue devices, it being resentfully accepted that the *Yanki* were ahead in plasma-screen technology, even with the latest Chinese improvements. Officially, digital readouts and touch screens were regarded as unnecessary luxuries. Li was ready at the engineer's console, and Nininze in the copilot's seat.

"Glad to get the cargo stowed," the Georgian said. "It must be important, not to be sent down with a cargo pod to Cosmograd. I wonder what it is?"

The pilot grunted. It *was* important, which was exactly why Nininze shouldn't have asked that question. But the Georgian was short, dark, lively, and talkative—exactly what a Georgian was supposed to be like. Binkis knew he was an equally archetypical Lithuanian in looks, tall and ash-blond with pale gray eyes, and just like the stereotype he was also closemouthed. Li was from Canton, and doll-pretty; she was also even more silent than the pilot, except where her machinery was concerned, and he was fairly sure she reported to Base Security.

"Part of it is computer parts," Binkis said. "Let's get the checklist completed."

Li and Nininze nodded with a chorus of, "Yes, Captain." The "Comrade" was best left off these days except on formal occasions.

Otherwise you were likely to be suspected of left-deviationist hankerings for the old days, which wouldn't do your career any good. A sensible man kept up with the changes.

"Poor Alexi," Nininze said, after they finished the run-through on the maneuvering jets. "Three more weeks up here, and not even any brandy!"

Binkis grinned as he watched Li finish the checklist on the navigational computer. He happened to know that a friend on the last visit of the nuclear-boost ship *Zuhkov* had left several bottles of quite good Stolichnaya with Alexi in return for a small stuffed pterodactyl, priceless on the black market back home if you could get it past the inspectors, or cut one of them in on the deal. Anyone who thought they could forbid liquor traffic in an organization founded by Russians was crazy. That didn't stop Security from trying, of course, and even trying to prevent people from making their own untaxed hooch down planetside, which showed you how in touch with reality *they* were. Of course, the current Security chief was a German named Bergman, with a spring-steel poker up his arse.

He'd been a compromise after the Chinese wouldn't accept a Russian and the Russians balked at having the commandant *and* the police general Chinese.

"Cosmograd Control, this is *Riga-alpha*, reporting all systems functional for descent," Binkis said.

On the second try, the message went through. Venus had a turbulent atmosphere with a great deal of radio noise; it made long-distance communications awkward. He used Russian, which was still the common language of the EastBloc space service.

He'd also meticulously checked everything twice, most particularly the parts that were the Station chief's responsibilities.

Alexi is a good man to have a drink with, but at seventh and last, he is a Russian, and thinks machinery will perform if you give it a good kick. A Russian is a Mongol with blue eyes—halfway to a black-arse.

There was the odd token Tajik or Uzbek, but the core of the program was still Slav, with a fair sprinkling of minor Soviet nationalities: Balts like him, people from the Caucasus like Nininze, plus plenty from the other Warsaw Pact countries ... and an ever-increasing percentage of Chinese. It was all supposed to show true internationalism at work. He liked the Chinese more than the Russians on the whole; they were better at detail work, and they took the new regulations on private initiative to heart rather than grumbling at them. Since a couple of them had started restaurants, you could finally get a decent meal in Cosmograd that you didn't cook yourself, and it was also now possible to get a broken light replaced without waiting three weeks.

The accented voice of the Hungarian duty officer groundside crackled through the speakers: "Cosmograd Control here. You are cleared for landing, Captain Binkis. Transmitting code."

"*Spacebo*," Binkis said

For a moment he looked at the great mottled disk of Venus through the windows, thick white cloud-masses and thinner upper-level haze and streaks of blue below. *Coming home, Jadviga*, he thought, and punched the *execute* button.

A loud *clunk* sounded from above as the docking collar disengaged. They were already weightless, but there was a peculiar feeling in the inner ear as the big gyroscopes whined and twisted the nose of the *Riga* to the proper alignment.

"Commence," he began. Then a startled obscenity: "*Pisau!*"

The ripple of action on the dials showed the firing sequence for the retro-rockets! "Li, override that!"

The Chinese woman's hands danced on the flight control console. "Negative, Captain," she said tonelessly. "The flight computer is not responding."

Binkis slapped the main manual override switch. He couldn't do a reentry burn by hand, but he could stop it until they'd figured out what had gone wrong. Nothing . . . and then the huge, impalpable hand slamming him back into his seat as the retro-rockets blasted and the view ahead vanished in a haze of burning gas.

Trilinkas sau ant kelio triesk! he screamed mentally at the useless controls. *Fold yourself in three and shit!*

Then with an effort that made sweat break out on his forehead: "Li, see what trajectory this puts us on."

For as the rockets killed some of its orbital velocity, the *Riga* had begun to fall.

CHAPTER TWO

Encyclopedia Britannica, 16th Edition
University of Chicago Press, 1988

VENUS: History of observation

. . . in 1927 and 1928 ultraviolet photographs were taken by the American astronomers William H. Wright and Frank E. Ross. The first studies of the infrared spectrum of Venus, by Walter S. Adams and Theodore Dunham (also of the United States) in 1932, showed that the atmosphere of the planet was possibly an oxygen-nitrogen one. Observations in the microwave of the spectrum, beginning in earnest in the late 1940s, provided the first evidence of the Earth-like surface temperatures.

The greatest advances in the early study of Venus were achieved through the use of unmanned spacecraft. The era of spacecraft exploration of the planets began with the Soviet *Pioneer* orbiter mission to Venus in 1960, which placed a spacecraft in orbit around the planet and sent four entry probes deep into the Venusian atmosphere. The entry probes provided data on atmospheric structure and composition, while the orbiter observed from above. The orbiter also provided the first high-quality map of Venus' surface topography and resulted in the naming of the continents, oceans, and major islands. Most important, it also provided the first positive indications of intelligent life . . .

Venus, Gagarin Continent—south of Jamestown Extraterritorial Zone

The night would be cold, but at noontime in the canyon the late-summer heat was dense enough to cut, trapped by the fifty-foot walls of dark rock on either side. Beech trees lined the edges of the cliffs, and arched over the narrow slit in the rock; bright sunlight filtered through the drying fall leaves and turned daylight into a green-gold twilit shade; enough of the leaves had fallen to make gold drifts along the banks, and more floated downstream past the feet of their *churr.*

The stream was low now, trickling ankle-deep over brown polished rock, but you could see that the winter torrents stretched halfway to the top of the cliffs and across the full twenty-yard width of this water-cut groove in the earth. The *churr* of the five riders were panting a little, tossing their shaggy blocky heads and stopping frequently to lap from pools; the beasts smelled hot and musky, like overworked dogs, and they panted with tongues the size of dish towels. Now and then one would snap at a passing insect with a wet *chomp!* like a door slamming.

The five riders kept going even when they took swigs from their canteens or gnawed biscuit and dried fruit. Three were Terrans in outfits of camouflaged parachute cloth, and two were hunters of the Kudlak tribe in straw hats like Earth's Chinese coolie type and knee-length leather pants held up by cross-belted suspenders. The Venusian tribesmen had quivers over their backs and short recurved bows made of laminated shamboo and *tharg*-horn in their fists, with steel trade-knives at their belts; the Earthlings carried their rifles across their saddlebows. Humans and *churr* all looked tired and worn, sweat cutting runnels in the dust on faces, brown fur matted and dusty.

Marc blew out a long sigh of relief and blinked in the bright sunlight as they came out into a broad open circle where a sinkhole had collapsed long ago.

"I was beginning to doubt my memory," he said thankfully. "*Mais*, here we are."

The depression was a mile or so across, an irregular oval with walls that were near-vertical in parts, in others collapsed into steep scree covered in thorny bushes. The little river spread more broadly here, in wide, shallow pools edged with rushes; those were dry with autumn, their tops shedding white seed-fluff that mingled with insects whose wings glittered gaudy or iridescent, many of them six inches across. The largest of all were the dragonfly-like predators; those buzzed like miniature crop dusters as they swooped, feeding, in lethal arcs. Birds larger still had been taking all of them impartially; they exploded upward in a multicolored swarm as the humans came into view, and the noise level dropped. Cliffsides were streaked with droppings, the guano adding an ammonia pungency to the air and showing where rookeries were in the spring, but the big, shaggy twig-bundles of nests were unoccupied right now.

Cynthia Whitlock pushed back her sweat-stained bush hat and glanced at Marc sharply. "Did we just escape something?" she asked.

"Not exactly," he said, scanning for the good campsite he remembered from his previous visit.

There were a couple of running springs around the edge of the sinkhole even this late in the year, each marked by a clump of trees and bright green grass and bush. The best was at the top of a short rise, on a knee of rock more than head-height above the level floor. A steady trickle of water as thick through as a man's wrist fell down into a pool before draining farther down, providing clean water and a ready-made shower. The cliff overhead was steep, inclined inward towards the base, which would give shade. Just beyond was a section that had collapsed into a steep slope, which gave a route out if necessary.

"In other words, yes, there *was* something to worry about," Christopher Blair said dryly. "Was that why you've been pushing us so hard?"

Marc shrugged. "*Weh*. Thing is, it's getting on towards the winter rainy season. That usually starts with cloudbursts up in the hills before the lowlands get any rain. Flash floods can come down this way *fast*."

Cynthia Whitlock had trained as a geologist. She looked at the way the rock had been gouged by water and nodded.

Zhown nodded, too, as he dismounted, looking around. "*Toob! Toob!*" he said, pointing at the canyon they'd just left, then around at the sinkhole and up at the cliffs around it. "Bad, *much* bad in narrow place if rains come. Better here. Better still if we go up there."

Blair raised one blond brow. "You might have mentioned that before we spent two days in a bloody wadi with no way out, old chap," he said to Marc.

"Dr. Feldman and Cynthia thought it was important to get those samples. So it was worth the risk to save a week's travel time," Marc retorted. "I was keeping an eye out for clouds, and I knew we'd reach this opening today. Otherwise we'd have had to wait until the next dry season."

I like Cynthia, Marc thought. *Hell, I like Zhown and Colrin. Blair . . . I don't know exactly* why *I don't like him. Well*, weh, *I do know* why, *but it's not* just *that*.

There wasn't any flotsam on the knee of rock, and there was enough level ground for themselves and their beasts as they set about making camp. That didn't take much time. They unsaddled and hobbled the riding-*churr*, unloaded the four pack-*churr* and hobbled them, and turned them all loose to browse. At sundown they'd give the *churr* some of the smelly, oilseed-oats-dried-offal pellets and scraps. *Churr* would eat nearly anything, and until then they'd have plenty of browsing around the spring-fed pools and along the ponds.

With rain unlikely the humans didn't need a tent, and setting out bedrolls took only a moment. Last spring's floods had left plenty of deadwood around the perimeter of the sinkhole, and they soon had a campfire going. Colrin put a pot of water on to boil, and started stringing lumps of meat from a small antelope they'd shot earlier today on skewers, along with chunks of onion from a sack they had with them, then set the meat and onions in a plastic basin and poured beer, chopped garlic, and ground *eesum* spice in with them. The kebabs, some it-might-as-well-be-rice and dried vegetables and fruit would make a good enough meal. They'd also dug a couple of sacks' worth of tubers from a vine that grew along sandy riverbanks. Something very close to it was a cultivated crop called a breadnut. The tame variety was about the size of a fist, while the wild ones were the size of walnuts, but both tasted a lot like potatoes with a sweetish overtone when roasted in the embers.

After their meal, they got to work, each group in its own way. The two native hunter-guides unlimbered their horn-and-shamboo bows and started shooting at stumps and logs. Archery was new to them, introduced by the Earthlings—nobody on Venus had invented the bow yet, as far as they could tell—and so was riding on a *churr*'s back rather than in a chariot behind it, but they'd taken to both like Russians to strong drink, and practiced relentlessly. It was something they understood and could copy themselves, and it was a tactful way for the Earthlings to refuse to sell them guns.

The Earthings got out their rock hammers and sample boxes.

"Is Zhown and Colrin's Kartahownian as lousy as it sounds to me?" Cynthia asked, as they walked towards the southern rim of the sinkhole.

The hills rose steeply there, several hundred feet; the knife-edged cleft where uncounted seasons had sliced through the rock showed bands in colors from fawn through dull yellow to black. Marc kept up a wary scan and the rifle in the crook of his arm ready to go, which wasn't easy as the footing changed from rock and mud to stream-smoothed rock alone. The stones rattled under the tough ceratopsian-hide soles of their boots.

"It sure is," Marc said. "It's not their native language, either, and some of the sounds are hard for them."

"It's related," Blair cut in "but distantly, much the way English is to Russian."

"*Weh*," Marc agreed. "A few of them learn Kartahownian so they can trade with the river valley people, but not that many. They're herders and hunters, mainly."

Blair stopped. "And how are their relations with the city?"

The Englishman had spent a lot of time in Kartahown's territory since he'd arrived, which was to be expected of a linguist and anthropologist.

Marc's duties as a Ranger took him more among the wild peoples. With a shrug, he replied, "Like bedouin or Mongols in the old days back on Earth. Sometimes they trade or work as caravan guards and suchlike; sometimes they raid and steal stuff; sometimes they and the sedentary peoples fight big-time. There's some inter-marriage, too, along the edges."

"That's roughly what I thought. Whose idea was it to teach them how to make bows and ride?" Blair asked, flushing under his tan. "Is someone trying to re-create Genghis Khan?"

Cynthia looked at Marc, too. He shrugged again.

"The high command sets the policy—we've given the city-folk a lot of new ideas, too. Personally, I approve. The nomads can be almighty rough, but they need an equalizer. To the city-folk here you don't have any rights unless you're a free Kartahownian or a damned powerful foreigner. They think the nomads are monkeys from the wilds and treat them like dirt if they can get away with it."

"Most of this planet is pre-agricultural, not even as far along as the Neolithic," the Englishman snapped. "Civilization is a new and fragile thing here. It can't take chances."

Marc grinned innocently. "Guess us Americans just can't help sympathizing with a bunch of wild-ass cowboys," he said. "Even if they *are* wearing lederhosen."

Cynthia snorted laughter. Marc bowed, and then turned to the Englishman. "Scissors-paper-rock for who keeps first watch?"

They both turned their backs on Cynthia. *Now, what do I think Mr. Bloody Blair will pick?* he mused. That needed only a moment's consideration: He flattened his hand.

"Marc has paper; Chris has rock," Cynthia said, her voice care-fully neutral. "Let's get going."

Marc nodded easily to both of them as he and Cynthia leaned their rifles carefully against a boulder, keeping his smile from get-ting too broad. Blair had certain things going for him; he was smart and handsome and charming and well educated and hardworking and smooth. His big drawback was being an arrogant son of a bitch, of course.

But you can't fault his bushcraft, the Cajun acknowledged reluc-tantly. *That's a good position and he's keeping his eyes open.*

Marc and the scientist went to work. The banded rock stretched a hundred and fifty feet above them, sheer except for a couple of cracks and fissures. They worked their way up cautiously, driving pitons deep with blows of the blunt hammer sides of their picks, testing them carefully, and then reeving the knotted climbing rope through the spring-loaded loops on the ends. After an hour they had a secure pathway from top to bottom for someone who knew his or her way around a rock face, which they both did. Marc did wish he had goggles, since the limestone they were working on tended to chip and powder, but he didn't want to restrict his peripheral vision. He felt even better about that when something tugged at the corner of his eye and he lashed out with the sharp end of the pick. There was a *crunch* and a rattle and he held up a scorpion the size of a small bread plate on the point. The stinger on the end of its tail lashed around in dying reflex, and Marc jerked back to avoid a drop of the poison.

Cynthia looked at it from her perch about fifteen feet away. "I think I recognize that from the briefing you guys put on. Is it the one whose venom is deadly in thirty seconds?"

"No, that's the little black one, worse than a black mamba back on Earth. These big ones, it's more like a minute or even two. You've only got about thirty seconds to inject the antidote, though."

"Thank God there is one!" She shuddered slightly. "I'm not equipped to blanch, but consider it done."

"I am so equipped, and I'm doing it!" Blair called from the ground. "This ecosystem is simply far too *energetic* for my peace of mind!"

After that, the afternoon went quickly and relatively peacefully. Rock-climbing could be fun, if you knew what you were doing, although dangerous wildlife made it a little more nerve-wracking than Marc really liked. Mostly he went where the scientist sent him and chipped out what she wanted him to. That could be real work when she wanted a chunk as large as his head, but the samples were mostly smaller. Every hour or so, Blair spelled him; Cynthia quelled his attempts at lighthearted repartee. At last the thirty-hour day drew to a close, and they laid the samples out on a tarp in the open where the sunlight still reached, away from the shadows pooled at the base of the cliff; the limestone itself had a yellow tint, like the rock that built Jerusalem.

Cynthia peered at the rock samples as if they should be subject to a pooper-scooper law; Marc had seen her getting more and more intent—and discontented—all afternoon.

"What's the problem?" he asked.

She made a hissing noise. "I'm starting to get really annoyed. I'm going to start sounding like Sam Feldman, pretty soon."

"Oh, I doubt it," Marc said. "You'd have to have five o'clock shadow to make that scratchy sound Doc does when he rubs his chin."

Cynthia gave a quick, unwilling grin. "Point. Okay, I'm getting frustrated like he was. Look at that cliff. You were right—good strata. Nice marine sedimentary limestone, uplifted when those mountains south of here got going."

Thirty miles south of Jamestown, the land rose from the coastal plain into these rolling hills, divided by occasional flattish valleys, oak savannah gradually turning into low mountains forested with beech, then pine and fir, and then becoming alpine meadows. The hills got steeper still south of that, and the rivers cut into them in spectacular fashion. The current theory was that Venus had bigger mountains because the continental plates were thinner and the magma beneath hotter and more liquid. Plates slipped around faster and collided harder.

"Reminds me a bit of the Dordogne country," Blair said.

"Or the Kentucky pennyroyal," Marc answered.

"Yup, similar in both cases. Except for the mountains, of course."

Some of the tremendous peaks that floated blue against the horizon had snow half the year. On Venus that meant *high* mountains; only the Mother River pierced them anywhere near here, the one that Kartahown sat on.

"Okay," Cynthia continued, "so first off, this is the best undisturbed but sufficiently exposed set we've got so far. I'd guess it covers, oh, one to two hundred million years. Down to the Jurassic in Earth terms. Plenty of fossils just like you said. As good as we're going to get until we get up into the mountains or the Eastbloc start sharing their data from their base."

"One would be ill-advised to hold one's breath waiting for that," Blair said. "Amazing how selfishly capitalistic those Johnnies can be, since they decided, quote, *It is glorious to get rich*, unquote."

"And they're *still* paranoid as hell," Marc added.

Cynthia nodded. "Yeah, most of the old bad features and a lot of new ones. So the big news is that this pretty stratigraphy has got the same things we've been finding everywhere, only all together and less ambiguous."

She pointed at a dark layer six inches to a foot thick at the bottom of the cliff. Below that the stone was also dark, but denser-grained and shiny.

"There it is."

"Sam's famous organic boundary layer?" Marc said.

"Yeah. One hundred fifty to two hundred million years ago, as far as we can tell, you get this layer everywhere that was underwater then. Basically it's a sort of quasi-coal made of solid blue-green and red algae and plankton, coccolithophorids-sort-of; there's nothing quite like it on Earth. It's like someone dropped the first ones into a planetary-sized nutrient bath to watch 'em go *fizz*! Then you get massive limestone—limestone's usually a biological product, and this *sure* is, calcium carbonate with some phosphate, lots of seashells. The isotopes look like the atmosphere was anaerobic at the beginning of these strata, mostly CO_2 and thick, nitrogen only a trace element, but then it gets much more Earth-like, as if biological action suddenly pumped the carbon out of the atmosphere and oxygen into it. It happened fast, couple of million years tops, and when it was over, this planet had an oxy-nitrogen atmosphere pretty much the way it does now, only with even more oxygen. That's an eyeblink. Then a little bit up from the atmospheric transition phase, as soon as there's enough oxygen around, you get—"

She pointed at a fossil. It was about a foot long and looked roughly like a curled nautilus.

"You get things like that. It's an ammonite, near as I can tell identical to a couple of the Earthly varieties from the Sinemurian strata of the Jurassic, two hundred million years old. No antecedents, no equivalent of the Triassic or the Burgess Shales, suddenly you go from single-celled organisms, mostly plants, to stuff like ammonites and"—her hammer pointed at another shape—"belemnite cephalopods and fully developed teleosts, fish with bony skeletons and jaws. That one there looks like a shark. And corals. And dammit—"

They both chuckled at her Feldman imitation.

"—I think *that's* part of the skull of a marine crocodile. Hell, for all we know there are *still* ammonites around on Venus. How could we tell? All we've seen is a thin sliver of what's equivalent to Hudson's Bay, and this planet has relatively more ocean than Earth does."

Blair grinned. "There are certainly some very large marine reptiles out there, crocodilians included," he said. "That's why the Kartahownians are so precocious with their catapults. I wouldn't care to go sailing in these waters without one!"

Marc nodded. "Point," he said unwillingly.

"And that's how it goes, all the way up," Cynthia said, swinging the hammer up to where the cliff tops were catching the sunset. "Suddenly you get new species, every couple of million years, very, *very* similar to critters from Earth. Some of them persist; some don't. Some of the older ones persist; some don't; some evolve into new types . . . same with the land fossils. We've established some tentative sequences. Sam, Dr. Feldman, has found what looks like a proto-*churr*, about half the size and much more carnivorous than the modern type. As far as we can tell, the fossil record is as screwy as the contemporary ecology here, with sauropods and saber-tooths and antelopes and hominids all mixed up."

"Well, that's the word," Marc pointed out. "*As far as we can tell.* How many thousands of rock hounds have been collecting fossils all over Earth for how long now? Whereas we've had six or seven people doing it for six years on Venus. That makes 'sampling error' pretty well automatic."

She shot him a look that made him regret speaking. "But what they *don't* have on Earth is this," she said, pointing to the shiny rock that underlay the whole limestone formation. "That's metamorphic. Sort of a sulfur-rich basalt. And it's goddamned *everywhere* we've been able to look, at about the same age."

"So what do you and Dr. Feldman think it means?" Blair asked, as they packed the samples in shamboo caskets and lugged them back to the campsite.

The native hunters gave them an incurious glance and went about their work: Everyone knew that the Sky People, while wizards of great power, were raving mad. Filling a sack with useless rocks and treating it like a treasure was typical of them.

Cynthia was silent until the task was done; Marc was startled when she finally answered. "Sam thinks . . . and I think . . . that two hundred million years ago, in the earliest Jurassic . . . this planet was different. Radically different from what we have now; as far as we can tell, it didn't have life at all. And we don't have any idea what changed it."

Venus, EastBloc Shuttle *Riga*—Low Venus Orbit, Surface

It isn't being dead that is so bad, Captain Binkis thought, as the shuttle *Riga* began its unplanned reentry.

His father had been a teenaged partisan in the war, and had always told him that. He ought to know, as many as he'd seen go and helped on the way.

No, it's the dying *that hurts*.

At least he didn't have to wait too quietly. The *Riga* was beginning to shudder as they struck denser air—still a vacuum by ordinary definitions, but when you were traveling at orbital velocities, it didn't take much.

"We're going to skip," Li said. Her short hair was plastered to her forehead in little black rat-tails, the lilt stronger in her Russian. "The angle of approach is too shallow."

Lights winked. "*I have the controls!*" Binkis said, half a shout of triumph.

He did, at least the manual ones. *Much good it will do us*. But whatever had frozen them out was gone, at least for the present. The shuddering grew worse; he fought with brief bursts of the altitude jets to keep the *Riga* from tumbling, which would smear them in glowing fragments over half a hemisphere. Deceleration slammed them savagely into their couches, and he felt the world go gray and vision narrow to a tunnel; something warm and salty ran down over his upper lip, tasting like iron as he reflexively opened his mouth.

If he breathed blood back through his sinuses and choked on it, they would all *certainly* die. Gently, gently, keep the ablative plating on her belly at maximum aspect to their path of descent . . .

Weight lessened; in an instant they would be in zero-G again . . . for a very short while, as they bounced off the atmosphere like a flat rock thrown along the surface of a pond. Li was still conscious, though blood flowed from her nose, too, and from the corners of her eyes like red tears. Nininze hung limp in his harness, and might have been dead except for the bubbles in the blood that trickled out of his loose mouth.

"Get me a descent vector," Binkis said to Li in a voice like an ancient rusted gate opening, wrung beyond exhaustion by the mental effort that had saved them.

"Where?" she asked faintly, her voice dull and flat.

"One that we can survive, *kale*!" he rasped. "We're not going to the Cosmograd landing field anyway!"

He could see the curving cone of possible trajectories on one of the screens, one that hadn't been affected by whatever-it-was. Already the whole east-central part of Gagarin was out-of-bounds, impossible for something with their speed and position, forbidden by Newton. Hands moved on the console. The schematic of the *Riga* turned on the central screen, and a course appeared, with the alphanumeric bars beside it listing the rate of descent and angle. He forced his hands to suppleness on the control joystick. A series of blows hit the underside of the craft as the vast white-blue disk steadied ahead of them. Then they merged into a juddering rumble, a toning harmonic that made the stainless-steel fillings in his back teeth ache. Flickers of incandescence began to show around the edges of the blunt, wedge-shaped prow ahead of them; he ignored them in favor of the instruments as the heat built in the little cabin.

"Here, sir."

Binkis' lips skinned back. "That is in the Prohibited Zone." He shook his head. "No matter. It is not nearly as prohibitive as death."

Figures, figures of life and death, edging up towards the redline limits. He could *feel* the air begin to take fire—

And they were through it. His whole body shuddered, and sweat washed the dried blood down until thick drops fell off his chin. The rudders began to bite air, a little mushy at first, then more definitely, and the ceramic underbelly of the shuttle started to generate lift as well as shielding them from kinetic energy turned into heat.

"Now get us down, you *keshke shunsnukis*, you dog-faced whore," he begged the craft he'd piloted so many times. "My sweet *Riga*, you can do it!"

They were still at better than ten kilometers up, but descending steeply. He wrestled the clumsy craft into its optimum glide, which wasn't much. As an aircraft it had all the grace and nimbleness of a cow falling off a cliff, particularly under manual control. The radar showed tangled mountains ahead, and a hint of flat sea off to his right, to the north; at least they hadn't overshot the whole continent and wouldn't be forced to come down in the open ocean. Drifting in a rubber raft fifteen thousand kilometers from base . . . that would just make an interesting bit of foreign food for the plesiosaurs. And they had seagoing crocodiles here twenty meters long. Of course, coming down on dry land that far from Cosmograd, assuming they lived, wouldn't be much better. He'd seen an allosaurus snap up a saber-tooth once, toss it in the air like a tidbit, and then bite the massive predator in half as it fell and pace on like a lizard from Hell, bits dropping from its jaws. . . .

Focus. If you die in the next five minutes, there won't be pieces big enough for anything but bacteria to squabble over.

Li spoke, startling him. "Captain, the radio is still dead. I think I could trigger the distress beacon, though."

"Do it. At this altitude, they may be able to track where we go down."

And walk all the way to get us? his mind gibed at him. Then: *For our cargo, possibly, they would, if it is what I think it is.*

Down, down. The land ahead becoming less and less of a map, less a blue blur and more mountains, plains, rivers. The *Riga* would come in hot, faster than a speeding car; it needed a long runway or they'd smash and roll. Nothing would be smooth enough except water.

There. A long lake, like an L with a tiny, shorter arm. Kilometers of it, like a fjord between high country, and smooth, smooth to the radar eye. He shouted in triumph and increased the rate of descent.

I will flare her up to kill speed just before we strike and then nose down before we stall, he thought. That meant handling the heavy, low-lift rocket-plane like a light aircraft. *Since the alternative is death, I am sure that I can do it.*

Lower and closer, and suddenly it was a real world out there, not an abstract painting. Through the layer of haze-cloud, and then the forested hills just south of the coastal plain were below them, shockingly close. The lake had low, rolling downs on one side, higher, shaggy heights to his left. No islands, no obvious reefs, and kilometers of water.

But fast, much too fast, he thought. *If we touch down at this speed we will spin like a tossed coin.*

"Li," he said, over the thuttering of cloven air. "Get ready to help me with Nininze if we have to evacuate quickly."

And . . . *now.*

He hit the *override* button to cut out the subsystem that usually prevented suicide moves, and then hauled back on the joystick, unconsciously straining at it as if it were connected to the control surfaces by something besides electrical impulses. The blunt wedge of the *Riga* turned its nose up and up, as if it were trying to climb back to orbit. Speed was transformed into altitude in a few instants of savage deceleration, and his abused body screamed to him in protest. Adrenaline overrode it as he fought for life. There would be a precise instant when the *Riga* was about to stall and acquire the aerodynamics of a large brick tossed into the sky.

Now.

He pushed the joystick forward. There was a heart-stopping moment of zero-G when it seemed the craft would fall hopelessly stern-first.

"*Shudas!*" he blurted.

They *were* going to stall. Then the controls moved, and the *Riga* lurched. The nose went down. Potential energy became speed once more as they fell. The lifting-body shape of the *Riga* functioned once more, and the rudders bit the air. But the speeds were lower now, much lower—still too high for a wheels-up landing, but not certain death. The lake grew to a long blue bar before him.

"*Velniai griebtu!*" he swore exultantly, and then they struck.

The ceramic belly of the *Riga* was still hotter than molten lead, glowing white and red, just below its certified failure state. A huge cloud of steam exploded out from it as they hit, along with the spray. It wasn't—quite—enough to flip the shuttle on its back. It did mean they rode forward for better than a kilometer on a pillow of superheated water vapor, an almost frictionless bed that sent the *Riga* squirting forward like a bead of mercury sliding over dry ice. That meant they were traveling fast enough to let the fins bite, and he was able to keep the *Riga* pointed west in a swooping, side-to-side, snake-track way. Just when the hilly western shore was starting to look uncomfortably close, the belly dropped into the water proper with an ominous series of crackling noises—the heat-shield snapping as differential cooling stressed it beyond its parameters. The ride became rougher as well, like a sled traveling over dried corrugated mud.

"Here we go!" Binkis shouted.

The shore loomed up. He steered for a cove with a sloping muddy shore and waving swamp reeds behind it, throwing a huge rooster tail of spray as the flat-bottomed craft careened across the calm blue water.

Then they struck. A feeling of huge inertia, pushing him forward intolerably against the straps . . . and blackness.

BOOM!

The first thing Binkis was conscious of was the smell, something like burnt sewage with an undertone of rank greenery. The noise that had awoken him was the explosive bolts throwing up the emergency escape hatch; it stood up now like the lid of a box, and smoke poured in, making him cough with the thick rankness. The *Riga* had run through the swamp and up onto the edge of firm land. The nose was canted up over a massive root and a towering tree overhung the cockpit; the angle made the acceleration couch seem like a bed. Every inch of his body ached as if it had been stretched out to twice its proper length and beaten with oak rods, and dried blood coated the lower half of his face like a sticky mask. He managed to wipe some of the sludge away and gasped for breath, but the effort was too much for him, and he slipped gratefully back into the velvet darkness.

When he woke again, Li was flipping water from a canteen on

his face. He saw that Nininze had been laid out on the narrow strip of floor between the workstations, resting on an inflatable mattress.

"Thanks," Binkis croaked, and took the canteen, gulping hastily and then coughing before a steadier drink. "How long?"

"I came to about twenty minutes ago," Li said. "It is four hours since we crashed."

"Landed, Li. Landed. We're alive, so it was a landing."

She nodded with her usual expressionless calm; he had to admit she looked better than he felt, moving fairly gingerly but with her face washed clean of blood.

"It was an inspired piece of piloting, sir," she said.

Binkis nodded. *Although . . . for a moment there, it was if Someone Else was at the controls.* He groped at his waist for the first-aid pouch, but Li silently held out two painkiller tablets. The pilot washed them down with more water, coughed again, wiped his face, and went on:

"What's our situation?"

Surprising him, she smiled. "We are stranded a very long way from home, Captain." Then, serious once more: "We grounded on a spur of firm land—relatively firm land—near the western end of the lake, where the short arm running north–south meets the long east–west one. There are cliffs about two kilometers south of here and extensive swamps to the north and west. I saw plentiful wildlife but no large sauroids. Lieutenant Nininze remains unconscious and is apparently concussed."

Binkis swatted at something on his neck; it squished unpleasantly against his skin. "We'll have to get out of the *Riga* and set up a camp on dry land," he said. "Then we can see about cobbling together a radio and getting in touch with Cosmograd."

They set to work. There was a spring not far south where a rocky shelf about twelve feet high rose from the soft ground, with a small clearing surrounded by huge evergreen oaks. They unpacked the survival kit, which included machetes, and chopped a way through the undergrowth of tall ferns to a game trail that led to the clearing, set up their tent, and then began the difficult business of hoisting the unconscious Nininze out without hurting him still more. Everything was slowed by the battering and bruising their own bodies had taken; neither of them was technically concussed, but you didn't get knocked unconscious without feeling well and truly miserable. The air wasn't too hot, around twenty degrees, and the extra oxygen helped, but it was thick, humid, and still, and insects buzzed about their ears ceaselessly. After a while, the sweat seemed to help, as if Binkis were sweating out the poisons of fear and pain.

Halfway through the process, Nininze began to come to, but was semiconscious and weak, not seeming to know where he was or able to talk coherently.

"*Prakeikimas!*" Binkis swore mildly. "Damn!"

"Shall we sedate him, Captain?" Li called through the roof-hatch. "I've already given him the painkillers."

"No, I don't want to waste drugs unless we absolutely must," Binkis said. "It's not a good idea with a concussion, anyway."

There were loops along the edges of the inflated mattress. He used his belt-knife to cut a set of restraints free of one of the acceleration couches and improvised a set that would immobilize the injured man at shoulders and waist and legs; then they rigged a block and tackle from the overhanging branch. Binkis stripped off his shirt to pad his hands and braced himself beside the semiconscious man.

"I'll hoist him," he said. "You swing him out on the top of the hull—make sure he doesn't land facedown."

"I will be careful to orient him properly," Li said. "Laying him facedown would aggravate his injuries."

As usual, Binkis couldn't quite tell if she was completely serious. He snorted and took a careful strain on the rope until the mattress began to lift, raising the Georgian's head and shoulders first. When the tail of the mattress had cleared the perforated metal plates of the deck, Li took up the slack on her secondary line, which prevented it from swinging like a pendulum bob.

"Carefully . . . carefully . . . *carefully!*"

Binkis shouted it the last time; the weight had come right off the rope suddenly. Then it burned through his hands, almost fast enough to burn through the cloth wrapping.

"To the devils!" he shouted. "What are you doing, Li, you *kumelé!*"

There was silence above, then a scuffling, and an earsplitting shriek of agony—beneath it a rumbling bellow, and a snarl like dogs. An instant later something fell through the hatch. It took him a moment to realize it was Nininze's foot, still in its boot, raggedly hacked free of the leg. Binkis froze for a fraction of a second, then snatched up the assault rifle, leaped for the back of an acceleration couch and up onto the roof of the *Riga*.

Two dozen brutish figures had swarmed up onto the upper surface of the shuttle, massive, hairy, slope-browed, snarling, with thin-lipped chinless mouths full of tombstone teeth; more dropped down from the tree as he landed. Several were dragging Li away; her eyes bulged over a great hand clamped across her face. Another knelt with a mouthful of Nininze's thigh in his mouth, straining backward with powerful neck-muscles while he sawed his sharp-edged obsidian knife back and forth to free the gobbet of flesh; half a dozen others waited to feed.

Binkis screamed and shot, the long chattering burst from the AK-47 sending a bright spearhead of flame into the olive gloom under the tree, the strobing light flashing on the startled faces of the savages and their painted, mud-streaked bodies. Two of them fell dead; another screamed and sprattled before the bolt clicked open. A score of the apish shapes scattered in panic flight, leaping outward into the swamp in huge bounds from the shuttle or running up the tree with the agility of monstrous giant squirrels, but more screamed and crowded closer, brandishing weapons. The pilot fumbled for another magazine and clicked it home just as a thrown club struck him in the knee. He heard the *crack* of breaking bone an instant before the pain doubled him over, and then he fell as the smashed joint buckled beneath him.

Binkis waited for death. One of the Neanderthaloids stooped over him: an older specimen, the hair-beard on his face and the tall topknot of reddish locks streaked with gray, the left eye an empty mass of scars. Tall feathers were tucked into his hair, and the mobile lips elongated into an *O* of astonishment as he examined the human's gear. The Neanderthaloid plucked the assault rifle from across Binkis' chest and brought it up to his broad blobby nose, sniffing and grimacing.

Another quasi-human pushed close, snarling; he was younger and stronger, with a knob-headed club in one hand. He pointed at Binkis and swung his bludgeon up. The older one made a gesture of negation and continued to examine the rifle. Somewhere Li was screaming again. Binkis choked a little on the rancid musk-stink of the figures around him, and watched stolidly as the length of hardwood rose to crush out his brains for the feasters.

Braaappp!

The AK-47 fired off most of its magazine before the older Neanderthaloid released the trigger. Five of the rounds blasted into the one about to kill Binkis, a row of black holes turning instantly red from crotch to sloping forehead. The sixth took the top off the head of one of the ones sitting chewing around Nininze's body, and the rest clipped down bark and twigs from the trees.

The new-made gunman hooted with delight as his fellows cowered. Then he made an imperious gesture, and four of them scuttled forward to lift the pilot in the air. He screamed once as the broken knee-joint twisted, and then fainted.

His last thought was a deep wish that he never wake again.

Venus, Gagarin Continent—south of Jamestown Extraterritorial Zone

Marc woke a little past the middle of the night. *What a dream!* he thought.

A face with slanted blue eyes and wheat-colored hair framing a high-cheeked, snub-nosed countenance. A diadem of shimmering silvery metal about her brow, and a chill wind from a glowing nexus of light behind her.

"Whoa!" he exclaimed, sitting erect.

He'd thrown back the top of the bedroll while he slept. *No wonder I made* un-transport *just now,* he thought. *Who could stay still with a dream like that?*

Perhaps the sudden drop in the air temperature had prompted it, just before it woke him. *Or maybe it's all those books I read as a kid,* he thought with an inner smile.

He rubbed his eyes with the heels of his hands and then blinked at the fire, dazzling in the darkness even though it had died to a bed of low coals that reflected in red-orange flickers from the rock overhang above. The Terran looked out into the dark; it was near-impenetrable, with no moon and even starlight a rare treat. His internal clock told him it was very late, that he'd been asleep six or seven hours; it was accurate again now that he'd adjusted to this planet's thirty-hour cycle. Like most people, he'd simply taken to adding a few hours each to his waking and sleeping.

Call it four hours to dawn.

But looking south towards the mountains, Marc caught a faint flash of light. And noise, more felt through the air than heard, under the constant splashing of the spring into its pool.

It was Zhown's watch, the elder of the two tribals. He was squatting well away from the fire, wrapped in a blanket with a short spear ready to hand, more useful than his cherished new bow in the inky darkness. Marc had slept in his clothes, but he walked barefoot into the dark.

"You walk quietly, for one of the Sky People," the guide said softly.

Marc could sense the grin in Zhown's voice. They spoke in a mixture of English, Kartahownian, and the hunter's native language. Marc wouldn't like to try discussing philosophy in the garbled pidgin, but it did well enough for practical things.

"The sky woke me," he said. "What do you smell? I hear thunder, maybe."

There were only a few real differences that they'd found so far between Venusians and Terrans. Two were that the locals had a distinctly superior sense of smell and somewhat better night-sight; not dog-sensitive noses, but several times better than Marc's equipment, and a slight but distinct advantage in darkness. And the Earthlings had keener hearing. All that made sense, given the thicker atmosphere and the lack of a moon or much starlight in the hazy nights.

"Hard to say with all this water close," Zhown said. "I think a storm passes from the sea southward, though. Rain there before daybreak, maybe already-now in the mountains."

Marc grunted, which was a polite acknowledgment in Zhown's language and an insult in Kartahownian. You had to keep in mind that a world the size of Earth or Venus was a big place. . . .

"No sense in waking the others," Marc said at last. "I wouldn't like to try the slope in the dark, not with *churr.*"

Zhown grunted in turn, which was reassuring. The native wouldn't have kept quiet if he disagreed; he thought the Terrans were among Those Others—spirits, quasi-elves, the specialists weren't quite sure what the term meant yet, except that it was associated with the supernatural. But he didn't have all that much awe of them just because they *were* supernatural, either. Apparently Those Others turned up all the time in his people's stories, and he was perfectly ready to argue with the Sky People in his own area of expertise. In fact, he thought most of them were klutzes away from their town and machines; Marc was quite flattered to be classed as a promising amateur at bushcraft.

He got his rifle and put on his boots, after carefully checking them for scorpions and similar manky nuisances. Then he took a position not far from Zhown and waited, squatting easily. The night was full of sounds once you quieted your mind and really *listened*: clicks and buzzes and rustlings, once a huge *hooo-hooo* in the distance like a Brobdingnagian owl, occasional howls and screeches. A little like the bayou country—once there was something like a bull gator calling his territory to the night.

But not much like, and Marc grinned to himself in the darkness. This was *exactly* what a younger Marc Vitrac had wanted as he read lurid pulp adventure stories with a flashlight beneath the covers back in the family house on the Bayou Teche. His grandfather had built that home, hand-shaping the cypress joists, and his father had trapped nutria from it in between spells as an oil-platform roustabout. Neither of them had had much understanding of the dreams that shaped Marc's generation.

The news from the first probes, still more the pictures from the second wave, had made all the old classics new again, inspired an ever-swelling stream of imitators, and set every boy and most girls on Earth to dreaming those particular dreams. Most of them had to content themselves with books all their lives, and bad movies, and documentaries.

But I made it, he thought.

Marc chuckled aloud. His own picture was probably on the bedroom walls of millions of hero-worshipping kids, and he was undoubtedly the thinly disguised hero of countless trashy novels and bad TV shows by now—and the illustrated heartthrob of countless girls. If he were somehow returned to Earth, he could write his own ticket and have hot and cold running starlets as long as he wanted.

Not that it mattered; barring some unlikely chance, he'd leave his bones here. You didn't ship people between worlds casually, not at fifty million a ticket each way.

But no leaving the bones just yet, he reminded himself, as a rumble of thunder came from the south, definite now, not an if-maybe.

That woke Corlin. Zhown chaffed him in their own language, and the younger guide stoked up the fire. Marc put a clay field oven full of balls of biscuit dough in it, using a green stick through the handle to lift it in, and set a potful of water to boil for zulk-tea. By the time the smell of scorched frying pan and antelope-breadnut-and-onion hash was wafting across the campsite, the gray light of a chilly overcast morning was as well, and the other two Terrans were up. Marc threw a double handful of crumbled zulk-leaves into the water, and a rich nutty scent was added to the smells of rock and water, vegetation, *churr*, and imperfectly clean human.

"God, that smells good," Cynthia said, as he passed her a cup. She sipped. "God, it tastes awful."

Marc poured shamboo-sugar into his own and stirred it with a twig. "Not that bad," he said, sipping. "Sort of like chicory."

Christopher Blair wasn't a morning person. "Chicory," he said, with a wealth of loathing in his voice. "God, never to taste a decent Darjeeling again, or even Blue Mountain coffee . . ."

His back was to Marc as he spoke, looking out over the breadth of the sinkhole. The river and pools grew visibly as they ate. By the time the pots were scrubbed out with sand, a three-foot surge had crossed the width of the sinkhole, lapping at the foot of the rock knee they'd camped on and boiling white across at the northern exit. Water filled the canyon they'd traveled to get here six feet deep, a deep rushing and gurning that toned in the rock beneath their feet. Fresh debris washed in by the minute, including whole logs with their root-boles exposed, and one great, turtlelike shape with a spiked dome of armor over a back the size of a family sedan. A desperate-eyed bony head reared above the surface, and it gave a mournful hoot like a terrified steam locomotive as the current swept it whirling into the canyon: probably the dinosaurian equivalent of *ooooohhhshiiiiittt!*

"Perhaps we might have risen a bit earlier," the Englishman said, as the rain started.

Marc shrugged and pointed. Just beyond the overhang, the cliff-face had collapsed long ago; the rocky slope was about forty degrees, and climbable by agile humans. The clawed, padded feet of *churr* could usually follow where men could go.

"Didn't want to try that in the dark," he said. "And we might as well have a hot breakfast. It may be a cold camp tonight if the rain keeps up."

"What's that?" Cynthia said, cutting off Blair's possible reply.

That was a balk of timber, most of a tree trunk, with leaves still fluttering from some of the boughs. The main north–south path across the sinkhole was a plunging, swirling cataract by now, but the balk of timber spun out of the current towards them, traveling more slowly for a little before it was sucked back into the torrent. A length of sodden black fur was caught in the branches—

"Greatwolf bitch," Marc said, shielding his eyes from the increasing rain. "Probably got caught underwater when the trunk rolled over."

He could just see the long yellow-white fangs, caught in a final snarl, but the animal lacked a male's massive shoulders and mane.

Though if you want to get technical, it's a canid or caninoid and most closely resembles the Miocene predator Epicyon haydeni *rather than the any type of wolf in the strict sense,* he thought with an inner grin; a lot of Doc Feldman had rubbed off on him. *But we call them greatwolves because they're doggie-looking pack hunters and the native names are all hard to pronounce.*

Then, aloud: "Hey, that's a pup!"

"Poor thing!" Cynthia said. "She must have carried it up the tree, to try and get it out of the water!"

Something whined and struggled feebly amid the tattered leaves. Decision came quickly; it wasn't too far away, no more than twenty or thirty feet, but it wouldn't stay there more than a few seconds.

"Get a rope ready," Marc said, stripping off clothes.

"I say, old boy, that's not such a good idea," Blair began, speaking mildly for once.

By then Marc was down to his boxers. He hit the water in a flat running dive and immediately wondered if Blair wasn't right. It wasn't all that deep right here, barely six feet, but Marc could feel the strong rip currents tugging and dragging at him as the floodwater surged over hidden boulders.

In for a penny, he thought, and struck out.

Foam slapped him in the face and tried to fill his lungs. The water was *cold,* too, as cold as any he'd felt since survival training on the Big Sur coast back Earthside, sucking at the strength of his muscles. But he'd been raised amphibious, long before diving became a favored sport, even longer before Aerospace Force training. You didn't fight the water; you eeled through it, rode it, sleeked along to make it take you where you wanted to go. . . .

Still, he clung and panted a moment when he grabbed the trunk, blinking and feeling a few spots where things had grazed him. There wasn't much time to rest, though, not if he was going to get back to the others before this thing was sucked into the vortex at the canyon-mouth; as more and more water poured into the sinkhole it was ponding back from the single narrow exit, turning that into churning rapids. Hand-over-hand he pulled himself along the tree trunk until he came to the corpse of the greatwolf. It was about as long as he was, and probably weighed as much, a great shaggy-black mass with fangs the length of his little finger. The pup was a male and probably just weaned, from the state of the mother's dugs, which meant he weighed fifteen or twenty pounds. Luckily, he was half-drowned, trapped among the alder's branches in a position that made him scrabble and strain to keep his nose above the churning water. That left him too feeble to struggle when Marc grabbed him.

"Sorry, little feller," Marc grunted, tracing the branches with his hands and visualizing. "Okay, hold your breath."

The cub rolled his eyes and snapped valiantly at Marc. He took a deep breath of his own and bobbed down, letting the current pin him against the wood. The greatwolf pup had to be pulled straight down to get him out of the cage of broken wood that held him; there was a nasty instant when Marc thought two branches had scissored around his own leg, and then he pulled free and broke the surface again. At his side the cub kicked feebly, his disproportionately large paws scrabbling over Marc's abused skin; he shifted his grip to the back of the pup's neck, which had the added advantage of making him go limp, as he would have when an adult's mouth seized him there for carrying. Then Marc switched to a sidestroke, pumping his legs against the grip of the water. That was the only practical way to travel, with the weight of the cub hampering him, but he was uneasily conscious that he couldn't see anything ahead through the increasing cross-chop of the flood and the rain that hissed into it, and even more that the water was full of things that could hurt him, and hurt him with no warning at all. A solid knock on one ankle sent a warning shaft of fire up his right leg, but he couldn't slow down and live.

He was starting to *really* worry when a braided lariat fell out of the air into the water before him. A frantic grab caught it, and he poured his will into the muscle and tendon of his right arm and hand. Then the wet leather snapped out of the water, pulled so hard that moisture squirted out of it under the tension, and he was dragged forward with a jolt that nearly pulled his arm out of its socket. That gave him warning enough that he had his feet under him when he came to the shallows and avoided being dragged over rock. As he'd expected, Zhown had the other end snubbed to the saddle horn of his *churr,* and had walked the beast away from the water to drag Marc out.

Blair tried to say something, but Marc ignored him as he staggered out of the water and under the overhang; the rising flood was lapping at the edge of the rock platform and would be over it in a few minutes. In the meantime, he'd risked his life for the sodden bundle of fur in his arms, and he wasn't going to waste it. The pup made a wet *splat* sound as Marc laid him on the stone and began rhythmically pressing on his chest. He coughed, sneezed, retched water, and nipped painfully at Marc's half-numb hand as soon as his eyes opened. A full-grown greatwolf could be five feet at the shoulder and outweigh a grown man, higher at the shoulders than the rump and with a head like a split barrel lined with fangs.

And this little critter is already sharp-toothed and has feet the size of dinner plates, Marc thought, as he shook off drops of blood and wrapped the shivering form in a blanket to keep him quiet and keep him warm. *He's going to be a big 'un, him.*

"Hold still, you little son of a bitch," Marc said, as he stuffed the wiggling bundle into a burlap sack and hung it from one of the packsaddles.

The *churr* shied a bit—they were among the greatwolves' natural prey, though that wasn't much of an honor, since a pack would kill and eat anything from rabbits to the smaller types of dinosaur. Once the job was done, Marc began to struggle back into his sopping clothes—not much of a comfort in the cold rain, but better than standing and letting it run down his naked skin. That gave him a little leisure to pay attention to the rest of his party.

Zhown and the other guide just looked at him as if he was strange; they probably thought he had some impenetrable spirit reason for doing what he'd done. Cynthia, a bit to his surprise and annoyance, was giving him the sort of glance a rambunctious four-year-old brother might expect. Blair was simple pinched disapproval.

"I must formally protest, Lieutenant," he said. "You have endangered the mission, and as your superior officer—"

Marc finished pulling on his waterproof poncho. "I'm not in your chain of command, Wing Commander," he said. "And on this expedition, *I'm* in charge of the non-scientific aspects."

That shut the Englishman up at the price of a look of white-lipped fury. Marc felt a bit guilty; it *had* been a damnfool stunt, and he'd be in some trouble back at Jamestown if the man made an official complaint about it. Marc was grateful when everyone quietly pitched in to the task of getting the *churr* up the talus slope, slippery as it was with rain. They carried the gear up to the top, then rigged ropes anchored there. Each secured a safety line through the thick metal ring on the horn of a saddle; then they kept someone ahead of each beast with the cord snubbed around a convenient rock as the *churr* made the climb. When the last left the campsite, it was ankle-deep. Marc followed it up, helping with a shoulder against its backside at a difficult spot, as it snorted and squealed and scrabbled its big blunt claws against the rain-slick rock. When they'd heaved the creature up another dozen feet to where the rope was snubbed, Marc and Zhown took a breather.

"I am glad you came un-harmed from the water," the native said.

"With the help of my oath-sworn friends," Marc replied.

"With my help," Zhown replied. "And Corlin and Night Face," which was what the locals called Cynthia. "Sun Hair did little but stand and shout loudly and move about."

"You say so?" Marc said, shocked, and got a brisk nod that sent drops flying from the edge of the straw coolie hat.

He knew the native guide didn't like Blair—significant in itself—but he also knew Zhown wasn't in the habit of slandering men, either. *But he's no less inclined to see what he expects than other men,* Marc thought. *And so am I, and I've never liked the* de'pouille, *and hope to beat him out with a woman, which is still more reason to think badly of him.* Marc put the matter from his mind.

"Let's get this whore where she belongs," he said instead.

Hours later, when they were camped in a shallow cave on a hillside several miles northward, he let the thoughts trickle back. The problem was that he still didn't have any evidence, except for Zhown thinking that the Englishman hadn't been very enthusiastic about rescuing Marc—and all he could really say was that Blair had tried to stop him taking the risk in the first place and criticized him for doing it afterward. Who could say if there had been room for another pair of hands in the effort of getting a rope out to him while he struggled in the flood? If there hadn't, then trying to pitch in would simply have hindered the first comers. And Blair had an excellent record; he'd been crucial in repairing the *Carson*'s damaged reactor, from the reports.

Leave it, Marc thought. *Just keep an eye on him.*

There was enough work to keep them all busy. The cave was a thumb-shaped indentation in a steep hillside, extending upward like a crack in the rock, with an overhang in front where their hobbled remuda could get some shelter from the weather. Soon they had a comfortable blaze going, always easier on Venus than Earth. Nothing carnivorous was likely to try to take shelter here from the rain, because even the biggest 'saurs were afraid of fire; given the higher proportion of oxygen in the air, wildfire was a terrible menace here. That was about the only thing they *did* fear, that and the predators whose shape evolution had hardwired into their pigeon-sized brains. Fortunately, they were a thousand feet higher here than Jamestown, and the season was further along. The cold-blooded giants and the big meat eaters that preyed on them avoided these coolish heights in fall and wintertime.

The party from Jamestown hung their wet gear from wooden stakes driven into the cave wall's cracks, changed into dry, unrolled their bedding, and prepared to wait out the rain; it rarely fell for more than a day at a time this early in the wet season, even in the hills. The cave was even comfortable if you were used to fieldwork and didn't expect it to warm up like a house. They put heated rocks in their bedrolls to get those toasty for bedtime. Cynthia set out her samples and went on with cataloging and note-taking. Blair talked with the guides and murmured a report on their language into his pocket recorder; the tribesmen saw to the *churr*. After Marc had built a cage of trimmed branches tied together with tough bark he considered what to do with his greatwolf cub. Now that he'd gone to so much effort and risk to get the cub, turning him loose to starve or be eaten seemed a bit wasteful. And he was too cute to turn into a specimen in Doc Feldman's collection, eyes big with terror and body quivering, whimpering what was probably a continuous cry of: *Mom! Come get me, Mom!*

Hasten slowly, Marc thought, and decided to ignore the cub until dinnertime. He might as well get the meal going. *Nothing like a long, cold, wet day for an appetite. Probably true of the little beastie as much as it is of us.*

They had a big aluminum pot along with them. Marc filled that with water and set it to boil, along with salt and a couple of meat-extract cubes he crumbled into it. There was a fair bit of antelope left; it was at its best now, since they'd drained it thoroughly when he'd gralloched the kill, but it wouldn't last much longer before it went off and had to be fed to the *churr*. He cut the meat into bite-sized pieces, dredged them in *nurr*-flour, browned successive loads in the frying pan along with some garlic, and then tossed it into the water to simmer. Raw breadnuts went into the stew next, as well as dried beans and vegetables from their stores, handfuls of wild greens picked up along the way, and Kartahownian spices that tasted a bit like curry powder and something like sage.

"Needs a good brown roux and some okra or *filé*," he said, tasting it. "Except for that, not bad."

For most of the afternoon, the pup cowered in the darkest, rearmost corner of his cage, growling whenever anyone came near, otherwise nothing but a black shadow and occasional glitter of yellow eyes and a whimper of bewildered grief. The preparation of the evening meal brought him forward to stand with his muzzle pressed against the latticework, wrinkling his wet black nose and licking the latticework as he drank in the fascinating novelty of the scent of cooking meat. The savory odors mixed with wet almost-puppy and drying cloth and leather and wood smoke and *churr.*

"Take over for a minute?" Marc asked. "Our furry guest probably likes his pretty rare. Damned if I'm going to swallow it and regurgitate it for him, though."

"Sure, I'll do it," Cynthia said, setting aside a rock. "This isn't going to make any more sense because I stare at it."

She stirred the stew and threw in a little more salt, then mixed a bowl of flour with baking powder, setting it on a griddle over the fire where it began to rise and bubble, browning. Marc snagged gobbets of meat on a sharp twig, piled them on a bark plate, and waved it around until the food was warm rather than hot; he added some rich marrow from cracked bones. Then he carried it over to the cage, lifted one edge for an instant, and shoved the plate through beneath. The greatwolf cub retreated again, then came forward belly to the ground, growling in a tenor voice. A slight quiver ran through his tail as he sniffed at the warm meat. Then he darted forward despite Marc's looming presence, gripped a chunk, and dashed back to the far corner to bolt it down. Another and another . . .

Good thing meat's cheap here, Marc thought, grinning at the supper-dance.

"Me Grug," Cynthia said from over by the fire, making her voice deep, and pounding a fist on her chest. "Grug mighty hunter. Grug *tame* dog!"

Blair surprised Marc by laughing. "Take it young, feed it, and see if that makes it love you—classic domestication."

"Hey, whatever works," Marc replied mildly.

Eventually hunger overcame caution, and the pup stopped retreating to eat, standing over the plate and bolting his contents in place. He growled and snapped again when Marc pushed an arm into the cage, but more as a warning not to touch the food than in a serious attempt to harm.

Still, begin as you mean to go on, Marc thought.

His hand darted down and took the cub by the ruff at the back of his neck; Marc shook the young beast gently when he tried to turn his head and bite him, and used his other hand to flick the cub's ear—the same methods his mother would have used to discipline him.

"No!" Marc said firmly, keeping his hold until the cub stopped squirming and trying to bite. Then: "Good boy!" as he released the cub and stepped back.

The twenty-pound puppy whined and laid his ears back, then returned to eating. When he was finished, his stomach was notably rounder; he pulled the good-smelling bark plate back with him to the blanket in the rear corner of the cage and settled down again, going to sleep with a limp totality, his mouth slightly open and pink tongue-tip showing.

"Charming," Blair said dryly. "But probably not as practical when it's bigger. And it will be. Very *much* bigger."

"People have tamed wolves back on Earth," Cynthia said. "And I think it's cute. I miss dogs."

Jamestown had cats, but no Terran dogs as yet; they didn't take to zero-G well, and weighed a great deal more. Interplanetary transport made every ounce count, particularly living ounces.

"People have tamed wolves, my dear," Blair agreed. "However, they're always more dangerous and unpredictable than dogs—and wolves don't grow to be two hundred and fifty pounds, and they can't take a man's leg off with one bite."

Marc shrugged. That was true enough. Greatwolves weren't just big; their broad wedge-shaped heads gave tremendous areas of attachment for jaw muscles, and they ould crack a *tharg*'s thighbones the way a kid did a candy cane. A pack of them could take down a medium-sized 'saur.

"If it becomes dangerous, we can always shoot it," Marc pointed out. "It's a lot harder to un-kill something than to kill it in the first place. And the species isn't common around Jamestown. It'll be useful for Dr. Feldman's study program."

"What'll you call it?" Cynthia asked.

"I think . . . Nobs," Marc said, and joined her laughter.

Blair seemed as much puzzled at their amusement as the natives, and a good deal more resentful. Marc was a little surprised. Was there anyone who'd been a kid since the 1960s who *didn't* know that reference? Surely *everyone* read Burroughs now?

"No, actually I'll call him *Tahyo*."

"What's that? Some tribal name?"

"It's Grand Isle for *Big Hungry Dog*. And he is, him!"

She was still chuckling as she tasted the stew and pronounced it ready. Everyone ladled one of the molded-leather bowls full, took a chunk of the hot griddle cake, and sat down to eat. Marc nodded at compliments, although the natives were like most primitives and preferred the stronger-flavored organ meats to the muscle cuts the Earthlings liked. The natives sighed after the heart and liver and sweetbreads, and didn't mind hinting that with their wonderful rifles the Terrans could supply an endless series of such treats, leaving the steaks and chops to the *churr*. They also had a ruthlessly unsporting and practical attitude towards hunting, again much like Earthly primitives; if they were economical with game, it was because hunting was dangerous hard work, not from conservationism. Give them a rifle and a motive, and they'd slaughter anything that moved like berserkers on speed.

"I'm not going to shoot a five-ton 'saur so you can have kidneys and brains," Marc said with a grin.

"Why not?" Zhown asked. "Those are the best parts, fried in oil, with crinkletongue spice."

That didn't keep him from scraping the bottom of a second bowl and belching hugely and politely.

Venus, Gagarin Continent—Far West

I'm glad that poor bitch Li is finally dead, Binkis thought. *I didn't think anyone could scream so long.*

That had been . . . how long ago? Since then his leg had healed somewhat, enough that the knee was merely constant grinding pain rather than agony. He could even move about a bit, on the crutch that A'a had made for him.

The *A'a* sound meant something like *Old One*. Or possibly *Wise One*. Binkis had tried hard to learn the Wergu language, but that combination of sounds and gestures was more alien than any human language could be, and he'd only had . . . months . . . weeks . . .

It couldn't have been years, could it? I have lost track. Perhaps I am going mad. That would be best . . . Now I will go and bathe in the springs.

Binkis couldn't smell himself much, though he knew he stank;

it was lost in the stunning urine-feces-rotting-food-sweat fetor of the Wergu village; one had to call it that, since there were hundreds of them here. He clawed himself upright along the side of the hut. It had been built of rough fieldstone, then plastered smooth on the inside; he didn't think the Wergu had built it, and they'd certainly patched the thatch badly, and let the windows of thin tanned gut rot and rip to tatters. It wasn't even all that uncomfortable, once he'd scraped the worst of the filth out and collected some dried grasses to lie on. The vermin that affected his captors wouldn't bite him, or at least the body lice and fleas wouldn't—the roaches and flies were inescapable. Dozens were swarming around the scraps of his dinner in the gourd bowl by the door, consuming the last of the rancid fish-and-roots stew. A'a had his females feed the captive well and regularly, the same diet he ate himself; they'd also hauled the prisoner to the hot springs and applied poultices of chewed roots to the knee.

The crutch leaned against the wall by the door and the raw deerhide that covered it. He stuck the padded end under his armpit and brushed the hide aside, blinking a second in the bright sunlight. Outside, the Wergu children played their stalk-and-pounce games, females tended what camp chores there were—they made the crude tools and weapons as well—and a few cripples or older males slowly starved to death.

Except for A'a. *Except for the Old One.*

The Neanderthaloid was carefully field-stripping the AK-47 as Binkis had taught him. His fingers were too large for some of the smaller parts, but he patiently picked up each one and cleaned it again until they all fit. The Lithuanian had known soldiers a lot less careful about it, when he'd been a young conscript. One of A'a's . . . acolytes, perhaps, at least one of the younger males who hung about him, was watching, enthralled, occasionally making a fascinated hooting sound and slapping himself on the head with a solid *thock!* sound. Now and then he would submissively groom A'a's bristly hide.

The Wise One looked up. He finished snapping home the receiver of the assault rifle, clicked in a magazine, and rose, slinging a webbing bandolier full of magazines across his barrel chest. A'a lived in the biggest of the huts now, and the back was stacked with crates of rifles and ammunition. The chief of the band hadn't even objected to moving out to the second-biggest that A'a had used before.

"*Come!*" he said/signed to the human; there was a gesture, combined with a grunted imperative that turned it into an order. "*Show!*"

"Show what?" Binkis replied fearfully. "Show *rifle?*"

A negative; he'd already taught the witch doctor everything he could about firearms, which was why he'd been afraid he'd go into the pot soon. And the word meant *explain* as much as *show*. Perhaps *show how* . . .

"Show! Come!" A'a said, and turned to walk away.

The Wergu led him out of the clutch of huts, past the turnoff to the hot springs, and then uphill towards the caves. After a struggle that brought a sweat of pain to his face, Binkis made an inarticulate sound of protest. A'a shrugged and threw him over a massive shoulder, trotting effortlessly upward; the jolting ride was only slightly less painful than climbing himself. The Wergu was scarcely breathing hard when he set the human down again; even given the lower gravity of Venus, the Neanderthaloids were stronger than any man, beast-strong, gorilla-strong, their great muscles anchored on massively thick bones that gave broader areas of attachment.

"Cave strange show!" A'a said.

As far as Binkis could see, it was just a cave; the limestone cliffs around the lake were full of them. He knew better than to disobey the Wise One, though. He waited while the Wergu shaman kindled a torch, and then followed him, his crutch thumping on the sandy floor in rhythm with his wheezing breath. The ceiling swelled out above them, thick with stalactites. Bats rustled up there, and the acrid sweet-sour guano stink of their droppings was thick. After a while A'a stopped and gestured to the walls.

"Stickmen make," he said.

Binkis stared, jarred out of his own misery for a moment. The walls were covered by paintings in an eerily naturalistic style, *tharg* and *churr*; antelope, saber-tooths, cave-lions, raptors, giant ceratopsians and duckbills and mountainous titanotheres, ochre-brown, green, crimson, blue. The irregular surface of the rock was used to add life to the images, like an endless band of bas-reliefs, and streaks of soot from animal-fat stone lamps rose above the scenes like exclamation points. In places the images had been crossed over with broad splashes of what looked like dried blood, and handprints in the same material. There was a smell of old blood, and of fat and smoke, and cold, wet rock.

"Strange cave. Come, show!"

The cave narrowed, until Binkis was stooping over and hobbling painfully. The torch guttered low, but the light seemed to be growing.

No.

The captive blinked. It wasn't as if there was actually a light, more as if he was somehow seeing without it. *I am* mad. *Good.*

A'a stopped, raising his torch and squinting as if into absolute blackness. "Show! *Show!*"

The poor beast wants me to explain *this,* Binkis thought with an involuntary giggle as he limped forward into the white not-light.

The stone vanished beneath his bare feet. What replaced it seemed to be soft and yet firm, like some resilient synthetic, but at the same time there was no sensation of contact beneath his feet at all.

At last the white light shone through his own body. He lifted his hand, watching bone and tendon move and flex. The pain had vanished in a scent of strawberries, and his fear with the taste of sour cream and springwater. Radiance shone through his skull. A voice louder than God's whispered behind his eyes: *Satisfactory.*

CHAPTER THREE

Encyclopedia Britannica, 16th Edition
University of Chicago Press, 1988

VENUS: History of observation

PROBES: By the early 1960s, orbital observations had confirmed that Venus, like Mars, was a life-bearing world, and further that at least one apparent city existed on the edge of a river delta near the northeastern edge of the continent of Gagarin. Atmospheric probes had given extensive details on composition, but only surface observation could begin to solve the puzzles that had aroused the anxious curiosity of all mankind. Foremost among these was the unmistakable shape of irrigation works, roads, and settlements. Expectations were high that the human race would soon contact its first alien intelligence . . .

Venus, Gagarin Continent—near Kartahown
Early Winter, 1988

Tahyo wiggled and whined a little, sticking his head out of the sad-dlebag. Marc dropped his hand to the greatwolf pup's head and gave it a swift, hard rub with the tips of his fingers, the short mot-tled brown-and-black fur rough under his touch. If you concen-trated just behind the crest that ran along the top of the skull. . . .

The pup sighed and let his head loll back in ecstasy, tongue drooping from the corner of his mouth. The Doc said it was a good bonding mechanism; it was certainly a good way to contain the pup's bounding, chew-the-landscape restlessness. The only draw-back was that it made him slobber, too.

Cynthia, who was riding a little behind Marc, chuckled. "That thing gets bigger every day," she said.

Marc nodded. *Hey, a dog's a great icebreaker.* *"Weh,"* he said. "Re-ally sharp growth curve. Doc Feldman's real interested, but I told him no dissection."

"This climate really *is* a lot like Spain or Italy," Christopher Blair said from his other side, changing the subject with . . .

Dogged determination, Marc thought with a slight smile. *He's been sort of nervous about me since we got back from that trip. And well he should be!*

"You get occasional nice days even in the winter rainy season," the Englishman said.

"I'd say more like California," Marc replied gravely. "Even though it's as far north as Hudson's Bay."

Blair shot him a dirty look. Marc returned it with a bland smile and took a deep breath of air scented by the sea that lay in a white-flecked blue expanse to their left. They rode their *churr* in a loose clump down the eastward track on a day cool but brightly sunlit, with stretches of almost-blue sky between the clouds and haze above. There had been a pathway here before the Terrans came, but it had grown wider—and rougher and more rutted—with the new traffic. They passed a train of ceratopsians pulling massive wooden wagons with six man-tall wheels, coming back to Jamestown with grain and cloth and bulk goods. Marc waved to the drivers, and reflected that *they* didn't have to worry much. The city-folk had learned not to run screaming at the sight of a 'saur with a human being on it, but they were still in sufficient awe that trouble was unlikely.

He'd have preferred personally that nobody but contact special-ists be allowed into Kartahown, but nobody had come to Venus to be confined to base . . . and Jamestown was a *small* town. You could study data in safety back on Earth, if that was your preference—there was only an hour-and-a-bit lag on a video circuit, after all. People came here to do and see things themselves.

There were five riders from the Earthling base; he and Blair were supposed to be riding herd on the others. Marc had no qualms about Cynthia, but the husband-and-wife team of power-plant techs was disconcertingly touristlike . . .

They came in on the same ship as Cynthia and Blair, Marc thought. *Why is it they seem a lot greener?*

A perfectly nice young couple, excited to be finally traveling to the city and snapping pictures of everything that moved with a fancy digital camera from the latest cargo pod to arrive from Earth. Marc had to admit that the gadget was nifty; it had an interior mem-ory and you could download the pictures to a computer for printing, which saved on shipping film out. Although the camera was also large and clumsy, about the size of an unabridged dictionary not counting the plug-in screen.

Sort of science-fictional, Marc thought. *But then, we're exploring an alien planet, eh?*

A lot of equipment Jamestown got was like that, things that wouldn't be on the general market back on Earth for years. It con-trasted with the Great White Hunter look of the rest of their gear: high-laced boots of greenish-yellow 'saur hide, pants with cargo pock-ets, bush jackets, and floppy hats, and automatic pistols at their belts.

But . . .

"Hey, Tom, Mary," he said. "Careful where you point that cam-era, okay? The locals are already convinced we're sorcerers—and there aren't many good magicians in their view of the world. Plus they tend to think anything new is likely to be unlucky."

Blair nodded. "You don't know what 'conservative' means until you've experienced Kartahown," he said.

"Do they think, what, cameras steal the soul?" Tom Kowalski asked.

"They do think that pictures have power over the thing depicted, but they're not likely to realize that's what a camera does," Blair said cheerfully.

"Yeah, but they *do* know what guns do," Marc said, tapping the butt of the 10-mm Browning Hi Power he wore at his waist, as they all did—it was regulations. "And that thing looks a little like a gun, and a lot of these people aren't all that fond of us, might want to *faire la misère.*"

Blair nodded; Marc felt a little disconcerted at how often they were agreeing.

Mais, we agree the planet is round, too.

The Englishman continued, "Kartahown doesn't have police or anything like them—well, London didn't until 1832, either. No courts, either, really, just prominent people who may settle a dispute if the parties agree to let them. The king's soldiers, noblemen's retainers, and temple guards kill bandits, and they may crucify a thief if someone brings one to them, but it's friends and neighbors who retaliate for murders and robberies."

Marc decided to hammer home the lesson. "And *we* don't *have* any relatives in Kartahown and not many friends."

The Kowalskis looked suitably alarmed, and Marc went on, "Now, don't get too spooked. The kings have 'put their hand' over us, which counts for a lot. And the locals are terrified of us, which counts for even more. Just be polite, cautious, unobtrusive, and if someone acts seriously threatening, shoot them down like a dog."

Tahyo chose that moment to try to scramble out of the saddlebag again, and the tension dissolved in laughter.

Twenty miles from Jamestown, a big square fortress of rock and adobe stood where a spur of higher land swung towards the ocean, the tail end of a ridge of hills stretching inland and shaggy with forest. Bronze gleamed ruddy on the spearheads of soldiers behind the pointed crenellations along the walls, and a thread of smoke rose in a column that bent towards the sea. Down by the roadway, three hundred yards or so from the fortress gate, waited a unit of thirty men. Ten wore cuirasses and helmets of 'saur hide shaped by boiling and nearly as strong as metal; the leather was polished and oiled and had an almost liquid-looking russet sheen. Their weapons were long, bronze-headed spears and short, leaf-shaped swords; they leaned on tall, oval shields that were made of the same thick leather set on wooden frames.

Nobody here had invented standing to attention yet, but they looked alert and tough, with scarred eagle-nosed faces, their legs and arms knotted with muscle. Another fifteen were slingers, lightly equipped in sandals and cloth tunics, with daggers and big pouches for the pebble ammunition of their craft. They carried two slings each, one the simple leather type tied around their brows like a headband, the other with a yard-long wooden handle to anchor the thong.

Marc eyed them with respect; a staff-sling could spatter a man's brains at well over a hundred yards, after cracking his helmet first, or give a Quetza all the trouble it wanted. The soldiers were used to Terrans pretty well, but they gawked at Tahyo's alertly curious head examining everything around. Marc took advantage of the moment to swing down from the saddle and lift the solid fifty-pound weight of the young greatwolf out of the leather carrying bag. The pup ran around his feet, sniffing frantically, looked at the strangers with frosty suspicion, then trotted off to a large rock to pee enthusiastically.

"Heel, boy! Heel, Tahyo!" Marc said sharply when the beast was finished.

The Kartahownians gawked even harder when Tahyo trotted obediently back to sit behind Marc's right heel. Some of the signs against wizardry got pulled out again, but a few grinned delightedly. Tahyo tended to have that effect on people.

It's the big head and big eyes, Marc thought. *Hardwired. Although the teeth are something of a put-off, the way they come over the lips.*

The officer in his two-*churr* chariot wore 'saur-hide armor as well, but his had gold clasps and studs, as did his sandals, and his helmet was of worked bronze, with a high crest of enormous feathers each two feet long or better, iridescent blue and green. He smiled broadly at the Terrans. So did several of his men. A few others had carefully blank faces that probably hid hostility. The rest showed varying degrees of fear and awe.

"The kings greet their friends," the officer said, which probably exhausted his English; he brought his clenched right hand to his forehead, an acknowledgment that the Friends of the King were of equal status or higher.

"*imiAmerican imiKartahownRis fiwas, fornas-hoon shoom'n,*" Marc said in return. "The Americans greet the kings of Kartahown with respect, and also its people and the gods within its walls."

He returned the gesture; Blair did, too, and the other three Terrans followed suit a heartbeat later. The nobleman's smile looked a little more genuine as he realized the Terran could speak his own language fluently, although accented with the nasal whistling tone of all the Sky People.

"Pass, then, in peace and friendship," he said. Less formally: "Enjoy yourselves. Visit the Temple of the Bride. A stranger brings double luck, and surely one of the Sky People will bring four times the good fortune from the goddess."

As the spearmen stepped aside, Cynthia raised a brow at Marc. "What's that about the Temple of the Bride? She's their local fertility-and-hearth goddess, isn't she?"

"Ah . . ." Marc paused, embarrassed.

Blair smiled. "As I understand it, women here have to sacrifice their virginity in the Bride's temple before they can marry, with whoever fortune sends along. A number of ancient peoples on Earth had similar customs," he said. "I've never been there myself, but perhaps Marc . . ."

Marc busied himself by lifting Tahyo back into his carrier, one hand on the loose scruff of his neck, one under the butt. The greatwolf laid his ears back but submitted with another loud sigh. The *churr* snorted, a sound that involved a *fluppppttt* of lips against blunt omnivore fangs; the riding-beast was willing to tolerate the smell of greatwolf, but only just. It was as unnatural as putting a tiger on an ox.

Then Marc laughed ruefully and shook his head as he swung back into the saddle. "It's far too public for my taste," he said. "Worthwhile from a tourist's point of view, though. Makes Bourbon Street look like a convent."

"I can imagine," Cynthia said dryly.

"Well, the locals get upset and insulted if everyone stays away." Marc cleared his throat and pointed southward. "And there you've got another fruit of our technical aid program," he said, with pardonable pride; he'd been involved in the negotiations.

The cluster of buildings was at the edge of sight; they could just see the white water of a millrace turning an overshot wheel, and three furnaces like squat pyramids with the tops lopped off. Two of them were being blown in, and trailed their own thick columns of sooty smoke into the blue-and-white sky.

"The new smelters," he went on. "Eighteenth-century-style charcoal-fired blast furnaces. Those hills have beds of hematite ore in them, sixty or seventy percent pure iron. We're already setting up an electric-arc furnace in Jamestown to turn the pig iron into steel; there's plenty of surplus power from the reactor. It'll be operational in a couple of weeks."

"I remember hearing about it," Cynthia said. "It'll certainly be massively helpful when we've got more basic tools. Right now it's a catastrophe to lose a rock hammer or a piton."

Blair scowled slightly. "I wonder what effect it will have on the local people," he said. "Dumping a new technology like that into an early Bronze Age culture . . . at best, there will be massive disruption."

"It certainly will change things, podna," Marc said. "What did that historian call iron? The democratic metal? You've been in town talking to the priests a lot, haven't you?"

"Yes," Blair said, seeming genuinely enthusiastic. "Trying to get into the archives, and making a fair bit of progress. Fascinating stuff there, absolutely fascinating. We know virtually nothing about the history of Kartahown yet . . . and even with this syllabic alphabet, some of the earliest records show how the language has changed."

Marc nodded. "*Weh*, I'm sure it's all real fascinating. But notice how the priests and the kings and nobles and their hired soldiers get all the metal here? The peasants cultivate with tools of wood and bone and stone, because bronze is so damned expensive."

"Tell it to your precious nomads when the Kartahownian kings get armies with steel armor and weapons," Blair said, then gestured at the northern sea. "And the islanders out there, when they find schooners full of Kartahownian slave raiders arriving."

Cynthia winced. They fell silent for a while, the loudest sounds the jingle of harness and the muffled thump of padded *churr* feet on the dirt, and an occasional startled *wulf* of interest from Tahyo when he saw or scented something new. The road dipped downward as they moved farther east, the rolling plain turning to flatlands where sluggish streams flowed seaward; sometimes they ponded back behind the coastal dunes and turned into vivid green marshes alive with birds that looked very much like duck and snipe and flamingo. Some of those were a deep crimson save for black and yellow heads; when they took off in mass flight the air seemed to turn to a moving sunset.

The land had patches of cultivation around dun mud-brick villages, but mostly it was rolling green pasture for the herds of king and noble and priest: *tharg* and *churr* and sheep, and pigs eating acorns under the oaks—or things enough like swine and sheep and oaks that they hadn't bothered taking up the Kartahownian names. The herds had guardians armed with long pikes and slings; the forts and fortified manors and temples had paddocks with stout walls and lattice roofs of thick oak beams. Fields grew more common and the road broader, with more traffic on foot and in chariots and little ox-carts and then . . .

"*Shoodak w'zaa hotl*," Blair said. "The Barrier That Guards the World. Impressive, isn't it?"

It was: a massive, sloped rammed-earth wall that stretched out of sight in either direction, bristling with sharpened tree trunks and studded with forts at intervals, guarding the inner lands of Kartahown from nomad incursions, and even more from the bigger and nastier forms of wildlife. When you considered some of the things humans here had to live with, it wasn't really surprising that they were just getting around to civilization.

What's really impressive is that this was all done by hand, wooden shovel, basket, and pickaxes made out of animal bones, with oxcarts for high tech, Marc thought. *They didn't even have wheelbarrows until we showed them how to make 'em.*

The gate was a V-shaped notch in the earthwork, one that could be quickly blocked with massive spiked balks of timber, with forts on either side. There was also a big canal that served the fields that stretched to the edge of sight in every direction, save where a few sloughs held livid-green reeds and stretches of water. In one of them, a pair of children in a small canoe dipped out a net full of wriggling things much like crawfish.

"Remind you of home?" Cynthia said, half-mocking.

Marc shook his head. "The swamps do; there's more of them further in towards the Mother River. This here is more like the delta country north of Baton Rouge, all the way up to Memphis. The air's a lot drier though."

The drained alluvial delta had black, waxy-looking soil that did remind him of the Mississippi; the road was the same material, but piled up like an embankment and reasonably dry. Ditches and canals divided the fields into long rectangles, misted with green where the *nurr*-grain was sprouting, or flax or shamboo, or orchards and palm-groves and garden-plots bearing various things leafy or rooty or bushy; peasants were out with wooden spades and mattock-like hoes made from sticks and large seashells, weeding and at the eternal task of digging out the canals. Women carried the muck away in straw baskets on their heads. Both sexes wore simple loincloths, but females sometimes added a calf-length tunic to show that their families ranked a little bit above the commonality.

There was an intense and almost meaty scent from the dark, moist richness of the soil but not much reek of livestock, except for the *tharg*-oxen who pulled carts with twin solid wheels or turned water-pumps, and the odd chariot pair of *churr*. Enough people, pigs, and gaudy domesticated birds the size of turkeys swarmed around the habitations to produce a gagging stink of garbage and ordure from the frequent mud-brick villages. This was a man-made landscape, swarming with a dense mass of peasant families, fertilized with their night soil, and it smelled like it.

"Let me guess," Cynthia said, gulping slightly as they rode through one of the teeming hamlets. "Don't drink the water."

"Not without using your water-purification pills," Marc replied soberly.

Blair nodded. "Not anywhere in the delta."

The stink was also the first thing you noticed about Kartahown, already bad when it was only a line on the horizon northward: sewage and middens and stagnant water mainly, and wood smoke and burning charcoal, with undertones of sweat and seldom-washed bodies. The road rose gradually, and the ground about grew even more thickly peopled. The crops were mostly vegetables for the city trade. Now and then they glimpsed buildings bigger and gaudier than the peasant huts, roofed in reddish tile and with brightly painted patterns on their whitewashed sides. Those were surrounded by mud-brick walls, and within those were gardens and trees; they could glimpse flower beds and ornamental pools laid out in geometric patterns.

"Country places for bigwigs," Marc said. "And that boxy thing with the columns is a temple. There's an interesting procession in spring, when they bring the image of the god out on a sort of giant sledge and haul it into the Temple of All Gods in the city center— the Temple of Koru, the big *papère* of the pantheon. The people line the way and strew flowers and herbs on the road and sing hymns."

Cynthia gagged again, for real this time. "I hope the herbs and flowers cut the stink."

Marc grinned unsympathetically. "After a while you don't notice it so much."

She shuddered. "What a thought! I'm going to check my toes for malignant blue fungus after I leave." She nodded towards the temple—Kartahownians considered pointing at the image of a god blasphemous. "*That's* certainly impressive, though."

The temple was a rectangular box, a brick platform twenty yards by thirty supporting a roof on six huge granite pillars floated down the Mother River on barges. The pillars tapered from base to plinth and were polished to a high gloss inlaid with silver and ori-lachrium and gold, mostly in the spiky, blocky-looking script this civilization used. Long banners woven from feathers in iridescent colors hung between the pillars. When one blew aside you could glimpse the brass idol within; it was in the form of a squat, muscular man twenty feet high, carrying a spiked mace and with the head of a carnosaur, all gape and red tongue and long white teeth, with a horn on its nose. Men in flounced robes were busy about the pronaos, and in the other buildings grouped around it. The smoke of sacrifice rose from an altar in front, where an apprehensive-looking pair of sheep lay struggling, legs bound.

Blair nodded in that direction, too. "That's Thunderfist, the god of war and kingship," he said. "Unfortunately, he's also one of the ones they sacrifice humans to on their high holy days."

Everyone fell silent for a moment. The Terrans had some influence with the monarchs of Kartahown, but not nearly enough to fiddle with the religious basis of their power, not yet at least. The more so as most of the priestly caste ranged from suspicious to hostile.

Tom Kowalski whistled. Cynthia and the others who hadn't been to the city before looked impressed. As usual, pictures couldn't really prepare you for what it *felt* like. A moat fifty feet wide surrounded the whole; most of the water was covered by floating plants with broad platelike leaves and big white-and-blue flowers. That was good, considering what else tended to be floating in the water. A long, sinuous shape glided up in an arch.

"Legless crocodiles," Blair said. "Twenty feet long and better, with teeth like steak knives; they swim in from the Mother River. Don't fall in."

A sloping earth berm fifteen feet high rose on the inner side of the moat; on top of that was a brick wall thirty feet high, five feet of baked brick on either side sheathing a twenty-foot core of adobe, with an octagonal tower half as high again every sixty yards. The outermost layer of brick was glazed, and it made patterns in blue and green and yellow and purple, geometric shapes interspersed with fantastic beasts and birds. Atop the wall were pointed crenellations, with guards pacing back and forth; the roadway ran over a bridge to the wall, then turned sharply left. That exposed an attacker's unshielded right side to stones and javelins from above. Then there was a section where the wall doubled, one stretch overlapping the other, with a gate at each end and a narrow tunnel-like stretch between walls studded with towers.

"*Mais*, here's the big city," Marc said. "Remind *you* of home, city girl?"

"Shee-it, no," Cynthia said honestly, then grinned. "Not even the 'hood I came from was like *this*."

Set into the walls beside the entranceway in three-quarter relief were polychrome statues of bearded, armored men raising bronze swords aloft and trampling enemies below their feet. Each wore what looked like a Plains Indian war bonnet on a helmet, and around them were the symbols of the Kartahownian gods—a sun-disk, a tooth, a spade, a lightning-bolt, a dozen others—each with a stylized open hand beside it.

"Showing the kings are 'under the hand' of the gods, you see," Blair said, in a voice with more than a touch of the lecture-hall in it.

I knew that, Marc thought, as they exchanged salutes with the guards on either side of the gates. *But I knew better than to say it.*

"Well, I'm off to the temple," Blair said. "Enjoy yourselves, children."

Marc nodded. The Englishman had an audience with the High Priest of Koru, about the only possible excuse for not seeing the kings first.

"Enjoy the archives," Marc said.

Venus, Gagarin Continent—Far West

Teesa blinked. The sights of many fought within her mind, blurring the green fronds before her eyes-of-the-flesh; the feel of air on skin, the scents in the noses of as many bodies overpowering her sense of self, of the smooth, narrow shaft of the blowgun beneath her hand, the rank green smell of ferns crushed beneath her knee, the presence of her warriors hiding about her.

Mother, you died too soon! You did not teach me all that I must know! she thought, groaning within as she resisted the temptation to tear the band from her brow.

Here near the Mystery, the featherweight of the Cave Master seemed greater than mountains. To the eyes-of-the-flesh it was a simple circlet of light-colored metal with a green gem above the wearer's brow, no more mysterious than a silver gewgaw such as the sea traders brought in her mother's time. But not even the hottest fire or the heaviest rock could mark or mar it; and somehow it always fit perfectly, whoever wore it.

That was the least of its wonders, if you were of the sacred blood.

With a focused effort she pushed the experience of bodies not hers out of her mind. Instead she drove her will outward in a simple command *nothing to fear*. Birds and fliers near the Cloud People band grew quiet, went about their daily rounds; a ground squirrel walked by within arm's reach, giving her a casual sniff and glance.

Closer and closer came the footfalls of the beastmen. She could hear their voices grunting and hooting, unlike any tongue of men—

but still more than those of wordless beasts. Sense them, sense them, the scent of each slow alien mind—

Her hand went out beside her, fingers splayed and then clenched three times, then two held out: *three-hands-and-two of them.* A little more than twice her band's numbers. Then a gesture with her thumb across her own throat: *We take them.*

Through the broad leaves of the ferns she could see the packed earth of the trail, below them on the slope. Across it was an old statue of the hunter god as a hawk-headed man with a spear, skillfully carved but neglected and moss-grown. Her eyes prickled for a second; without their children to tend them, how could the shrines of the gods and the graves of the Ancestor Spirits be strong enough to ward the Cloud Mountain folk?

Beyond the trail were only glimpses of pine-trees and oaks and beeches, down to the valley where the Cloud Mountain People had once dwelt in pride and happiness. The river was hidden from her, nor had she ever seen it, but she knew every bend of it, where each family and clan had fishing rights, and the caves in the cliffs beyond, and the place where the huts and gardens had stood, the holy lake, and the very Mystery itself. All swarmed by the beastmen and their shes now, all defiled by their filth. Her people remembered, though, they remembered very well, and repeated the tales for each new generation over and over again.

The raiders lay completely still. Teesa blinked her eyes closed, seeing each mind in her mind, like glowing lights. When the lights were in the right place—

"*Arag!*" she screamed, leaping upright: *Kill!*

Her blowgun came to her lips. A blob-nosed beastman face filled her gaze, not twenty paces away. Thin lips skinned back from menhir teeth as the thing screamed, threw aside the great haunch of meat he carried, and reached for the club and shield slung across his shoulders. She filled her lungs as her lips clamped on the carved ivory mouthpiece, then surged the air out from the bottom of her chest, clenching her gut to give it added force.

Phhhtt.

The bone needle had an amber bead on its rear to stabilize it in flight. The curve it made between her blowgun and the beastman was a single blurred streak, and then the creature tried to scream with eight inches of sharpened *tharg*-shin through his throat—not for long, because the grooves at its tip were coated in the crystallized venom of the black spider. Teesa's hand whipped down to the little pouch at her waist-belt made from the hide of a whole marmoset, with the head-cover folded back. The six warriors with her had shot at the same instant, and four of the beastmen were down dead; another had a needle through his arm and would die in less than a minute. Already his eyes glazed and foam dripped from his lips.

The Cloud Mountain warriors snatched up spears or obsidian-headed axes and charged screaming the war cries of their clans, and the remaining beastmen surged to meet them. Teesa ran behind them, ready.

Phhhtt.

This time the needle sank to its bead beneath the beastman's ribs. The hairy torso convulsed, and the Cloud Mountain warrior's axe slammed into the side of his head an instant later. Beyond him a beastman had cast aside his weapons and grappled with one of her people, taking him in a bone-crushing bear's grip and snapping at his throat. Teesa dodged in and laid a hand on the bristly, sweat-slick hide and *pushed* with her mind.

"Ai!" she screamed, staggering backward.

The air filled with the stink of fear-loosened bowel as the beastman collapsed backward, head nearly touching heels as every muscle in his body convulsed, breaking bone and ripping loose from it as well. Teesa shuddered and staggered herself, forcing the death-fear out, a black tide that had nearly consumed her as well as the enemy fighter; the Cloud Mountain warrior dropped to his knees and panted like a *tharg* run to earth by hunters, caught by the backwash.

Using the Cave Master to kill was *dangerous*. Her hand fumbled a little as she shoved another dart into the blowgun.

Then a noise struck her, a long *braaapppp!* It was nothing she'd ever heard before, something like a grove of shamboo breaking in a bad storm, something like two rocks striking together again and again . . . and not like them at all. A hot, acrid stink came with it, alien, making her nose wrinkle.

It was the last of the beastmen—by the feathers in his topknot and the necklace around his corded throat, their chief. Jondlar of the Axebeak clan was in front of him, the point of his spear almost touching the beastman's breast, but somehow his own back had erupted into a mass of blood and bone.

No! she thought, as time seemed to stop. *Not my man! No!*

Jondlar was falling, falling backward; as he did she saw a row of holes across his torso, much smaller than the ones in his back and just turning from black to red. The beastman held a . . . *something.* It was the length of a club with a forward part a little like a blowgun, and a sheen as of metal—but no metal she had ever seen before. From below it a flat boxlike curved shape jutted out, and he fumbled at it—

That is a weapon! she knew suddenly.

Action followed thought; there was no *time* for grief. The curved shape came free of the weapon and the beastman snatched for another like he held in a vest across his body, but her blowgun was already at her lips.

For my beloved! she cried within, and shot.

The beastman chief threw up his arms as the dart slammed home into his eye. That close to the brain, the poison killed in the space of a double blink, and he fell limp as a wet rope.

Teesa looked around. Her warriors were wide-eyed, shaking, on the brink of flight. Ordinary death they did not fear overmuch, but magic was another matter. There was frank terror in their eyes as she held the strange weapon of the beastman chief in her arms.

When there is time I will learn its secret, she told herself. That which slew her man would avenge him. Aloud she said, "Be brave! You are the Cloud Mountain People, clans of the Axebeak, the Raveners, the Winged. Be brave!"

She could see the words take effect and feel them through her mind as she relaxed the screens that kept the death-anguish away from her.

"Gather up all their gear that is strange—that is a new-thing. And some food; we will not be able to stop to hunt and forage while we run."

The men obeyed, though they held the new-things gingerly. Taldi showed her a knife as long as a man's forearm, of some shining metal. He touched it, and then pulled a callused thumb back in surprise as it sliced deep enough to bring a thin line of blood.

"This is cursed!" he said.

"No, fool," she said, overcoming her own impulse to flinch. "This is *sharp*. And tough; see—"

She rapped the flat of the blade hard on a rock, and it rang with an odd vibrating call like nothing she had ever heard before

"—it does not shatter, as obsidian would. Bring all such here."

She waited impatiently; while she waited, it was harder to fight back the tears. Then she passed her hand over first the Cave Master's jewel and next the plunder.

"See, I take away ill-luck by the power of the Mystery. Now we must go. The beastmen will be here soon. I can hide us on the track, but not if they see us from a distance first."

Venus, Gagarin Continent—Kartahown

"You are of the *imiAmerican*," the High Priest of Koru said.

He sat motionless on his throne before the great gilt solar disk of his god. Spicy and bitter smoke from burning incense-resin coiled up to either side of him from censers held by motionless underpriests.

"Why should we trust your word, you deceivers, blasphemers, violators of all good custom and decency?" he went on in excellent English.

Christopher Blair—or Christophé, as he thought of himself most of the time—felt a fine bead of sweat break out on his forehead. He forced himself to take a long calming breath and lean back in the shamboo chair. That was a sign in itself that Tau'tan wasn't as hostile as he acted. Chairs were a luxury here, reserved for the elite, and that Blair had been given one was a good sign—although not as good a one as refreshments would have been. That would make him a guest, and as such absolutely sacred in theory . . . though Kartahownians were human, and hence didn't always put their theories into practice.

"In every people, there are factions and divisions," he replied. "Are all the men of Kartahown as one in all things?"

Tau'tan smiled thinly and tossed his head, the local gesture for *no*. "Truth," he said. "There is some truth in what you speak."

"Thin" was the word that came to mind when you saw the ecclesiastic. He was tall, an inch over six feet, and gaunt to an almost skeletal degree. Green eyes burned in the face of an ancient eagle; the resemblance was increased by the roach of hair down the center of his shaven scalp, short at front but longer at the rear and slicked up with wax into a crest that curled forward. The sun god's gold glittered from rings and bracelets and a broad rayed pectoral; his robe left one shoulder bare as was common custom, but it was ankle-length and covered with shaggy tufts of wool dyed yellow to show his office and allegiance. Besides being chief hierarch of the Great God, he was a cousin of the Left-Hand House, one of the city's royal families, and a major noble in his own right.

For a long moment the green eyes bored into Blair's. Then Tau'tan waved a hand. One of the shaven-headed acolytes standing behind his chair turned and padded away, his feet silent on the white-streaked black stone of the floor. When he returned it was with a servant who bore a tray with bread, honey, fruit wine, water, and cakes made from something like dates and something very similar to walnuts. Blair sipped and nibbled; it was difficult with a throat clenched tight, but necessary. The cakes were palatable, and the fermented fruit juice awful beyond description.

When he had eaten and drunk enough to satisfy ceremony, he went on: "Nor are we who have . . . come to this land . . ."

He didn't say *world*. That was one of the sore points with the priests of the sun god; the notion of other planets sharing the light of the sun struck them as obscenely blasphemous.

". . . all of one people, really. We are of . . . different cities. Not all are willing allies of the Americans, an arrogant and thoughtless people."

"Ah. Restive subject-allies," the Kartahownian said; *his* city had conquered most of the Mother River's valley in the past two centuries and had plenty of experience with the attendant problems. "I understand this. What then do you offer? Can you remove your polluting presence from the Land Beneath the Hand of the Gods?"

Blair sighed and shook his head. "As well ask your mariners to cease sailing to the northern isles," he said. "If one city of the Land ceased, would the others?"

Tau'tan's lips narrowed. The Kartahownians had been sailing to the archipelago off the northern coast of Gagarin for a long time, and "islander" meant much the same to them as "wog" had to a Victorian Briton. Then the priest controlled his temper.

"We have heard of this other settlement of Sky People, far south of here in the upper basins of the Mother River," he said. "Cosmograd, is it not called? And we have heard there is no friendship between it and Jamestown. Are you of that folk?"

Blair shook his head. "No. There are many, ah, cities and kingdoms among the . . . Sky People. Mine is neither of the *imiAmerican* and their allies nor of those who rule Cosmograd. We are a people of more ancient culture and wish only friendship with the people of Kartahown."

Tau'tan grinned like a shark. "And to outdo your rivals for trade and wealth and glory and mastery," he said. "Yes. Perhaps we *should* discuss this further."

He snapped his fingers again, and a cup carved from a single carnosaur tooth was placed in his hand, full of the revoltingly thick, sweet fruit wine.

His other hand waved. "You may speak freely. None of my attendants understands your tongue."

And with nothing recorded . . . what do les Américaines *call it . . . plausible deniability?*

I hope *that's not symbolic,* Marc thought, as the Left-Hand King of Kartahown brandished a new steel sword, smiling at the American guests. Tahyo pressed himself back against Marc's leg, silent but tense.

Unlike the first steel sword—the one the king had worn for years—this wasn't a gift brought from Earth. It had been made by his own Terran-trained smiths from ore smelted right here on Venus.

Maybe we should have insisted that the first load from the smelters be made into plowshares or frying pans. Oo ye yi, I hope he doesn't decide to chop someone up to test it!

"Wonderful!" the monarch said. "And my *blacksmiths*"—he used the English word, horribly garbled—"tell me that soon there will be many more!"

Marc could have sworn that Cynthia raised one slim dark brow ever so slightly at the exchange; she certainly coughed slightly, but that might just be from the strong bitter smell of incense.

The King of the Left Hand was a man in his early forties, middle-aged by local standards, his hair and curled beard shot through with gray though he had most of his own teeth; the spare tire around his middle was a carefully acquired mark of status. The King of the Right Hand was sitting more quietly, clean-shaven as befitted an unmarried youth. He smiled at the Earthlings as well; most of his closest advisers were priestesses of Owl Eyes, the goddess of agriculture and wisdom, and the friendliest of the religious hierarchy to the Sky People. Both kings wore pleated cloth-of-gold robes to their feet, and towering headdresses of green and scarlet feathers in crowns of gold set with uncut gems.

The thrones they sat in were of wood, a dark near-ebony thickly set with polished, sectioned scutes from the belly-armor of a type of 'saur. They were cut thin enough to be translucent, spreading in a high arch behind the seats; they looked a little like the spread fan of a peacock, and something like stained glass or the wing of a butterfly, glowing with the light that shone through the windows behind them. A few shipments sent back to Earth by solar-sail cargo pod had been auctioned after study, for publicity and to support the space program; the price they fetched had actually paid for the shipping costs, or nearly. Here on Venus the material was much less expensive, merely worth several times its weight in gold.

At that, this was the *informal* throne room, probably being used now to make the Terrans' refusal to make the customary prostration less offensive to traditionalists. It was merely twenty yards by ten, with a high, arched ceiling. The yard-thick walls were rammed earth around a matrix of shamboo, sort of a primitive equivalent of ferroconcrete, pierced with tall, narrow windows and smoothly plastered and painted with colorful murals in a blocky, half-stylized fashion. They showed the kings and their ancestors at war, the hunt, or sacrifice; the gods of Kartahown hovered over them, smelling the smoke of the offerings, shedding blessing and help. The floor was some highly polished dark stone, slick underfoot. Warriors with gilded armor and painted shields stood around the edge of the room; within milled a crowd of nobles and functionaries and priests in a blaze of bright cloth, feathers, and silver and gold.

Only the Queen Mothers and First Wives sat, besides the kings, and on stools rather than chairs, but those were important posts, making the holders powerful in their own right. Clerks, some of them women, stood by the more senior officials and commanders, their reed pens ready to write on palm-wide strips of shamboo; lean, muscular runners in loincloths and complex leather hats stood poised, ready to dash off with messages. The lands ruled from here covered an area the size of California, with a population several million strong.

It would all have been more impressive without the smell, which the incense cut only a little, and minus the flies. The kings and Queen Mothers and a few other bigwigs had servants behind them with billowy fans of feathers on long poles; most of the rest made do with whisks. Marc felt himself beginning to twitch like a horse in a summer pasture, sure that something was going to crawl up his nose soon. Occasionally Tahyo's jaws went *clop* on a passing bug.

"Once again we see that it was wise and good of the Gods to send the *imiAmerican*, the Sky People, to us," the senior king said.

His colleague nodded agreement. So did everyone else—if you didn't think the monarch's words were inherently wise you were well advised to conceal it in this time and place. They had an intensive zero-fault tolerance policy here. One of the Queen Mothers smiled benignly and sent a couple of the servants with fans over to the Terrans to keep the bugs off; she was delighted with the great-wolf pup, even after they'd declined several broad hints that Tahyo would make a wonderful gift. Marc *had* given a quick résumé on his pup-rearing program, and he suspected that huntsmen would be out fetching equivalents before the day was over.

The king continued, "Let these *sorkisun*"—which meant *noblemen*—"be our guests while they are within the walls. Let none hinder or harm them; our hand is over them, and those of the powerful Gods who stand our friends. Hear! Fear! Obey!"

"*Hear! Fear! Obey!*" the crowd chanted.

Even informally, the going-away ceremony took time, and even after they were out of the throne room it took a while to get out of the palace, which was a huge, sprawling warren of courtyards and colonnades, residences, chapels and gardens, workshops, barracks, and storerooms. It was full of messengers, soldiers, servants, workers, visitors, and ambassadors. Take a wrong turning and you might end up in a dim space where acolytes groveled before some half-human idol, or in a big, sunny room where women sat at their work and looms made a rhythmic thumping under a chorus of song. Tahyo kept trying to lead them towards the kitchens; Marc pacified him with an occasional scrap of dried meat from his backpack. The young beast's powerful jaws shredded the leather-tough stuff with cheerful abandon.

"I wish it was respectful to have someone show us out," Cynthia muttered, as they backed out of the last wrong turn. "Even for court etiquette that's weird. There was someone to show us *in*."

"*Mais*, it is polite to have someone show us out, if the people showing us out are a nobleman and their entire retinue with a crier going ahead blowing on a trumpet," Marc replied. "Anyone less who acted as an usher would be an insult, and the full dress would take all day, believe me. *On time* just isn't on these folk's memory disks. Ah, here we are!"

Guardsmen crashed long steel-headed spears in salute on their tall oval shields of 'saur hide, a heavy drumbeat sound. Just then a messenger ran up panting and handed them all fly whisks with carved ivory handles, a gift of the same thoughtful king's mother. A file of the soldiers trotted out after the Terrans as they left the palace grounds, which did have the merit of keeping the crowds in the square at bay and away from the sharp pointies. Freed of royal decorum, Tom and Mary began snapping digital pictures, exclaiming happily at the scenes caught in the plug-in screen behind the gadget, which Marc had to admit was nifty.

"Now, let's take a look at the only real city in the world!"

CHAPTER FOUR

Encyclopedia Britannica, 16th Edition
University of Chicago Press, 1988

VENUS: Biology

The first detailed studies of Venusian ecosystems revealed features which seem to mimic the fossil record of Earth. However, while individual species are closely similar to extinct and extant terrestrial types, the interactions themselves were obviously different. The coexistence of dinosaurian and mammalian species, and of both with birds and pterodactyls . . .

Venus, Gagarin Continent—Far West

To sleep with the Cave Master on one's brow was to invite visions. Teesa had never done it herself until tonight, but her people's need was strong.

Now she stood outside the Cave, the Mystery itself, but in her dream it blurred. Not from any fault of her eyes, but as if the dark pit in the limestone cliff were many rather than one. One moment her own people passed by, then the beastmen, then strangers in odd costumes, all fading into one another as if one had *become* the other.

A voice spoke to her: her mother's, in memory. *"The Cave Master can show you what has been, and what will be—and what* might *be."*

Then one of the strangers turned to look at her. He was a tall man with short-cropped dark hair and an alien cast of features, but with a warrior's build. His eyes were dark and they looked at her with—

Fear, she thought. *But he is not afraid for himself.*

Light pulsed from the Cave of the Mysteries, as her mother's tales said it did in rare moments. And that light *pulled . . .*

With a cry, she sat bolt upright on her pallet, tearing the diadem from her brow. Her sister stirred likewise, words of concern falling soundless. Gradually Teesa's breathing slowed to normal, and she wiped at the sweat on her face, staring out into the night.

I expected the visions, she thought. *But I did not expect them to be so much like life.*

Feelings still made her heart pound, the breath go quickly between her lips. Fear. Love. Hate. Yet the things that had caused them slipped away as her memory grasped at the contours of her dream, like clutching at the reflection of a light in water.

All that was left was a heavy sense of *consequence.*

"You died too soon, Mother," she whispered again. "There is so much I do not know!"

Venus, Gagarin Continent—Kartahown

"Kartahown!" Marc said grandly as they emerged from the palace, and waved an arm.

Cynthia sighed quietly, a sound of awed satisfaction; Marc smiled to himself at the sound. It *was* quite a sight, the great sprawling mass of the palace behind them, and the Temple of Koru before—a mass shaped liked a stepped wedding cake or a minor Tower of Babel four hundred feet high, ten broad level steps with each joined to the next by the long processional staircase that ran from base to summit. Each of the ten levels was a different color, shades of black and brown, green and purple and crimson and silver-gilt. On the top, the great sun-disk blazed in the hazy sunlight like a beacon; on each level below, another great idol of a major god caught the light as well.

It took a while for the rest of the scene to register, in the face of that huge monument to an alien faith. The main square of the city wasn't square, more of an irregular rectangle covering twenty or thirty acres. It was paved by cobbles long since worn flat, and mostly covered in booths, light structures for selling a hundred hundred goods, from piled melons to smoked sausages to fine cloth to shoes and 'saur feathers.

Marc snapped a lead to Tahyo's collar before they ventured into the warren; he didn't think that anyone would try to steal a greatwolf—or that they'd come away with both hands, if they did—but it was best not to take chances. The structures were temporary, shamboo poles and reed matting taken down every evening, but the places were inherited, even the seasonal ones, so that for generations on end a summer booth for selling *nurr*-flour could give way to a winter one for comar-fruit . . .

"Speaking of which," he said, and tossed a bit of copper to a vendor.

Comar were sold on their stalks, and looked a bit like a vegetable edition of the German stick grenades in old war movies; you peeled off the mottled, greenish-brown rind with your thumb, and then pulled off circular sections of fruit from the top down, each like a small, flat donut. The taste was something like a tangerine, something like pineapple with a hint of cherry, and something indescribable, with a strong spurt of juice when you bit down. Marc grinned as the other three Terrans exclaimed over it, and they strolled through the narrow laneways between the raucous crowds of buyers and sellers and pack-oxen and *churr* and sheep and wandering pigs.

"Why don't we grow these?" Tom Kowalski asked.

"Or at least import them," Mary added.

"The tree takes six years to start bearing, and the fruit don't travel well," Marc said.

Though they made a great fruit brandy, and seeds sent back to Earth were being nursed with care, to see if they could adapt to the thinner atmosphere and shorter day. Marc foresaw a major industry there if they could. He dropped a section into Tahyo's waiting mouth; the greatwolf crunched down, stopped to consider the unfamiliar taste, then wagged his tail. He didn't butt his nose into Marc's palm for more, which meant he thought it was just so-so, but then, he was a carnivore.

"Where the hell is Blair, anyway?" Marc went on. "He was supposed to be paying a courtesy call on the High Priest of Koru, not getting into a research session."

"Koru?" Mary asked.

"The sun god. Heap big chief deity," Marc said. "They tend to be a bit resentful of us, because they've been rivals of the kings for a long time—centuries, probably—and we've been strengthening the monarchs and the priesthoods of Thunder Fist and Owl Eyes."

"Chris has been getting some wonderful stuff from their archives," Cynthia said. "All the history of Kartahown's there, dating back hundreds of years. Maybe thousands; it's hard to tell because their calendar is so screwed up. He's even getting a handle on the origins of their writing system. This is like time travel, no shit!"

Marc made himself nod. *All of which they've never allowed us to look at before,* he thought sourly. *Must be that frat-boy charm of his.* Sometimes you could forget that the purpose behind Jamestown was knowledge, and that all the other activities were here to support the research.

They had the same problem on Mars, from what he'd heard of the research station there, only more so, since more of the scientists spent long periods living among the natives, who had been building cities and doing calligraphy when the cutting edge of Earthly technology was the spear-thrower. Anthropologists there had to be handy with dueling-swords and needle-guns as well as getting used to being looked down on as monkeys from the wilds.

The Terran party managed to leave the main square without more than a little jostling, taking a good many souvenirs and even more pictures. The streets beyond were narrow and crowded, and wound as if they'd originally been laid out by wandering livestock, but they didn't have quite the pulsing sweaty hive-swarming of the main marketplace. Mud-brick and shamboo-earth walls rose two stories on either side, topped by another of woven shamboo, often bulging out in balconies; some walls were whitewashed or painted, but most were left in the natural dark brown color. The streets were dirt here, too, sometimes with a winding strip of cobbles down the center.

"I don't know whether being able to see what you're stepping in is good or not," Cynthia grumbled, half-laughing, as they skirted a noxious shin-high heap black with insects.

Tahyo found the smells fascinating. A couple of skinny pigs closed in on the refuse after the Terrans went by, snapping at a local who kicked at one of them. Which was one more reason buying shish kebab from the street vendors was a *bad* idea . . . unless the vendor had managed to kidnap one of the clean, pampered *pet* pigs the wealthy sometimes kept here. At least you didn't have to be afraid it was "roof rabbit": There weren't any domesticated cats on Venus, or at least hadn't been until the kings got a basketful of kittens.

Marc grinned to himself. Space travel had solved a lot of ancient questions, among them the matter of how cats would react to zero-G. It turned out that their basic response was to swim through the air towards the nearest human face, latch on with all four paws, claws out, and scream their heads off.

Only doors opened on the ground floors of houses; those might conceal anything from crowded tenements to the mansions of the wealthy centered around courtyards, since they didn't have anything corresponding to zoning here.

The Terran party passed peasants with loads of onions and herbs on their backs, water-sellers with hooked poles clattering with clay cups, skin containers on their backs and lying cries of "Fresh! Clean!" on their lips. A portly merchant passed in a striped robe and flared leather hat with a ring of little scent-filled metal balls dangling on strings from its brim; he went pacing along ahead of his train of pack-*churr* and hirelings, holding his long walking-staff as if it were a spear. Housewives with children clinging to their tunics fell silent and drew aside as the Terrans approached; a painted harlot in a gauzy garment slit up the side and eye-paint that made her look like a raccoon did the same, then muttered an automatic invitation.

Second-story windows were narrow slits; only on the third floors were there broader ones. The buildings leaned inward slightly, so that those overhung the streets. People leaned out of many of them, mostly women chatting with their neighbors. Then a cry of "*Shu-maaaaa!*" came from above.

"Look out!" Marc cried, and Cynthia on his heels—which was

pretty much what "shumaaaaa" meant, or possibly *look out below!* was closer.

Glad she *was listening to the lecture!* Marc thought, as he yanked Tom back by his belt. Cynthia did likewise for his wife, and the two rescuers grinned at each other as the power-plant techs swore at the way their boots had gotten splattered with the contents of the chamber pot.

"Worse if it landed on your head," Cynthia said unsympathetically. "It's a bit more disgusting than the pictures, though, isn't it?"

"My romantic heart, it says no. *Mes pattes*" he tapped his boot against the wall to show which paws he meant—"they agree!"

The Kowalskis perked up as they came into a slightly wider street, one broad enough for three men to walk abreast, stretching in a long, shallow S-curve before them. This time the houses had openings, long narrow chambers giving back into the depth of the buildings. A *tink-tink-tink-tink* of hammers sounded, for each of them held a smith, coppersmiths with trays beaten and engraved with scenes from myth or legend, enameled fancies and plain pots and pans, bronzesmiths offering knife and spearhead and beautiful leaf-shaped swords, and silversmiths and goldsmiths plying their trades. 'Saur scutes glowed, and raw jewels were polished until they shone crimson and green and aquamarine against the flash of precious metals. The air was hot with the small forge-hearths many of the shops contained, kept red-hot with charcoal and draught blown by apprentices through shamboo tubes.

A crocodile of children—not only boys, either—on their way to school paused to exchange mutually intrigued looks with Tahyo; then their pedagogue, a grave bearded man in a robe, got them going with a flick of his shamboo switch.

The Kowalskis plunged into bargaining. They had enough Kartahownian for the numerals, and satchels full of things to trade. The locals hadn't invented anything like coinage yet; there were brokers who specialized in elaborate multiperson swaps, but straight barter would do here. In the end, the Kowalskis exchanged two nylon scarves and a tea towel printed with the Golden Gate Bridge for a pendant of fretwork 'saur ivory set with turquoise.

"I'm happy just looking," Cynthia said.

"And that's Crashing Voice, the god of smiths," Marc said after a few minutes more wandering. "This is sort of a chapel, not the main temple."

The building was a U-shaped niche with the open end towards the street; there was no house attached to the shrine, nothing but the *temenos*, the sacred precinct, which meant the priest's job was probably held by local heads-of-household in rotation on a part-time basis. The floor was brick-paved and scrupulously clean; the image was on a stone block and a little more than life-sized, a bronze of a man sitting cross-legged, tapping with a hammer on some piece of work on a board across his lap. His head looked normal, until you realized that his hair and beard were made of hundreds of miniature knife-blades and spearheads. The altar before it was a low, rectangular block; it held a stone dish with the ashes of an offering of incense, fruit, flowers, a bowl of boiled grain, and the body of a bird with black-and-purple feathers. A couple of beggars squatted and waited; one of them had a black and a white thread side by side on his one good arm as he looked at the fly-swarming but not too rotten sacrifices.

"Why's he doing that?" Mary Kowalski said.

"Anything left on the altar after sunset is theirs," Marc explained. "And it's officially sunset when you can't tell a black thread from a white one. First come, first served. The bird may not even get cooked."

The two techs nodded wisely. "I read about that in the handbook," Tom said. "Say, that statue's a really nice piece of work—lost-wax method? It reminds me of some old Khmer stuff on Earth."

"You've lost me," Marc said.

Cynthia snorted. "You make the statue in wax and then cover it in clay," she said. "Then you heat it until the wax runs out and pour in the molten metal. And yes, Tom, they do use that. Chris tells me there's a vegetable wax they use instead of beeswax, and it's fairly common and cheap here, so they came up with the technique earlier than people on Earth did. It makes good candles, too, better than beeswax."

"Ah," Marc said wisely, suppressing an impulse to kick something.

"Next birthday, I'll buy you a soul, Marc," Cynthia said.

"This'll make a great picture for our niece and nephew back

home," Tom said. "We can send it back as a data packet and have it developed there. Mary, why don't you set up the tripod?"

Marc opened his mouth and then closed it again. There was no reason they shouldn't. True, a crowd was beginning to gather, but it seemed mostly curious.

"We seek to do honor to Crashing Voice, patron of makers," he said aloud to the bystanders. "Since we of the Sky People are also makers and craftsfolk."

A few of the metalworkers had stopped to watch, and some of their families had followed suit, and passersby were slowed by the knot of people in the narrow way. The soldiers of the escort were lounging easily among them, mostly trying to strike up conversations with women. Mary and Tom got out their shamboo tripod; they'd been carrying it broken down and slung in a leather tube over Tom's back. The mounting had been made in the Jamestown machine shop, and it held the digital camera in a firm clamp.

"Here," Mary said.

She pulled something else out of her backpack, a thin plasma-screen display device, slotted it into the framework, and plugged an extension cord into the side of the camera. The screen lit with a sharp image of the altar and the statue of the god. A man in the robes of a priest of Koru pushed through the crowd and stood staring as she programmed the camera and then trotted over to join her husband. They stood on either side of the cult-image, smiling and waving at the lens as the automatic flash lit the dimness of the *temenos* three times.

"Look!" the priest suddenly screeched, pointing at the screen. "It is true what the other one said! The *imiAmerican* steal away the image of your God!"

"Oh, you *couyon*!" Marc swore, as he saw a knot gathering, jabbering and pointing at the screen. His pistol came out, and his left hand drew the bowie-style ratchet knife slung at the small of his back. "Tom, Mary, get back here *now*," he shouted.

Tahyo crouched and growled between Marc's feet, his thin juvenile's mane standing up around his neck and shoulders. The two technicians looked bewildered, staring around as the crowd grew with the eerie speed of crystals in a saturated solution, and the noise turned hostile. Out of the corner of his eye Marc saw Cynthia draw her pistol and jack the slide to chamber a round, holding it down in a two-handed grip. Beyond her, a royal soldier who'd been chatting with a housewife staggered forward as someone thumped him between the shoulders . . . and then fell forward on his face, with a knife-hilt standing in the back of his neck and blood spilling red in the afternoon sun.

"*Tau'wan hubimi!*" someone screamed. "*Kill the witch-folk!*"

"*Merde,*" Marc said comprehensively.

Time to flip the switch to us-or-them mode, ran through him grimly. *I usually like these Texians, but when it's us or them, I don't need to think very long, me.*

Then he barked: "Take my back!"

The camera went over with a crash and tinkle and pop of components shattering under feet and sticks. The Kowalskis hadn't drawn their pistols in time, and a dozen rioters from the crowd-turned-mob were trying to drag Mary away from her husband, while as many more belabored the man with fists and sticks and feet. If it hadn't been for their assailants getting in one another's way, they'd have died before Marc and Cynthia could cover the twenty feet to them. Time separated into stuttering instants, strobing flashes that some part of his mind knew even then would come back to him later, mostly when he really didn't want them.

Crack. Recoil slammed the 10-mm pistol back in his hand. A round blue hole appeared in the back of a head, and blood and bones shot out through a fist-sized gap between the man's eyes. *Crack,* and Marc fired with the muzzle inches from a man's ear.

A curved bronze knife slashed at him. He caught it on his own blade; an instant later the man folded over with an *oooff* and fell, a patch of his tunic on fire from the muzzle-blast of Cynthia's pistol. Marc ignored that direction as a ripple of *crack-crack-crack* sounded and then a second's pause as she ejected a magazine, slapped in another, and let the slide run forward to chamber a fresh round. Evidently *she* hadn't wasted her time in the self-defense course.

Marc kicked, a short snap that hammered the toe of his boot into the side of a man's knee. It broke with a wet, crackling snap like green shamboo, an ugly sensation that shivered up Marc's foot.

The man let go of Mary Kowalski and dropped to the ground, shrieking, the insect-thin sound lost in the white noise roar that echoed from the high, hard walls all around them. The Cajun thrust with the knife and jammed it up under the short ribs of another man, firing over his shoulder at one who was about to brain Tom with a knobby oak bludgeon set with sharp obsidian flakes. Tahyo's fangs clamped on the face of another who'd come crawling with a knife clenched between his teeth; he dropped that, flailing at the young greatwolf with hands that rapidly weakened.

The pistol clicked empty; Marc dropped it, pulled out the one Mary hadn't used, and wheeled.

Suddenly they were in the middle of a bubble of empty space. Tom Kowalski reeled backward and sat down, hands to his bloodied face. Mary wasted an instant crossing her arms over her bare scratched breasts, then picked up the oak club and held it like a baseball bat, glaring. Cynthia snapped a fresh magazine into her pistol, standing beside him with the weapon in the precise range grip, raised to eye level, left hand supporting right. Dead men lay sprawled with the wide-eyed look of surprise they always had, and wounded ones twitched or whimpered for their mothers or tried to crawl away like broken-backed snakes. Tahyo growled and bristled and licked the blood off his chops at Marc's feet, making little two-step rushes whenever he saw movement. The crowd filled the exit from the U of the shrine, glaring back; there was a heaving stir and a couple of the royal soldiers rammed their way through to join the Terrans.

The soldiers looked bloodied and battered, too, but their tough 'saur-hide armor had protected them, and from the look of their spear points and swords they'd quickly switched from crowd-control bashing with the flat and the butt to nice, deep, soul-satisfying thrusts and jabs.

"Kill them all, these alley scum, lord!" the senior survivor snarled to Marc, sounding quite like the greatwolf for a moment. "Smite them with your wizardry!"

"Don't get in front of us or it'll smite *you*!" he snapped to them. To Mary: "Drop the club and get my pistol there, and Tom's ammo." And at last to Cynthia: "You all right?"

"Apart from being about to die at the hands of a mob of screaming savages?" she said. "Yeah, doin' just *fine*, bro."

Her eyes went up to the flat roofs around them. He glanced that way himself without moving his head: flickers of robed figures ducking behind the parapets. Pretty soon they'd start throwing things, or the mob would realize that there were a lot more of them than the Terrans could shoot before they were overrun; already there was a ripple along the front as those safely behind pushed those in front. That was the problem with superstitious awe about firearms. It wore off too quickly.

Then a trumpet blared. Marc let out a long *whoosh* of relief at the sound of stout staffs thwacking on heads and shoulders from farther down the street, to the accompaniment of deep uniform shouts. The mob wavered and then began to run, flowing out of the narrow entrance to the shrine like a film of water running downhill, only played backward. The heads bobbing about half-seen on the rooftops around them vanished, and windows were shuttered with quick, decisive slamming sounds.

For a moment Marc's stomach twisted as he became aware of how close death had come, and a sheen of cold sweat broke out over his skin. He took another deep breath, mostly through his mouth to ignore the fresh smells of death, and holstered his pistol—without, he noted with a slight flush of pride, letting his hands shake. A squad of burly Sun Temple guardsmen trotted up to the entrance to the shrine; they were armored much like soldiers, but bore quarterstaffs rather than spears and shields. The bronze-capped ends of the six-foot staffs were mostly splashed red; now and then one would jab down to make sure a rioter was dead, with a nasty *thock-crunch* sound.

At their head walked a tall blond man, twirling a staff in effort-less figure eights with one hand, whistling, ignoring the trickle of blood from a pressure-cut on his forehead.

"I say, you chappies look as if you could use a bit of a hand," Christopher Blair said cheerfully.

"*Merde,*" Marc muttered again. *It's better to be rescued by him than not be rescued. I suppose.*

CHAPTER FIVE

Encyclopedia Britannica, 16th Edition
University of Chicago Press, 1988

VENUS: Biology

After the landing of the first manned EastBloc (1981) and American (1982) expeditions to Venus, a torrent of discoveries renewed Earth's waning fascination with her sister world. The greatest single shock was the extreme similarity of Venusian life to that of Earth, not only in gross anatomy—the unmanned probes had made that obvious as early as the 1960s and 1970s—but in detail, even at the cellular and molecular levels. As was the case with Mars but to an even greater degree, the fundamental mechanisms of cell division, DNA/RNA operation, and serum immunology seemed closer to those of terrestrial life than could be accounted for by any amount of parallel evolution.

Venusian life even proved to be edible, apart from a few poisonous species and a modest range of allergic reactions, greatly aiding the establishment of research stations. The enforced 4-

year span of isolation before surface-to-orbit facilities were established at Cosmograd and Jamestown gave a welcome quarantine period; experience showed no great bacteriological or viral threats to the base personnel, and great care was taken under the UN Extraterrestrial Protection Act of 1980 to ensure that no pathogens were transmitted by interplanetary travel . . .

Venus, Gagarin Continent—Jamestown Extraterritorial Zone

"Hey, growing fast, you," Marc said, taking a deep breath of the crisp morning air and letting his greatwolf out into the front-yard run.

Tahyo was already as high as the Earthman's waist, and the size of his blocky wedge-shaped head and enormous platter-shaped paws showed he'd be bigger yet. The body between feet and fangs was still gawky-gaunt, but it weighed more than half what the man's did. The legs were thicker relative to their length than a dog's, which was to be expected in something that would be as heavy as a small lion when full-grown, but otherwise Tahyo's layout wasn't far from the canine-wolf basic pattern. Right now the whole stern was wagging along with the tail, and then he stuck it in the air and bowed over his forepaws, looking up. Behind him, the sun was rising on a long Venusian day, turning the western horizon salmon pink. There was a deep hush to the air; Jamestown hadn't really quite begun its working routine yet.

"Note for Doc Feldman: classic canine let's-play behavior," Marc said, and reached down to ruffle Tahyo's ears.

"Classic drooling, too," he went on, as the not-really-a-dog licked enthusiastically at any part of the man he could reach.

Marc grabbed the beast by the ruff, rolled him over, and stared straight into his eyes, making his voice deep: "Who's the boss, eh, you? Who's the boss?"

Tahyo made a whimpering sound and tried to lick the hands that held him, then lay back in splay-legged submission, which was a good enough answer for government work. Marc stepped back and let the big animal rise; when he showed him the leash, Tahyo began to leap and wiggle in midair again.

"Heel!" he said, and Tahyo did. "Sit! Good boy!"

Marc tossed him a treat—the bones from a rack of *tharg*-ribs he'd brought home from the base mess hall yesterday. Today he'd be cooking at home, and not just for himself. The greatwolf made short work of them, crunching them with the relish of a kid with a piece of hard candy; even as a semi-pup, the strength he could bring to bear on the crushing and shearing molars at the back of his huge mouth was impressive. Marc had rigged up the front yard as Tahyo's territory; it was a half-acre, walled in adobe and, unlike the back, not planted to anything but a couple of big oak trees that had been here before the house. It was pretty bare now—it turned out greatwolves were enthusiastic diggers, but as an added bonus they were easy to housebreak and naturally buried their own wastes.

"Stand!" Marc said as he opened the front gate, slung his rifle, and clipped the chain leash to Tahyo's collar. "Let's go!"

Instead of the wild lunge of the first few times, the greatwolf trotted along beside Marc as he jogged, obviously wondering why he was going so slowly, and equally obviously resigned to the foibles of the boss. They passed a few pedestrians and one woman mounted on *churr*-back; Tahyo behaved perfectly, and Marc felt a glow of pride. The process was mutual, too. People were getting used to seeing a man running with a young greatwolf, and even the locals weren't quite as weirded out as they had been at first.

"They wanted me to have you Iced," he told the dog as they passed the tannery, which Tahyo found fascinating. "Not going to turn you into an electronic zombie, boy. So you be good, eh? No gobbling people's cats or *bebettes*."

Out past the tannery he turned south, into the pastures outside the town proper. They were still well within the boundaries the kings had granted Jamestown—which covered an area about the size of Delaware—but they weren't liable to run into anyone while Tahyo was excited.

"*Weh, neg*," he said, and unclipped the leash. "Go, boy! *Go!*"

Tahyo shot away across the rolling grass, green and up to his back and starred with big crimson flowers; a trail of butterflies and bugs shot into the air in his wake, and occasionally he'd leap his own length into the air with a tombstone *clomp* of jaws to catch one, or just for the hell of it. On all four paws he had to keep his head up to see where he was going, and sometimes he disappeared for a moment as the stems closed over his back.

"Stop!" Marc called.

The greatwolf did, albeit with a glance over his shoulder that said plain as words: *Do I have to?*

"Sit! Lie down . . . up!" Marc threw a stick. "Fetch!" For an hour he worked the animal with basic commands.

"You're smart, you," he said, when Tahyo lay panting beside him beneath an oak tree. Tahyo looked at him again and put his head in Marc's lap. "Doc says you should be a stupid one, eh, primitive form of mammal . . . but wherever your *pawpaws* came from, your family's been here a long time, eh? Dodging the 'saurs and catching dinner. So you've got as much brains as any mutt I've had. Which is a good thing."

Usually Tahyo paid close attention when Marc was talking, waiting for one of the words he understood, or just focusing on his parent/pack leader/god. Now Tahyo glanced away, the happy sagging grin on his chops disappearing as he raised his head. Then he came to his feet and turned, and suddenly his body was one quivering arrow of attention, his wet black nose wrinkling at the end of his blunt, broad muzzle.

"Eh, you scent something, you?" Marc said, using the *tu*-form.

He came up to one knee himself. The wind was from the west, as it usually was this time of year, and it rippled the grass across the broad pasture. This stretch was empty, but a hundred yards farther on was a board fence. Behind that, a herd of *tharg* was scattered through the grass, the small domestic variety, up to their chests in the tall herbage, since the settlement had far more grazing than it did stock to keep the growth down. A herdsman watched them, a Kudlack hireling mounted on *churr*-back, a javelin in his hand and several more in a hide bucket slung across his back, whistling a tune that could just be heard against the sough of wind through the vegetation.

Marc took his rifle from where it leaned against the tree, working the bolt, then trotted towards the fence. The greatwolf followed, black fur bristling on his shoulders, fangs showing, and the beginnings of a growl rumbling in his chest.

"What's got you upset, *neg?*" Marc said.

A quick scan up showed there weren't any Quetzas or lesser

predators of the air around. Nothing big showed on the ground, either . . .

"Except that grass there is moving *against* the wind!" Marc exclaimed, and threw the heavy weapon to his shoulder, letting the crosshairs fall on the patch until he saw a flicker of movement there.

CRACK!

He swayed back against the recoil and worked the bolt with a quick flick of his first three fingers. A body exploded out of the patch of tall grass he'd aimed at. It was a biped, about his own size and covered in yellow-green feathers except for a crest of crimson plumes that snapped out in reflex as the lizard body writhed in death. The jump put it a good twelve feet into the air; a good deal of its length was the powerful digitigrade legs, each with a great sickle-shaped claw held up against the hock. Those flashed out in equally automatic reflex as the vicious predator struck out in one last attempt to disembowel whatever had hurt it. A steam engine hiss escaped the long-fanged mouth, scarlet-purple within, and a spray of blood came with it from the lungs shredded by the powerful expanding bullet.

"Raptor pack!" Marc shouted to the herdsman.

The yell—or possibly the sight of that leap into the air not twenty yards from him—brought the mounted man to full alertness. His javelin cocked back as the first of the feathered killers burst from cover and launched themselves at him with huge bounding strides; raptors were smart like parrots, and knew they'd have the run of the herd without its guardian. They'd probably associated the death of their pack-mate with the man, too. The steel head punched into the breast of one. The crosshairs of the scope brought the other vividly close, the long feathers working and their hairlike filaments fluttering with the speed of its passage. A raptor could outrun a *churr;* they'd been clocked at fifty miles an hour for short sprints.

CRACK!

The heavy, hollow-point bullet punched the predator just before it began the killing leap towards the herdsman. The *tharg* herd was reacting with bawling panic, but also by forming a circle around the calves and yearlings, tossing their long moon-shaped horns. And Tahyo . . .

. . . gave a roar behind him.

Marc wheeled with fear-driven speed. Another raptor had crept up through the long grass, eeling on its belly until it was within leaping distance. Tahyo's jaws were closed on its hock just above the six-inch dewclaw; the other poised to kill as the raptor screamed frustration.

CRACK!

A quick check showed the other half-dozen raptors heading south at full speed, leaping fences with no more effort than a man clearing a croquet hoop; they'd been out for food, not a fight, and had had enough. The herdsman waved at him.

Tahyo lay with his jaws still locked on the dead raptor's leg; there wasn't much left of its head, after the 9-mm big-game round hit. Marc gave the hairy form of the greatwolf a quick check-over. There was no obvious damage.

"Heel, boy! Sit!"

Slowly, licking his chops and glancing back at the carcass, Tahyo obeyed. Marc scavenged up his spent brass and drew his knife to open the body.

Then he stood back. "Go to it, Tahyo! You earned it."

The run back to town took more time; the young greatwolf had eaten until his stomach bulged like a beach ball, and obviously thought it profoundly silly not to curl up near the kill and keep napping and eating until even the bones were gone. He obeyed, though, and sat politely when a slightly nervous Maria Feldman came by down the street, leading her toddler.

"Hello, Marc. How's it going?" she said, as they cautiously introduced two-year-old to greatwolf.

Tahyo showed intense interest; Marc could see the *it's-a-puppy!* reflex kick in after the initial is-this-interesting-or-edible curiosity, and the play-gesture followed. The toddler stuck a dubious hand in his mouth, and then reached out to pat the terrible head.

"Oh, just routine, today," Marc said. "Got to go—big dinner tonight!"

"With that nice Ms. Whitlock?" Maria asked with a smile.

Marc's own mouth quirked. "Among others."

Venus, Gagarin Continent—Far West

Teesa sat under the thatched overhang at the front of the Chief's House, sitting cross-legged on a rug of skins and examining the death-thing that had killed her Jondlar, nostrils twitching at the faint remaining scent, acrid and fiery. It carried like a minor key through the stronger smells of the village, wood smoke and cooking, sweat, dung, drying hides tacked to the log walls, and the warm, clean forest-smell from the mountains above.

The death-thing had a wooden part at the rear, made to fit against the shoulder, and another where a hand would support the front, but the most of it was the strange, blue-silvery metal. It was heavy, like stone or bronze, but harder than either; cautious tests on the big knives of the same metal had shown that they could nick bronze, and the tube that spat death was harder still. Hard stone would grind the edges of the knives sharp, as with a bronze blade. It was more work, but warriors had nearly come to blows over the having of them.

None had wanted to touch the death-thing, which might well be laden with misfortune.

Jondlar's brother Taldi thought it was cursed, of course. But then, Taldi thought having a whitefeather shit on his head or letting his fire go out meant a curse.

This is cursed, that is cursed, he's not happy unless he has a good curse on him, Teesa thought. *Though perhaps all of us are under a curse.*

She sighed and let the death-thing rest across her lap as she looked up. The village was about its work. There were a dozen houses like hers scattered on either side down half a mile of pathway, differing only in that each held several families while in hers only she dwelt with her little sister, Zore. Each house had walls of oak logs chinked with mud and sticks on a base course of fieldstone carefully fitted; the roofs were high-pitched and neatly thatched with greenish-gold reeds cut into decorative patterns. In this mild, comfortable summer weather, the reed curtains that covered windows had been rolled up and the shutters were open. Every house had a space in front where the roof was continued out past the walls, and where a hearth burned in a circle of stones. Each also had a post planted in the dirt, twice a tall man's height, carved to show which of the clans of the Cloud Mountain folk dwelt within.

In a wider open spot was a bigger, round building, roofed but open-sided save for the supporting pillars. That was the Gathering House for ceremonies and meetings; a spring welled up in the middle of it, feeding a pond from which all could draw water, and a mossy stone-lined channel carried the overflow away. The whole was hidden in a circular depression of the hilly plateau. Above, to the south, reared the mountains. Every settlement of the Cloud Mountain People had to be hard to reach and hard to see these days.

Most of the men and some young women were out hunting; children wandered about, playing or doing chores in the small gardens behind the houses, or among the free-ranging knee-high flightless purple-and-green housebirds and small pigs with black and yellow stripes on their bristly hides. Here and there an adult knapped obsidian or flint, or shaped wood and leather and shamboo into things useful or beautiful. One old man, his yellow hair turned silver, bent with exquisite care over a small pot filled with the poison sacks of black spiders, boiling them down into a tarry sludge in which the points of blowgun darts would be dipped. The empty traps and the bodies of the noxious palm-sized insects were piled nearby.

Teesa bent her head back over the death-thing. Only after days of study had the various shapes and bits come clear to her eyes, so alien were they. She pulled back on the little lever on the right side, feeling a smooth, heavy resistance as if she were pulling up a bucket on a rope. Inside was an empty space, and the other end of the tube. The thing went *click* as well, and the little finger-sized lever inside the metal loop ahead of the grip made for a hand came forward.

Zore leaned forward, nostrils flaring. There was an oily scent from the complex interior; it looked—

"I am *tired* of thinking that this looks like nothing else in the world," Teesa said.

Zore giggled. She was just fifteen sun-turnings, and squatted naked save for a string of beads around her neck and some body-paint, her shock of tousled white hair falling loose down her back.

"But it *does* look like nothing else," she said, and craned nearer. "It looks like the insides of an animal," she went on. "If only the insides of an animal were made of this strange metal."

Teesa opened her mouth to tell the young girl to be silent, then closed it again. *That is quite clever!* she thought instead. *I have been spending too much time angry since the raid, and not enough using my wits. I should let Jondlar's spirit go, if I can. It is enough to avenge him.*

She forced his image out of her head—thinking about a ghost could summon it—and held the death-thing up to look down the tube from the rear. It held spiraling grooves cut into the hard metal.

"This must be like the dart for a blowgun," she said, fingering one of the little things the beastman chief had had in a hide pouch.

There were several hundred of them, small cylinders about the size of a finger and colored like copper. She brought one up to her nose and sniffed deeply; yes, there was a smell, something strangely like the lingering scent in the tube. A touch of the tongue confirmed that it was copper or bronze or something like; the sharp taste was unmistakable. Teesa held the little cylinder to her forehead and concentrated on her memories.

"When the beastman used this death-thing, many of these little tubes were cast out of the side of it—here, where you can pull back on this lever and look down the tube. But"—sweat broke out on her forehead as she forced the details back—"they were shorter. Part of them was missing!"

Zore turned one of the little tubes in her fingers. "The pointed part at this end, or the round-and-flat part?"

"The pointed part was gone! That must be the dart-that-kills! And a magic breath to push it!"

She leaned over and gave her sister a hug for an instant. Then she returned to the death-thing. "So the dart must go in *here*, with the pointed end first."

Fumbling, she slid the cylinder into the opening and let the moving part run forward; it pinched her finger a little and she sucked at the minor hurt as she thought.

"Then he held the wooden part against his shoulder, so, and—ah!"

Peering down the tube, she saw there was a notch and a blade that came into alignment. "How clever! It is by this that you see where the dart will strike!"

The way the rear sight could be adjusted up and down puzzled her for a few minutes, but the Cloud Mountain People were familiar with the concept of "aiming up" when trying for a long-distance shot with a blowpipe. At last she clicked the sight down flat for point-blank range and looked around.

A pig was walking down the beaten earth of the street not far away, with only empty savannah and scattered trees beyond it. Teesa brought the blade into the notch and moved them until they rested just behind the pig's shoulder, then put her hand to the grip and pulled the little curved lever before it.

Crack!

Teesa toppled backward as the death-thing punched her shoulder with a sharp pain like a fist striking; the acrid smell was back, overpoweringly strong. Lying on her mat, she saw and heard as the pig sounded a single short note of agony and dropped, blood pouring from a hole in its side. Others ran squealing and squawking; children screamed; adults sprang up with weapons in their hands. Zore leaped up and yodeled delight, turning cartwheels as the crowd gathered and babbled questions.

Slowly, for the first time in weeks, Teesa began to smile.

Venus, Gagarin Continent—Jamestown

"Save early, save often," Marc muttered to himself; the rich brown chicken-stock-frying onions smell from the kitchen was getting to him.

And while Ametri is a pretty good cook, she ain't Cajun, her. Can't trust her to make a good roux. Got to do that myself.

He tapped the button at the side of the keyboard. The computer whirred softly to itself; just for safety's sake, the same procedure saved a copy of his report on the wild *tharg* migrations to the base mainframe and its ROM disks. Venus could get some humongous thunderstorms and electronic storage had to be redundant. Then . . .

"Oh, hell, it can't hurt," he muttered to himself. "It's just the public records. Or the semipublic."

Wing Commander Christopher Blair, he typed. *Selection history.*

The usual stuff: high marks at Eaton, Sandhurst, Olympic-level fencer, marksman . . . something sprang out at him.

On the Beta list until departure minus twelve, when Commander Jason Brady killed in auto crash on M1 north of Milton Keynes.

"No," Marc said, slapping his forehead with the palm of his hand. "You are not going down that route, *P'tit Boug*," he said to himself. "You know why you don't like him. People die in traffic accidents. Down that route lies madness and bad, bad things. This place, it's too small for any of us to go crazy."

He flicked off the computer, rose, and stretched, looking around and smiling wryly. Jamestown wasn't all that short of housing; adobe brick was—

Cheap as dirt, he told himself.

And they could hire local builders for not much more. Anything that came from Earth was expensive and in short supply, of course, which made for some odd contrasts. The computer was connected to all the others in town with the latest in fiber-optic cable, but the water system was based on shamboo pipes and elm logs bored hollow and pegged together.

The rugs on the tile floor of the big living room/office would have fetched plenty on Earth, and the furniture was handcrafted of tiger-striped woods; lustrous furs covered the benches built into the walls. The windows were of thin-scraped 'saur intestine, and translucent rather than clear; the available glass was better, but not much—the first Kartahownian shops were just getting the knack, and it was wavy and full of bubbles. The heating system was an arched kiva-style fireplace in one corner, where a low fire of split oak soaked warmth into the massive walls and radiated out again, keeping the raw chill of the winter day outside at bay. A special research effort back on Earth had been necessary to produce the everlasting fluorescent lights above. It was cheaper to make lightbulbs that cost thousands of dollars each to send to Venus, rather than send replacements for forty-five-cent ones that burned out. Even so, residents were "encouraged" to use alcohol-fueled lanterns as much as possible.

The kitchen/dining area was behind a doorway closed with strings of wooden beads. It had the same mixture of luxury and primitivism: broad counters and an island of polished honey-colored wood whose grain swirled with scarlet streaks, but the stove was built of brick, its main luxury cast-bronze disks set in the top. He'd hired some kitchen help for today, a middle-aged woman named Ametri and her daughter. They were chopping vegetables as he came in, and looked mildly scandalized as he moved over to the oven—in Kartahown, cooking was woman's work; there weren't even male chefs. Both of them wore simple ankle-length gowns of what amounted to linen; Ametri had her hair up under a kerchief as befitted a widow, but her teenaged daughter wore her long black locks tied back with a headband and woven with scarlet ribbons.

The stock for the gumbo was nearly ready—simmering away in an eight-quart clay pot, with ten pounds of browned chicken parts, necks and bones, the onions and garlic, parsley and celery, all scenting the air even more delightfully than the loaves of fresh bread beside the earth oven. The simmering had been going on for four hours; now he dropped in the *sachet d'epices*, and put the shrimp shells and heads on a small cutting board, ready to dump in.

"You should hire my daughter Talti as housekeeper," Ametri said, as she sliced tomatoes. "Then you would not have to cook— she learns quickly your way of cooking, and already she is good at our way. She is a hard worker and clever to learn your customs, always clean and neat, and so pretty! It's not right for a *sorkisun* like you to live by yourself without a woman."

"Sokisun" was Kartahownian for *nobleman*. Trying to convince Ametri that he wasn't one was as futile as trying to tell her General Clarke wasn't a king. Marc groaned inwardly; Talti was about seventeen in Earth-years, and built like something from the latest *Beach Blanket* movie, which was uncomfortably obvious under the thin almost-linen of her gown, and she was giving him a big white smile as her mother tried to . . .

. . . *well, not exactly pimp her. Being a* housekeeper *for someone well-off is a recognized sort of relationship in Kartahown, a way for a poor girl to earn a dowry.*

A couple of guys did have "housekeepers" like that, but it was officially frowned upon, a policy he agreed with . . . or at least the part of him above the neck did so. Dr. Feldman was eagerly awaiting conclusive evidence on whether the Terran and Venusian varieties of human were interfertile; if so, it would screw up the biology even worse. It hadn't taken nearly as long for someone to prove that Part A fit Part B.

A sound came from the front yard: not quite a bark—greatwolves didn't—but at least a long *ooroorrrff* by Tahyo, followed by happy thumping noises as his tail beat against the wooden gate, and then more as someone thumped his ribs. Marc smiled; that more or less settled who it was. The pup's run was in the front yard, so he wouldn't destroy the potherbs and truck out back, and while he'd learned not to growl at people who came through the gate, there were only a few he fussed over.

Then the bell over the door tinkled and the someone came in, "Damn that dog and his slobbering jaws of love!" Cynthia said. "I brought this dress from *Earth*!"

"Hi, podna," Marc said mildly.

"Podna my ass!"

He heard her go into the bathroom and the water run. Ametri and Talti scowled as Cynthia came back to the kitchen, and ostentatiously turned back to their work.

"Lord Jesus, but that smells good," Cynthia said, sounding a bit mollified.

She was dressed in a simple, sleeveless brown dress and a pair of gold hoop earrings that did wonders against the long, slender ebony neck. This was a semiformal occasion after all, although she looked nearly as good in field overalls . . .

Down, boy! he told himself, and returned her smile.

"What's for dinner?" she went on, taking a piece of celery and nibbling on it.

"Shrimp, chicken, and andouille gumbo, dirty rice . . . well, sort of rice . . . fresh *wheat* bread, and wop salad. Comar tarts for dessert."

"Wheat bread? My, my," she said, raising one slim brow.

The first experimental plots were just now yielding something beyond enough seed-grain, finally acclimatized to the shorter year here. She went on, "And it would take someone from New Orleans to make a salad into an ethnic slur."

He flashed her a grin as he combined the lettuces, not-quite-olives, and tomatoes and dressing in a large bowl, then tossed and divided the result on eight plates.

"I'm not from the Big Sleazy; I'm a bayou boy, me," he said. "And at least I haven't started calling you *ma negresse,* eh?"

"And you'd better not!" she said, sounding as if she were only half-joking.

He gave a mock whimper as he laid two anchovies and one boiled shrimp across each salad, then added a spear of boiled shamboo-sprout.

"Plus the General is coming," he said mischievously.

The celery stopped halfway to Cynthia's full lips. "Are you bullshitting me?"

"I said a few section heads were coming," Marc put in reasonably. "One of them turned out to be the Commandant. Want to help get ready?"

"As long as it doesn't involve ruining my only Earth-made dress," Cynthia said. "You didn't tell me the *General* was coming. Shee-it!"

"*Mais,* would you mind putting out these and the salsa and chips and drinks? The next part here in the kitchen requires the skills of a joint chief and a choreographer."

Marc whistled silently to himself as she worked. He could imagine them doing this for themselves, a family dinner. . . . The whistle became audible as he beat the roux with a whisk and waited while it turned to the proper chocolate brown color for Cajun Na-palm. The nickname wasn't given idly, and you had to be careful not to get any on your bare skin. He added it to the stock; this part *did* require focus.

Forty minutes later, he stepped back, dusted his hands together with satisfaction, and began to pull off the apron. The doorbell tin-gled again. His smile turned a little gelid when Chris Blair's face showed beyond the door, and they did the squeeze-the-hand thing. Doc Feldman and his wife, Maria, followed, then the General and his spouse, an elegant woman in her late thirties who ran Jamestown's information systems. General Clarke was in his early forties, lean, square-jawed, and energetic. Marc liked and admired him, without the element of awe that a lot of the older hands felt; most of them swore the man would have been president someday if he hadn't volunteered to lead the First Fleet's landing team.

Possibly. But I don't think he made much of a sacrifice in taking this position. There's not much call for generals back home, except for the Army Corps of Engineers.

After all, the United States hadn't fought a real war since Korea, and none looked likely anytime soon; nuclear war was mutual suicide, and neither the Americans and their Commonwealth allies nor the Russian–Chinese alliance wanted to risk it by clashing directly. For that matter, apart from some ongoing squabbles in Africa, nobody on Earth had fought a serious conflict since . . . when had that last one in the Middle East been?

Nineteen sixty-seven, he remembered. *Twenty years ago and change.*

The EastBloc and the U.S. had stepped in after that and imposed a settlement, and the place had gone back to being a sleepy backwater, only marginally more important than Africa itself. With two entire habitable—and inhabited—planets at stake, everyone who mattered was too focused on space anyway.

Even the French and their pissant little European Union.

According to the news, they were busting their asses at that base in Guiana and their little space station, but it would be years before they could do anything interplanetary, and by then they'd be a distant third fiddle.

So the General probably made a pretty good career choice if he didn't want to sit in the Pentagon and shuffle paper clips or in Jerusalem with the International Force.

Still, he was intelligent and hardworking and a good commander, if a little fond of thinking of himself in the history books. Right now he was playing Man of the People, with a Hawaiian shirt under his coat. His enthusiasm for the gumbo as they moved to the table was probably genuine, though. Jamestown's food tended to the three B's: Big and Bland or BBQ. You could get decent ribs, but the main alternatives to military-flavored American were Aussie Vegemite and Brit meat pies and soggy sprouts. And he was a fascinating conversationalist, particularly when he got on to the first couple of years here at Jamestown and the desperate struggles involved, which he made seem heroic and funny at the same time.

When the fruit tarts were there and the zulk-tea poured, Clarke's manner changed. "You heard about the EastBloc shuttle that went down two months ago. Venusian months, that is—forty days."

Everyone around the table nodded. Strictly speaking, it had been the upper stage, not the whole shuttle, but without the rocket-plane that rode it piggyback, the first stage was simply a big supersonic jet without much purpose in life. The loss hadn't been quite the disaster it would have been for Jamestown; the Sino-Russian base was bigger and had four surface-to-orbit craft to Jamestown's pair. It was still a massive setback; a new one would have to be shipped from Earth by solar-sail freighter, assembled in orbit, piloted down . . . and the loss of the highly trained crew had been almost as bad. Even just in money costs, sending three more people to Venus would cost nearly as much as the rocket-plane.

Clarke went on: "Well, my counterpart at Cosmograd, General Wang Enlai—amazing how the Chinese tail is wagging the Russian dog these days, isn't it?—has given me some news."

Dr. Feldman snorted. "That's a first. Usually they treat the sun setting in the east as a state secret."

Clarke gave him a quelling glance. "They've heard from their crew. They're still alive, out there in the far west. The radio beacon was triggered last week."

"They want us to help, and they're offering something in return?" Marc said.

Everyone looked at him, and then Clarke smiled grimly. "Bingo. In fact, they're offering to share their biological and geological research files."

"I'm surprised," Marc said. "We had that *potain* with them just before I left, when they tried to say we should 'discuss' our operations on Venus with them before we did anything, because they got here first."

"By six months," Clarke snorted. "And President Dole told them to go pound sand. Which is why I'm *not* surprised they're being reasonable. To them, reasonable is what you do if you can't get away with barking out orders. Push back, and they respect you; act soft, and they push harder."

Sam Feldman looked as if he were going to drool into his empty plate. "They've been operating in the interior highland, which means they're observing different strata and a different local ecology. Getting their data would more than double our knowledge base overnight," he said. "That's a prize worth having."

"How *exactly* do they want us to help them, sir?" Chris Blair said.

Brownnoser, Marc thought. Although the Englishman might just be formal by reflex.

"Nothing they have has the range; the crash site's way out at the western end of Gagarin, six thousand miles from here," he said. "That's a bit far to walk."

Everyone nodded or murmured agreement. The equivalent of New York to San Francisco and back, across trackless wilderness swarming with savages human and quasi-human, not to mention a bellowing profusion of wildlife like nothing Earth had seen in geological ages. Clarke continued:

"They want us to send one of our blimps for their people. None of theirs have the range; they're all turbine-powered. I'm inclined to agree. I need two lighter-than-air-qualified pilots and an information and power systems specialist. Volunteers, of course."

Marc and Blair looked at each other; for once they shared a thought, and a quick slight nod. Cynthia was grinning openly.

"Sir," Marc said, sincerely. "I got into the volunteering habit thirty million miles away and it's too late to change."

"That's good," Clarke said. "I hope you get along with the EastBloc member, too." He laughed at the fallen faces around the table. "Be glad I hung tough. They wanted to put a whole crew of theirs on our airship!"

"Oh, great, some stone-faced Slavic goon with degrees in engineering and toenail-pulling," Cynthia said.

Clarke shook his head. "I think you might be surprised. For one thing, she's qualified as lighter-than-air crew—they've got a blimp of their own, even if it isn't as long-ranged as ours."

"For one thing?" Marc said curiously.

"Ah, caught that, did you? Well, her last name is Binkis—same as the pilot of the *Riga*. Guess they picked someone with real strong motivation to help the mission."

The *Vepaja* was six hundred feet long where she swung against the west wind at the mooring mast over the gathered crowd. The airship was a smooth orca shape two hundred feet through at its thickest point a third of the way back from the blunt prow, with an X of control fins at the rear and the gondola built into the lower hull. The frame was a geodesic mesh of shamboo sheathed in varnished parachute cloth—and you needed *tough* cloth to brake a cargo pod coming down from orbit. The upper half was covered in a shiny black material, amorphous-silicon solar collectors originally developed for the space program and adapted to power the four ducted-fan electric engines slung on either side of the hull's centerline; fuel cells inside ran on hydrogen and provided backup for night work or in cloudy weather. In the bright morning sunlight the airship looked light and festive for all its bulk, the colors and lines of it bright and sharp.

"Home sweet *Grand Beede*," Marc murmured, looking up.

"As in?" Cynthia asked, seated next to him on the bench.

"Big, clumsy guy," he replied. "Or in English, a blimp."

"Rigid airship, old boy, not a blimp," Blair said from Cynthia's other side. "And could we be spared the backwoods pidgin French just for once?"

"*Weh*," Marc said amiably, being rewarded with a slight grinding of perfect white teeth and a chuckle from Cynthia.

Jadviga Binkis just looked at him, blinked once, and then looked away, but the EastBloc observer hadn't said much except in the line of business and not much then. She was a round-faced blond woman of about thirty, looking stocky and competent in her green overalls, and she'd checked out well at everything she was supposed to know. Everyone assumed she was secret police, but Marc had his doubts.

Of course, they have to have multiple specialties, too, I suppose. They're not quite as shorthanded as we are, but it's close.

Captain Tyler silenced his crew with a glare and got ready to clap. The General was finishing his speech at the podium in front of the shamboo bleachers, usually used for the audience at pickup softball games and now holding most of the adults in Jamestown not busy with something that couldn't be put aside. He did it rather well—invocation of international friendship away from Earth's rivalries, praise of the volunteers, reminding God that help would be welcome right now, and a spare ironic joke that got a ripple of laughter from the bleachers. Then the crew filed down in front and he went down the line of them, with a firm meet-the-eyes handshake and a bit of talk for everyone who'd be going.

"I envy you, Lieutenant," he said to Marc. "This will be one for the history books—the first round-trip to the western tip of the continent. Lewis and Clark all over again. No relation," he added with a grin. "Mostly my ancestors were tailors in Lithuania back then."

"*I'd* envy me myself if I wasn't going, sir," Marc said in reply, and felt his answering grin get broader.

It wasn't the first time he'd flown out in the *Vepaja*, of course. That was one of his rated skills; he'd helped take her out to the islands, south to the mountains, and east and west on field trips—but never more than a few days overall. He'd enjoyed it thoroughly, and seen a fair number of things no Earthman had before. You couldn't explore a planet the size of Earth in a hurry; the policy was to build capacity and do things methodically. Which was sensible . . . but the General was right: This was one for the history books.

Marc went on aloud, keeping the impulse to burble with enthusiasm under firm control: "But we'll be flying, not walking, sir, and it shouldn't take more than a month."

He was glad when the brief ceremony was over and there was only Sam Feldman left to say good-bye. "Yes, I'll remember to keep an eye out for specimens," Marc said. "Keep up the good work, boss. You've got the honor of Brooklyn to think about, you."

"And you be careful, you bayou rat," the older man said gruffly, slapping him on the shoulder and then surprising him by a swift, hard hug.

"Hey, that's my job!" the General's wife said.

Captain Tyler had a fond father's pride in his eyes as he looked at his command and a look of resignation as he glanced back at his scratch crew: Cynthia Whitlock, Christopher Blair, and Marc Vitrac. Tyler was older than the other men by about five years, with a leathery-tanned face and sun-faded sandy hair cropped short, an old Venus hand who'd landed with the General and lived in a grass hut while they struggled to get things going.

Two rated lighter-than-air pilots, one of them a Ranger, and a qualified power systems specialist, Marc thought, reading his mind. *Enough for a long trip—just. Oh, well, it's not as if we can afford a standing crew anyway. And the EastBlocker, for what she's worth.*

"Let's go," Tyler said, in a neutral Californian accent—his family was from San Diego, something involved with shipping, though he was an Annapolis ring-knocker himself.

There were enough of them to stand watches on a long voyage, and less of a loss to Jamestown than the regular full-time crew if the *Vepaja* was lost on its long, long voyage. Its sister-ship the *Duare* was in the hangar for maintenance at the moment, and there were enough spare parts and local supplies to build another at a pinch. They absolutely needed at least one professional airshipman, so Captain Tyler *had* to go along; apart from him all of them were about as expendable as people who were worth shipping out from Earth could be, which was a testimony to the General's judgment, in a rather disagreeable way.

"Heel, boy!" Marc said, as the four of them started up the curling spiral staircase within the mooring tower.

Tahyo came over, tail wagging slightly, wedge-shaped black head up and yellow eyes gleaming with interest. Captain Tyler gave him a glance then shrugged; the issue had been settled some time ago. Blair's lips tightened. He just didn't *like* the young greatwolf, but he was too smart to make much of it. Cynthia gave the beast a thump on the ribs and was rewarded with a head-butt under her hand.

The staircase went up and up, until the little adobe town was laid out like a diorama below, with the ragged circle-shaped crowd of humans below reduced to waving dolls. A hundred feet up, the docking ring at the *Vepaja*'s nose slotted into the movable collar of the tower, and below it, a strip of the forward hull lowered to make a catwalk leading into the gondola. They walked along that in a creak of bending shamboo and into the gloom of the interior keel deck, then up a short ladder to the rear of the control bridge. That was brightly lit by the inward-sloping windows that surrounded the U-shaped chamber on three sides; there were railings all along the edge except where the three workstations and the helm stood, so you could look down. Behind them were the living quarters and galley; the level below held the batteries, storage, and ballast, and there were hatches up into the main body of the craft and the gas cells made of 'saur intestine, as well as another ladder to an observation bubble on the top of the hull.

It all had a faint odor of ozone now, and fresh paint from the touch-up, and the pleasant almost-cedar smell of well-seasoned shamboo. By now, after a week of intensive refresher-training, they all knew where to go; even Tahyo headed straight for his padded basket and curled up. Jim Tyler cracked his fingers and smiled as he sat down at the consol at the apex of the control deck, glanced either way, and began to press switches. Marc sat and strapped himself into the copilot's position to the right of the helm, with Blair at the navigator's console on the other side, and Cynthia behind him holding down the flight engineer's station. In theory, one man could handle the *Vepaja;* the controls were all fly-by-wire through the ship's computer. In practice, for such a long journey . . .

Mais, *me, I'm even glad we've got Jadviga along. It's going to be a risky trip.*

Cynthia's voice was firm. "Power systems on. Solar collector input at ninety-nine-point-seven percent of optimum for ambient light. Batteries at full charge. Fuel cells active on trickle and all nominal. Hydrate reserve fully charged."

"Navigation and communication systems are green to go," Blair said crisply. "Wind seven knots, north-northeast. Visibility unlimited. . . ."

"I confirm all systems ready," Marc said, after the Englishman had finished listing the barometric pressure and the rest of the data, his eyes flicking over the boxes and alphanumeric readouts on his own screen. "Captain, the ship is cleared to go."

"Prepare to cast off," Tyler said. "Prepare to valve ballast." He touched a button, and his voice boomed out through the speakers below: "Clear the launch tower! Clear the area unless you want a shower, people!"

Marc glanced aside; the crowd below was dispersing nicely. Tyler's right thumb moved a wheel set into the joystick, and there was a whine from behind them as the four engines pivoted, then a rising hum as the propellers built speed. The Cajun kept his hands firmly clamped to the armrests of his seat; they itched to be on the controls themselves. The captain's left hand tapped deftly at the panel.

"Casting off!"

A thunk-*clunk!* as the docking collar released.

"Valving ballast! Netural buoyancy at three thousand feet."

A deep rumbling sound as water spewed out of the valves set into the ship's keel. There was a sudden rising-elevator feeling, and the ground grew farther away, people shifting from full-sized to dolls and then ants.

"Left full rudder, up all, all ahead one-quarter," Tyler continued, using the trigger-throttle set into the joystick and twisting it to control the rudder-elevators.

The *Vepaja*'s nose turned upward, pressing them back as they rose. The engines gradually tilted back to the horizontal as they leveled off, and then Tyler brought the craft onto its course. With the wind behind them on their right, they had to head a little north of west to keep from making leeway; the coast headed that way in any event. Marc watched the captain set the course into the autopilot— that was something he needed a little more work on—and lean back. He turned and grinned at each of them in turn.

"Prepare for boredom," he said.

"I thought this was supposed to be an adventure?" Cynthia asked, raising a brow.

"Adventure is what happens when someone fucks up, pardon my French," the airshipman said. "Like *someone* in Maintenance was doing, given all the things that went wrong before we got this tub ready. Boredom is what happens when everything goes right."

He pointed down below. The rectangle of Jamestown with its fields and pastures and the three-quarter-circle bay it sat on were falling behind them . . . slowly. The white sand of the beaches stretched in either direction, green water curling in silver foam, shading out to deep blue on their left. Ahead, the coast stretched out, green-and-tawny grass, tendril-like lines of forest along watercourses that glinted silver when the sun struck them, and other copses standing tall on the north-facing slopes of hills. The road heading west dwindled away into a game trail; the *tharg* and *churr* of the nomads were ant-tiny, hard to distinguish from the wild game that swarmed over the rich savannah, but now and then they could see the circle of a thornbrush enclosure and tents within. Off to the south, the white peaks of the Coast Range showed at the blue edge of sight: the Mother Ocean stretched to the north. Between here and there was a chaos of forested hills.

"We're making,"—Tyler glanced at the instrument board—"thirty-two mph ground speed. We can't go much faster than that without a boost from the fuel cells—which would mean running down our hydrogen, which would mean stopping in one place and cracking more, right?"

Marc and the others nodded. Marc was a little annoyed; Tyler was coming at it as the heavy old Venus hand, repeating commonplaces. Solar collectors just weren't very energetic, even a rectangle five hundred feet by a hundred, even this much closer to the sun, and even the highly efficient variety made in orbital fabricators.

"So we can't go faster than about thirty miles an hour—we're getting two from the tailwind. So, we're going six thousand miles—call it seven with the way we'll have to jig out around those mountains two thousand miles west of here—at thirty miles an hour. Call it fifteen, because we can't travel at night on the collectors . . . so that's four hundred hours of flying, and four hundred hours of mooring at night, plus additional unscheduled downtime, and so, my children, prepare to be real bored."

CHAPTER SIX

Encyclopedia Britannica, 16th Edition
University of Chicago Press, 1988

THE SPACE RACE

The history of the space race is marked by a very high degree of parallelism. The early EastBloc lead in heavy multistage rockets and the early American perfection of reusable two-stage winged shuttles were both temporary. Given that both competitors were operating within the same framework of natural law, and that both were prepared to commit very large resources, this was perhaps inevitable. On Venus, the United States even planted its initial manned base (Jamestown) fairly close to that of the EastBloc (Cosmograd), and within a year of the founding of the latter. Ostensibly this was to leave the possibility of mutual support open, though there was widespread speculation that the real goal was to limit any possible EastBloc territorial hegemony.

The EastBloc has never revealed why it decided on a location for Cosmograd so far from the landing sites of its initial probes . . .

Marc checked the sensor in his hand again. It obstinately refused to show anything but absolute normality; he tucked it back into the leather sheath at his belt and crawled forward over the surface of the gas cell. That was like being a bug on an air mattress, if you allowed for the net of soft, strong rope over everything. He advanced with a hand or foot always hooked under a length of it, since the 'saur intestine of the gasbags was both shiny and slippery-slick. Then he checked the valve and piping . . .

Zip, he thought disgustedly, and swung down the side of the cell until he could reach across and clip his safety line onto the vertical ladder that ran from the top of the gondola to the observation blister. Inside the gloom of the *Vepaja*'s main hull, the creaking of the shamboo ladder was lost in the muted groaning chorus that the airship's fabric always made when it was under way. The interior was hot and stuffy as usual, and saturated with an olive gloom and the smell of well-cured 'saur intestine, the local equivalent of goldbeater's skin used for the big donut-shaped gas cells that filled most of the interior. The cells surged a little inside their confining nets, billowing on either side of him as he climbed past the axial girder that ran down their centers and up towards the observation blister. He heard the voices long before they could be aware of him.

"Do we really have to talk about him?" Blair said.

"You're the one who seems obsessed, Chris," Cynthia retorted.

Works okay. Tone far too friendly.

"All right, then, let's talk about you and me," Blair continued smoothly.

"In other words, you don't want to talk about yourself—you want to talk about how I feel about you."

Blair joined in the woman's teasing laughter. "I'm certainly interested in how you feel," he murmured.

Cynthia groaned in mock agony. A moment later her breath caught. . . .

Marc felt himself flush in the darkness. *You stay any longer,* p'tit, *you're going to be a* dominon, *and Peeping Tom isn't your name.*

He slid back down the ladder hastily, his boots thumping on the roof of the gondola before he swung into the control room. Tyler looked at him and raised his brows.

"Anything wrong, Lieutenant?"

"No, sir. The main valves all check out and the hand sensor says there's no excess."

Tyler frowned at the gauges. "That's odd. We're showing what should be a trickle leak."

Unexpectedly, Jadviga Binkis spoke up; her English was excellent, though thick with what Marc thought of as a Boris-and-Natasha accent.

"When gauges disagree with physical inspection is good idea to trust physical inspection," she said.

Tyler nodded politely. "Well, everyone keep an eye on it," he said.

Just then Cynthia slid down the ladder, using the fireman's grip with hands and feet on the uprights, bypassing the stringers.

Either that was very quick, or things haven't progressed as far as I thought, Marc mused to himself. Then, Mais, *none of your business, boug!* He still had to fight down a grin when Blair slid down after her, looking flushed and frustrated in a way Cynthia wasn't equipped for, and running his hands through his shock of yellow hair.

"Did I hear you say there's a gas leak, sir?" Cynthia asked Tyler.

Nobody took a hydrogen leak casually on Venus. The denser air combined with the greater partial oxygen pressure to make fire a worse hazard than it had been on Earth since the Cretaceous, when Earth's atmosphere had been similar. Forest fires here had to be seen to be believed.

"The computer says it's drawn down 2 percent of bottled reserves to maintain cell pressure," the captain of the *Vepaja* said. "But I just had Lieutenant Vitrac do a visual and hand-sensor check on all the cells and the valving."

She gave Marc a hard, quick glance as he nodded, then listened with interest.

"There's no excess hydrogen in the upper hull," Marc assured them, and everyone showed at least a little relief, even the stone-faced EastBlocker. They were all on the same flying bomb, after all. "No leaks that I could detect, and no mechanical fault in the valves or the vents."

The airship had six lifting-gas cells, each with its own main valve opening through the upper keel. In addition there were latticed vents all along the upper surface, with fans to maintain a continual throughput of air inside the hull, from bottom to top and out.

"All those *p'tit* h'atoms," Marc murmured.

He got a quelling look from Tyler and a quick grin from Cynthia; Jadviga just looked puzzled. Blair was doing his imperturbable-Englishman routine again, above such things as mere anxiety. Hydrogen atoms would leak through nearly anything, eventually; they were just too small to be completely contained. Fortunately they leaked *up*, and if you could make sure they went outside the hull, there was little chance of getting the sort of hydrogen-air mixture that turned you into another martyr to the cause of interplanetary exploration and incorporated your remains into the base of the Venusian food chain.

"Still," Tyler went on, "I'm not going to take any chances. We're only four hundred miles out. We'll find a good mooring spot and spend the rest of the day and as much of the night as we need in an inch-by-inch inspection of everything. The gas cells, the reservoir, the piping, and everything between."

Nobody so much as frowned. Flying on the *Vepaja* was just as boring as Captain Tyler had promised; and besides, it was their lives. Marc called up a map of the area on his screen; it was all satellite imagery, since they were well west of any area that had been overflown from Jamestown before, much less walked on. Photography from the space station could show you the general outlines of things, but experience had shown that the devil was well and truly in the details.

"Haul away!" Marc said into the handset.

They all stepped well back as the electric winch hummed in the *Vepaja* above them. The dead tree they'd clipped the cable around was massive, the stump thicker through than a man's body at chest-height where they'd secured the hitch, and tapering to a pointed stub not much higher. The wood was weathered enough to be iron-hard but hadn't been dead long enough for the roots to rot. It held with a creak, and the airship sank by the nose as the braided 'saur hide came taunt. As it did, the gas pumps on the roof of the gondola chugged, compressing the lifting medium in the cells into a much denser, non-buoyant form in the steel storage tanks along the keel. That was always preferable to valving off gas to descend.

At last the orca shape hung two hundred feet up, streaming out behind a long curve of cable; it could pivot around the anchor point in a complete circle if the wind veered, and it would be over water for most of that—the tree had grown on the tip of a spit of land running out into a lake five miles across and ten long.

"Go for it, boys," Cynthia said cheerfully. "Just watching all this honest work makes me feel better. A little sweat never hurt anyone."

She was keeping watch with one of the heavy game rifles in her arms. Jadviga Binkis stood behind her, looking in the other direction and holding a chunky automatic shotgun loaded with heavy rifled slugs. Back home, police used those for breaking through thick, locked doors; they were an acceptable way to knock down something large, living, and mean at close quarters. Mostly what was in view was the water of the lake they'd christened Myposa, reed-grown close to shore, blue with small whitecaps farther out. Rolling open downs surrounded the water on this northern shore, with thick forest in the valleys and scattered trees on the downs; the tall grass rippled like long, slow ocean waves. Most of the birds and beasts had fled when the airship came close, but they could see moving dots on the edge of sight.

Marc and Blair lifted the pump with a grunt, walking it between them with a careful shuffle until they had it resting securely on the graveled beach. Then the hose and power cable came down, and they snapped the connectors home.

"All clear, Captain," Marc said again.

The pump started up, its mechanical purr oddly alien among the creak and rustle of vegetation, the cheep and buzz of insects, the rustle of beasts too tiny or too witless to be alarmed by the huge shape in the sky passing through grass and brush. Hand-sized fliers with triangular wings and long tails tipped with miniature rudders and mouths full of tiny needlelike teeth flew among the bugs, snapping up prey and leaving legs and bits of gauzy wing to flutter downward.

The airship bobbed a little closer to the ground as water flowed into the ballast tanks. The rest of the afternoon, sunlight falling on the great hull went into cracking for the hydrogen, to fill the cells and cram into the reserve tanks.

"Captain, I'll take a gander around and maybe get us some fresh meat," Marc said into the handset.

"All right, Lieutenant," Tyler said. "But don't go out of visual range of the airship; that's an order."

"Roger, Captain."

Blair frowned. "It's an unnecessary risk," he said.

Marc shrugged. "*Mais*, so's getting out of bed in the morning," he said. "And we should conserve our preserved foods."

"Trivial."

Marc shrugged again. "Since I'm cooking tonight, let me get some decent ingredients. The dried stuff . . . is it desiccated or desecrated?"

"I'll take a turn in the galley, if you wish," Blair retorted.

Nearly a week together in the *Vepaja* had revealed that the Englishman was rather proud of his cooking skills. He *was* much better at it than Marc had expected, in a rather academic, by-the-book way, and could manage a fairly good omelet as long as their fresh eggs held out. While Jesus might be able to turn water into wine, even he couldn't have done anything worthwhile with dried, powdered eggs.

"But we don't have any Brussels sprouts for you to overdo, old boy," Marc said blandly.

The blond man flushed and took a step towards him. Cynthia cleared her throat and said, "Let's get to work. That inspection won't do itself."

Marc waited while the basket was lowered from the cargo doors on the *Vepaja*'s keel and the other three hoisted up into their craft. As the doors closed, he pulled a mottled length of parachute cloth out of a pocket and tied it around his head like a bandana, knotting it at the back of his head.

Then he whistled sharply and picked up his rifle; he didn't bother with the bush jacket; just buckling on the belt with pistol and knife and machete, and slinging the bandolier with its cartridge loops over one shoulder. Tahyo's gangling form rose out of a clump of grass at the signal. He trotted over, as always covering the ground fairly fast even though his legs and paws and head still looked far too big for the awkward rest of him. At the sight of the rifle and the sound of Marc working the bolt to chamber a round, Tahyo's goofy eagerness sank into a quivering joy. He had never had the slightest doubt about what he was supposed to do for a living, and he loved his work.

The yearling greatwolf was already a bit above his master's waist at the shoulder, his barrel head nearly breastbone high as he took the air that was blowing from a bit west of north. He followed obediently as Marc walked in that direction, keeping the breeze in his face and carefully to the open ridges where he could see the *Vepaja* clearly. Grass still green enough to smell sweet when it crushed underfoot waved around him, waist-high to chest-high most of the time; there was an undergrowth of herbs, some prickly, some with small blue-green flowers.

The trees on the higher ground were smallish, flat-topped thorny acacias, and Marc kept a wary eye on them; leopards and other medium-sized predators liked to use them as convenient points from which to drop in for dinner.

Unfortunately, keeping to the high ground meant everything else could see the airship, too, and one another—and most animals felt sort of exposed on a ridgetop; the ones that didn't were the ones that didn't mind being seen, which usually meant *big and dangerous*. After a half-mile, Marc stopped before the ridge ahead of him sloped up and the grass grew shorter.

"Stay!" he said to the greatwolf, and went forward stooping, and then snake-crawling.

When he was on the top of the ridge, the grass was just tall enough to hide everything but his head, and the bandana would break the outline of that. Before him, the ground broke away to a low swale covered in forest, rising to more grassy hills on the other side; the strip of forest followed a creek to his right and left. An infinite freshness rolled in towards him, and for a moment he simply lay and enjoyed it. Here he was an atom among atoms. There weren't any complications out in the bush, just a million million creatures going about their lives, willing enough to treat you as you treated them . . .

Then he sighed: back to business. "Tahyo!"

Behind him, the greatwolf came to his paws, head quivering with eagerness.

"Circle wide, boy!" A hesitation, and Marc gestured. "Circle wide!"

Tahyo shook himself as if in understanding and cut off to the right, loping through the tall grass down the hill and disappearing among the trees. Marc lay, neither tense nor relaxed, simply waiting, not even really watching, just letting his gaze drift. If you tried to see everything, you saw nothing; his father and uncles had taught him that a long time ago, and training later had only sharpened it. What you needed to do was know what the patterns were, and see only the *breaks* in the pattern, the things that didn't fit.

"Like that thrashing in those brushes," he murmured to himself, very softly, watching leaves shake and insects rise in a glittering cloud.

Then he heard Tahyo's cry—something between a howl and a roar, with more than a bit of puppyish yelping still in it, what he called *wulfing* to himself. The bushes were around man-high, with long, narrow leaves and pink trumpet-shaped flowers; at this distance he wasn't quite sure if they were really bushes, or vines growing over something else. The things that came out of them were equally unfamiliar; their voices were like terrified brass trumpets, honking and echoing across the grassy hills.

Some type of 'saur, he thought. *The warm-blooded kind.*

Small ones, smaller than him but a little bigger than, say, Cynthia; bipeds that ran like ostriches on two muscular-thighed hind legs, a resemblance increased by the long hairy feathers that covered their bodies. The thick tails and the yellow crests on their sheeplike heads were pure Venus, and the front limbs were shorter and held close to their chests, with long gripping fingers ending in blunt claws. The teeth in their open mouths confirmed it: flat shearing and grinding plant-eater equipment. The herd had about a dozen adults and juveniles ranging down to knee-high hatchlings.

Marc grinned at their bulge-eyed panic, and gently released his hold on the rifle. Tahyo appeared behind them, *wulfing* and leaping and snapping, darting back and forth. Greatwolves were pack hunters and they used exactly this sort of tactic, a noisy pursuit driving prey on to a hidden ambush. The herd—or flock—was stampeding up the hill in honking, gobbling panic, like a cartoon of six-foot Thanksgiving turkeys.

The first of the 'saurs came by on either side, biggish adults that probably outweighed Marc. He ignored the grown ones, and the others with the distinctive crests; those were probably the males, and would taste rank. He took one long breath and let it out, then another and coiled ready without moving. Just there, a plain, uncrested, medium-sized one—

Marc exploded out of the grass, the machete free in his hand. The oncoming 'saur reared back in terror, screaming like a steam whistle and rearing back on its tail; one foot pistoned out in a kick that might have been dangerous if he hadn't dodged. That put him in position for a quick, flicking sweep with the two-foot blade, twisting with a grunt to put the weight of his body behind it. The impact made a heavy, slightly soft catch in the arc of the shining steel, and the head fell with a thump a few feet away. The headless body ran on for six steps with a bright red spray of arterial blood spurting up in twin jets before the 'saur fell forward, flat on its . . .

"Headless neck, eh?" Marc said to himself, chuckling as he wiped the machete clean on a handful of grass. Tahyo came bounding up the hill, bristling and rolling his eyes and exuding a general air of *God, that was fun; let's eat!*

Marc met him with a stern "sit!" before letting him have the head. The rest of the 'saur herd went honking off northward, apparently not noticing the *Vepaja* floating in the sky. Marc looked up carefully; there were plenty of birds and pterosaurs around, including one variety he'd never seen before, with a four-foot wingspan, black and white stripes on its fuzzy body-fur, and a long row of spike teeth in its beaklike mouth. It sailed in and clung to the side of a boulder not far away with its feet and the claws on the leading edge of its wings, watching him intently, or more probably watching the bleeding carcass at his feet.

None big enough to worry about—except possibly a dot too high to make out, which might be anything. Prudently he dragged the sixty-pound carcass over to a flat-topped acacia and hoisted it up by the surprisingly chickenlike feet to butcher down to something more portable. Tahyo came crawling on his belly, grinning and wagging his tail, but he waited until told to dive into what a greatwolf considered the real treat, the multicolored and rather stinky guts.

"Just don't roll in it, you dirty *saleau*, you," Marc said. "Or I'll give you a bath."

The greatwolf understood "bath" all right, and gave a placatory whine at the dreaded word. When the butchering was finished—Tahyo completed his meal by eating the feet, crunching them like candy-sticks and belching contentedly—Marc packed the remaining meat in a roll of canvas and paused for a moment.

The sun was down nearly to the horizon in the east, sinking far beyond Jamestown—beyond Kartahown, beyond civilization, beyond the maps. The clouds there were like frothed castles of white whipped cream, just starting to get a ruddy tinge.

"Me, I'm sticky and tired," Marc mused. "But it's a *good* day."

He'd enjoyed wilderness back on Earth . . . but even if you were out in the bayous beyond Grand Isle, you always knew that you were really in an island of wild in a sea of civilization. Here it was exactly the opposite. There was a *world* out there, and the base or even Kartahown and the Mother River and its cities were the islands. Tiny little islands, in a sea of living things, all of them mating and killing and eating just as they always had. If you wanted to know what was over the hills, you had to go there yourself.

"So I can advance the cause of science and civilization without being around to see the consequences, eh, Big Hungry Dog?"

Tahyo looked up at him, thumped his tail on the ground, and quickly gulped down a last bite of giblet with a slightly guilty look. The greatwolf looked relieved when the human made no attempt to take the savory morsel, and then sighed with resignation when Marc rose with the bundle of meat on his back and a tumpline to bear the weight across his forehead, took up his rifle again, and trotted back towards the anchor point by the lake.

"*Gar ici*, I'm glad to have you along," he said to the animal running beside him. "Keep a nose out for anything that might like to snack down, eh? We're smelling of blood and meat, us."

Animals were beginning to filter back into the area, losing their initial fear of the shape of the aircraft when nothing particularly bad happened. Besides small game like a tiger-striped looks-like-a-rabbit, he spotted half a dozen varieties of antelope, a troop of man-sized tailless baboons, wild hogs four foot at the shoulder and stripped with patterns of tan and yellow, and once something huge raised its head over a fifty-foot tree for an instant and then crashed away, invisible save for the heaving of the vegetation. Farther in the distance came the appalling squall of a saber-tooth, either celebrating a kill or working off frustration from missing that last infinitely satisfying leap-and-plunge-in-fangs.

The rest of the crew had completed their inspection and were making a temporary camp. That meant mainly doing their laundry, digging a fire-pit, and bringing down some cooking equipment; they'd spend the night in the *Vepaja*, a safe two hundred feet above the bugs and beasts. Marc silently rubbed the 'saur with the spice mix and set it to roast over coals already giving a nice white glow. Things burned faster on Venus.

And from the silent, troubled looks Cynthia is giving me, that's not all that heats up quickly. Mais, *get over it*, boug. *It's her life, and if she doesn't feel the same way about you, that's just the luck of the draw. Thinking otherwise, that's obsession and madness country. So what if there are only a hundred and thirty of us locked up together on the same planet? You're supposed to be the pick of ten million volunteers. Act like it!*

It was still intensely frustrating, if you were a healthy twenty-five-year-old.

Maybe I should take up that offer of a housekeeper. He grimaced. *I'm not prejudiced. I just think that sex with the locals is . . . creepy.* Weh, weh, *they're human beings, or near as no matter, but . . . and you can get the fleas out of their hair . . . but can you get the ghoulies and ghosties out of their minds? I'm not sixteen anymore. The thought of sleeping with a woman I can't really talk to puts me off.*

After the cooking was started, he headed down to the water with soap and a towel, after giving it a *careful* checking-over. These upland lakes were usually pretty free of parasites, but that didn't mean there weren't other predators. When he'd waded out, dried off, and switched to some clean fatigues, Cynthia came over.

"Marc—," she began.

He grinned and shrugged. "It's okay, Cyn. I'm a big boy and I know how things work."

She smiled, though with a wince-inducing amount of relief, and changed the subject. "I'm glad we had time to check things over before we got impossibly far from base."

Marc picked up his rifle and they walked back towards the fire; a mouthwatering smell was coming from it as wafts of blue smoke drifted skyward.

"Me too," he said. "I'd be even happier if we'd found what went wrong and knew we could fix it—or not."

"*Passé, passé!*" Marc mumbled in his sleep.

Tahyo whined again; he understood *get lost, dog!* quite well by now. He still stuck his nose—cold, wet, healthy, startling—in his master's ear once more.

Marc threw off his light blanket. The interior of the *Vepaja*'s gondola was an oval about a hundred feet long, with a lower level half that length fared into the middle for the ballast and reserve-gas tanks. The interior partitions were shamboo wicker covered with coarse cloth on both sides, enough for privacy—if your hearing wasn't very good. Their merit was that they could be easily re-arranged to suit a specific mission. For this one the central corridor had the galley and head opposite each other right behind the control chamber, then five small rooms, each with a narrow bunk and not much else.

Marc yawned and stretched in the stuffy dimness, lit only by starlight through the round porthole, open now for fresh air. Even that wasn't much, with the usual high haze and no moon. Nights on Venus were darker than on Earth.

"If you think I'm taking the basket down to the surface just for you, you're crazy, Tahyo," he said. "You can use that litter box we set up and learn to like it."

Then he grimaced. It was a smelly, messy procedure, and the one argument that had almost persuaded him to leave the young greatwolf behind on this trip. Tahyo didn't like it, either; it offended his sense of propriety to unload in the airship, which he evidently considered their den and thus sacrosanct. Doc Feldman thought it was an instinct not to mark a lair with scents another predator might follow to vulnerable nursing mothers and pups.

Usually Tahyo would endure a heroic degree of discomfort to

wait for the morning, but this time his anxiety didn't seem to be quite the Oh-God-I-just-can't-hold-it-boss type of stress. Instead he was bouncing back and forth between the narrow cot and the door. Marc yawned and blinked and began to swing out of the bunk. Then he froze. The airship had swung out over the water during the night; all the better, security-wise. But there was just enough starlight on the still water to see it was a *lot* too close; and now they were down by the nose as well.

The alarm went off just as he reached for the button by the head of his bed—it was the steady *whoop-whoop-whoop* of the manual override, too, not the choppier sound of an automatic warning, so someone had slapped *their* emergency button.

Marc jumped for the corridor, almost tripped over the hysterically *wulfing* Tahyo—the greatwolf hated what the mechanical wail did to his sensitive ears. Marc plunged past the galley and into the control room, to find Blair in the commander's seat; he was on watch right now, and frantically pressing buttons and screens. The water was starting to fill the view through the slanted windows.

"Main valves on the forward three cells open. Can't get the buggers closed from here," he said, loudly but tonelessly, without looking up from the urgent futility of his task.

Marc whirled and flung himself at the ladder, vaguely conscious of others following him. There was no time for anything else; if they came down in the water here they'd be lucky to make it to shore naked. Trying to walk three hundred miles back to Jamestown that way . . .

Up through darkness lit only by the dim red of the night-lights, with the gas cells of the airship looming around him like monstrous, pillowy giants from a child's nightmare. A turn and twist, and he scrambled lizard-style over the upper surface of the donut, the net-covered surface feeling palpably looser and less taut under his body than it had earlier in the day. Then he was at the top, where a short tube joined the cell to the valve in the hull surface above. His hand slammed at the switch there to close it; he could hear the hiss of escaping gas.

"*Shit!*" he screamed, as nothing happened. "Use the manual override! Use the manual override!" he shouted, to whoever was . . . please God . . . on the second and third cells.

That was an aluminum lever. He grabbed, pulled . . . and felt the servo working against him, keeping the valve open to the alien night. He reached across without hesitation and pulled the power connector. It might spark and blow them all to the afterlife, but that was an acceptable risk right now.

There. The heavy three-pronged plug came loose; his hand flashed back to the manual lever and yanked. A *clung* from above, and the rubber-edged rectangle thunked closed.

"Number One cell secured!" he called.

"Number Two secured!" Jadviga Binkis' voice.

"Number Three secured!" Cynthia.

Just then a rumble came from far below them; the emergency ballast was dropping hundreds of gallons of water a second into the lake—the same water they'd expended precious time and power to pump *up* that very day. The fabric beneath him began to bulge and grow resilient once more as emergency hydrogen from the tanks flowed through.

"*Pouponer,* old girl," Marc gasped. "Make yourself nice, eh?"

He lay for a moment in sweating exhaustion on the top of the cell. Much as he loved the Venusian wilderness, he had *no* desire to die in it trying to fight off a 'saur or a saber-tooth with an improvised wooden spear.

Then he forced himself to swing back to the ladder and down into the control deck. Captain Tyler was back in his seat, though, like Marc, he was wearing nothing but his boxers. Cynthia and Jadviga came through an instant later, nearly as undressed. Only Blair was still in his uniform, looking white-faced. Outside, the water of the lake receded with smooth grace as the *Vepaja* regained buoyancy; they could see it clearly now, since one of the prow searchlights had been switched on.

After a moment Tyler nodded and turned the swivel chair to face the rest of them.

"There wasn't any alarm until Wing Commander Blair noticed what was happening—," Tyler began.

He gave the Englishman a glare. Marc did, too; he hadn't noticed too damned much, since he was supposed to have been awake and alert. *Tahyo* had turned out to have more on the ball.

"Sir, as you said, there wasn't any alarm from the automatic systems. And all the gauges remained steady—I *did* keep an eye on them, I assure you."

"—and as he says, there's something amiss with the computer," Tyler finished. "Miss Whitlock?"

"I'll check it, Captain," she said. "But offhand I can't think of anything spontaneous that would cause precisely that cascade of errors."

"Of course is not spontaneous," Jadviga Binkis said.

Marc started slightly; she was usually so quiet you could forget that she spoke at all. She went on:

"Is sabotage, wrecking. As was crash of *Riga*. There is conspiracy at work here."

"Perhaps," Blair said. "But a conspiracy by whom, and to what end? I can think of any number of motives—for example, having lost their shuttle, the EastBloc might wish to see *our* base suffer a corresponding loss."

The others looked at one another, dismayed. Captain Tyler nodded slowly. "They say the third time it's enemy action. I'm not inclined to wait that long." He looked around. "It's my decision, but I'd like to consult. Who's for returning to base?"

Oh, that's a toughie, Marc thought unhappily. *On the one hand, I don't want to miss this trip—and Jadviga's husband and his crew may be alive. On the other hand, I'm not real eager to die, either. Difficult enough just making the trip, but what if the next bit of sabotage is a fire?*

His hand twitched; then he pressed it firmly down by his side. Stillness held for a second; then Blair's hand went up and, more slowly, Cynthia's.

Tyler smiled grimly. "Well, I say we're going on, but it's nice to be in the majority."

A pause, then: "And here's how we're going to do it from now on. Obviously, single watch-standers are out . . . except for me. I'll set up a roster. For starters, since you were so alert, Lieutenant, you and Wing Commander Blair can share the rest of the night watch."

"Captain," Cynthia said. "I'd like to get to work right away on the computer's programs."

"Can you tell who did what?"

"Ummm . . . no. I mean, I may be able to find out what's been f—screwed up in the program, but code doesn't carry fingerprints."

"The morning will do, Ms. Whitlock," Tyler said calmly. "After losing so much gas and ballast, we're not going anywhere tomorrow. And I want to consult with General Clarke."

Suddenly Jadviga spoke: "You assume saboteur is among us, Captain?"

Tyler nodded. "From the non-fatal nature of the sabotage, yes," he said. "Whoever he or she is, they'd want a chance of getting out. Which is why I've decided on continuing with the mission. The further we get from Jamestown, the less likelihood of whoever it is acting again. Unless they're not just nasty but suicidal."

He spoke calmly, but Marc was glad *he* wasn't the saboteur. He suspected whoever it was wouldn't live long after Captain Tyler found out their name.

And no suicide will be needed.

CHAPTER SEVEN

Venus, Gagarin Continent—Far West

"Run! Run!" Teesa shouted.

Her sister, Zore, scampered by, burdened by her fluff-tail. The little spotted animal had its claws fixed in her shoulder, hard enough to draw beads of blood, but the girl scrambled on, clutching it to her and her blowgun pumping in her other hand. The last few of her people followed, out of the village that had been their home since her mother's time; some had bundles in their arms, many nothing, not even a loincloth. An old woman knelt, singing her dying-song, then thrust a long shamboo knife up under her ribs and collapsed, kicking.

Smoke blew in, hot, acrid clouds of dusty-black smoke, from roofs set alight before they fled—nobody would leave more than they must to the beastmen.

The *crack . . . crack . . .* sound of the new weapons echoed from the northward, firing in the slower way. Teesa moved the little lever ahead of the handgrip to the bottom position that launched one dart every time you squeezed the lever.

But I have so few of the darts! she thought desperately.

Taldi limped up, blood streaming from a cut on his leg. "We cannot stop them," he croaked.

Teesa took down a section of shamboo pipe and gave it to him. He knocked out the bung and let the water run over his face, gulping and coughing. Then he unhitched a leather bandolier full of the boxes-of-loud-darts and tossed it to her.

"These are cursed, but you wanted them," he said. "Take them and go—give me your blowgun darts first. I will hold them as long as I can. You are our people's guardian."

Her eyes prickled, but there was no time for tears. Instead she touched his shoulder.

"I hail you, brother of my mate," she said formally.

Then she took down the Cave Master and set it around her brow. The familiar shiver ran over her skin; she looked south through a hundred eyes, felt the fury and fear and pain of men and beastmen fighting and dying. And . . .

A mind. Not a beastman—true-man, but of a kind she had never met before. And familiar in another way; it was a mind that had been touched by the Mystery, as she had.

But it was mad.

Her world swam about her, and she almost fell to her knees with her hands clutched to her temples. That brought the loud-death against the Cave Master with a cold *clink* that startled her back to awareness. She *pushed* with her thoughts, and the babble receded to a background gabble. She pushed again, and saw from Taldi's eyes that he could not see her. He smiled grimly, hefted the pouch of blowgun darts she'd given him, and settled himself behind a stone wall. The Cave Master told her of parties of Cloud Mountain warriors falling back southward, harrying the beastmen to keep them off the fleeing females and children.

And every little while, one would flare and die, making her wince.

She took a piece of burning thatch and set it to the weathered, tinder-dry wood of the spirit-poles before the house where she had been born and where her mother lay buried beneath the hearth, then turned and trotted southward herself.

There was good ground a few miles from here. There she could use the loud-death and stand revealed.

We can live in the mountains, she thought.

It would be hard, without their stocks of tools and stored food, but it could be done—her folk were skillful hunters, and they could gather acorns and leach out the tannins with water, if nothing else.

But what can we do there but live from one kill to the next, without houses, without the graves of our kin or the company of our spirits? Will we be any more than the beastmen themselves?

Then she shook her head. Time enough for such questions later. Now was a time to kill.

"*Ça va, Christophe?*" Marc asked idly.

"*Comme ci, comme ça,*" Blair replied, in faultless Parisian, not looking up from the recorder and laptop. "*C'est la Venus, eh?*"

Marc laid down his load of firewood by the stack he'd built and raised a brow, rubbing fragrant resin off his sweaty arms and then pulling up a swatch of tall grass to clean his palms.

"Didn't know you spoke French," he said.

Blair shrugged and frowned. "My dear fellow, give me credit for a certain degree of education," he said.

Marc grinned. "Funny, where I come from, people consider speaking French the mark of a swamp rat."

"If you can call *that* patois French," Blair said.

"Well, Texans claim that what they speak is English," Marc said equably. "When it isn't Spanish."

Cynthia gave a subdued groan. She and Jadviga were spreading the reserve mats of solar-power sheeting on the hillside just inland of the *Vepaja*'s anchor point. The material was a thin, flexible backing supporting foot-square tiles of the actual accumulators; those were flexible, too, but less so, and they were about the thickness of a sheet of cardboard. The combination was only about as heavy as a blanket of the same area, but there was a *lot* of area, and her ebony skin shone with the sweat that made her halter and shorts cling. Lacking nature's sunblock, the Lithuanian woman had kept to long sleeves and looked even more uncomfortable.

Marc and Blair had muscled the rolls to the locations, but the two women were in charge of opening them out and attaching them to the power cords that climbed up the airship's anchor cable. The expedition carried the spare sheeting to make repairs if the layer on the upper hull was damaged, and for making up the loss if they were forced to valve gas in quantity. Tyler wanted all storage back up to maximum before leaving, and Clarke had backed him up. Marc didn't blame them, but it was a lot of work, and he could see that Jadviga was itching to get going.

Well, if I was married to someone lost out there, I would be, too, he thought charitably.

Tahyo looked up hopefully as Marc stretched and worked his arms; he'd been rather crushed since the women forcefully rebuffed his attempts to "help" with what they were doing. Marc ruffled his ears as he went by, then snapped the connectors onto the sheets and the power cable.

The handset at Cynthia's waist buzzed. She put it to her ear, nodded, and waved at the windows of the control chamber.

"Power's flowing," she said.

A moment later the pump began to hum and chug again. Cynthia added, "Captain Tyler repeats that none of us is to get out of sight of the others."

"*Weh,*" Marc replied. "That's reasonable."

"And he won't let me work on the computers alone," she said unhappily.

He spread his hands, and she nodded. Then he looked around. The camp was set up, complete with tents; they weren't going to sleep in the aircraft until they got under way again, either. He suspected that Tyler had had to bend Clarke's ear a good deal to get permission to keep going, but he wasn't taking any unnecessary chances. The process of filling the ballast and reserve-hydrogen tanks was pretty well automatic; he picked up his rifle and fishing rod and headed over for the lake.

"The fish here aren't much," Cynthia said casually, strolling along with him.

"*Weh,*" Marc said again. "*Mashwarohn.*"

"Is that Kartahownian?"

"Grand Isle. But even as catfish, they aren't much."

They weren't; the commonest species seemed to be the equivalent of a mud puppy, with coarse, bland flesh. On the other hand . . .

"But Big Hungry Dog here doesn't mind," he went on.

Tahyo followed him, then went running off after something with glittery wings six inches across, leaping into the air and tripping as he came down. A few seconds later the greatwolf's head came up again, looking sheepish.

She hesitated, then went on: "Do *you* think whoever's responsible is . . . one of us?"

Marc sat down on a convenient rock, put a worm on his hook, and braced the rifle close to hand.

"Yup," he said. "I can think of two or three ways to make that jiggery with the computer fatal instead of just dangerous; can't you?"

"A dozen," she said, then winced.

Marc laughed. "Hey, podna, that proves you're either innocent or a real good actress. But if you're the Evil One, you'd have to be, no?"

She laughed unwillingly. "Unless *you're* the good *actor,* bayou boy."

He nodded, and then jerked the line sharply as the float bobbed. The reel hissed sharply for a moment, but the fight didn't last long. A fat, chublike fish was on the end when he used the net on its last pole, gasping and twitching the barbell-like tendrils under its jaw.

"Another mud puppy," he called, extracting the hook and tossing the flopping length into the air. "Tahyo! Come and get it!"

The big, lanky animal galloped over, stopped, judged distances, and opened his mouth. The fish disappeared in a snapping bite, except for its head; Tahyo cocked an eye at the ground and snapped it up, crunching it and licking his chops with a hopeful look.

"God, does that damn beast never stop eating?"

"*Mais,* he sleeps, too, yes," Marc said, and cast another worm on the waters.

Cynthia dropped her voice: "Do you think it might be . . ."

Her eyes flicked to Jadviga, who was methodically straightening out small rucks and creases in the solar collectors. She had a methodical neatness that Marc found a little surprising, given the number of disasters her side's space effort had endured. But then, she wasn't exactly a Russian, and he supposed the EastBloc selection process was nearly as rigorous as the one the Americans and their allies followed.

"Well, it's her husband we're trying to rescue," Marc said quietly. You had to be careful; sound carried better on Venus.

"If she's really Jadviga Binkis," Cynthia said. "Or if *anything* they've told us is true."

"There is that," Marc said. "Their shuttle went down, but beyond that it's all their word. *Mais,* hey, no information is no information." Cynthia made a frustrated sound, then looked a little doubtful when he added, "What does Blair think?"

"Well . . . Chris says that it's either someone back at Jamestown, or Jadviga. The slow leak was actually a good idea, he thinks. It would probably have killed us, or at least wrecked the *Vepaja,* but might have been classed as something natural even if we survived—we'd have had to get out too fast to investigate."

"Hmmm. Possibility," Marc said.

He didn't add: *Or your boyfriend might be the one. But who'd benefit? Maybe the EastBloc . . . but they've got Jadviga here anyway, and they'd only benefit if they've been selling us a line of goods about their crash. And why would Blair work for them, anyway? Money? That's ridiculous . . . isn't it? And it could be Cynthia, I suppose . . . but that leaves us with motivation again.*

"I can see we're all going to have a fascinating hobby to while away the hours," he said. "Unless we're all killed the next time."

Cynthia snorted and threw a tuft of grass at him. Just then the floater bobbed again. Tahyo *wulfed,* eyes fixed on the thrashing that broke the blue surface of the lake, making little abortive lunges as he waited for Marc to land the fish.

"Well, there it is," Captain Tyler said. "It blew up fast, but that's Venus for you."

They all looked over his shoulder at the main screen at the captain's position. The airship had VPS—Venus Positioning System— and satellite weather coverage direct from orbit. That gave them their own position, about three-quarters of their way towards the crash site. It also gave them an excellent real-time view of the huge, bruiselike, circular storm that was heading their way out of the north-polar ocean. On Earth they might have called it a typhoon or a hurricane, but the similarity was only a general one. Weather was a solar-driven heat engine. Venus got more solar insolation than Earth, and stored it in a thicker atmosphere; winds blew harder, and seas ran higher. Marc was profoundly grateful he wasn't out on the northern ocean in a single-sail Kartahownian boat under *that*.

Outside the control cabin, the sky was still clear except for the usual high haze, but the afternoon sunlight had an odd sulfurous light, almost like the old gold of sunset but with a sickly cast that set his teeth on edge. Occasional gusts of wind pushed at the fabric-covered hull, making the geodesic shamboo framing creak and moan softly, louder than the quiet humming of the engines.

"I used to think we got what we deserved," Marc said.

"Used to, Lieutenant?" Tyler said dryly.

"Yessir. But bad as we are, we aren't *that* bad."

"What's your explanation, then?"

"*Mais*, sir, I'm coming round to the view that God hates us."

Everyone chuckled, even the normally stone-faced Jadviga. "That would be funny, if only it were funny," Cynthia said, holding up her hands.

There were salve and bandages on the palms, fruit of an emergency tear-down-and-repair of Engine #4, when a casing cracked and it shorted out in the middle of a rainstorm. Every other system in the airship had hit collywobbles as well, despite the exhaustive rebuild before they set out.

Maybe it's just bad luck. We haven't found anything else that has *to be sabotage. On the other hand, we haven't been able to find out how our computers were fucked over, either. And first time accident, second time coincidence, third time enemy action.*

Tyler smiled and nodded back to the screen: "Emily there is moving at about our top speed, and we're only in slightly more danger if we go on than if we go back. The real question is, do we try to stake down, or do we ride it out in the air?"

"Stake down?" Blair said. "Not in the open, Captain."

"Christ, no, Wing Commander!" Tyler said impatiently. "But if we could find something on the order of a canyon, I'd chance it. I want you and Lieutenant Vitrac to go over the maps, such as they are—"

Both men nodded. Back home these days you could pretty well read a car's license plates from space, but the thick, turbulent atmosphere and the sparse network of satellites made observation from orbit a lot less efficient here.

"Ms. Whitlock, Ms. Binkis, you'll join me in visual observation, looking for a likely place. Gentlemen, ladies, let's get to work!"

The three of them sat at their workstations, each taking one of the hull-mounted cameras and scanning ahead and to either side of the airship. The fabric of the *Vepaja* creaked and groaned as Tyler pushed the engines to maximum, and from behind and below them there was an almost inaudible *thrip* sound as the pumps began to force hydrogen into the intakes of the fuel cells.

"I'm taking her up another three thousand feet and turning south to follow the coast," Tyler added. "We'll get a little more power from the collectors that way, and make better speed. If we can ride the southern fringe, it'll push us the way we want to go."

Unspoken in all their minds were the mountains even farther to the south. Chains lined most of the northern part of Gagarin, sometimes right to the edge, sometimes hundreds of miles inland. In places they were broken by sinks and depressions that gave access to the uplands in the interior, or even to the great coastal plains to the south; the big 'saur migrations followed those. Hereabouts, the mountains were a good two hundred miles south. Unfortunately, they were also an unbroken wall higher than the Himalayas; the highest peaks were nearly thirty thousand feet, high enough for eternal snows and even glaciers. Even the lower ones were well over the *Vepaja*'s operational ceiling of twelve thousand or so.

"Captain, perhaps I'd better make some just-in-case precautions ready . . . just in case," Marc said.

Tyler considered that for a moment, then nodded. "There's no point in pretending a crash isn't a possibility," he said calmly. "Storms like this are the biggest reason we haven't done really long exploratory flights before."

Marc didn't think anyone was too happy to have the possibility mentioned, but it needed to be done.

Correction, he thought. *Blair looks fairly happy. Which is odd.*

The man had been tense and nervous the last week, but he was calm now, flicking through screen after screen of stored satellite imagery with methodical speed, making a note now and then. He raised an ironic brow as he felt Marc's gaze.

"Do remember to pack some tea, old bean," he said, and went back to his work.

Marc licked a finger and made a *one for your column* check mark in the air; then he walked back through the corridor and down the stairs into the cargo compartment. Tahyo came over, whining; he could sense that something was wrong, and probably feel the way the barometer was dropping. The man took a moment to reassure him. It was easy enough; Marc felt a little guilty at the way the young greatwolf simply accepted that he could make things better.

They all had small survival packs ready; that was SOP. The problem was that in an airship wreck, if you threw things out the door, the ship or the remnant thereof tended to jump skyward, stranding the laggards to drift additional miles unless you were bailing out from high up.

No more food, he decided. *A couple of packages of the freeze-dried stuff will do.*

The closest thing to crashing on Venus was going down in Alaska or Greenland or Antarctica back in the 1920s. The biggest difference was that neither starvation nor attacks by crazed flesh-ripping penguins were much of a menace back there. Eating usually wasn't a problem in the Venusian wilds; the problem was avoiding *being* eaten by something; here a polar bear would be small game. Or avoiding being eaten by *somebody*, if rumors about quasi-human tribes were true—and the initial probes had certainly given that theory a lot of backup.

"Ammunition," he muttered to himself. "Weapons, tools. Fire-starter kit. Clothes, no; you can do without in a pinch. And some extra medical supplies. VPS units so you don't get lost. Copies of the *Shipwreck Handbook*. I hope to the good God we don't turn out to be the first people who really need it."

The handbook was a thick hardcover with plenty of illustrations; it was intended for someone unfortunate enough to be stranded a long way from Jamestown with no quick way back. Marc had had a role in the latest edition, which contained notes on everything from archery to how to break a *churr* to the saddle or perform an emergency appendectomy.

The cargo bay contained a number of large crates, woven shamboo strips on a framework of larger stems. He emptied four and began methodically packing. The extra two rifles and shotguns; the spare pistols; every last round of 10-mm pistol and 9-mm express Magnum. A couple of bows and quivers of arrows, which were reusable. Knives, machetes, hatchets . . .

"Aha!" Marc said.

A few ringing blows detached the heads of axes from their helves. In a pinch you could improvise a workable handle out of a branch in an hour. Out in the wilderness, the only way to get the *head* of an axe was to chip it out of flint. Beads and mirrors, the classic trade goods: They'd yet to find a hunting tribe here who weren't gaga over them. They had axes, knives, and spearheads of their own that worked, sort of, but they didn't have anything like plastic beads or anything that would give an accurate reflection.

Rope, binoculars . . . *And why not?* He added the *Vepaja*'s complete carpentry kit and all their nails.

"Now the brilliant bayou boy will show everyone how to get all this stuff *out* once buoyancy control has been lost," he said, bowing to the empty hold as if to an audience.

Not altogether empty. Tahyo found the whole process fascinating and thumped his tail on the deck in applause.

The airship came with plenty of rope, braided 'saur-hide cables and others down to heavy-twine diameter made from the scutched fibers of the immature shamboo plant. With hand and boot he wrapped each of the crates tightly in multiple layers, then joined each by a stout twenty-foot link.

"And now for the resistance piece, as my European ancestors would be horrified to hear me say," he said.

Tahyo seemed to agree that was funny; at least, he grinned and thumped his tail again.

"Ah, but you're not a tough audience, you."

The spare just-in-case anchor had been made out of sections of a cargo pod hull—the alloy was tough and flexible, though extremely hard to shape. The four spade-shaped blades were spring-loaded, too, ready to snap out and dig in. Marc secured the cable to the loop at the end of the anchor's short, thick shank, and then lashed it with a quick-release knot to eyebolts near the emergency keel hatch.

"There," he said, as Tahyo investigated with a quivering nose. "Kick the anchor out, and everything else follows."

It would be a stone bitch to get everything back in its proper place when the storm blew over, but not nearly as much as trying to get everything together at the last minute.

When he'd finished, Marc looked up, startled. *Didn't notice that,* he thought. The airship was pitching now, a slow nose-to-tail motion as if it were a land vehicle going up hills and over and down, again and again. Marc had compensated automatically while he worked, but now he lurched and grabbed for a stanchion.

There was a new noise under the ever-louder creaking of the ship's frame as well. Something like the wind crackling the edge of a sail.

Uh-oh.

That was the fabric panels starting to vibrate on the outer skin. They wouldn't rip easily, but the seams where they were sewn together and fixed to the hull frames were weaker. He muscled the greatwolf into a shoulder-and-chest harness and clipped it to a rope, then made sure he had a full water-dish available and the big crate full of dirt. The animal flattened again and looked at him imploringly.

"You're not going on the bridge in this weather, *cher,*" he said sternly, ignoring the pleading whimper. "And I'm not leaving you loose to get tossed around."

He climbed quickly back up the short ladder-staircase, this time keeping a careful grip on the rails. The *Vepaja* added a corkscrew lateral motion to the pitch, and the creaking and groaning added an ominous squeal. Occasionally one of the engines would surge, the usually near-inaudible humming rising in pitch as an air pocket left the propeller racing.

As he came back into the control cabin, Marc looked out through the slanting windows to his right and winced slightly. The whole horizon northward was livid black now. As he watched, lightning crawled across the surface of the clouds, horizontal and branching like the forks of a river delta. The flash threw the darkened control cabin into stark blue-white relief for an instant; the rumble of thunder that followed thudded into his chest and made the increasing howl of the wind seem almost quiet.

"So good of you to rejoin us," Blair said; he had to shout a little.

"Can that," Tyler snapped. "Get strapped in, Lieutenant."

Marc did, then pulled his earphones on—as much to drown out the rising whistle all around him as to hear the others, though that was a bonus. The air had a prickling smell that tingled in the nose, a hint of ozone and danger. The satellite feed of the storm was breaking up in the electrical discharges, though for now the VPS was still tracking them on the computer's map. He called up a schematic of the *Vepaja* and then the deformation gauges—lasers and mirrors on the structural members within the hull.

"Mr. Storm, he *en fâché*," he murmured to himself. A metal frame would have started to twist apart already, but the laminated shamboo bent like a bow. "Very angry indeed."

Tyler spoke in their ears. "I think we can abandon the search for a place to tie down," he said dryly.

The ground below was still visible through wisps of hard-driven cloud. It was tall forest, almost jungle, covering a maze of steep-sided hills. Some of the sheltered parts might have been possible . . . if the ground speed of the wind hadn't already been faster than the maximum the *Vepaja*'s engines could command. Trying to drop anchor would just tear the cable mountings out of the frames. Marc called up the feed from one of the cameras mounted in a blister on the keel, dialing the magnification, and blinked as a tree lashing on a hilltop below suddenly shattered, the massive crown flying along like a tumbleweed rolling through the air, shedding bits of itself as it went.

They'd had storms like this in Jamestown. They were alarming enough with a good, stout three-foot-thick wall between you and the outside. Suddenly the airship stopped feeling like a flying house; the shuddering, toning sensation that welled up through the chair and straps made it seem more like a chip in a spring flood. His hand moved on the trackball, and the camera scanned; just northward was the coast, and waves like flowing walls were crashing on . . . over . . . granite cliffs, breaking in vast torrents of white water and withdrawing seaward, carrying boulders and hundred-foot tree trunks with them like beach-wrack.

He glanced around the cabin. Tyler was totally focused on the controls. Jadviga was watching her screen intently, or appeared to. Cynthia lay back in her crash chair, arms behind her head; when he caught her eye she shrugged and smiled, as if to say, *Whatever.* Blair was occupied with some task involving multiple screens, until he gave a grunt of satisfaction:

"As far as I can see, the storm is pushing us almost exactly on course to where we were going," he said. "Although—"

Just then the light outside dimmed like a theater right before the curtain went up.

"—the trip is likely to be a bit lively. Ground speed around seventy mph."

"Here it comes," Tyler said, watching the onboard radar. "Just about—"

The *Vepaja* pitched forward, and then went tail-down. Mark felt his stomach lurch as the fall put him in free fall for an instant; then weight crushed him down into the cushions. A white noise roar overtook the howl of the wind, the sound of heavy rain drumming on the fabric; then a louder harmonic set his teeth shivering in sympathetic vibration as pea-sized hail began to lash it as well. The world outside was pitch-black now, except for the flashes of lightning—and those were coming at intervals of about four seconds. Marc tore off the earphones as a blasting hash of static nearly deafened him.

A second later, lightning flashed again, close enough to make the small hairs on his arms stand up and sparks jump nearby. The screens went crazy for an instant and then blanked. The *Vepaja* spun end-for-end, and then went through a corkscrew that threw them all against their harness like sacks of flour as the great flexible framework screamed in protest. Far away, something snapped with a monstrous *tunngggg* sound.

"Structural failure in ring seven! Hull fabric's going!" Tyler shouted. "Upper starboard quadrant. Vitrac, Blair, Whitlock!"

Marc hit the quick-release catch of his harness, then gripped the seat arms with paralytic strength as a rolling heave left his feet pointing at the opposite bulkhead for an instant. When *down* returned to the floor, he cast loose and clawed his way back to the exit.

"Ladies first!" he called, as Blair braced himself on the other side of the door. "Jadviga!"

The Englishman gave him a curt nod as they braced themselves with one hand on the bracket and the other outstretched to grab. The EastBloc officer let go of her seat and made a staggering run across the deck. Both men's free arms snapped out like mechanical grabs and caught her by the shoulders of her green overalls. Another surge tried to sweep her backward and into the forward windows of the control cabin; Marc felt his fingernails rip and his shoulder-joints crack as his hand closed with desperate strength. Then the *Vepaja* pitched back, and they half-threw her into the corridor. She tumbled bruising-hard against the wall, grabbed a bracket, and began to haul herself hand-over-hand towards the midships ladder.

"Hi, guys!" Cynthia called, half-heard through the roar of noise all around them.

Then she leaped. The timing was impeccable, but the airship spoiled it with an unexpected buck, and she slowed as if invisible bungee cords had suddenly snapped taut. Marc released his handhold, pivoted, and caught Blair's wrist. The other man's hand snapped closed on his wrist in turn, hugely strong, and Marc let the same surge throw him out into the cabin like a snapping whip. His right hand clamped down on Cynthia's wrist, and he poured all his consciousness into the need to *hold on* . . .

Seconds later the airship rolled back.

"Shee-it, that *hurt*," Cynthia shouted through the noise, holding on to a stanchion with one hand and shaking the other to restore circulation. "But going through the window would have hurt a lot more. Thanks, guys!"

She went down the corridor. Marc looked back as Blair swung him around again, and caught the Englishman's look of admiring relief at Cynthia's back as she preceded them. Then he turned to Marc for an instant, mouthed, *Thank you!* and made an after-you-Alphonse gesture.

Too cold, was Marc's thought as soon as they were all inside the loud cave of the hull.

He knew why: Pieces of the outer covering were off, and the storm-driven air ramming in was bringing the temperature down. They were high enough that they'd have needed bottled oxygen on Earth. Pressure fell off less rapidly here, which was a good thing, because they needed to be high lest they be caught in a sudden downdraft. Everyone strapped on padded helmets of strong, boiled 'saur hide with lights, loaded themselves with tools and kit, and headed up into the dark vastness of the hull. The headlamps speared through the dimness, flicking across the bulging surfaces of the lifting cells and the twisting regularities of the hull-frame and its bracing.

"*Merde!*"

That was Blair, blurted out in shock and surprising Marc a little even among the pounding urgency of the moment. He'd read the lips for the meaning. Being inside the hull right now was like being inside a darkened bass drum beaten by a million demented chimps. Jadviga settled for pointing with her headlamp.

Merde, Marc thought himself.

Number seven ring girder—one of the circular members that spanned the hull—had indeed cracked. And the splintered ends were rubbing against the surface of the adjacent gasbag. The problem was that the only way to get to it in the violently pitching aircraft was *over* the gasbag. They all climbed up the ladder to the axial walkway and paused for a second, clinging like baboons to a branch as the *Vepaja* heaved in three dimensions and looking at the rippling net-covered surface. A fine spray of water filled the air as they climbed, coming in bitterly cold through tears in the upper hull surface, and the slick surface of the cell glistened in the light of the headlamps.

Cynthia went first, jumping spread-eagled like a flying squirrel; there just wasn't time for the cautious regulation way. Marc felt his stomach lurch. She skidded over the flexing cell as the airship rolled to one side, then caught her foot in a loop, swung three hundred and sixty degrees, and stopped with arms and legs splayed like a spider's, the headlamp making a pool that underlit her contorted face.

Hey, podna, save some scared for yourself, eh? he thought, and leaped himself.

There was no time for safety lines or anything at all but going fangs-out and hair-on-fire. He scrabbled and caught at the net ropes, at the price of a broken fingernail. The sharp stab of pain barely registered; he tore the loose part free with his teeth and spat it aside. Blair made his jump, and Marc steadied him as the cell flexed and shuddered under the impact. Then they both did the same for Jadviga.

Back in the seventies on Earth, there had been a brief fashion for water beds, liquid-filled mattresses. Marc had tried one for a while, persuaded by a friend who said sex on them was like making love to a woman with infinite buttocks. It had turned out to be more trouble than it was worth, but crawling over the surface of the gas cell was disconcertingly like his memories of that brief teenaged experiment. And like that long-ago fashion statement, it made progress difficult; you couldn't push off the surface, even with your knees or elbows. The difficulty got worse as they headed down the side, until it was steep enough for them to have to reverse and climb down. Netting and cell membrane both were slippery with the moisture, and it was even darker here.

When they approached the broken section of rib, they *did* take a moment to snap their safety lines onto loops in the netting; the muscles in his neck relaxed at the feel of its tug as the *Vepaja* bucked and twisted. One slip and they'd hit the top of the gondola after an eighty-foot drop.

Communication was by hand signals. Marc managed to get across: *He and I will cut the rib; you patch the leaks.*

The *And everybody, for God's sake, no sparks!* had to be left to common sense. The broken rib was flexing inward, and the jagged ends had already cut the netting cords and made rents in the gasbag. Ribs were a triangular truss of three mature shamboo tubes fastened together, each the size of a man's leg. It took a lot to break full-grown shamboo; the stuff had silica fibers in it, making a sort of natural fiberglass. The problem was that that made *cutting* it nearly as hard.

Blair drew the machete across his back and tapped a point above the break; a cut there would leave the end out of reach of the gasbag, unless the rib fractured again. Marc did likewise below, and they both let themselves hang free, drawing back for the first chop. . . .

Twenty-six hours later, Marc jerked himself back awake. Captain Tyler was talking.

Christ, he's not human, Marc thought.

The captain of the airship merely looked badly beat-up—there were bandages over half his face, some of them showing red spots—and totally exhausted. The other three looked like the recently resurrected dead.

The *Vepaja* was drifting with the slow low-altitude breeze, just enough way on her to keep her stable. They still had two of the engines functional, but most of the solar collectors had been ripped off the upper surface, and hydrogen reserves for the fuel cells were low. At least the breeze was warm; he could feel it through the place where the control cabin's forward windows had been. That was where Tyler had gotten the cuts on his face, when a freak of the storm had stove them in with a balk of timber. A *lot* of water had followed, and about half the instruments were out for now, including the shortwave radio transmitter. Right now everything was pleasantly comfortable and above all *silent* after hours of nightmare struggle inside the pounding hull.

The General must be having kittens, Marc thought inconsequentially, then forced himself to alertness.

". . . seams on the gas cells," Tyler finished. "With that and the structural damage, we need to find a quiet spot out of the wind and do as near a complete rebuild as we can. At the very least, we have to get the cells deflated and flushed, then do some real patching. Otherwise the leaks will have us down within two days. I think we can get all four motors functioning again, but three will get us back, and we can use the emergency collector sheets to replace what we lost up top during the storm."

Marc suppressed a whimper at the thought of what they'd have to do to get the airship functional again. *It's just the exhaustion talking,* he told himself, blinking at the morning sunlight coming in through the space where the tough armor-glass had been. So tempting to breathe deep of the fresh-scented warm air and lie down to sleep . . .

"Captain," Jadviga said, frowning. "What about our mission? We are nearly at the location of the distress beacon."

Tyler nodded; exhaustion made his voice harsh. "*Nearly* as in *somewhere within a fifty-mile radius,* Mrs. Binkis. Two thousand square miles is far too much territory for five people to survey on foot. We'll do what repairs we can here, then proceed as seems best."

Marc blinked gummy eyes, nodding. The terrain below looked fairly hopeful—rolling coastal plain not unlike that near Jamestown, grassland with scattered oaks, with occasional higher hills and an escarpment inland rising to an uneven plateau. He could just catch glimpses of lakes and rivers there, and not far away a long waterfall drawing a silver line against black cliff and green forest at the foot. The mountains were far south beyond that, just barely visible even from three thousand feet. Intelligence and satellite photography said there were a couple of small cities—more like big walled villages—and some farming along the coast northward, but from where they floated nothing of the hand of man was visible.

Game was there in plenty, mostly mammals, with a clump of Volkswagen-sized armored 'saurs, like giant spiky turtles with bone clubs on the ends of their tails.

Tyler opened his mouth to reply. A flicker moved behind him, and then curtains of living leather blocked the empty windows, on either side of a lean body covered in pale fuzz streaked with jagged strips of brown.

"*Get down!*" Marc screamed.

Three other shouts tripped on the heels of his. Tyler began to lunge forward out of his chair, but not in time to avoid the stabbing beak of the creature that clung to the nose of the gondola. He screamed himself in shock and agony as the spearlike tip slammed into his shoulder blade. Bone cracked, and there was a wet snapping sound as the sharp peg teeth ripped at flesh and tendon.

Marc shouted wordlessly as he snatched up his machete and attacked, hacking at the thing's bony scarlet-crested head as it tried to drag the thrashing human back out into the air. It shrieked like a steam whistle, and again as Blair came in on the other side, the dulled edge of his weapon bouncing off the thick, coarse hair that coated the pterosaur's snaky neck.

Its taloned feet gripped the lower frame of the window, and the wings were folded to let the snakelike body worm its way into the control cabin. Three long claws tipped the joint of each wing, scrabbling at chair and control panel as it lunged. A carrion reek came with it, bits of rotting meat caught in the hair and teeth.

Both men struck again, and chips of bone flew. Marc grunted with effort as he smashed aside a darting strike of the beak. Tyler moaned as Cynthia darted in under the great head and pulled him free; Jadviga joined her to roll him on his face and frantically pack cloth into the gaping wound. Blood pulsed between their fingers.

"Come on, birdie," Marc crooned, as the thing recoiled a little from the menace of their blades.

"That's right, you evil, scavenging bugger," Blair said, standing at his shoulder. "Do stick your neck out."

They took a step forward, and then the muzzle of Jadviga's shotgun came past his shoulder.

"*Christ, no!*" Marc shouted, and wrestled the weapon away from her.

The red-dripping fanged beak drove for him again. Blair moved with savage speed, lunging with the point of his machete. It wasn't designed for that, but the rounded point was still sharp enough to gouge into one of the big slit-pupiled eyes of the pterosaur, and throw it sideways—for all its forty-foot wingspan and mad-weasel ferocity, the body between the great membranes was still only forty pounds. It hissed liked an infuriated air-compressor and thrashed itself backwards, hanging on to the sill with its hind feet.

"Let me shoot it!" Jadviga said.

"You crazy *couyon*!" Marc said, using his hip to bump her away from the weapon. "This airship, she's *leaking*. You fire a gun here and chances are we go up like a bomb, us!"

Cynthia and Blair called confirmation. Cynthia was still working over Tyler's limp form; the Englishman kept darting forward, holding the machete like a fencing-saber and making lunges at the animal that menaced them. It hissed back at his shouts and made stabs back; beak cracked on steel, and another chip spun away.

"There are more of them out there," Blair called.

"Damn! I know this breed; they hunt in packs. Flocks. Whatever."

He thrust the shotgun back at Jadviga, judging that her blood had cooled enough. Then he darted past the fallen man and into the arms locker. It held bows as well as firearms; arrows were reusable and perfectly good enough for hunting smaller beasts. The one he pulled out was a recurve—they could be left strung—of laminated shamboo and *tharg*-horn and sinew, with a beech-wood riser. He pulled it out of the clips and seized a quiver as well, hurriedly slinging it over his back.

"Do lend a hand here, old chap!" Blair called.

"Coming, coming," Marc yelled. "Hold your horses."

He edged around Tyler and Cynthia, and then stood behind Blair as the man barred the pterosaur's way with his blade.

Got to admit he's got guts, him, Marc thought, as he put a shaft to the cord.

"On the mark . . . *duck*!" he shouted.

Blair dropped flat to the deck. The pterosaur drew its long neck back in a triumphant S-curve, preparing to drive its bill into his back like a spear. Marc drew the arrow to the angle of his jaw, the bright, pyramid-shaped head shaped out of cargo pod hull material glinting in the dimness.

Snap. The string slapped painfully on his bare forearm. A fraction of a second later there was a *thump* as it slammed home into the thing's narrow chest, punching through the keel-like breastbone until the scarlet feathers stood out like a dot of color against the pale blue-gray of its skin. The animal fell backward, its talons in a deathlock on the sill of the empty window frame. When they loosed, the great, forty-foot spread of wings fell loosely open, and it tumbled away downward like a newspaper blowing down a street, shrinking to a tiny dot as it spiraled towards some waiting scavenger.

"Get out, everyone out into the corridor!" Marc said.

He set another arrow to the string. Four more of the big predators banked past the opening as he waited, one diving under the gondola and then flaring up, its feet thrusting out to grip the window frame.

Snap.

This time his arrow pierced its neck, and it launched itself out and away with another hissing screech. More calls answered it, around the gondola and from directions he couldn't see.

"We're out!" Blair called crisply.

"*Foutre!*" Marc panted as he thrust the light shamboo-wicker door closed. "How's the captain?"

"Weak, but I've stopped the bleeding," Cynthia said, looking down at Tyler with worried affection. "It'll be touch and go—I need to do some repair work there."

Jadviga nodded as she handed out the contents of the arms locker; everyone strapped as much as they could carry to their backs. Medical cross-training was common in Jamestown, and according to what Cosmograd had sent she had experience in the field, too. Just then they all looked up at a heavy *thump* over their heads, and a drumlike pulse as something heavy struck the fabric of the hull.

Blair trotted down the corridor and up the access ladder. He opened the hatch, looked up, closed it again, and jumped down after he pushed the locking lever home. It wouldn't do much good; the ceiling over their heads was wicker and fabric.

"That's not good," he said crisply. "There was one crawling in through a hole in the fabric while I watched, and several more holding on to the outside. Persistent buggers."

Marc nodded. "This breed of flier likes to mob the big pterosaurs, not the Quetzas, the other types that live off fish and such," he said. "They rip them up with diving attacks, force them down, and eat them. Individually they're not as bad as a Quetza, but they don't work alone, and they don't stop once they've started."

Cynthia looked up. "The airship doesn't look much like a pterosaur!"

"It's big and it's flying," Marc said. "These things, they aren't what you'd call too bright. Vicious, yes. Brainy, no. And they'll have smelled the blood—smelled us. They hunt ground-mammals, too."

Something hissed querulously from the other side of the thin door, and jumped back against the latch. A rank reptile stink filled the air around them.

"We'll have to abandon ship," Blair said, sounding indecently cheerful. And then, oddly: "And it's not *my* fault."

"Just bad luck," Marc agreed.

His mind was working fairly well, as long as he kept it focused, but that was adrenaline, and there were limits to how long you could keep going on that. Better to hurry. He looked into one of the cabins and pulled out the thin mattress.

"Get Tyler on that," he said. "Strap him down. This is going to be tricky."

Another thump came from the side of the gondola. He glanced back into the cabin; it was Jadviga's, and there was a picture of her with a tall, lanky-looking blond man and a small boy resting by the bunk. Just outside the porthole, a slitted yellow eye the size of his fist looked in.

He pulled the rest of the bows out of the arms locker, sharing them out—no sense in wasting them—and they all hustled down the corridor, lifting Tyler's unconscious body with them into the hold. Above them more thumps and hisses sounded as the monstrous flying vermin tore their way into the *Vepaja*'s hull and gondola, crawling with folded wings into its spaces.

Blair kicked the door closed behind the injured man. Tahyo had greeted the humans with a hysterical outburst of *wulfing*, roughly translatable as: *There are bad things out there! Bad! Bad!* A sharp command from Marc sent him flat on his belly, but a thin, anxious whining persisted. His tail wagged in feeble hope whenever Marc's eyes happened to cross his.

Blair and Marc nodded to each other and set about tearing up the railings to prop against the door. None too soon; there was a thumping and screeching from just beyond it seconds later. The hold was stuffy and dim. Cynthia's face almost disappeared in it, save for her eyes and the white smile she flashed at him with a thumbs-up.

Marc took a deep breath. "Want to do the honors?" he said to Blair.

"No, no, you can kill us all with my blessing."

"Oh, very much thanks," Marc said, feeling long-held resentment vanish, at least for the present.

He walked over to the curving wall of the hold. An aluminum

box was fastened to it, and an armored cable ran up from it. *Auxiliary buoyancy controls—emergency use only!* was stenciled in red over the gray surface.

"I think this qualifies," Marc said, and opened it. "Stand by, everyone. And pray these still work!"

Inside were a line of switches. Marc flipped the red one—the master-switch—then went down the row, *clunk-clunk-clunk-clunk-clunk-clunk-clunk.*

For a moment nothing happened; then a slight falling-elevator sensation began at the pit of his stomach. Jadviga leaned over the small port in the keel door.

"Well under a thousand meters," she said. "We are descending. Gradually—less than a meter per second. Open terrain with occasional trees . . . a small river . . . more steppes."

Below the switches that opened the exhaust valves on the upper keel was another marked: *Deploy anchors.*

Marc whistled lightly through his teeth as he looked at it. There were two anchors forward, lodged forward of the control gondola and secured to the reinforced structure of hull ring frame two. Normal procedure was to come into the wind and establish zero speed relative to the ground before dropping the anchors—and to put a landing party down first so that they could be secured manually before any strain was put on them. That wasn't really practical this time; he just hoped that they'd drop and not rip right out of frame two the instant the strain came on them.

"Everyone secure yourselves," Blair said. "And Captain Tyler."

"Good idea." Marc nodded.

They did, snapping their quick-release safety lines to one of the eyebolts that were scattered thickly around the hold, for good reason. Jadviga and Cynthia lashed Tyler down to the surface of the emergency hatch itself, which was an excellent idea. Marc unfastened Tahyo and brought him over beside the injured man.

"Down, boy," Marc said, before snapping the line from the greatwolf's harness to an eyebolt on the hatch surface. "And *stay.*"

"You've got that beastie working for you, haven't you?" Cynthia said.

"*Mais,* I'm lucky with canids." He added a chuckle, and found it was genuine.

"Five hundred meters. We are drifting at . . . I can't be sure. Perhaps five kilometers an hour ground speed, perhaps a little more. A rocky hill covered in brush. More grassland . . ."

Jadviga lay hugging the surface of the hatch as she kept up the commentary. It went on smoothly in her accented English, even when a beak slammed through the doorway that led down into the hold and withdrew with a crackle of breaking wicker. Tahyo whined louder; the hissing screeches were very loud now, and the stench of rotting meat. Marc came up to one knee and reached for an arrow. Blair did likewise.

"After *you*, Alphonse," Marc said.

"No, after *you*," Blair said.

They drew and shot together. Both arrows punched through the wicker without slowing perceptibly; the screeching on the other side went from loud to earsplitting, and a huge thrashing and thumping accompanied it. Ripping and tearing sounds followed, and blood leaked under the bottom of the door; at a guess, the rest of the flock/pack/whatever were dining on their fallen friend. That might just distract them for long enough . . .

"Not bad, Alphonse," Marc said.

"Not bad if I do say so myself. And I do; oh, I do!"

Jadviga's voice went on, flat and calm. "One hundred fifty meters. We are dropping faster. One hundred. Seventy-five. A large clump of trees. Fifty meters . . ."

Marc reached over and untied the slipknot that held the spare anchor. "Everyone get a hand on the quick-release catches," he said, stripping himself of all his gear and lashing it down to the hatch. "When I give the word, release them."

He stationed himself by the control box, his thumb poised. Jadviga's voice chanted as the distance to the ground lessened; the screeching hisses of the pterosaurs built to a crescendo, as they thought their prey was mortally wounded and falling fast.

"Ten meters! *Five!*"

Marc took up the slight tension on the button, feeing the ball of his thumb pressing against the hard synthetic. The keel brushed hard on the ground for an instant, making them all lurch. He pushed, and heard the double *bang!* of the anchors being fired by their explosive bolts.

"Now!"

Marc leaped for the hatch. He landed on it and grabbed for an eyebolt just as the smooth, gentle drift turned to a lurching twist. The *Vepaja* pivoted as one anchor caught and then the other; huge rending and crackling sounds came from up ahead. The hatchway came loose with a *crang* and dropped eight feet, striking the ground with a blow like being whacked full-body with an oak board. Everyone clutched his or her handholds as it slid backward and twisted, tobogganing down a grassy slope. Most of them yelled; Marc knew *he* did. Cynthia's cry was one of alarm as fresh blood broke through Tyler's latest bandage.

The spare anchor whipped off the hatchway, dragging coils of rope out of the cargo hold as the airship bucked and shot upward. The forward port anchor did rip loose then, with a gunshot crackle and a shower of fabric and frame scattering debris that fell or drifted like a midair explosion. The ship slewed around the hold of the starboard anchor, and as it did, the dragging emergency hook caught under a huge log. The four rope-wound wicker crates shot out of the hold and landed bouncing and rolling.

"Uh-oh," Marc murmured.

The *Vepaja* shot upward again, as weight came off faster than the emergency valves could bleed lifting gas. The last anchor ripped out of the frame, and the whole forward third of the airship forward of the gondola bent upward as the keels broke, two hundred feet arching up until the pointed bow faced the white-blue haze of the sky. Metal would be grinding on metal amid a miasma of hydrogen . . . what was known on Earth as a fuel-air explosive, only air was more reactive here.

"Look out!" he cried, and buried his head in his arms.

Everyone flattened themselves. Cynthia arched her body over the unconscious captain.

WHOOMP!

Heat washed over them, enough to dry Marc's eyes amid the sudden glare of orange-red light; he gritted his teeth against the expectation of pain, but his skin merely prickled. When he looked up, the airship had broken in two; the forward part was high in the sky, the pale hydrogen flame running over the surface as it drifted away westward and downwind. Dense black smoke came up from over a hill.

Some of the pterosaur flock had escaped; one crashed nearby as he watched, its body-fuzz charred black and smoking. The rest rose hissing from the airship wreck and vanished. A great silence fell, with the chorus of birds gone and even the insects distracted from their crinkling and buzzing for a moment. Marc felt his throat constrict for a second; it was only a machine, but it had served them well and kept them alive through the storm.

"Guys," Cynthia said. "Guys, this doesn't look good."

Marc felt a prickle of alarm. She was working over Captain Tyler again, and this time it didn't look like it was working. The man was conscious, but the last fall had jarred something loose—even hard pressure wasn't halting the bleeding. Into the silence, he spoke in a breathy whisper.

"Come . . . here."

All four of them knelt around the dying man. Tyler closed his eyes and gathered his strength for a moment. "Something . . . weird happened as we got close," he said. His voice was just audible if you strained. "Something . . . different. Like an autopilot we didn't have . . ." Another pause, and then he spoke more strongly for a moment:

"Lieutenant Vitrac, you're in charge. Get my people home. Tell my wife—"

A catch in the slow, labored breathing, a hesitation, another breath, and then it stopped. Cynthia checked the pulse, then sighed and closed his eyes. Marc crossed himself; so, somewhat to his surprise, did Jadviga.

He rose and looked around. "We'll make camp and scout around and see to our gear," he said. "Then we'll head towards the coast and back towards Jamestown."

Jadviga flushed. "But our mission—"

Marc raised a hand in a soothing gesture. "By the last VPS readings, we're just about on top of the shuttle crash site. But the satellites never got a visual, and we don't have an aircraft anymore. We'll do some scouting, but we can't delay long. The odds on us getting back alive are short enough as it is."

Cynthia frowned. "I don't suppose a rescue mission might come for *us*?"

She didn't look too disappointed when he shook his head; neither did anyone else. Their last message had them about to be hit in a dangerous storm; if a satellite happened to be overhead and managed to get an image through the haze, it would show the *Vepaja* crashing and burning. Sending the only other working airship at Jamestown to rescue the rescuers would be foolhardy, and whatever you thought of the General, nobody had ever called him that type of idiot.

"They'll cut their losses," Marc said.

Jadviga nodded; that didn't surprise Marc, either. By comparison with *her* bosses, the General was a save-the-baby-seals sentimentalist.

"It's up to us, then," Blair said quietly.

CHAPTER EIGHT

Encyclopedia Britannica, 16th Edition
University of Chicago Press, 1988

SPACE RACE: Implications for Earth

As the twentieth century enters its last decades, it has become increasingly clear that our focus on space has fundamentally reshaped our life on Earth as well. Most obviously, the knowledge that we were not alone in the universe has had a profound effect on Earthly philosophy, religion, and culture, compounded by the discovery via space-based telescopes in the 1970s that Earth-like planets with oxygen-rich atmospheres are common in nearby star systems. Technologies developed for the space effort shape our lives; increasingly, manufacturing in and energy from space affect the global economy.

However, the discoveries which began in the 1950s have affected us not only through increased scientific knowledge and technological spin-offs, but also through the shaping of national rivalries. Few now remember how real the threat of another global war was in the 1950s, or how serious conflicts on the periphery of the blocs remained as late as the early 1960s. Many contemporary analysts credit the Space Race, as much as nuclear weapons themselves, with breaking the twenty-year cycle of the World Wars.

The knowledge that life existed on both Mars and Venus prompted increased research spending, but proof in the early 1960s that *human* life existed on both planets made interplanetary travel a matter of maximum priority. As the 1960s wore on, spending on research, development, and deployment of space systems gradually came to match and then exceed that of the military budgets of the two great power-blocs.

The deaths of the two Communist dictators Joseph Stalin (1953) and Mao Tse-tung (1956) and their replacement by the relatively reformist regimes of Khrushchev and Chou En-lai assisted the deterrent effect of thermonuclear weapons and ICBMs in the reorientation of EastBloc policy away from direct military confrontation and into competition for space, under the slogan *Proletarians of All Worlds, Unite!*

Paradoxically, the increasingly severe competition to establish a presence in space and on Earth's sister-worlds led to increased pragmatism and cooperation on Earth itself, where both major blocs desired no distractions. Among the first fruits was the peaceful settlement of the Quemoy-Matsu island dispute in 1958. The USA/UK/USSR/PRC demarche which imposed the Treaty of Nicosia on the parties to the last Arab-Israeli war in 1967, and the inter-bloc peacekeeping force which enforced it, were among the most spectacular. The Middle East, a scene of instability throughout the nineteenth century and into the postwar period, became a sleepy backwater.

Similarly, the ever-closer integration of British Commonwealth and United States foreign policy after the joint intervention in the Suez Crisis (1956) received another major boost when the United Kingdom agreed to merge its space efforts with those of the USA in 1961.

More controversially, some scholars attribute the increasing neutralism of Gaullist France and its close European allies Italy and West Germany (and Spain, after the fall of the Franco regime in 1968) to the waning of the threat of invasion from the East. In recent years, the European Union, as this alliance has come to be known, has embarked on space efforts of its own. As yet these have produced little practical result . . .

Teesa scowled and stamped her foot. "When fire fell from the sky before, the beastmen got *these*," she said, waving the metal death-weapon. "Shall we let them have *more?*"

The women and warriors looked at her dumbly. They were a bedraggled lot. The attack on the village had come so swiftly that none had had time to do more than snatch up children and weapons, and the other settlements of their people were only a little better off. Now they crouched in the little hollow, bodies bare of ornaments, eyes of hope, despite the sweet warm wind of spring-time and the bright sun. She could tell that they only wished to flee misfortune.

Teesa's hand touched the pouch by her side where the Cave Master lay. *I could* compel *them*, she thought. Then with a shake of her tawny mane: *No. They are grown folk of the Cloud Mountain People. It would not be right.*

Besides, it wasn't reliable with so many. She did draw it forth, hold it high until all the three-score at the gathering had bowed their heads in reverence. Then she set it on her brow, checked that the curved-metal-pouch-of-darts was clicked firmly into the weapon, slung it over her back by the strap, touched fingers to her knife and blowgun and dart pouch, and turned to trot northward. She knew where she was heading, roughly; it was twenty miles, half a day's run without forcing the pace. If she sent out runners to other Cloud Mountain settlements and waited for fighters to come, it might take two days.

If anyone will follow me, she thought, anger burning bright. *If my own village will not back me, there would be little use in sending a summons to the others.*

Her sister, Zore, was the first to follow; Teesa could feel the girl's bright confidence in her, which was worrying in itself. Then a clutch of strong warriors came after, shamed that a girl-child should go where they feared. Most of the rest followed them, some more from fear of being left than from courage. By the time Teesa was half a mile from the gathering spot, the only folk left behind were mothers and some of the older fighting men to guard them back to the shelters.

Teesa halted in a dell, where a creek ran beneath trees and a cliff-side reared three times man-height above.

"I am glad you have found your courage, my people," she said formally; many winced or shuffled their feet. "Now let four swift runners step forward, Taldi first among them."

Her lost mate's brother *was* a good runner, particularly over a long track. And it would be a good idea to get his obsession with curses out of her war band; he wouldn't speak so before strangers.

"We've got one basic problem, and that's mobility," Marc said, sitting on a chunk of log not far from the fire, with his rifle resting between his knees.

"Well, yo," Cynthia said. "We're on fucking foot, man."

Even close to the cheery light, the campfire seemed very small and very lonely in the Venusian night; there was a cool breeze from the south, but above there was only darkness, with the haze too thick for stars. The circle of light at their hilltop camp showed a huge basalt column that made a natural polygon, lighting the dark rock and the small tree that grew in a crevice on its top. That was a palm of some sort, and its fronds rustled dryly, a background to the buzzing and clicking, the hoots and howls and occasional squalling roar. A brace of quail-like birds the size of small turkeys roasted at its edges; every so often one of the four Terrans would lean forward to give the green-wood spits a twist. Tahyo lay not far away, his eyes shining green-yellow when he glanced occasionally at the flames, licking his chops plaintively despite having crunched down the heads, guts, and feet. Marc still felt better with Tahyo's better-than-bloodhound nose at the ready.

All that Marc could smell himself was the spicy, cedarlike scent of the burning wood, roasting meat, and a bit of his own and his companions' sweat. Blair and Cynthia sat together on the other side of the round circle of stones that marked their temporary hearth; Jadviga was off a little to one side.

Leaving me on my lonesome, Marc thought with an inward smile. *Very neat depiction of our little social unit, eh?*

He prodded at the dirt with a stick, not exactly drawing, but as an aid to thought.

"*Weh,* we've got more gear than we can possibly carry ourselves," he went on. "But we're going to need every scrap of it to get six thousand miles east of here. I'd hate to be left standing with an empty rifle while a dire bear ate me only a week's travel from home."

Blair sat with his legs crossed and his fists on his knees; the firelight gilded the sparse hairs on the backs of his hands, turning them to little copper-gold wires.

"We could make for the coast and try to build a boat," he said. "That would solve our transport problem."

Cynthia looked at him. "Chris, have you *seen* the stuff that lives in the ocean here? I wouldn't try a long voyage on anything that doesn't outweigh the pleiosaurs—and that means a hundred tons displacement. With one big mo'fo' of a catapult on the foredeck and the stern."

Marc nodded. "Yeah, but granting that, a ship *is* a possibility. But we'd need a lot of native help, and we'd have to show them how to make the tools to make anything I'd feel comfy sailing in."

"A good point," Blair admitted. "And there are the storms to consider."

"Yeah," Marc said. "So, we could catch and break a bunch of *churr* for riding and pack-beasts, or some *tharg* and make an oxcart, or both."

Blair's eyebrows went up. "That would be a great deal of work for four people," he said.

"We could get some native help on that, too," Cynthia said. "If there's a friendly tribe nearby."

Marc shrugged. "Possible, but it'd mean months learning the language. Or we could Ice a couple of 'saurs. I've done it with Doc Feldman and we've got a kit along."

"Oh, great, the four of us are going to capture a six-ton ceratopsian!" Cynthia said, but she smiled as she did.

"Not impossible, I should think," Blair said thoughtfully. "A pit trap, perhaps?"

"Well, the *first* thing we've got to do is build a secure camp," Marc said. His smile became impish. "We'll call it *Fort Dinosaur.*"

Blair surprised him by being the only other one to laugh.

Tahyo gave Marc a look of profound disgust as he swung the axe beneath the warm spring sun. The young greatwolf had a thoroughly canine attitude towards pointless effort; he was against it. And if it wasn't concerned with hunting food or playing, it was pointless.

"You'll enjoy sleeping safe from the saber-tooths and 'saurs, too, you," Marc said cheerfully. Then: "Timbeeerrr!"

There wasn't anyone within twenty yards, but he said it anyway, for the sake of the thing. The slender young tree was only three or four times his own height, anyway; they weren't set up to handle real tree trunks. It came down with a crash and a flashing of pale green leaves, a sort of poplar, the wood creamy pale at the stump and the scattering of chips. It was easy to cut, but heavy and strong. The axe took the branches off with a steady *tick . . . tick* sound. When the sapling had been turned into a long tapering pole, he dropped a loop of rope around the butt and hitched it over his shoulder, leaning into it as he hauled.

Blair was doing likewise not far away. As they pulled their loads up the hill the Englishman began humming—the chorus from *The Volga Boatmen*, which Marc had watched, twice, on his own transit from Earth. Three months of mild queasiness in zero-G could make you receptive to about anything; he'd even read *War and Peace*, and then right after it *Jude the Obscure*, cover to cover. There were limits to how many times you could do *At the Earth's Core* or *A Princess of Mars*.

"He's getting a lot less tight-assed," Marc muttered to himself. "*Mais*, life is like that. Odd. I was *convinced* he was a son of a bitch until *after* that piece of sabotage. He was different after that."

The campsite was a semicircle fifty paces around, backed against the sheer basalt crag that topped the hill. They didn't have time or labor for a stockade; instead they were using an abatis of sharpened stakes, supported by Y-forked poles driven deep into the soil and the whole lashed together with tough braided rawhide.

Shamboo would have been perfect for the whole thing, but there didn't seem to be any growing within convenient reach.

Cynthia crouched by a low, hot fire, charring the ends of the stakes, turning the pale creamy wood to iron-hard blackness.

"Ah, the life of a research scientist on the cutting edge of Earth's technology," Blair said sardonically as he dropped his pole with the others.

The woman snorted. "Hey, lover boy, you noticed, didya?" she said with sardonic amusement; Marc also noticed the look she gave the Englishman's sweat-slick muscular torso. "We come here by nuclear-powered spaceship. Then we travel by bamboo . . . well, shamboo . . . blimp. Now we're down on our feet. Pretty soon it'll be chipping flint, you mark my words. And walking on our knuckles."

Jadviga laughed, which was unusual; she was braiding strips of hide not far away, her fingers moving with quick, strong flicks.

"Already you are making the wooden spears with fire-hardening," she said. "Was there not a discovery of such in Germany not long ago?"

Marc searched his memory. "*Weh.* Preserved in waterlogged caves—four hundred thousand years old. Proving that we were top predators even before we were human. Though here, with the raptors and allosaurs and Quetzas, the title's still open."

Jadviga finshed a strand and dusted her hands. "There. I have enough for a fleet—hundreds of meters!"

"Dozens of meters, at least," Blair joked.

I wonder why he said meters? Marc thought idly.

The Commonwealth countries had talked about switching to metric, but they'd never really gotten around to it, probably because the chances of the U.S. doing so were somewhere between zero and nothing, and the links of the Anglosphere had gotten steadily stronger over the past generation.

Mais, anyone in the sciences is used to using metric, too. Only polite to Jadviga, since she's not likely to know our system well.

Marc drank a dipper of water and asked, "Jadviga, podna, something I've always wanted to ask. This isn't far from where you people put down your first probe, when I was just a little *bebette.* Why didn't you plant your base here?"

Jadviga's face grew even less expressive than usual. "That was a policy decision," she said.

Marc shrugged; he could tell a silence that meant *Bug off, Yanki,* when he heard it. He switched the rope yoke and loop to the butt ends of half a dozen finished poles. That was a real load, but he only had to keep them moving fifteen yards or so. He stood bent over and panting with his hands on his knees for a moment, then got to work. The first rings of six- and eight-foot shafts already bristled outward. Marc trimmed rough points on the butt ends of the longer ones with his machete, and then rammed them as deep as he could before letting them drop into the forks. Getting through the tough sod was a bit of a struggle, but the earth beneath was dark and soft, and a few minutes of grunting effort sufficed for each. Jadviga had coils of the hide rope soaking in a bucket of water; Marc took a length and tied the shafts to their supports, bracing his foot and hauling with all his strength to get the knots tight. The leather would dry hard as iron in a day or two of this warm, dry weather. If they were here more than a couple of weeks, they could pour melted horn over it for waterproofing.

When he'd finished the set, Marc paused to haul up a bucket of water from the shallow well they'd dug, pouring it over his shirtless torso before drinking a couple of pints. The taste was clean, but with an earthy, mineral undertang. Then he checked on lunch: soup cooking in a leather trough suspended over a low, hot fire. If you made sure the heat only reached the portions with liquid inside, that worked well enough for a prolonged simmer. This was bird-meat with wild greens. He tasted a spoonful: ready in about another hour.

"I'm going up to have another look," Marc said. "Can't hurt, and it's my turn."

Jadviga cast him a glance as he slung rifle and binocular-case over his back. He suspected it was a sympathetic one, and winced a little. *Was my tongue hanging out that much?* he thought. *And here I thought I was being subtle.*

The ladder was made the same way as their abatis, two long saplings or youngish trees with stout branches tied across them for rungs. It bent with the springy resilience of nearly living wood as he went up it quickly, and he rubbed his hands on the seat of his cargo

pocket pants to clear them of sap before he unlimbered the binoculars. The top of the column was ten paces on a side, an irregular
tabletop with a few pockets where soil had accumulated and tough
grass and low bushes taken root.

It gave a magnificent view over the countryside around. That
was about half-and-half grassland and forest, with the woodland
like an irregular-meshed fishing net thrown over the green-tawny of
the open country. Southward, higher hills rose, dense with tall trees;
there was more forest and broken country to the east as well. As he
remembered the map, that was the crash site for the *Riga*, a long
lake about ten miles away.

"Those are real woods, there," he said to himself.

It was pleasant up here, sitting amid the quiet sough of the
wind as it dried his skin and hair. The *Vepaja* had crashed about a
mile and a half to the northwest; he could see the black stretch
where it had set woods and grass afire, but a quick scout had shown
nothing worth salvaging except pieces of twisted metal, and that
could wait.

Turning in a slow circle, he saw plenty of game. A flock of black
eagles came down a long vale, big birds with ten-foot wingspans
and talons like tigers. A herd of small antelope panicked and sprang
out in all directions as the birds went overhead, and they dove, tag-
teaming the little herbivores and settling down to eat pack-style,
and incidentally guard the carcass. In the next clearing over was a
herd of *tharg*, about two hundred of the big bovinoids . . . or
bovines, if Doc Feldman was right. They were scattered when
Marc first turned the focusing screw of the binoculars with his
thumb, but they stampeded to the other end of the open space and
formed a defensive ring.

A minute later he saw the reason: three spotted saber-tooths
cruising around the edges looking for a chance to cut one out, their
stumpy tails twitching in excitement.

"Just another day on Venus," Marc said to himself, grinning.

Then the binoculars tracked back. A pack of raptors exploded
out of cover, a dozen man-sized feathered sauroid predators. One of
them turned back to raise its crest and prance at whatever had
spooked them, leaping high to make a threat display with the long
sickle-claw that folded out from against its hock.

Crack.

Marc shot upright with an amazed curse, and refocused just in timed to see the raptor collapse limply, its long head and snaky neck flexing as it fell with what he could have sworn was a surprised expression. Looking down, he saw the others hadn't heard it; Jadviga would be jumping for joy if she had, because the only people besides them in this part of Venus who could possibly have guns were the crew of the *Riga*.

Marc kicked a rock off the cliff. The others looked up at that, all right. He made a broad gesture to the east, then a finger-waggle: *company*.

"Why are we acting as if this might be an enemy?" Jadviga complained. "It is Franziskus!"

Mais, it might be someone else from the crew, Marc thought. *But she's got a right to be hopeful while she can.*

All of them were outside the abatis, armed but looking friendly. Or all of them but Tahyo. The greatwolf was restless, slinking about in front of Marc's feet, whining and *wulfing* occasionally. The gentle slope of the hillside fanned out ahead of them, the waist-high grass billowing in the warm scented wind. It offered no cover within a thousand yards except for the grass and the odd scrubby bush, which of course was why they'd picked the spot.

Or, just possibly, might some local have gotten the ship's gun?

Not likely; even less likely that they'd be able to maintain it or hit anything they shot at, but why take risks?

"Call me an old lady," Marc said easily. "But this is the way we'll do it."

"I must call you *sir*, now," Jadviga said.

That's an actual joke, Marc thought, surprised. *From Mrs. Stoneface herself.*

Then he chided himself for an uncharitable thought; after all, she was probably going to see her husband again, which had been a major point of the whole expedition. And right now, Marc hoped so, too. Another three Terran personnel would make it much more likely that they'd get back to Jamestown uneaten.

The slope ended abruptly with a line of scrub along the edge of a tongue of high forest. Marc leveled his binoculars. The trees were draped with lianas and creepers, strings of hand-sized crimson flowers rising a hundred feet and more into the air as they spiraled upward around trunks; insects and hummingbirds buzzed around them, and around the white and rose and purple blooms on the bushes that made a wall along the feet of the big oaks and beeches and mahoganies. A fringe of dwarf palms only ten or twelve feet high was scattered out into the meadow, along with the odd live oak. Only insects swarmed around the corpse of the dead raptor, but those included dragonflies two feet from wingtip to wingtip.

Then a figure pushed through the brush, hacking left and right with a machete. Marc blinked in surprise; it was a tall man with unkempt ash-blond hair and a scraggly new beard, dressed in a hide loincloth, but with an AK-47 over his back, ammunition pouches and knife and pistol and scabbard at his waist.

"It's Binkis," Marc said. "Looks a bit gaunt, but otherwise healthy."

Jadviga made an involuntary sound of relief and checked her impulse to run forward with a visible effort. Her man strode out into the open and waved his machete overhead before sheathing it. Then he turned and made a curious beckoning gesture towards the scrub.

Marc whistled and handed the binoculars to Blair. "That look like what I think it looks like?" he said.

The Englishman slung his own rifle and took them. "Bloody *hell*!" he said after a moment.

"You Great White Hunters going to enlighten my humble Harlem self?" Cynthia asked sharply. "I can see there's some natives with him."

"Not just natives," Marc said, remembering what he'd seen.

Squat figures, built like barrels on thick, muscular legs, with arms like oak roots and hands like spades. Hair like a sparse pelt, say halfway between what a human had and what a chimp did—though perhaps not quite so much if you used an Ainu as your *Homo sap* reference. Big blobs of nose, little eyes under shelves of bone, beards half-hiding the fact that they had no chins.

"Neanderthals," Marc said, as more and more came into view: twenty at least . . . no, more like thirty now.

"And over a dozen of them have assault rifles to go with their spears and stone hatchets," Blair added dryly.

"You are *shitting* me!" the young woman said sharply, grabbing for the glasses.

When she lowered them again, they all turned and looked at Jadviga, who'd gone white under her tan.

"*Mais,*" Marc said slowly. "Could you start by telling us, Mrs. Binkis, what the *Riga* was doing with better than a dozen military rifles on board? And please don't tell me it carried them all up to orbit and back."

Jadviga flushed, but her voice was steady. "Like you we keep a number of firearms for protective purposes," she said. "The *Riga* was bringing replacements from Earth."

Cynthia cut in, "And what Captain Binkis was doing handing them out to locals? The Treaty *clearly* forbids giving Venusians firearms! Under *any* circumstances!"

The Baltic-born woman licked her lips. "I'm sure there an explanation is. Perhaps Franziskus was coerced . . ."

Blair had been using the binoculars again. "He's armed, and he appears to be in charge. At least, he's waving and they're spreading out in response."

Tahyo added his bit to the exchange, a bristling growl. His master went on:

"Those are very like the specimens I remember from the first EastBloc probe's pictures. Is there something you're not telling us, Mrs. Binkis?"

She shook her head. "I . . . I am as surprised as you are, sir."

"Don't bullshit me! You're surprised all right, but not *as* surprised."

Marc thought quickly. It didn't take a man long to walk a thousand yards, and half that would put the strangers within effective range. A quick glance behind him showed the half-completed abatis, but that had been built with wild animals or possibly spear-armed natives in mind. It was no protection against modern weapons at all. Running was out of the question; they'd be hunted down if the newcomers were hostile. Which left only one, very bad, alternative.

"All right, everyone, up the ladder. *Now!*" he snapped.

As he'd expected, Jadviga showed no sign of obeying. Cynthia and Blair did, snatching up a few things and then doing their best squirrel imitation. Marc waited an instant and then did a little snatching himself: a belt of ammunition, his quiver and bow, a couple of full canteens.

"Up, boy!" he barked. Then as the animal whined and hesitated: "*Now!*"

Climbing near-vertical ladders wasn't easy for a canid to begin with; their bodies weren't put together that way. Tahyo was at the awkward age, anyway, and each rung required a sort of lunging shuffle. With no fingers to grip and a ladder only slightly inclined in that meant he had to keep his paws from slipping by sheer pressure, and soon the beast's long legs were quivering. Halfway up, the young greatwolf began to topple backward with a yelping howl, plate-sized forepaws flailing at the air as he twisted sideways. Marc lunged.

"Jesus!" he shouted, as his hand closed on the falling greatwolf's ruff.

Tahyo weighed over fifty pounds these days, and the angle was awkward; the wiggling and thrashing didn't help, either. Marc jammed a knee around the rung he was on and felt his back crackle as he bent back, farther, farther, the gear slung across his shoulders pulling at him, the greatwolf's paws scratching bloody tracks down the right side of his torso.

"*Huhhh!*"

When he slammed forward again he clung for a moment, almost sobbing as he panted with relief. Tahyo clung as well, his jaws clenching so hard on the rung that the tough green wood splintered.

"Use this!" someone called from above—Blair, he thought.

A loop of rope dropped down beside him. After wrestling moments and one heart-stopping instant when he thought they were going to fall again he managed to get the noose up under Tahyo's forelimbs and snugged tight.

"Haul away!"

A few seconds later Marc threw himself flat on the rock at the top, panting and scratched and bleeding, the smell of his own sweat thick in his nostrils and the taste of vomit at the back of his throat.

Hey, you were nearly defan *Vitrac there; you're lucky you don't need new underwear. Not time to be a saint yet, you.*

Tahyo stood shivering in splay-legged panic for a while, then went over and christened the palm tree, trotting around the top of the column as he investigated their new surroundings. Marc suppressed an impulse to kick the gangling animal; the cold sweat was still pouring down his face.

"Sheee-it, that was scary!" Cynthia said, scolding.

"*Weh. Mais,* love me, love my dog," Marc said.

"Quite right," Blair said, and she glared at them both.

Marc controlled his breathing and took a careful sip from his canteen; the ones they had here might have to last awhile. Then he rolled to the edge and looked down.

"Jadviga's talking to her husband. She looks a bit worried . . . wait a minute. . . ."

One of the Neanderthals made a grab for the woman. Without even looking aside, Binkis drew the machete at his waist and cut backhanded. The man-thing's hand dropped in the dirt, and he ran off shrieking, clutching at the stump as it sent red gouts into the air.

"Shee-it," Cynthia said quietly, swallowing.

"This is odd," Blair said. "According to reports, Franziskus Binkis is, if not a mild-mannered pilot, an unexceptional one. How exactly did he come to be the Great White . . . er, how did he come to rule this bunch? They're not turning on him for lopping off a hand. Look at the way they're cringing, even that older one in the ritualistic gear."

Jadviga seemed to be having second thoughts as well. She shook her head, once and again, and began backing away from her husband. Then she turned and bolted for the ladder; Binkis made a gesture, and two of his followers leaped, brought her down, lashed wrists and ankles together, and carried her away.

The pilot himself approached a little closer. "Come down!" he called, his hands cupped around his mouth. "Come down, and you will not be harmed!"

"Said the spider to the fly, eh?" Marc called back. "Get those hairy goons away and we'll talk. We came here to rescue you, *vieux*!"

He suppressed a plaintive: *What the hell's going on?*

"Circumstances have changed," Binkis said.

Marc shivered slightly. There was something . . . strange in the

Lithuanian's voice, and it wasn't just the clotted accent. There was a flatness to it, a lack of affect. And the way he turned his head to look at the piled boxes of supplies had a mechanical quality to it—supple, but disconcertingly precise. He grunted and gestured. Half a dozen of the shambling figures moved towards the stacked crates of supplies.

"Can't let them do that," Marc muttered, and reached for his rifle.

Binkis turned as Marc leveled it, and brought the AK to his shoulder. Marc ignored him; a hundred yards away, a hundred feet down . . . with an ordinary assault rifle and iron sights, it would take a miracle for the EastBloc pilot to hit anything. Marc aimed instead at one of the Neanderthals, aimed for the ground at his feet. Shooting down a man who held nothing but a wooden spear and stone hatchet wasn't something he'd do if there was any choice, and the dirt spurting up at the man's feet ought to do it. Breathe out and squeeze the trigger—

A bullet went *crack* over Marc's head, close enough to feel the hot wind of its passage. Another struck not far from his face, peppering him with grit blasted free, making him claw at his eyes with a shout of pain. A third and forth struck the rifle from his hands. By the time he had cleared the grit from under his lids the irreplaceable weapon was tinkling in pieces over the rocks at the foot of the column.

"Down!" Blair shouted, suiting action to words; Cynthia followed with prompt prudence. "Flat!"

"Jesus!" Marc said reverently, looking at the blood on the palm he had wiped across his face. "There is something very goddamn wrong here, eh? *Nobody* shoots that good offhand."

"I should say so," Blair said. "I'd have a shot at them myself, but on second thought, no, perhaps not."

Cynthia crawled close. "Well, there's always this," she said, and pulled a canvas bandolier from around her neck. "From when we excavated that well." The plastique was in blocks about the size of an ordinary brick; the time-fuses were ready to cut.

"There won't be much left of the bally gear if we use that," Blair warned.

"*Weh*," Marc said, nodding once. "But we can't let that stuff fall into Binkis' hands, or his merry friends'. And we can't sit around and discuss it. Let's do it."

All three of them took out a block of the plastic explosive, pushed a detonator into the soft, doughy material, and pinched off a six-second length.

"You drop yours straight down, Cynthia," Marc said. "Chris, you go long. I'll aim right for the crates. One, two, *three*."

The woman rolled onto her back, pinched the detonator to start it, and tossed it gently behind her. The four-pound block of explosive cleared the lip of the column's edge with barely an inch to spare and dropped, trailing a hissing sound and a thin line of blue smoke. The men threw an instant later; Marc came up on one elbow and chucked underarm like a softball pitcher, and behind him, Blair came to his knees and used an odd-looking circular overarm toss.

"One, two, three, four—," Marc counted.

CRANNNG! Bits and pieces of boxes, gear, and rock fountained up, and the ladder disappeared in a whirlwind of splinters and chunks. The basalt of the column quivered beneath them; it was far too thick to be brought down, but the sensation was unpleasant anyway.

CRANNNG! CRANNNG!

The sound of the second and third blasts was a little flatter than the first, not being partially confined by the rock. They did have a background of screaming howls. Marc shook his head to try to clear the ringing in his ears, leopard-crawled to the edge of the column, and peeked cautiously over. Most of the Neanderthals who weren't down still or writhing were running fast. One of them had Binkis over a shoulder; no way to tell whether the EastBloc pilot was dead, or how badly he was injured if he wasn't.

And the piled boxes of supplies were shattered, and the remnants burning with the fierce bright flames that this oxygen-rich atmosphere bred. A firecracker ripple spoke of ammunition cooking off . . .

CHAPTER NINE

"Look!" Teesa cried desperately. "The beastmen flee! The fire-from-the-sky has struck them!"

Heads turned, and it was true; dozens of the Wergu fled across the open downs, howling witlessly. The sweat of fear still gleamed on the limbs of the Cloud Mountain warriors, its smell rank, but she could see the spirit return in them. Through the Cave Master, she could feel the fierce swell of their will to battle. And the mind—the strange mind, the one that had touched hers through the circlet—had flared and gone blank. Not dead, but . . . away.

"So come!" she cried, and clambered up to run forward.

The death-maker went to her shoulder. A dot appeared in her vision as she stared down the barrel; with the dreamlike certainty of the Cave Master she could tell that marked the place the little darts would fly.

Crack. A beastman toppled backward. *Crack*. Another. A third shot wildly at her, until a flurry of blowgun darts brought him down, convulsing as the black-spider venom had its way with him.

"Well, well," Marc said, looking down. "The day's full of surprises, isn't it?"

As he knelt, Tahyo stood beside him, nose pointed alertly and tail wagging slightly. The other two humans had a similar look.

The newcomers were putting out fires and looking around the former campsite. Others dragged the Neanderthal corpses together off to one side. And one stood below, looking up at him.

A true human, like the rest. Unlike most of the others, she was female: around twenty Earth-years, he judged, and near his own height. Slender, like a runner or gymnast, with long blond hair falling past her shoulders and confined by a headband of some silvery substance. She wore a loincloth of some tawny fur with flaps falling halfway to her knees before and behind, and a halter of the same, shaped like a sports bra. A machete rode at one hip, a bronze knife at the other, and a bandolier held magazines for the AK-47 she carried with easy assurance. Her face was alien, high-cheeked, snub-nosed, with a full-lipped mouth and pointed chin; her eyes were turquoise, bright against the honey-amber color of her skin.

Blair said thoughtfully, "Does that remind you of anyone?"

"She's a dead ringer for that woman in the fur bikini who ran past the Russian probe back in '62," Cynthia said. "Couldn't be the same one, she's too young, but she's definitely the same *type*. So are the spearmen."

"Not just spearmen," Marc said, watching one of them pull a long shamboo dart out of a Neanderthal corpse. "Those are blow-guns they've got slung across their backs, and poisoned darts, at a guess. And there are a few bronze tools there, as well as polished stone."

"High-grade hunter-gatherer culture, or maybe Neolithic, with contacts with someone more advanced. The coastal towns, at a guess," Blair said.

"Let's not assume they're friends, just 'cause they look pretty," Cynthia said sharply.

Below Marc, the yellow-haired woman gestured again: *Come down.* Then she pointed to her lips and spoke, then touched her ears. *We will talk.*

"*Mais*, we don't have a language in common, lady," Marc muttered.

Just then a pre-pubescent girl came up and stood beside the woman; they looked very alike, perhaps sisters, perhaps just members of a tribe with a limited gene pool. The older woman gestured again, and then turned to say something to one of the warriors; the man touched his spear shaft to his forehead and hurried off.

"Well, the young lady is in charge," Blair said, stroking his chin.

"Yeah, could be they're *feminist* cannibals and torturers," Cynthia observed dryly.

"I don't think we have much choice but to try and make contact," Marc said, a little reluctantly. "There's the enemy-of-my-enemy bit, and we don't have enough water to stay up here more than a few days. Plus we really, really need help getting back home now that all that gear got blasted to bits—and we need help finding out what the hell's going on here."

"I'm a linguist," Blair pointed out. Cynthia laid a quick hand on his shoulder, and Marc shook his head.

"I've had more experience with primitives. Let me down on the rope, and then pull it back up quick when I'm on the ground."

Both of them looked at him. Tahyo did, too, and whined plaintively; that made everyone chuckle. Marc stood up and shouted. The woman looked at him, and so did most of her followers. He ostentatiously set down his weapons, held up his hands to show them empty, and made an *I'm coming* gesture.

The woman froze for a moment, and then called an order. The young girl took her war-gear and walked back a hundred yards; the rest of the warriors backed off likewise, most of them squatting on their haunches and leaning on the shafts of their spears, apart from the ones on burial detail or camp-chores.

"*Mais*, that's a gesture, at least," Marc said.

"And only a gesture," Blair said.

Marc nodded at the warning. His two comrades reeved the rope through the loop of a piton driven into a fissure in the basalt near the lip, and Marc snugged the loop under his arms. It still felt a bit like walking naked out of an air lock in deep space when he slipped over the lip of the column, holding the rope and fending off with his feet as they lowered him down the steep rock, smooth and swift. Loose rock shifted among the scree at the base; he cast off the rope and turned around, walking down towards the . . .

Priestess? Princess? Whatever?

Teesa started as the stranger walked towards her. *That is the man I saw in my dreams!* she thought, awed.

She touched her hand to her forehead and bowed slightly. The stranger smiled at her and made an expressive gesture—shrugging his shoulders and turning his palms up.

That was so human and yet so strange that she fought back a laugh, and looked at him with fresh eyes. He wore odd garb: closed sandals that covered his feet completely, leggings of woven cloth joined together at the waist, a heavy belt. She recognized the 'saur hide of that and the boots, and her brows went up—his folk must be mighty hunters, and from the workmanship of the metal buckle also gifted makers. His build was much like men of her folk, muscular and broad-shouldered but lean and long in the limb, and he was not much different in the color of his sun-bronzed skin.

She judged that he would be a good warrior, strong and quick; right now he was bare to the waist, and showed the scratches and grazes that would come of fighting or fleeing.

Wholly alien was the cast of his features, and the darkness of hair and eye. Through the Cave Master she could feel the contours of his mind, and that was both oddly new and familiar. A smile dimpled her cheek as she felt his eyes on her face and body, looking at her as a man gazed on a woman, but without any hint of anger.

"Who are you, warrior, that you walk my dreams and hurl thunder?" she asked. "You are not as the one who now leads the beastmen against us—you are his enemy, is that not so?"

Then he spoke in turn, and she frowned in puzzlement. It was true speech, not beastman gruntings, but it was as alien as the talk of the coast-men towns. And though she knew only a few words of that, this was plainly something else again.

Need drove, despite the risk. She smiled reassuringly, and touched the Cave Master. Then she advanced, slowly, meeting his eyes as she reached out to lay fingers on his temples. He made no objection. With the touch established, she *reached* . . .

God, she's gorgeous, Marc thought. Then: *Down, boy! Concentrate on the job here!* And: *Hey, she looks a lot like the woman in that dream I had . . . looks a lot like the one the probe showed back in '62. Couldn't be* her, *of course.* . . .

Closer, he could see that she was close to his own midtwenties, with a few fine lines beside the slanted blue eyes. Her teeth showed white and even when she smiled; there was a smell of clean sweat, well-cured leather, and some spicy herb about her, as well as a faint hint of cordite. The leather of her garments was fine-grained, probably from some young antelope, and dyed along its edges with flowing patterns. Her hands were long-fingered and graceful as she gestured, the nails pared close and kept clean—cleaner than his, right now.

She spoke; the language was utterly strange, not even the sounds like Kartahownian or any of the tribal dialects he'd acquired a smattering of. Some people could pick up a strange tongue in a few weeks; unfortunately, they were extremely rare and none of them had the other qualifications necessary to get sent to Venus. So he'd be stuck drudging through more show-and-tell . . .

Might as well start with names, he thought.

Then the woman stepped closer. That gave him a better look at the headband she was wearing, and his eyes went wide. It wasn't copper or gold or bronze, and the lines of it were sleek enough to look machined. *And* the setting for the jewel at the center was smoothly seamless, not like anything he'd ever seen before.

The stone was a clear, translucent green, with depths that seemed infinite. Marc stared at it as the woman slowly raised her hands and set them on either side of his head; he could feel her fingertips searching through the close-cropped hair, settling into contact with his skin.

Then they clamped down hard. Marc opened his mouth . . .

. . . and staggered up from his knees. His comrades' voices came to him, hard with concern.

"I'm not harmed!" he said, turning and shouting.

Then his mouth and tongue froze, as he realized he'd spoken in a language he had never learned. Something went *click* in his head, and he called the same words in English.

"What happened?" Blair called.

"I haven't got the faintest idea," Marc called, feeling sweat breaking out all over his body.

His head . . . not ached. It felt *suffused*. And his stomach rebelled in sympathy; he barely managed to suppress it. Just what he needed to demonstrate his diplomatic skills: projectile vomiting.

"But *oo ye yi*, I'm going to find out!"

He turned back to the woman. She touched the base of her throat.

"I am Teesa, of the Cloud Mountain folk; my sign is the Eagle," she said.

And he understood her perfectly; even that her name incorporated her mother's, with a shift from *d* to a *t* sound, and that "folk" was an elided form of a word that had once meant *clan-hearth-in-common*, and that the sign was partly a totem inherited with the maternal bloodline, and partly something found in dreams and visions. . . .

"I'm Marc Vitrac," he replied, wincing at the cataract of data. "Ah . . . American, of the Terrans . . . the Sky People." *What did you do to me?* he didn't ask aloud.

Instead he went on: "How did you teach me this language?"

She smiled and made a soothing gesture . . . and he knew what the gesture, a sort of patting-the-air motion of the hand, meant, too.

"I gave you our speech and took yours through the Cave Master, which is the inheritance of my line, from mother to daughter from time out of mind," she said. "But now we must leave here quickly. We are too close to the hearths of the beastmen, and they have new and terrible weapons. Come quickly!"

Marc sat looking at the fire, kneading his temples. It was very dark, with not even the occasional glimpse of a star, with only the low light of the cookfires to show the sheltering circle of jagged rocks. The Cloud Mountain People had chosen well; the light wouldn't show outside the hollow. None of them were very close. They looked at the strangers with a mixture of awe and suspicion, and they spoke sparingly, their voices low.

But normally they're a talkative folk, and they'd be laughing and boasting of their deeds now . . .

"*Cho! Co!*" he groaned, clutching at his head.

When he looked up, he was uneasily conscious of how Blair and Cynthia sat together and stared at him a little fearfully.

"Hey, that's Cajun, not Cloud Mountain. Look, I'm still me," he said, his voice shaky. "Not pod people, Okay?"

Cynthia relaxed first. "You've got to admit something has been . . . hell, Marc, something's been *done* to you. To your mind."

Blair nodded.

Marc shrugged. "*Weh.* As far as I can *tell*, though, what's happened is that a new language got dumped into my speech centers. I still . . . feel like me."

"Well, you would say that, wouldn't you?" Blair murmured, and then held up a hand. "We'll have to go on the assumption that you *are* still you, old boy."

"*Weh.*"

I wish I was certain, he thought behind the mask of his face. *My head feels . . . too full. Like the contents got stirred around and reinserted.*

And cascades of new information seemed to fall into place every time he *thought* in the Cloud Mountain tongue. Not just information: When he used it he started to think *like* a native speaker. And that was very damned strange, when he tried to mentally translate terms like "life" or "death" or "time" or "cause."

He noticed them staring at him with concern again. "*Weh*, it's a bit startling from the inside, too, eh?" he said. "Like having a whole new world dumped into your head."

"I take it back," Blair said dryly.

"What?"

"Calling these people *high-level hunter-gatherer,*" he said dryly.

Cynthia chuckled. "I don't think they made the, umm, *Cave Master,* somehow," she said, waving around at the encampment. "All this looks a lot more like your first guess, Chris."

Not far away, Teesa and her sister sat by one of the fires; a tall yellow-haired warrior shared it, working with quick tapping blows from an antler pick on a stone tool held across his lap in a fold of leather, *tip-tip-tip*-tock*!* Then he shook the fragments out of the leather and began to bind the spearhead into a shaft, studiously avoiding Marc's eye. When he became conscious of the Terran's eyes on him, he deliberately looked elsewhere, making a covert sign as he wrapped the tools and a block of obsidian in the hide and tucked it away in a haversack made from the whole skin of some badgerlike animal.

The all-too-familiar *click* sounded behind Marc's eyes, and he knew the gesture the man had made was one against dangerous magic.

Bon, he thought. *My comrades are looking at me strange because I can speak Cloud Mountain, and* they *think I'm big bad* mojo.

The young girl came over to them with a sheet of bark. It held grilled antelope liver and breadnuts, and a twist of coarse salt in a leaf.

"Oh, in for a lion, in for a lamb," Marc muttered to himself, and brushed the fingers of his right hand down from his brow to chin, then moved his hand sideways.

"This traveling hunter thanks the she whose hearth gifts him with meat," he said in the girl's own tongue.

She giggled. "So polite! My name is Zore. I'm not polite, not often."

Marc grinned. "No, you are a *forrick*," he said.

The word slipped out almost before he saw the mental image, something like a miniature baboon with a bright red bottom.

"Well, I won't throw dung at you from a treetop," she said. "Anyway, my sister says she will speak with you tomorrow."

Marc watched her skip back to her sister's fire. "Cute little *babette*," he said, handing around the food.

They'd all kept their mess kits, since those folded around their canteens. Apart from that they had their knives, pistols, Blair's rifle and forty rounds of the powerful Magnum ammunition, and Cynthia's shotgun, unfortunately with nothing but the six rounds in the magazine. Marc still had his bow and quiver; from the burned and blasted gear they'd managed to rescue little besides the scorched metal parts of some tools, and a small steel box that Marc fervently hoped had come through undamaged.

They ate the liver in Cloud Mountain style, with trimmed

twigs as forks; the locals seemed to be a mannerly folk. The rich, strong-tasting organ meat went down well, after a long, strenuous day and nothing since breakfast. Their hosts had also added a pile of leaves the size of small towels, which was exactly what they used them for; the sap was thin and astringent and pleasantly scented.

"I think I've figured out something," Cynthia said at last. "Look, everyone, that damn thing the girl—"

"Teesa," Marc put in.

"Teesa, right. The thing she used on Marc . . . well, there's only two explanations for it. First, it could be magic. Second, it could be really, really advanced technology."

"There's a difference?" Blair asked.

Cynthia punched him on the shoulder, only half in jest. "You bet. Because that isn't the only evidence of advanced technology around. And I don't believe in magic."

"Isn't this sort of academic—," Marc began.

The black woman cut him off with a chop of her hand. "No, it *ain't*. Think about it for a second. The other evidence is this damn *planet*."

"You don't mean the aliens-did-it stuff, eh?" Marc said.

Silently, Cynthia pointed to Teesa and back to Marc. "You got a better explanation? And that explains a lot—how Venus has a fossil record that ends two hundred million years ago, and how you've got dinosaurs and people together at the same time. This place isn't a naturally living planet at all; it's a terrarium. A zoo. An experimental station. Give you odds Mars is, too. And somewhere around here is . . . I don't know, a watching post, an automatic alarm system, whatever. It *does* things. Give you odds that's why the EastBloc didn't set up their base around here. Those problems they had with their probes . . ."

Marc checked a surge of denial and skepticism; after what had happened to him, all certainties seemed shaken. Blair poked meditatively at the fire with a stick.

"It would take a technology . . . not just more advanced than ours, but one based on entirely separate principles, to create an entire ecosphere. On the other hand, so would instant imprinting of a different language on a human brain."

"*Weh*," Marc said. "But it would account for a lot. For the way *we* got here, for example. And why the *Riga* did. Sort of stretching co-incidence for us both to end up in the same neighborhood by accident, eh?"

Suddenly he felt his spirits lift. *I'm not just lost and in danger of death*, he thought. *This is adventure, by God! We've got a chance at one of the great puzzles of all history! Sure, it's sad Tyler got killed, but this is a dangerous planet.*

He tried to drag himself back to practicality. "We've got to find out more," he said.

"Yeah," the woman said, looking over at Teesa. "We do. 'Cause our little mission to rescue bro Binkis obviously isn't on anymore. Something else entirely got its hooks into him.

"Oh, and one thing—be careful what you say around Teesa there."

"Why?" Blair asked. "*We* didn't get the mysterious language lesson, old boy."

"*Weh*," Marc said, with a grim smile. "But she got English the same way I got Cloud Mountain. Or the Real Tongue, to translate."

Next dawning, Teesa watched in the bright early light as Marc used the . . .

"Bow," her new language supplied. Unlike many of the words, it actually meant something, something she could understand rather than just making her head hurt. The *bow* was made up of *laminations*, and bent to throw the *arrow*, which was much like a little spear or a giant blowgun dart.

The muscles stood out in his arms and shoulders in a sudden static wave. The string released, going *snap!* on the bracer, and the arrow hissed out, thunking into a tree forty yards distant.

Teesa walked over. Marc nodded to her, friendly but wary—she couldn't blame him for that. Most of her folk would have been frankly terrified at such close contact with the Mysteries, but his people had arcane knowledge of their own.

"Good shooting," she said.

He'd picked four trees, each another fifty or so paces out. The farther ones were far beyond blowgun range, but the closest—

She put the bone mouthpiece of the tube to her lips. *Ffffth!* The fire-hardened tip sank quivering in the creamy-colored bark. Just then a fluff-tail broke from cover behind a bush. Teesa's hand flashed down to the pouch at her belt, loaded, and *ffffth!* again. The little animal leaped, landed, kicked convulsively, and lay still. Marc grinned and bowed. They walked over to the tree; she picked up the fluff-tail on her way, hanging it from her belt.

"Mother of Fluff-tails, thank you," she said as she did. "For hide and meat, we thank you and your children."

At the tree, Teesa's blowgun dart stood beside the man's arrow. Marc reached out to pull it free, and she laid a hand on his arm to stop him. Even without the Cave Master on her brow, there was a peculiar feeling to the contact, as if her fingers grew warm. He must have felt it, too, for he moved aside a little as she plucked the dart free herself, holding it by the steadying-bead at the blunt end.

"This is a clean dart," she said, holding up the foot-long sliver. "See? The end is charred but not treated. We use for practice, and for small game. Now see this, but be careful!"

She returned it to her pouch, and—carefully!—drew free one of the dipped rounds. That had a thick tarry liquid on its end.

"The venom of the black swamp spider. Very dangerous and very hard to find, and how do you say . . ."

She thought for a moment. What would "boil down" be in the Sky People tongue? Ah, yes.

"Very hard and dangerous to *concentrate*. Very, you would say, *expensive*. But death to a man in a few heartbeats, and even to a large 'saur, in an hour or so if you hit a soft spot, around the eye or mouth, or the anus. We use in war, and to guard our homes."

"Not for hunting?" he asked, taking the dart with sensible, gingerly caution and examining it.

"No! The meat is deadly if not cooked very well, and even then too much may sicken you—make your hands tremble."

"Ah. Nerve toxin, and a bad one," he said. Then in her language: "A lasting poison."

"Yes." She looked speculatively at the bow. "Blowguns have short range, and will not pierce a shield or a leather cloak. Perhaps with those . . . why do you use it, if you have the death-from-afar?" She tapped his pistol.

He replied, "The *guns* come from our home." He pointed upward to show that he meant the place-beyond-the-sky, not the village to the east. "The *bullets* come from there also. We can make a *bow* here, and the arrows."

"Can I try?" she said.

He handed her the bow. She looked at it carefully; the handle in the center was mahogany, the limbs shamboo strips with *tharg*-horn on the inside, sinew on the outside, and a beautiful double-curve shape. It had the look of something well made for a purpose, though there was none of the little touches—decorative carving, perhaps some inlay—that one of her people would have used for something so valuable. As he had done, she held the grip in her left hand and tried to pull back the string.

"Like this," Marc said, standing behind her and setting her stance and hands in place. "Throw the left hand out, and draw back with your shoulders and stomach muscles."

Ah, she thought, grasping what he meant with her body as well as her mind—she was accustomed to hard, skilled work from earliest childhood. *Like this* . . .

With a long *hooosh!* of effort she managed to draw the string to the angle of her jaw; her right arm trembled a bit, and the twine bit into her fingers despite the work callus. She would need a bracer on her left arm and a shooting glove on her right fingers such as Marc had, but those looked easy to make. She let the bow relax and handed the weapon back to Marc.

"Very nice," he said over her shoulder. "That is a heavy bow."

She grinned to herself; the musky scent told her he found more than her strength and skill interesting. Of course, he could probably tell the same of her . . .

Except that his language is strange—it has so few words for scents, she thought suddenly. *And they are . . . vague. Why would that be?*

"Now let me try with an arrow!" she exclaimed.

"Well, just once," he said. "You need a bow tailored to you, and some gear. Try that closest tree first."

It was a big one, with white bark that shed in long, curling strips. She did again as he had shown her, conscious of the closeness of his body until she pushed that and everything else out of her mind with life long discipline.

Snap. The string stung her forearm. There was a sweet surge through the bow, and the arrow flashed away—faster than a thrown spear, far bigger and heavier than a blowgun dart. And . . .

"I hit!" she said, jumping up and down and waving the bow. "I hit!"

Only just, though: The arrow stood through the edge of the tree, through the bark and just a bit of the wood. She could tell from his raised eyebrows that Marc found it surprising she should hit with her first try. They grinned at each other. . . .

A grunt, and a whistling of cloven air from behind her. A javelin arched over their heads and slammed into the tree with a heavy *thunk* of cloven wood. Taldi strutted past to pull it free, which needed a foot braced against the trunk and care taken not to snap the triangular stone head; he took the arrow, too, and handed it to Marc.

"Here is your toy," he said, contemptuously at first, then with a little quiver of fear in his voice as the greatwolf stuck his head around Marc's thigh and bared teeth at Taldi.

"Heel," Marc told the animal, and turned back to Taldi with mild amusement, which clearly made the Cloud Mountain warrior angrier than ever. Then Marc added, "Circle, boy!"

Tahyo gave a deep sound: *Ooooorh*. Then he dashed off down the stretch of grassland and into the thicker brush beyond.

"My thanks for fetching my toy," Marc said, taking it from Taldi's fingers and setting it back on the string.

Just then, a striped wild pig broke cover. It was a small one, less than knee-high, and it dashed between two of the trees and beyond. Marc pivoted smoothly, drawing to the angle of his jaw and tracking the animal with the point.

Snap.

Teesa found herself holding her breath. The arrow soared out in a blurred arch, and . . .

"You hit!" she cried, jumping up again.

The animal went over with a squeal, kicking and thrashing. An instant later Tahyo appeared, throwing himself on the pig and seizing its throat in his already-powerful jaws. When it went still he sat back, licking his chops and looking hopefully at the man a hundred yards away.

Taldi flushed, going dark red under his amber skin; the range was far beyond javelin throw.

"It is a bad magic, to ensorcell a greatwolf," he snarled. "The Father of Greatwolves must be angry with you . . . and any that shelter you! They will be under his *curse*!"

"Thank you, hunter," Teesa said hastily to Marc to put him under the protection of ritual. "We accept your gracious gift of meat."

Taldi stalked off, which was bad manners—he should have helped them break the kill. Teesa and Marc dressed it out, washed their arms down in a nearby stream, and carried it back slung from a branch between them. Cries of welcome greeted them; quite a few had observed the shot from a distance, and fresh meat was always welcome, when you'd been living on trail-jerky for days.

"Do you often use the, ah, the Diadem of the Eye to learn new languages?" Marc asked, as they recovered the other arrows and headed back to camp.

"Never before," she said cheerfully, and laughed as he looked at her wide-eyed. "It is too dangerous, and we seldom meet outsiders."

"Too dangerous?" he asked.

"Yes. My mother died when I was very young, before I could learn all she knew, and even if she had taught me all her skills, the Diadem of the Eye is *dangerous*. To touch a mind with it is . . . full of perils. Sometimes both the wearer and the one touched may . . . how do you say?"

The concepts that flooded into her mind were so strange; there was no way to really say *be taken by the bad spirits*. She sorted through them, and smiled as she found the words she needed.

"Yes, *go hopelessly mad*."

"Urk!" he replied.

The gently rolling land grew steeper to the southwest; the ridges and hilltops were still in grass, but thick forest crept upward, foretelling the solid mantle of trees that covered the foothills and lower slopes of the great mountains on the horizon. The two-score of Cloud Mountain warriors walked in a rough line, with scouts ranging out to the front and behind and on either side. The others moved at a ranging, swinging walk, stopping every hour or so to rest for a few minutes and drink water. The air was warm and soft, enough so that their near-naked bodies gleamed with sweat as the hours of the long Venusian day wore on.

Marc put one foot ahead of the other and concentrated on his breathing; he was in hard, good shape and had the advantage of muscles and lungs that had evolved for heavier gravity and thinner air than this, but he still had to admire their stamina.

"And the way they keep off the ridgelines and don't leave much track," he said quietly to the other Terrans as they got back to their feet after the latest rest period.

"Yeah, they're the Last of the Cloud Mountaineers and every one of 'em's an Eagle Scout," Cynthia said, wiping the sweat off her face and directing a stream from the canvas water-bottle into her mouth. "You bet—Davy Crockett and Dan'l Boone would have loved 'em."

Zore went by, her tame fluff-tail at her heels, chasing a butterfly with orange-black-blue wings nearly as broad across as her head. Tahyo started off after her, and then returned at a sharp command to *heel*. Marc had noticed that the locals were uneasy around the young greatwolf; they knew his kind, but only as dangerous predators and hunting rivals. A greatwolf who ran with human beings was big mojo and it made them uneasy.

"Not too far off, from what Marc tells us," Blair said.

"Yeah. And I'm not enthusiastic about getting involved in their quarrels," Cynthia replied quietly. "Even if they seem a lot nicer than the Neanderthals. It's against doctrine . . . and it's sort of skanky. I never had any desire to be the first Negro conquistador."

Marc shrugged in agreement: Non-interference as far as humanly possible *was* official doctrine, and generally speaking, he supported it. *Odd, I actually* like *Cynthia better now that I'm not in the running, so to speak*, he thought. "Evidently the survivors from the *Riga* are at this place where Teesa's people used to live before the Neanderthals came . . . the *Wergu*, they call them."

"What does that mean, exactly?" Cynthia asked.

"Errr . . ."

He concentrated; he was getting the trick of stepping back from *knowing* the language to knowing *about* it. When he'd managed to transpose the sounds to shapes in his mind's eye he went on:

"Ah, *beastmen*. '-Gu' is the suffix; sort of 'men' in the sense of a generic term, as in 'Englishmen,' or 'people.' 'Wer,' beasts; 'gu,' men: beastmen. These guys are the *Nesbergu*. Cloud Mountain People. Or possibly the Misty Hills Folk, something like that. Humans in general—our type of human being—are *firigu*. True-men."

Blair missed a stride, almost stumbling. "Excuse me? 'Nes' is cloud and 'ber' is mountain? How would you spell those?"

"*Weh*," Marc said, and did, transliterating phonetically.

"Extraordinary," Blair breathed. "Of course, it could be a coincidence."

Cynthia and Marc looked at him. "Sugar, what *are* you on about?" she asked.

"Those words . . ." He turned to Marc. "Could you tell me a few other common words? Numerals, that sort of thing?"

"Sure. Counting up, *ai, tah, tro, keti, pekki, sews, eff, owok, neh, tek*—"

For the first time, he considered the shape of the language he'd acquired in a finger snap. His jaw dropped as he mentally transposed the syllables into phonetic print.

"—hey, wait a minute! You're not serious!"

"What's 'mother'?" Blair went on.

"'Ma.' But hell, that doesn't mean a thing. The *Chinese* for 'mother' is 'ma.' *Bebettes*, they all say that."

Blair nodded, a hunter's keenness in his handsome face. "Give me a few common words."

"'Piwur,' father. 'Taiz,' sky. 'Tektek' for one hundred . . . that's not . . . wait a minute; 'ten' is 'tek'! Holy shit!" he said, awed. "Chris ol' buddy, your fame is made!"

"Initial *d* becomes *t*!" Blair shouted, running in a small circle and punching his fist into the sky. "Consistent sound shift!"

A few of the Cloud Mountain folk looked over at him, puzzled; others leveled their spears and looked around for a threat or danger.

"*Will* you two jokers tell me what's going on?" Cynthia complained.

The two men halted and began talking; Blair was actually waving his hands in excitement, and Marc let him take up the thread. It was his field, after all.

"None of the languages we've met here on Venus—or on

Mars—has any relation at all that we can find to any of the languages on Earth," he told her, words stumbling over one another.

"Well, yeah," she said. "They're different *planets*, dude! Thirty million miles distance."

"Hoist by your own petard, my dear," he said, grinning from ear to ear. "*You* were the one going on about how the life-forms here were too similar to Earthly ones and that it made some sort of alien intervention the only believable explanation."

"Mostly *extinct* Earthly ones, yeah," she said cautiously. Then her eyes went wide, white in the ebony face. "Wait a minute!"

"Yes! Yes! *Yes!* This language *is* related to one on Earth!"

"Which one, lover?"

"To ours. To French and Latin and Hindi! It's an Indo-European language, I'd bet the skin off my arse! Kentum subfamily at that! One of the sound shifts is identical to one in Proto-Germanic, but that could be a coincidence."

He grabbed Marc by the arm. "I've got to learn it! You've got to teach me! Or could *Teesa* do the same thing with me—"

Cynthia stared at him. "Oh, shit," she said quietly after a moment.

Blair's grin faded slightly. "What's the matter?"

"I thought aliens must have seeded Venus and Mars, right? Transporting all those life-forms here. And human beings, too, or at least hominids; theoretically they could have evolved into full sapients here. So all that means the unbelievably powerful aliens were in our solar system within the last couple of million years."

"What of it?" Blair said, visions of Nobel Prizes all but dancing in his eyes.

Marc saw the point first. "Chris, old bean, how recently would the . . . oh, call them the Lords of Creation . . . have had to bring people here for this language to be recognizably Indo-European? What's the possible time frame?"

Blair's scholarly ecstasy faded. "Oh . . . difficult to tell . . . offhand I can't say if it's related to any known daughter language . . . if it is, quite recently, a few thousand years. If it's not, then possibly as much as six thousand years, or perhaps a spot more or less, depending on how you date the period of Proto-Indo-European linguistic unity."

"*Weh*," Marc said. "Which means *aliens* have been visiting Earth within *historic* times. And grabbing people from the Volga steppes and dumping them here."

"Does this alarm you, old chap?"

"'Cause if it don't, it should," Cynthia cut in. "Because it means they're not some ancient millions-of-years-ago thang. It means they could come back *tomorrow* for all we know, and find us camping out in their zoo, prodding the exhibits with sticks and doing barbeques. And hey, we're exhibits here, too—does that give you a clue about our status with the Man?"

Teesa came running back along the line of her tribesfolk. "What is the matter?" she called to Marc in English—with a distinct Cajun accent, he noticed again. "Is there some danger?"

Weh, *there is, here*, he thought. Cynthia shot him a warning look. *And* weh, *yes, I realize we have to be cautious. That Cave of the Mysteries you've got, it's one scary place!* Aloud, he explained, "My companion is happy because he has found new knowledge. He is..." Marc searched his new tongue for a word. "He is a loremaster, a *scholar*; we Sky People would say. And he has found that your Cloud Mountain tongue is kin to ours."

"Really?" she said, obviously interested. "Languages have kinfolk?"

Just then Tahyo decided the stranger was too close to the boss and growled at her. "Friend!" Marc said sharply, and grabbed him by the ruff, shaking him sharply. "Let him sniff your hand," he went on, poised to grab.

She did, fearlessly, which made him sweat a little. Having the bearer of the Mystery's hand taken off at the wrist didn't bear thinking about. The animal put his quivering black nostrils to her slim fingers, then looked questioningly up at Marc. He supposed she and the Cloud Mountain People all smelled a little different from Terrans.

"Friend!" he said firmly.

Tahyo sniffed the hand again, then did the same with Zore. His *it's-a-puppy!* reflex cut in, and he made the play-gesture. The two dashed off, Zore squealing with glee. Marc hoped sincerely that the greatwolf wouldn't decide that the tame fluff-tail looked too appetizing.

"How do you make a greatwolf obey you?" Teesa asked. "That is a strong magic."

"It's no magic. I rescued him when his mother was drowned in a flood, and fed him and disciplined him as his mother and her pack-mates would have done. So to him, I *am* his mother and his father and the leader of his pack . . . his clan, his tribe."

Teesa frowned. "That *is* a strong magic," she said. "So . . . could you do that with any animal? With the great chieftain-lizards? The *raka-ewhin*."

Marc shook his head. Blair's ears pricked up as she dropped a Cloud Mountain word into her English. The term for "chieftain" was "raka," and for lizard "ewhin."

"No. They're too stupid, and they don't live with their parents. And they're too big. What I was speaking of works best with . . ."

Marc paused. There wasn't any way to say "mammal" in the Cloud Mountain tongue—

Wait a minute. There is.

"—with animals-of-fur."

The Cloud Mountain woman nodded. "Do your people uummm—"

A faraway look came over her face; Marc suspected it was the same one he wore when he was consulting his new language for something unfamiliar.

"Do your people, ummm, *tame* many animals so?" She wrinkled her nose and laughed. "Like Zore and her fluff-tail. Or like the pigs and fowl we keep around our settlements?"

Marc chuckled with her. "Perhaps it started that way, very long ago. But yes, we raise dogs, which are like greatwolves, but smaller—"

"Good!" she said. "That Tahyo of yours, he will be *very* large!"

Marc nodded; something the size of a small lion didn't have to be malicious to do damage, just startled or angry for a moment, and he worried about that.

"—and we use them to guard, and hunt with us. And *churr*, we ride on their backs and make them carry loads for us. Tharg too, to pull loads, and of course we eat them."

"You don't have to hunt them?" Teesa said. "They just stand there and let you kill them?"

"Well . . . we keep the *tharg* in fenced enclosures, and take one out when we need it."

"And riding on the backs of *churr*!" Teesa marveled, her turquoise eyes sparkling. "I would give much to see that! I would like to *do* that. It would be like . . . like being a bird! If folk could ride so, they could hunt so much better, and they could carry their kills further . . . and different clans could trade with each other so much more easily . . . and many, many other things they could do . . . that would be a great thing!"

Weh, *that settles that; she's sharp as a tack.*

"Perhaps you can show me, when we've driven out the beast-men and taken back the Cave of the Mysteries," she said happily. "The very Gods have sent you to help us!"

Cynthia and Blair turned and glared at him. Marc winced.

CHAPTER TEN

Encyclopedia Britannica, 16th Edition
University of Chicago Press, 1988

TOURISM: The first paying tourist flight to Earth orbit took place in 1981, when four passengers paid two hundred and fifty thousand dollars each to spend three days at America's von Braun Station. Curiously, the next flight was from Baikonur, as the EastBloc offered discounted tickets to help with their ongoing foreign-exchange problems . . .

Jadviga Binkis shivered as she stumbled along. The filthy village of the subhumans was terrifying as they straggled up through the little valley towards the cave-pierced cliff, with the stench of excrement and sweat and rotting meat and badly cured leather, and the human skulls and bones fixed over the doorways of the stone huts. The females and young clamored about the warrior-hunters as they returned, screeching, grunting, and howling in a demon chorus that stunned her ears. Some—probably those whose mates had not returned—made little rushes towards her, black-nailed hands outreached. The males beat them off, with fists and kicks and blows from the shafts of spears—one gray-haired female fell senseless with her split scalp pouring blood.

The gray-haired, one-eyed elder male who seemed to be senior among the Neanderthals grunted and gestured. Franziskus replied in the same manner, and her scalp crawled to see the casual fluency he used. Then he waved towards a hut larger than the others; it was enclosed with a head-high palisade of shamboo, and the surroundings had been swept clean. The elder and her husband led the way in under the shade of a veranda. The Neanderthal crouched on his hams; Franziskus sat in a chair of shamboo and hides, and indicated another for Jadviga. She sat in it, clenching her hands on the rests.

A young Neanderthaler female came at a clap of Franziskus' hands and set out wooden cups of clean water and a jug made from a section of shamboo. Then she took the man's weapons and scuttled away with them into the hut. Jadviga drank thirstily and poured herself more.

"Franziskus . . . ," she said in their native language. "What . . . what is going on?"

The familiar face turned towards her. He was in good condition—his skin was glossy with health, and his naked torso had more muscle on it than his usual lanky thinness. Yet his face looked . . . *was* . . . a death-mask carved out of lard, and it turned towards her like a turret.

"Security precautions are taken," he said. "Disturbances have required the expenditure of energy. Levels of awareness have been updated with data stream."

Then, for an instant, something flickered in the gray eyes, a hint of life, and a living man's inflection returned to his voice. "*It* is waking up."

"What is waking up?"

Franziskus went blank again. "Primary subroutines have been reactivated prematurely. Maintenance is overdue. Protocols have been violated. Corrective measures are required."

"What do you *mean*?" she shouted, then sank back, appalled.

The dead eyes looked at her, then blinked. "Semantic efficiency is insufficient. Receptor memetic-nets encountered are paradigmatically inadequate for metastochis. Low-level subroutines are incapable of sufficient discrimination to avoid undesirable contacts due to this contamination. Decision trees must be consulted. Primary subroutines may require contact with the primary species. Information has been transmitted."

Oh, my Franziskus, what have they done to you? What has reached out of the Forbidden Zone to touch you, as it touched our machines?

Minutes crawled by, and the dead eyes watched her. At precise intervals they would blink, as if some program was keeping the surfaces of the eyes moist according to a timetable. At last the old Neanderthal grunted something; Franziskus answered with two sweeping motions of his hands and what sounded like a dog barking. The one-eyed one went outside and began calling to the others. Franziskus resumed the eerie stare.

"Come," he said abruptly, rising. "You are the pair of the dyadic unit. Your presence will increase unit functionality. Genetic algorithms must be accommodated in this scenario." A pause. "And you may have valuable data. Interface is inadequate. Holographic data storage has deteriorated as the unit is neurally stressed."

He seized her by the arm and pushed her through into the long, dim interior of the hut. Her eyes took in a neat shamboo bedstead, racks, bits and pieces of equipment from the *Riga*. And against the far wall . . .

"*Kad tave zheme prarytu*," she whispered. "Let the earth swallow them indeed! The fools sent it! They really sent it!"

For a moment Franziskus was her man again. "Yes, they did. Velnio Ishpera—devil's spawn that they are. But—" His face crumpled. "I don't know what *it* will do with this. Help me, Jadviga! Help me!"

"Pretty," Cynthia said, a bit grudgingly.

Marc suspected that she was getting annoyed by children daring one another to rub at her arms and legs to see if the color came off; the third time, she made a horrible face and growled, and the toddler sat down abruptly, began to bawl, and then ran off screaming for its mother. Apart from that, the Cloud Mountain brats were fairly mannerly. The mother in question scooped her two-year-old up and gave it one smart slap on the bare fundament.

The settlement on its bare hilltop was obviously temporary, but equally obviously put together with care and skill. A small river dropped over a steep cuesta a quarter-mile to the eastward; the pool at the base was reserved for drawing drinking water, and all the residents washed daily downstream of that. Butchering and anything else smelly took place downwind and downslope, so the flies weren't too bad—and the wind of the uplands kept many others at bay. The huts were made of saplings bent into U-shapes with each end in the ground, and covered by woven mats of green reeds. Those had been trimmed into attractive patterns, and the cooking area in front of each had a neat hearth of stones and a bare area kept swept of rubbish.

The Cloud Mountain folk had put up two for the newcomers, one for Blair and Cynthia and one for Marc and Tahyo. Tahyo found that thoroughly satisfactory; he had a strong territorial instinct. Marc was a little less enthusiastic, and not only because the greatwolf snored and twitched in his sleep and had a tendency to flatulence, but such was life.

"Okay, we've got to take stock," Marc said abruptly, putting down his wooden cup of herbal tea. "We've got two jobs here: We've got to find out what the hell's going on with the, ah—"

"Alien artifacts," Cynthia said helpfully, leaning on Blair's shoulder.

"*Weh*. And then we've got to get home to tell the base."

Blair poked at the low embers of the fire; local custom was to not let those go out, though it was a clear day and comfortable even here in the uplands.

"Or, I suppose, we could simply go home with what we know, and let the proper authorities handle it," he said with a trace of reluctance in his voice.

Marc snorted. "Heck, Chris, you don't believe that. First, we can't get home unless these folks help us. Want to try walking five thousand miles with just the three of us?"

"I must admit, even Burton and Speke would have a problem with that."

Marc nodded. "And the Cloud Mountain People are not going to help us unless we help them. They're in too much of a fix to do that even if they felt like it. Second, none of us could live with ourselves if we just bugged out."

Blair shrugged. "Well, there is that, I suppose, but the issue had to be raised."

"Okay," Cynthia said. "Let's tally our assets and theirs. The Wergu have hundreds of warriors, and forty or so assault rifles. Plus there's something very goddamn strange about friend Binkis."

"Something which is the alien artifact at work, and which means he can shoot to ten-tenths of his weapon's capacity," Blair said thoughtfully. "*We* have one rifle, twenty rounds, one shotgun, eighteen rounds, and our pistols, with one spare magazine each—twenty-eight rounds. And however many there are of the Cloud Mountain People, which I assume is less than the Neanderthals. And that's assuming they all continue to like us, which is a bit optimistic."

"Oh, we've got something more than that," Marc said, grinning.

"There's our matchless knowledge and skills," Cynthia observed dryly. "We're Earth's elite, after all."

"*Weh*, but besides that, one bit of our equipment seems to have survived. The Ice gear."

"And just how do you expect to use that without the trank gun and capture kit?" Cynthia asked.

"I don't know. But I'm thinking hard on it."

Half the encampment was grouped around the impromptu bowyers' shop the Terrans had made of a spare hut, squatting and pointing and occasionally commenting. The matting of the hut had been rolled up to let in light and the mild, sweet upland air. From outside came a cheerful brabble of voices, children at play, and the smell of the noonday meal cooking. The sky was nearly blue, with only a trace of the usual high, white haze, though clouds hid the snow-peak heights on the southern horizon.

"You come from three different tribes, then? You and your friends?" Teesa asked.

"Not exactly," Marc replied, lashing the riser of the bow into the clamp and adding weights to the basket attached to the center of the string. "Cynthia and I are of the same tribe—"

"You don't look much alike," Teesa pointed out. "Here, mostly people from the same tribe look alike. You look like the coast-town people. Blair looks a little like us, his hair and the color of his eyes, but not really—the eyes are the wrong shape and his skin is that funny pink color where he isn't sun-browned, and his nose is so big, like yours. And I've never even heard of any tribe that looks like his woman."

"Ah . . ."

How to encapsulate United States history?

"Our American tribe is made up of people whose ancestors came from many lands. Blair comes from a kindred tribe allied to ours—they speak the same language and many of our people came from his tribe's territory in past times."

"Our tribe adopts outsiders, too, sometimes," Teesa said. "True-men, of course."

Marc nodded, and adjusted the improvised tillering device—it was basically a frame with an adjustable weight, to test that a bow's limbs were of the right resistance and evenly stressed.

"So, tell me of your mother and sire," Teesa went on.

Marc chuckled. "Only if you tell me of yours," he said.

"I know little of them. My sire died while I was in the womb, and my mother when Zore was born."

"Mine—," Marc began. A good deal of conversation later he went on: "*Mais,* this looks good," and took the bow out of the frame.

A couple of dozen Cloud Mountain warriors squatted on their heels around him. They watched with interest as Teesa took the weapon. It was her own height, five-nine, and he'd adjusted the draw to seventy pounds, using his own longbow as a template. The riser-handle was a hard, glossy, local wood he couldn't identify, yellow-brown with black stripes in the grain; the tribe was used to working it, and they'd done so astonishingly fast with only stone tools. The limbs were nicely tapered shoots of second-year sham-boo from a wild stand that had died out at that stage, and they'd required very little working. At each end was a cap of notched antler to hold the string.

None of it had been very difficult. Blair and Cynthia were running their own classes, and the locals were already highly skilled woodworkers with access to first-rate materials.

Marc smiled to himself. Chris was still trying to figure out why the Cloud Mountain People didn't have the bow already; it was a Mesolithic invention, long pre-dating the Proto-Indo-European period. He was also already writing up his notes on the language, using sections of smooth bark for paper and a quill pen with homemade ink. Some of the tribesfolk were interested in that, too—particularly the shamaness-midwife-herb-doctor ones, who had a system of pictographs used as mnemonic aids. It wasn't anything like a writing system, but they'd grasped the concept and seemed quite taken with it.

The warriors had focused like gimlets on the bow-making. Marc suspected every male in the tribe would have a longbow in a couple of months, and a lot of the women, too. It took a long time to train an archer from scratch, but these folk were already all strong and highly skilled with throwing spears and blowguns; they'd learn quickly.

Or at least most of them would. Taldi stood with folded arms, sneering.

"What need have Cloud Mountain warriors of such a new-thing?" he asked, his lip curling slightly. "Perhaps it is cursed. He consorts with a greatwolf—perhaps he is a creature of the Father of Greatwolves. For that One is no friend to our folk; his wrath bears a deadly curse."

Some of the watchers snorted or laughed; evidently Taldi's obsession was well known. Some looked slightly frightened, and a few thoroughly so. Teesa frowned, obviously troubled.

"He is challenging you," she said, leaning close and speaking English. "I cannot forbid him—but that means he accepts you as a warrior worthy of challenge."

Blair looked at him from the corners of his eyes. "Can I be of any help?"

"No!" Teesa said. "Such challenge must be met by each man alone, with weapons or hand-to-hand, between the trees—on the field of the warriors."

"A man's gotta do what a man's gotta do," Marc said, mouth slightly dry at the suddenness of it.

Then he remembered: *He would* like *to share her hearth. The dude's jealous, even though he's got nothing to be jealous about.* Mais, *nothing much, yet.*

Marc straightened up and handed the bow to Teesa with a slight bow. She smiled at him, plainly confident, the turquoise eyes calm. That heartened him for some reason, and there was a small smile on his mouth as he turned to Taldi.

"You are a fool, and a liar," he said in the Cloud Mountain language. "You want this woman, and you fear to lose her, so you close your mind to truth, and do harm to your own tribe and clan, lying as to the real reason for your challenge."

Taldi's face went pale under its natural umber color. Folk scattered as he turned and walked towards the Terran, then drew the stone-headed hatchet and threw it into the ground at Marc's feet. It struck with a hard, dry *thunk* in the packed soil and stood with the polished handle quivering.

"At dawn!" Taldi said, and stalked away.

Dawn was clear and mild as the sun rose to their west. The tribesfolk woke with the sun anyway; this morning they were up even earlier. Some went chattering and eager to the field of short, dense turf spotted with evergreen oaks. More were grave and subdued, for while a fight wasn't something very unusual, it wasn't common, either—and this was against one of the probably magical visitors, and those under the protection of the Guardian of the Mysteries. *She* was there when the earliest spectators arrived, burning a small fire of sweet-smelling herbs and chanting.

Taldi got a fair share of scowls and covertly hostile gestures as he stood with his arms crossed, black and red chevrons painted over his cheekbones and his long golden hair clubbed back in a fighting braid. A core of friends stood by him, leaning on their spears and scowling back at the critics.

Marc ignored him as he walked out and began some stretches. A flight of long-tailed scarlet birds soared up from one tree as the three Terrans approached, screeching and hooting. The hot yellow sunlight flared on their crimson feathers and a tumble of trumpet-shaped blue flowers below. Marc eyed the bees buzzing around those with wariness—the last thing he needed now was a stinger in the butt, and Venusian bees were the size of your thumb and made the African variety look like harmless butterflies.

The more so as he'd decided on Teesa's advice to wear Cloud Mountain costume of breechclout and short, soft moccasins. It made him feel hideously conspicuous, though fortunately he wasn't as parti-colored as Blair would have been, not being so pink by nature and taking the sun fairly quickly.

The Englishman held out his field belt; Marc drew the machete in his right hand and bowie in his left.

"Do I have to kill him?" he said to Teesa.

She blinked in surprise. "Don't you want to? He wants to kill *you*."

Marc's mouth crooked slightly. "Do you want me to kill him?"

"Well . . ." She hesitated. "No. He is my mate's brother and he has been a good friend to me, a good hunter, and a good warrior for our folk. If only he were not so foolish."

"Does the law say that I must kill?" Marc asked.

"No—we are not so many that we can afford to lose strong men often. The law is that one or the other must die, or flee, or surrender, or be too badly wounded to fight," she said. "But Taldi will not surrender—and he is a fine fighter, brave and strong and quick. He will fight to kill, and will take no mercy from you."

"*Weh*, we'll see," Marc said.

Cynthia's breath hissed out as the Cloud Mountain man drew his obsidian knife and flint hatchet, crouching slightly with his left foot forward. She drew her pistol and quietly thumbed off the safety. Marc met Blair's eyes and nodded very slightly; if he lost, they might suddenly find themselves fighting their way out of a hostile settlement.

And I'd be dead, he thought. *This guy doesn't look like he's in a winning-on-points mood.*

Taldi was two inches taller than the Terran, and built of whipcord and gristle. He looked to be about Marc's age, which meant he'd managed to grow to manhood in this place of savage half-men and even more savage beasts; the scars on his arms and chest and face told the story of it. And the way he moved, light on his feet, watching his opponent's eyes, not his hands.

On the other hand, Marc thought grimly, as he drew his knife and machete. Ten million people had tried out for the slot he'd won. *So I'm the product of a rigorous selective process, too*, non?

Taldi's lips spread from white, even teeth in a carnivore grin as he circled and Marc turned on one heel to face him. The triangular blade of the volcanic glass knife moved in a small, precise circle, the edges sharper than a razor, sharper than a surgeon's scalpel. The tomahawk's business end was thicker, a rectangle of polished flint lashed into the end of a yard-long handle. From the way it twitched back and forth, the tribesman knew exactly what to do with them. He waited until the sun was in the Terran's eyes before he sprang.

Gotcha! Marc thought, watching for the tensing that came before motion, watching through carefully slitted eyes.

He swayed left. You didn't have to see every detail to know when a man was going to jump you. Taldi's ferocious swipe with his hatchet made an ugly wind six inches before Marc's face, but the Cloud Mountain warrior recovered with supple ease. It still left him vulnerable, and the obsidian knife shattered as he used it to block a swipe of Marc's machete, with a sharp *crack* and a spray of fragments.

The crowd roared and swayed as Taldi leaped back in a panther bound; Tahyo was *wulfing* hysterically and lunging against the stout rope that bound him to the tree. Marc grinned and tossed his own bowie aside, thankful that the weather was warm—not all the sweat on his face was from exertion or heat. That stone had come *far* too close to taking off his nose.

There was a murmur from the spectators at the gesture of renunciation; a Cloud Mountain woman's voice cried out, "He is a warrior!"

He thought Cynthia chimed in, too—something on the order of "He's an idiot!"

Focus made the noise a distant murmur, shrank the world to a pair of blazing blue eyes. Taldi had been startled at the blow that broke his knife, but he wasn't in the least daunted by the machete's two feet of sharp steel. Marc could see his eyes narrow; that brief exchange had also given him an idea of the Terran's speed.

And I got some idea of his, and I don't like it, me. This guy's made out of springs.

The men circled again, slightly crouched, their feet scuffing in the dirt and grass. Now that neither had a knife, Taldi spun the tomahawk from one hand to another and back again in a quick blurring snap. It was showy . . . but it also made the sudden backhand chop at Marc's temple frighteningly unpredictable. He turned it with a wrench and a sweep of the machete, and flint struck sparks from steel, a flat, unmusical *kwranggg!* of sound. Blows went back and forth with blurring speed; steel sparked on flint again, cracked on hard wood. When they backed off and circled once more, blood trickled down Taldi's chest from a shallow slash, and a raw red graze showed on Marc's left cheek.

He lunged, and Taldi parried. The blade of the machete struck the fire-hardened wood of the tomahawk shaft and slid over the bone rings that covered it, with a tooth-jarring vibration. Taldi punched at the Terran's face and Marc twisted his head to let the fist go by; then each grabbed at the other's weapon-wrist, and the men pushed chest-to-chest, straining against each other as their feet churned at the dirt. There was no subtlety or skill to this; it was raw strength against strength, like two rutting stags in season.

Taldi grinned in triumph; they had similar builds, but he was three inches taller than the stranger, and thicker through the arms and shoulders. Marc smiled back and gripped until wrist bone creaked beneath it and *pushed.* The tribesman's blue eyes went wide as he felt the strength in his opponent's limbs—muscles bred on a world that pulled more heavily than this, and a body selected from millions. Slowly, slowly, Taldi's own arms bent back in the iron grip.

Christ, this fucker's strong, Marc thought, as the breath wheezed between his clenched teeth. *But I'm stronger.*

Back and back the tribesman's arms twisted. Then suddenly he threw himself back and whipped a knee up at Marc's groin. The Terran twisted to catch it on the point of his hip; that was painful enough to make the breath hiss out between his teeth, but it brought a yelp of pain from Taldi as well. Another flurry of movement and they broke apart and faced each other panting, their bare torsos gleaming with sweat and blood; the tomahawk lay on the ground, and the machete still rested in Marc's right fist.

"Yield!" he called. "You fought well, Taldi of the Badger totem, but you're beaten. I don't want your life. Yield!"

Voices from the crowd joined the call; evidently they'd been impressed. Taldi looked around with a desperate, hunted expression.

"Kill me!" he said to Marc.

"Why should I kill you?" the Terran replied.

He looked aside; there was a young live oak not far away, perhaps ten yards. He flicked the machete across his body and to the right; it turned once as it flew, the honed edge glinting in the morning sun, then sank into the wood with a heavy *thunk* and a malignant humm as the blade quivered for a few seconds. A flight of small yellow birds burst out of the branches, cheeping and weaving in and out in a mass of avian panic.

Taldi blinked, then screamed, "You scorn me!"

Marc shrugged and made a beckoning gesture with both hands. He wasn't surprised when the other man gave an incoherent shriek and leaped to attack once more. Instead Marc grabbed an outstretched arm, locked it, turned, and bent and twisted. Momentum turned into flight, and the Cloud Mountain warrior crashed down flat on his face. He had grit; his nose was streaming blood and his eyes were glazed, but he pulled himself to his feet and began to stagger forward.

"*Co faire te en colaire?*" Marc said in exasperation; it was what his father had said to him when he threw a tantrum as a youngster. "Why you getting angry, eh? I'm *trying* not to kill you!"

Taldi wound up for another haymaker. It was a clumsy blow. Marc wasn't surprised at that, either—apart from the way the man was battered to reeling incoherence, in his experience Venusian tribesmen were deadly with weapons. Outside Kartahown they hadn't developed much of a martial arts orientation yet.

Marc's own left blocked the punch, sweeping a knife hand to the inside of Taldi's forearm. In the same motion Marc drove an extended knuckle into the soft spot of the solar plexus just under the breastbone, into the inevitable gap in the steely muscle that sheathed the other man's stomach.

All the air went out of Taldi in a single agonized *ooofff*. The involuntary downward motion of his face met the Terran's swift uppercut with a crunch of snapping cartilage as his nose flattened—Marc took the sharp pain in his knuckles rather than risk shattering the tribesman's jaw or smashing in his facial bones with a knee strike.

Taldi collapsed, curling up like a shrimp and struggling to get air into his paralyzed lungs. Marc picked up the man's own hatchet, stepped forward, and ceremoniously, lightly, touched the edge to his fallen opponent's neck. Then Marc stood and tossed it aside once more.

When he straightened, Blair and Cynthia were looking *very* relieved. Marc nodded to them, then gravely to Teesa's beaming countenance, and waved to the cheering spectators as he walked back to his comrades. Even the clump who'd been yelling for Taldi looked impressed, and a few of them nodded soberly in his direction. Tahyo tried to lick Marc's grazes and minor cuts when he walked into range, flattening his ears and looking aggrieved when told *down;* after all, he'd only been trying to help.

"Water," Marc croaked, and drank deep, coughed, drank more.

It tasted delicious despite being lukewarm and having a strong mineral tang, but it stung when some ran out of his mouth and into a shallow cut over his collarbone he hadn't even noticed. His hand started to shake as he remembered the flint whipping by the end of his nose, and how easily his hacked body could be out there right now, twitching . . . or possibly screaming for his mother and waiting hoping to die quickly.

But I didn't lose, he thought. *Phew!*

Teesa came up. "You fought very well," she said seriously, and handed him a gourd with a glossy green-and-white skin.

"Better than him," Marc said, laughing, and she gave a sudden brilliant grin and a nod.

"And very . . . very *cleverly*. I saw how you led Taldi on. That took both skill and courage."

Marc took the container and put it to his mouth. The smell told him it wasn't water: some sort of berry wine, acrid but not unpleasant, and with a kick like a cotton-field mule. It helped relax the knots in his gut and back. He'd never wanted to be any sort of a soldier, but fighting now and then was part of exploring Venus. Having Teesa beam at him wasn't hard to endure, either . . . and oddly, it made him feel better to know she liked him the more for *not* killing Taldi.

"Thanks," he said a bit hoarsely.

Then he looked over to where the fallen man's friends were

tending to him—mostly by pouring water on him. He coughed, choked, and then sat up with one helping him and holding a cup to his mouth. He looked worse than he probably was, although his nose wouldn't be the same again, and it was pouring blood down the lower half of his face and beginning to swell and turn purple. One of his companions held a swatch of some fiber—like an enormous cotton boll—to it, and Taldi came out of his daze with a start as it touched the tender flesh. He grabbed it and then held it to the injury himself, with a tender, tentative dabbing motion.

In a story I'd go over and shake hands and we'd be friends, or he'd be a faithful Tonto type, but I don't think that's in the cards, Marc thought. *Look at that glare!*

"You have made an unforgiving enemy," Teesa said, as Taldi came to his feet and was led stumbling towards his hut.

"Better that than he makes me an unmoving corpse," Marc replied, in her language—it sounded funnier that way, and Teesa gave him another of those wide white grins.

"But you have won respect from most," she said. "You were feared for your magic, but now you have shown you are a strong fighter . . . and a merciful one."

"Hey, let us in on it, man," Cynthia said sharply.

"According to Teesa, we've gone up in the eyes of the locals," Marc said.

She muttered something; he thought it was, "One of them, at least."

CHAPTER ELEVEN

Encyclopedia Britannica, 16th Edition
University of Chicago Press, 1988

SCIENCE FICTION

A literary genre developed principally in the twentieth century, dealing with scientific discovery or development, often set on other worlds . . .

. . . a great boom in the popularity of science fiction following World War II however, coupled with the public realization that many, in fact most, of the spectacular advances of modern science had long been anticipated by intelligent writers of science fiction, led to a gradual reappraisal of its status. This trend was greatly accelerated by the discoveries of the late 1950s and early 1960s which confirmed many of what had previous been regarded as the most lurid and improbable predictions: life on other worlds and human cultures on Mars and Venus. In the 1970s, proof followed of a multitude of Earth-like worlds orbiting nearby stars. By the 1980s, science fiction's status as the characteristic and dominant form of twentieth-century prose fiction has been widely accepted, arousing considerable resentment in some literary circles marginalized by this development; the petition drive against the assignment of what they called "pulp trash" as the basis of university English courses earned Norman Mailer and Truman Capote a brief reprise of their former fame . . .

Teesa took up her bow and strung it with an ease that still surprised Marc; it had only been a couple of weeks since the first time she touched one. Marc laid aside his improvised bowyer's tools and walked out of the hut, ducking his head under the rolled-up matting of its sides.

"Getting diplomatic again, eh?" Cynthia said, winking at him as she ran several of the locals through the art of trimming feathers to fletch arrows. "Going to do some more *negotiations*?"

"I am above your coarse suspicions," Marc said loftily.

He ignored her snicker. His ears *did* flush when she added:

"You're wearing a *breechclout*, man—everything shows. It's a certainty, not a suspicion."

The Cloud Mountain People learned quickly. Teesa waited; she already had a bracer for her left arm, a shooting glove on her right, and a tube of boiled hide slung over her back as a quiver. Leatherworking was another skill with which the Cloud Mountain People had no problems. The quiver even had an attractive decorative pattern of looping and running tendrils tooled into the surface. The arrows were a dense, hard, pale wood like ash, neatly fletched with colorful feathers and with beautifully worked triangular obsidian heads—and several of them were dipped in the deadly spider venom.

"Let us go and practice more!" she said eagerly. "This is a great thing!"

The warriors watching solemnly dipped their heads in the tribe's gesture for *yes;* some of them made a palm-down sweeping motion, one they used for emphasis. Most of them had their own bows now, and a few had *made* their own. He got the impression that the sort of concentrated effort they'd been putting in wasn't normal for them. They weren't farmers; hunting peoples usually worked in bursts, separated by long periods of ritual, song, storytelling, fooling around with things they did for fun, or just plain loafing. But for this, they were willing to work their asses off.

And not just for this. A little way off, a circle of them were watching Christopher Blair give a little lesson in unarmed combat. A young man went flying with a yell and thumped down on the mats of the improvised open-air dojo. Hoots and laughter followed, and Blair took his pupil-victim through the move more slowly. Somewhat to Marc's surprise, he'd turned out to be a good teacher, patient and cheerful . . . at least with the Cloud Mountain folk.

Makes you wonder . . . where has the sour, arrogant Blair of old gone? he thought. *Maybe it's love.*

Tahyo jumped up eagerly and followed them, tail wagging. *I could swear he's gotten a third bigger in the month we've been here,* Marc thought, thumping the broad head. A little of the gangly skinniness had left the animal, and his neck and shoulders were beginning to develop bands of muscle and the first faint bristle of the adult mane. The greatwolf's tongue lolled over his terrible steak knife teeth as he grinned up at Marc. A pat from Teesa was accepted with equanimity. Tahyo was still young enough to have that *but-of-course-everyone-loves-me* puppy/cub reflex, since he was designed to grow up in a pack's warm bath of affection.

"You have given my people more than this," she said, holding up the bow for an instant.

"What, then?" Marc answered in her own language.

"You have given us hope," she said gravely. "Now we will not lose the memory of our holy places, our long home."

The long, sloping meadow this camp of the Cloud Mountain folk used for target practice was littered with big basalt rocks, the occasional low-growing tree, and patches of brush. That was deliberate; they wanted training to be as realistic as possible. Marc heartily approved. Nice, round bull's-eye targets were seldom edible, and in his experience never attacked with intent to kill and/or eat you. Instead, they used wood or wicker outlines of probable targets—antelope, a saber-tooth, several different varieties of small-to-medium-sized 'saurs, and a startlingly realistic Neanderthal, which he'd thought for one queasy-making moment was a real one, stuffed. Teesa put an arrow to the string of her bow.

"Like this," Marc said, standing behind her, even though it was no longer strictly necessary to correct her stance. "Draw. . . ."

Halfway through the second hour she shook out her right arm, flexing the shoulder. "I had better stop now. Any more and I would be learning bad habits. I will not become skilled in one day."

Marc nodded soberly, his respect for her wits going up a notch. She walked downslope, towards the river and the woods; he followed, and Tahyo cast back and forth as he trotted ahead of them. The Terran envied the greatwolf. To him, things were as they were; as long as he had Marc and enough to eat he took each moment as it came, letting the past vanish and looking forward to an interesting smell or sight.

"Let us go walk in the meadows by the river," she went on.

Not that there aren't interesting sights around here, he thought, watching Teesa's swaying walk, which the local garb showed off to best advantage.

"Down, boy," he muttered to himself, watching the shapely muscles clench and unclench. "It's not enough you're stranded thousands of miles from home, and that you've just discovered the most dangerous secret in the history of the human race, but you want to get into *that* sort of trouble, eh?"

Worse, when Teesa threw a smile at him over her shoulder, he had an uneasy sense that she knew exactly where his gaze had been directed.

"So," he said, trying to change the—unstated—subject, "the Wergu took the Cave of the Mysteries away from your folk?"

"In my mother's time." She nodded, serious again. "They came from the south, from the high mountains; no one knows why. Many and many of them"—she made a gesture of opening and closing both hands—"beyond counting, fierce and full of hate for all truemen. They took the sacred valley and the caves where we had dwelt from time out of mind, and the places roundabout where the other clans of our people lived. Many of us were killed: my mother's mate, my sire, and many-many. Since then we have dwindled; those were good lands, easy to protect from the animals-of-scale-and-feather—"

'Saurs, he translated mentally.

"—and with good soil for gardens, and many other things." She touched the necklace of gold nuggets on her bosom. "And there was the heavy metal, which we traded to the coast dwellers for many things, bronze tools and weapons. Above all, there we could do the proper rites that made our Ancestor Spirits strong to protect us and brought the favor of the Gods. There we had much time for making things that were beautiful and useful, or pleasing to the Gods, and for rituals and song."

Her face lit as she described it . . . described, he realized, as a lost paradise she'd never seen herself. Then she sighed sadly.

"Since then we are becoming mere rude hunters, like the high-landers or the tribes to the east."

Marc nodded gravely. *Looks like Blair was right*, he thought. *High-level hunter-gatherer, pretty well sedentary already, and just beginning to hit the Neolithic, on the fringe of civilization.*

That was hard for humans here, with ten-ton critters to keep off the crops. It was probably no accident that the only civilization this planet had produced so far had arisen on the northern coast of the northernmost continent. Whatever they'd been like back on Earth— and the paleontologists were still arguing about that—the biggest 'saurs here weren't endothermic, warm-blooded. The smaller varieties with feathers *were* warm-blooded, hideously active all year round, and an infernal nuisance, but the titanosaurs and other massive types mostly stayed south of the mountains or migrated in through the passes only in summertime, which kept down the numbers of elephant-sized predators following them. That seasonal presence was bad enough, together with the hordes of meat-eating flying things that the thicker air and lighter gravity made possibe.

I've thought before that this planet isn't really suited to human beings, Marc mused. *But then, if we're right, it really isn't. It's a zoo.*

He didn't really like thinking about that. It gave him a sick, cold feeling in the pit of his stomach. They'd come to Venus—Mars, too—as explorers at the cutting edge of the human story. When he considered what the world would be like if Cynthia's theory was true . . . well, it was a lot less glamorous to be someone who'd just paddled his dugout canoe into Manhattan and was getting the first chill realization that the skyscrapers weren't natural.

With an effort, he pushed the musings aside. Until the Terrans had more information, it just wasn't worth the effort to keep the mental wheels spinning pointlessly.

They came to the side of the river; it was a hill stream, about ten yards across, mostly fairly shallow above a bed of colorful egg-sized rocks, but with the odd deeper pool. They sat below a stretch of rapids—or a man-high waterfall—where willowlike trees and live oaks provided shade, but not so much that there was no breeze to keep the bugs down. Teesa put her arms around her knees and watched the falling water for a while; Marc leaned back on his elbow and watched her—or, when he felt too self-conscious doing that, watched Tahyo chasing dragonflies. Some of them were big enough to give him a bit of a fight, and made gruesome crunching and squishing sounds when he ate them, but they kept the other flying beasties down around here.

Mind you, watching them catch and eat small birds was sort of disturbing.

After a moment Teesa spoke: "I am made . . ."—she used a word that could mean *yearning* or *uneasy* depending on the context.

"Why?" he said quietly.

"For all our generations, we Cloud Mountain People tended our gardens, hunted, wrought tools and houses, raised our children, did honor to our ancestors and the Gods, and this we thought was as life would always be in the world of men."

His mind did a mental skip; the term meant *two-footed ones*. It was worse than thinking in a foreign language, more like having his concepts switched on him without warning.

"We were the greatest of all tribes, because we had the Diadem of the Eye and the Cave of the Mysteries. Even when the beastmen came and drove us away, we *knew* that if we could but take our heritage back, then all would be as it was."

She turned her head and looked at him. "But now you come, Marc, you and your Sky People, and suddenly all that we have and are . . . it seems so small. You tell me stories of worlds beyond the sky, and mysteries deeper than any of ours, and the knowledge I took with the Diadem of the Eye shows me that this is true—truer than perhaps I can grasp with the fingers of my self. If you go . . . if you go away, will this world of ours seem ever after small and dull and far away from the things that move the worlds? Like a small cave, after you came through with a torch."

Despite himself, Marc chuckled. She frowned and asked, "Why do you laugh: because we are so much less than you?"

He shook his head. "No! Because I tell you, this Diadem of the Eye, the Cave of the Mysteries . . . these are things that daunt *us*. They are beyond our ken and fill us with fear and wonder. And I was just thinking within myself how our pride is put down by that."

Teesa chuckled in her turn. "Yet from what you say—what the Night Face and her man say—these aren't really *ours*, the way we thought."

She made a whirling gesture with one hand. "And we ourselves, our first ancestors, were brought here from your world beyond the sky, your Earth, the blue star."

"By beings whose arts are as far beyond ours as ours beyond yours—further."

Her mouth had a rueful twist. "How? You too can travel between the lights-in-the-sky, you say."

Marc pointed northward. "From there, on the edge of the great salt water, this land looks high—like *that*."

Now his arm swung around to the south, where the fangs of mountains higher than Everest floated on the horizon, whiter than salt.

Teesa frowned. Her face had an odd innocence when she concentrated like that, and he had to restrain an impulse to reach out and smooth the lock of blond hair back from her brow with a hand. Slowly, she spoke:

"As a babe might think a toddler of three seasons and an adult much the same because both had learned to walk?"

"Very much," he said. "You are as wise as you are beautiful, Teesa of the Cloud Mountain folk."

She shook off her mood and smiled. "They have sweet-tongued men on the blue star, then, with words like the honey you find in an old tree."

He leaned closer. Some distant part of his mind was yammering about doctrine and consequences and a number of other things. The turquoise eyes came closer . . .

And she was past him. "We should swim!" she said, from the edge of the pool.

Two swift movements and she'd skinned out of the halter and taken the water in a clean running dive.

He followed suit—jumping into the water even faster than she had; the one real merit of the Cloud Mountain breechclout was that you could shed it quickly. He was grinning as he came up and saw her sleeking back her hair under the waterfall, looking at him out of the corners of her eyes. The white water foamed around her shoulders, and . . .

"Some things don't change between planets," he muttered.

That was a pose he'd seen more than once in a teenager's favorite recreational graphics. And very effective, when a woman wanted to get someone's motor racing and had a waterfall handy. Which hadn't actually happened to him in real life before, but there was a first time for everything. Their eyes met and they both laughed in mutual understanding.

"Mmmm," Teesa said, her head lying on his shoulder.

"Mmmm," Marc replied, grinning up at the hazy blue of the sky and pulling a stem of grass to chew on.

I suppose my pa would have smoked a cigarette, he thought. *Though it's not worth the way he died, him.*

"It has been many seasons," Teesa said sleepily. Then she laughed; he could feel her breath on the wet skin of his chest. "For you also—unless you are truly a *wirdvas.*"

That meant something like a male succubus known for insatiable appetite and stamina; he grinned harder at the compliment. Not far away, Tahyo was waiting with heavy patience, chin on the ground—and a rope leash tying him to a small tree. A curious cold, wet nose was *not* what you wanted applied to sensitive parts of your anatomy at some of life's more intense moments.

I guess she really *likes me,* Marc thought. *She didn't crack up when I jumped and yelled.*

Although he would have liked a blanket for the time spent on land. Even soft spring grass could get sort of prickly.

A voice broke through his reverie. Teesa looked up at him, puzzled, as he sprang up; then her face changed as she heard it, too. They sprang for clothes and weapons, scrambling to dress.

"The beastmen! The beastmen come!" Zore shrilled. "Quickly, quickly!"

Marc had never seen Teesa so shaken. She pulled the silvery circlet from her brow and turned to him, her turquoise eyes enormous in her amber face.

"Nothing!" she said, her voice low and rapid. "I cannot see . . . feel . . . there is *nothing*! It is as if the Diadem of the Eye has been—" She swallowed and dropped into English. *"Turned off."*

Marc cast his mind back to his last sight of Franziskus Binkis. "I think that may be just what's happened," he said. "But you have to act as if it hasn't, Teesa. You must, or your people will lose heart."

And we'll all die, he didn't add aloud. *Besides, I really do like these folk.*

The command group stood on the lip of the hill, with the hollow holding the village behind them. The land rolled northward, falling in a tumble of bare ridges and forested slopes. The nursing mothers, the pregnant, the children, and the old were already gone, running for the hiding spots in the hills that had been prepared against this chance—save for a few near-adolescents like Zore, ready to take messages. The fifty or sixty warriors were massed on the slope below. A thread of smoke stood tall in the sky behind him, signaling the other Cloud Mountain settlements that enemies were come.

Hopefully, they'd answer.

Teesa nodded crisply and put the Diadem of the Eye back around her brow; only Marc was close enough to hear the strain in her voice, or see the prickle of sweat that broke out on her brow. It must be shattering, to have the certainties of a lifetime disappear—as if a devout Catholic had suddenly lost faith in the Mass.

"Warriors!" she shouted. "Once again we face our ancient enemy. But this time we have strong friends, with new weapons!"

The Cloud Mountain warriors cheered. *Good men*, Marc thought—and that included the scattering of unwedded women. *They've been beaten before, but they're ready to try again.*

They shook weapons in the air as they shouted; many of those were their new shamboo longbows. Others drummed war spears on their shields, a harsh, booming sound through the sough of the wind and the cries of the birds that burst out of the trees around them.

Marc looked aside at his Terran counterparts. "What's wrong with this picture?" he asked.

"What did that old French dude say?" Cynthia replied.

"Old French dude?" Blair asked.

"Talleyrand." She cocked a thin, sardonic brow at her lover. "I *did* take history as well as paleontology, Chris."

"Sorry. Ah, when he was briefing his staff for the negotiations after Napoléon's fall. *And above all, gentlemen, no zeal.*"

"Yeah," Marc replied. "That was more or less what I had in mind. Now we've got them all hot *en colaire*, we've got to make 'em remember it's not how hard you fight, it's how smart you fight, that counts."

He glanced at the contorted faces, the feathered headbands, the patterned hide shields.

"We've got some work to do." He looked a question at Teesa, and she nodded. He raised his voice to address the tribesmen:

"Warriors of the Cloud Mountain People! You do not go to fight."

A puzzled buzz came from them. He continued, "You go to hunt beasts. Beasts that walk like men, but *are they not beasts?*"

"Beasts! Beasts!" the crowd screamed, drumming on their shields once more.

"Then we should not fight them as men do, honorably, face-to-face, but instead stalk them, like—"

"Beasts! Beasts! Death to the beastmen!"

Teesa stepped forward to take up the harangue. Blair raised an eyebrow at him, and Marc shrugged. Cynthia had the last word:

"Hey, it's a *damn* good thing you didn't stay home on Earth and go into politics!"

"The bewitched one is not with them," the scout said, pointing down the long open slope towards the forested river.

Teesa frowned and looked at Marc; he made a gesture—*later.* The man went on as Marc knelt and sketched in the dirt. "They come all together, up the valley here. The ones with the thunder-sticks come second, spread out, *so,* where the trees don't cramp them. The rest come first with club and spear."

"How many?" Teesa asked.

The man held out his hands and clenched and unclenched them twelve times, then one hand once: a hundred and twenty-five.

"Twice our numbers," she said. "And how many with the thunder-sticks?"

This time his fingers flexed once, and then he held out a hand with the thumb tucked away; fourteen.

"And we have four," she said. "Though thanks to our friends, we understand them better."

And "we" know how to clean them now, too, Marc thought, looking up for an instant into the hazy brightness of a Venusian morning. *It's amazing how fast crud builds up in this climate; the extra oxygen makes things rust faster.*

"Here's how we'll do it," he said confidently.

Mais, *I* would *come up with a scheme that leaves me in the front without a gun,* Marc thought sourly on the open grassy slope, feeling even more naked than he really was in the tribal breechclout. *Not a château general, me.*

He could smell his own sweat, rank and musky. *Well, no wonder. It's hot, and I'm terrified,* he thought. For some reason that made him chuckle a bit . . . silently.

A fluting cry came from downhill, an oddly musical hooting like nothing that had ever come from a human throat. From a tree ten paces over a Cloud Mountain warrior flashed him a grin. Marc responded in kind and reached over his shoulder for an arrow.

Carefully, he reminded himself as he set it on the string of the bow: The twenty-four in the quiver were all dipped in the black-spider venom. *Wouldn't want to nick your hand, eh? Glad they're good with leather here.* He had a stout antelope-hide glove on his left hand, where the arrowhead would rest close.

The Neanderthals seemed to have a fair grasp of what their new weapons could do. From the reports, they weren't even wasting ammunition by firing away on full-auto . . . though he suspected that Binkis, or whatever was running Binkis, simply hadn't shown them how to push the selector to that notch. They *did* realize that the weapons had about three times the effective range of a Cloud Mountain blowgun or four times that of a thrown spear, and that they'd go through a shield handily.

And they could shoot surprisingly well, considering how long they'd had the weapons.

So . . .

He was carrying his pistol, which wouldn't be much use unless things got uncomfortably close and personal, and his binoculars. Those he could use; he unlimbered them and scanned downslope. A face rose over a bush of greenish-yellow leaves . . .

Great shelf of bone above the eyes, huge, coarse blob of a nose, protruding mouth, chinless behind a sparse brush of reddish-brown beard . . . easy enough to see why the Cloud Mountain folk called them beastmen. The face was painted, streaks of black soot and red ochre, for some esoteric purpose or perhaps just as camouflage. A long bone dagger was thrust through hair drawn up in a topknot on the long head, and a smaller sliver pierced the septum of his nose. He carried a long oval shield in one hand, and a long club of some glossy dark hardwood with an end shaped into the likeness of a clenched fist.

His eyes scanned about; then he hooted again. At that instant the brushy tree line was empty of anything but birds and insects; then a wave of beastmen with spear and knobkerrie came out into the open, grassy hillside. There were about forty of them— the number of the whole Cloud Mountain force, until the other settlements sent their fighters. At least Teesa was out of it for now . . .

Uh-oh, he thought, at the rush of protective tenderness, blinking a little in surprise. *That wasn't just a roll in the hay—though it was that, literally.*

"Now!" he shouted, stepped out from around the tree, and drew to the ear. A score of Cloud Mountain warriors did the same. *Snap*, and the string of his bow slapped against his bracer.

Twenty arrows slashed out over the hundred yards or so between them and the beastmen. His own hit, just, slicing across the first Neanderthal's arm. The beastman took three steps forward and then stopped, going rigid; then he screamed, with froth spraying from his lips, and sank down in convulsions that shook the tall grass over his body for a few seconds. Two more arrows went home, one right in a Neanderthal's chest, the other through a leg—both deadly hits thanks to the poisoned arrows. They didn't have enough of the poison for all the arrows they'd made, not nearly enough, so they'd been told to use them for the first volley.

Two hits was good practice at this range and with men who'd only been training for a month. You could become a fair or at least middling rifle shot in a month, but even practicing ten hours a day wouldn't make you more than a novice with a bow; that took thousands of hours. The Cloud Mountain men screamed their joy and shot again and again, as fast as they could draw.

Most of the enemy raised their shields and rushed forward, bellowing, as they would have against a shower of blowgun darts. That did them less good than they'd thought it would. For one thing, they had a wider killing ground to cover than they would have with blowguns.

For another, a string under a hundred pounds of tension could punch a couple of ounces of arrow a lot faster than your lungs could push a dart. Arrows hit *hard*, and harder still as the enemy got closer. Marc drew and shot, drew and shot, distantly aware that he was glad of the activity distracting him from the fact that scores of gorilla-strong humanoids were rushing at him with intent to kill him and eat his flesh, and not necessarily in that order. The noises they made were louder than any a human could have made, coming from those barrel chests, but they covered a smaller and deeper range of sounds. It was rather like being charged by a line of carnivorous foghorns.

Crack. One of his arrows punched right through a shield. The beastman held it by a single grip in the back, but it must have gouged through far enough to scratch his sweat-slick skin, because he stumbled and went to his knees, then began to shriek like a teakettle and jerk and twist as the nerve toxin did its work.

Thud, and another sank through a massive hairy torso; that one would have been fatal even if it weren't poisoned, but inside the body cavity, the venom killed between one stride and the next, and the creature flopped down as boneless as a dead chicken. Four or five other beastmen were down, dead or badly wounded.

"Pull back!" Marc shouted, and did just that, running up the open slope behind.

The beastmen had been hesitating a little. Now they bellowed more loudly still and rushed forward. A few threw their knob-headed clubs at fleeing humans; one struck at the base of a skull with the *thock* a maul would make on hard oak. The man flopped down as limp as the beastman who'd taken Marc's arrow through the chest.

"*Now!*" Marc shouted, more loudly this time, as his foot came level with a short piece of peeled willow wand. "*Down!*"

As he threw himself flat he *really* hoped everyone remembered what to do.

Ten feet ahead and several feet above him on the slope four Cloud Mountain fighters came erect, holding the AK-47s they'd taken from the Wergu. The lids of turf and grass on wicker that had covered the holes that concealed them flipped back like the covering of a pot, and each had a solid place to rest their elbows as they took aim, firing with the steady shoot-breathe-pick-target-aim-breathe-out-and-shoot rhythm the Terrans had taught them.

"Although I wish we'd had more ammunition for practice," Marc said to the roots of the grass under his nose. "At least they don't have to adjust the sights—"

Crack. Crack. Crack-crack-crack—

The bullets went through the air just over his head; there was an overwhelming sweet scent of crushed grass in his nostrils, but a thin, bitter-acrid scent of nitro powder under that. He began crawling—leopard-crawling, with his belly kept firmly pressed to the earth and his chin touching it as well. He could see Teesa firing as he'd taught her, carefully, picking a target and concentrating, squeezing the trigger gently as she exhaled. The range was only twenty yards, and the targets were standing up; she and the three men *had* to be hitting. Once Marc was past the line of gunmen and out of the line of fire he could rise again and look.

The Cloud Mountain fighters *had* thrown themselves flat when he yelled, crawled as he had, and they were all out of the way now. Most of them were on their feet again and bending their bows; that reminded him to do likewise. Just then the remnants of the Wergu turned and ran; his arrow sank six inches into the hairy buttock of a beastman, and the hominid ran a dozen paces before the poison knocked him down.

About twenty of the beastmen were down altogether, half of the forty or so who'd come out of the woods. That was shocking casualties to a tribe of primitives; Stone Age warfare could kill plenty of people, but it usually did so one or two at a time rather than all at once.

"Cease fire!" Marc shouted, going down on one knee. "Now let's see if they do what we want them to," he added more quietly to Teesa.

She grinned at him as she pulled the magazine out of the assault rifle, took a handful of loose rounds from a pouch, thumbed six into the magazine, and reinserted it with a practiced twist and smack and *click* sound.

The archers filled their quivers from adolescents who dashed forward with reloads. Zore brought Marc's, giving him a thumbs-up signal; she'd probably picked that up from Blair.

"Speaking of which . . ."

The Wergu were running, but they slowed down as they approached the forest, throwing themselves down and helping their wounded, which mostly seemed to consist of pressing handfuls of grass to the wounds, pulling out arrows, and—he checked through his binoculars—actually *licking* the wounds, much the way a dog would.

"*Zeerahb,*" he heard Teesa mutter.

That made him smile a bit. The word meant *disgusting* . . . in Cajun-French dialect. The version of English she'd picked up from him was definitely what he'd learned on Grande Isle from his *maw-maw*, rather than the school version he used most of the time.

"Here come the gunmen!" he called out as the brush stirred behind the defeated Wergu. "Remember the plan!"

"Marc," Teesa said.

He glanced over at her; her face was sober, and her eyes steady. "Why is the possessed one not here? Why does the Diadem of the Eye no longer answer to my will?"

Marc licked his lips. "I can't be sure—"

"Tell me! I can see from your eyes that you know!"

"I don't *know*. But I think that . . . there is a thing in your Cave of the Mysteries that works through the Diadem of the Eye. It is that which has taken Binkis . . . the possessed one. It uses him for some purpose . . . I don't know what. That's how he can do impossible things. He isn't here because without the Diadem of the Eye, it can't control the man so far away from the Cave of the Mysteries. And it's . . ."—he dropped into English for two words—". . . *shut down* the Diadem of the Eye."

Teesa's face crumpled. "The Mystery has turned against its people?" she said, her voice trembling on the verge of tears. "We who have served it for so many generations?"

"I don't think it has. It just works with whatever's closest . . ." He thought quickly as her face showed stricken grief. "If we can take the Cave of the Mysteries back, I'm sure"—*or at least pretty sure*—"the Diadem of the Eye will work the way it did before."

She took a deep breath and nodded. "I will trust your word, my beloved," she said.

Marc turned back towards the slope and the forest below. He didn't want to see her wince, and he didn't want to look at her face right then, either.

Instead he looked as the Neanderthals with Russian assault rifles—*and isn't that a sight*—came out of the brush. They looked as if they knew what to do, as well; they strung themselves out in a line and began to crawl forward, shooting to pin the four Cloud Mountain guns down. Scores more with shield and club and fire-hardened spears appeared on either flank, hooting and stamping as they worked themselves up into a frenzy of bloodlust.

"*Weh*, someone told them how to do it," Marc muttered as the first shots cracked out. "Pin us down, then send the clubs in to noogie on us."

He flattened himself to the ground again. Teesa popped back out of her hole and shot; before the brass cartridge had sparkled its way down to the dirt she was hiding again. And as well she did; three or four bullets kicked up little spurts of soil from the ground all around her. . . .

Marc waited; then he waited a little more. Wergu riflemen ran from tree to tree, rock to rock, or crawled more through the long grass. That wasn't as good concealment as it might have been; the breeze was from the south, but eeling through the grass on your belly made it ripple against the wind. The Cloud Mountain fighters knew all about that, and the pits they were standing in still gave them a good view downslope, as well as protecting most of their bodies. Two of the beastmen with Terran weapons died before the rest were within fifty yards of the foxholes.

But one of the Cloud Mountain shooters did as well, with a round blue hole between his eyes and the back blown out of his head. Teesa had a long scratch along one arm from a fragment spalled off a rock by a bullet; three inches to the right and it would have gone through her chest. Marc tried not to think of that, and kept asking himself whether it was worth the risk to stand and use his bow.

Probably not, he thought, as a tribesman not far away stood and loosed a shaft, and then pitched over backward as a Wergu shot him through the stomach. The noises he made grew less human, and then he started to scream.

Marc checked his watch—it went rather oddly with the Cloud Mountain breechclout and sandals, but there you were. It was set to Venusian hours, fifteen minutes longer than the Terran variety. It was ten o'clock now, only about eighty minutes since the whole thing had started, not even noon yet. The Wergu were getting very close . . .

Crack. Something went over his head, barely a foot away and making a malignant *peewwwww* sound as it went away.

They're bad shots, but this is getting too close. It's time; it's really time. I'm not letting being nervous about Teesa—or myself—cloud my judgment.

He pulled his handkerchief out of his pocket, tied it to the end of his bow, and waved the long stave in the air without getting up. Marc was lying on his back as he did so, looking upslope. About eight hundred yards away, halfway back up to the crest, was a dark lump of basalt boulder with a V-notch in it. As he watched and waved, a flash of reflected sunlight came from there, either Blair's telescopic sight or Cynthia's binoculars—she was acting as spotter and calling the shots for him.

Then there was a flash of brighter fire, a muzzle-flash, faded in the bright Venusian sunlight but still discernible, followed a fraction of a second later by a *crack* deeper and longer and louder than the sharp, spiteful snap of the assault-rifle cartridges, halfway to a *boom*. Teesa gave a gleeful whoop; Marc rolled over and looked downslope, just in time to see one of the beastmen catapult backward, turning as he went. Marc winced slightly. What one of those heavy, high-velocity, soft-nosed big-game bullets did wasn't pretty even when an animal was on the receiving end, and the Wergu were close enough to human to make it plenty gruesome.

The heavy, deep *crack* came again, and a beetle-browed head dissolved in a pink mist. *Crack*, and another gun-wielding Wergu went down, his right arm torn away. *Crack*, and this time it was right through the sniper's triangle, the point right above the breastbone. *Crack* . . .

The Wergu didn't run; they'd had just enough exposure to firearms to lose their first fear of them, without knowing much about them. Instead they snarled and hooted and bellowed, and then they began firing at the sangar from which Christopher Blair was savaging them with the single surviving game rifle. Hugging the ground, Marc gave a grin that would have done Tahyo credit. At better than eight hundred yards, the heavy, scope-sighted weapon in expert hands could punch the pips out of a card. With an AK, you weren't much better off than you would be throwing spitballs.

Teesa looked at him, her eyes peeking over the edge of the foxhole. Marc waited an instant and then chopped his hand down. She rose and started shooting again; an instant later the two surviving Cloud Mountain warriors did as well. Seconds later, only half a dozen of the Wergu riflemen were still standing; they wavered for an instant and then turned and ran; the waiting horde with clubs did likewise.

Marc leaped to his feet, drawing his bow. "Come on, you Texians, let them have it!" he shouted. Then, as the last of them fell: "Get the guns! Get the guns!"

Teesa leaped out of her foxhole and flung herself at him. He returned the embrace . . .

"You really want to go through with this?" Blair murmured to him beneath the chanting, speaking behind Cynthia's head for an instant.

"I think we have to. We're in good with these people, but turning them down . . . that would be an insult."

Blair smiled slightly. "It's just that I feel hideously self-conscious, don't you know."

"Lover, if you think *you* feel conspicuous!" Cynthia said, staring straight ahead and not turning her head to meet the eyes of either man. "I just hope the folks back home in Harlem never hear about this."

"You look very fetching," Blair said loyally.

"I'd never live it down—it feels like bein' a cross between Josephine Baker and the Queen of the Zulus in this getup."

Since the getup consisted of a breechclout made of bright crimson and green feathers sewn on a leather backing, a halter of the same material, bands of colorful monkey-fur at elbows and knees and wrists and ankles, and a towering headdress of orange plumes and 'saur teeth, Marc could scarcely blame her. He and Blair were in much the same, except that they didn't have to wear the Barbarian Sports Bra. Their chests and faces *were* covered with swirling designs in chalk, black greasepaint and orange spots, which they'd spared Cynthia, probably because the color contrasts wouldn't work.

Night lay heavy on the Cloud Mountain settlement. The great bonfire at the center threw the patterns in the curved roofs of the huts around into sharp relief and cast a column of sparks into the blackness of the sky, filling the air with the spicy smell of burning pinewood. The warmth of it cut the coolness of the highland night, and palm-broad insects with wings that glinted like flying jewels circled it and then threw themselves to frenzied death in the flames.

Ranks of women surrounded the fire, drumming on tall, hollowed-out logs topped with taut hide. Their faces were painted in halves down the centerline, robin's egg blue on one side, white on the other, with their long yellow hair flying wild around their heads as they dipped and swayed their faces to the beat. The sound throbbed like the heartbeat of a giant, until even the pulsing of the fire seemed to throb in time with it. Naked children a little too young to be with the drummers dashed through the crowd, blowing handfuls of powder at the adults—Marc caught some that Zore blew at him, grinning behind a mask of face-paint that made her look like some mad blue-eyed raccoon.

"*Tchew!*" he sneezed involuntarily.

It smelled like not-much, a sort of burnt pollen scent. Then his nose began to tingle . . .

"Uh-oh," he said. "*Mais*, I think that stuff's got an active ingredient."

Teesa appeared. Her face was painted, too, with a band of black across the upper half that made her eyes glow like jewels in the fire-shot dark. The Diadem of the Eye was on her brow the green jewel at its center shining with an inner light, and a cloak that looked like the throat of a hummingbird swirled around her as she danced, at once slow and sinuous. Behind her the Cloud Mountain warriors came, threading about the drummers, their feet stamping in unison and their spears rippling like the antennae of some great beast.

"Here's our part," Marc said.

The three Terrans moved forward. Marc concentrated on his part in the ceremony—it felt rather like amateur theatricals in high school combined with choral dance, though he'd never done the bit where you cut your arm and dripped blood in a bowl of berry wine and then everyone drank it before. At last Teesa raised the empty bowl.

"*Their blood is ours! Our blood is theirs! They are of the folk!*" she cried, and threw the bowl into the flames.

They flared up to meet it. For a moment Marc felt sadness; it had been a nice piece of woodcarving, and the cream-and-orange striping of the wood was beautiful. Then he staggered slightly.

"Wow, that powder stuff has quite a kick," he muttered.

He'd smoked grass once or twice in high school, but it hadn't been anything like this. The whole world looked as if it were painted in bright primary colors on a pane of glass, with light shining through it. At the same time, every sight and sound seemed *heavy*, as if they carried a freight of incommunicable knowledge that he was just on the verge of understanding. Everyone here was his brother, his sister, his father and mother; the entire universe was linked to him as if with chains of silver light as the Cloud Mountain folk gathered around and began patting the Terrans on the back or giving them quick hugs.

"It's an honor," Marc said, sincerely.

Suddenly Blair began to weep. The sight was an overwhelming sorrow to Marc.

"Hey, podna, what's wrong?" he asked.

Cynthia used the plumes of her headdress to tenderly wipe the Englishman's tears away. "Lover boy, it's all right. *Everything's* all right!"

Blair shook his head, and covered his face with his palms. "Oh, *mon Dieu*, I should have told you! Even though it wasn't my fault, I should have told you when we crashed! I am a *cochon*! A bad, bad man!"

"Why are you swearing in French?" Marc asked.

It didn't seem all that important. Off to the side Tahyo was in a pen; he'd seemed interested and just a bit frustrated at not being allowed to join in. Now he was bristling, every hair on his head standing erect and his teeth showing . . . and Teesa screamed.

At first it seemed part of the rite; then Marc saw how the tribesfolk were recoiling in horror. He started forward, then stopped as if he'd run into a brick wall as he saw the anguish in her eyes and the carved-stone immobility of her face. Blood sprang from under her nails as she tried to tear the Diadem of the Eye from her brow, but even though the muscle corded like flat straps in her forearms and her fingers crooked like talons, she could not force them the last inch towards the circlet of metal.

"*Run!*" she screamed. "Oh please, beloved, *run*!"

Marc gaped at her; his limbs felt heavy, weighed down with the hostility of a universe. Then her arms fell to her sides, and she spoke again. This time it was in Russian—which he understood, well enough to know that she was speaking it with a strong accent. Somehow that made the whole process more horrible.

"Disposition of experimental subjects is unfavorable," she said, in a monotone that somehow managed to sound irritated without any inflection at all.

Her head turned, tracking like a radar-controlled gun. "Data input on new stimuli is suboptimal. New sources must be accessed where bandwidth is available."

Decision firmed. Marc leaped towards her; if *she* couldn't take the damned thing off, he could do it for her.

Time seemed to stretch. For all that she moved so stiffly, Teesa wasn't there when his body hurtled through the space she'd occupied an instant before. Instead a foot seemed to come from

nowhere and slam into his solar plexus; all the breath in his body
went out in a single *ooof*, and his diaphragm spasmed, paralyzed and
unable to draw in more. He rolled almost to the edge of the fire, and
would have rolled into it if there hadn't been a lip of earth buildup
there. As it was, he could feel his hair begin to smolder in the seconds before he could gather strength to roll over.

That let him see Blair try to seize Teesa from behind. One fist
snapped back, and suddenly the big blond man was bent over and
clutching himself. The Cloud Mountain shamaness turned and hit
him behind the ear; the blow looked as if it had been executed by
some piece of digitally controlled machinery, precise and fluid.

Tahyo was going hysterical in his pen, throwing himself at the
slats and roaring, foam flying from his teeth as he splintered the
tough wood. The Cloud Mountain folk were tumbling over one another in panic flight, all except Zore, who stood crying and calling
out her sister's name.

Cynthia was much cooler; she stooped and picked up a nice fist-
sized smooth rock, hefted it thoughtfully, wound up, and lofted it at
Teesa's head.

The long yellow hair flicked as her head moved aside just
enough to let the rock pass. Then she took two quick steps and
clamped a hand on the top of Cynthia's head. The black woman
reached up to knock the grip aside . . . and then froze, immobile,
scarcely even breathing.

"Satisfactory," Teesa said in the same dreadful monotone. "Full
data transfer will require locational access to the central node. Follow me."

Teesa turned and walked into the darkness. Cynthia followed,
marching with the same robot precision.

CHAPTER TWELVE

Encyclopedia Britannica, 16th Edition
University of Chicago Press, 1988

INTERNAL CONTROL DEVICE: method of controlling animals through electrical signals conveyed via electrodes implanted in the brain tissue. Initial experiments in the 1960s were pursued with some vigor when the projections for the Venusian bases showed that the cost of shipping heavy earthmoving equipment was prohibitive, even without the necessary support infrastructure . . .

Cynthia Whitlock came to herself with eyeblink suddenness. She staggered, and a hand grasped her arm.

"Be calm," an accented voice said.

Jadviga, she thought. *Where—*

Memories crashed into her mind. The firelight, Teesa suddenly turned into a flesh-and-blood puppet, then the grip on her head and a blinding pain, and when she was aware of anything it was walking with something *else* moving her limbs—

Her knees buckled. She sat on a rough stone bench covered in furs, blinked, choked back a heave of nausea. Jadviga handed her a gourd of water, and she drank thirstily; it was clean and cool, and soothed a throat she realized was dry as mummy dust.

The light was dim, but she could see that they were in a circular fieldstone hut—a good-sized one, ten paces across, with a quartet of carved poles in its middle holding up a roof of poles and branches covered in thatch; a rock shelf covered in skin rugs ran all the way around the interior, save for a door curtained with another hide. There was a rock-lined hearth in the center, and a smoke hole above, but both were empty right now. There was a faint smell of old smoke. The hut itself smelled clean, with scents of leather and food and the sweet scent of fresh rushes on the packed-earth floor, but somewhere not too far away was the garbage-and-sewage stink of a settlement of primitives whose customs didn't include much washing or cleanup. Leather bags hung from pegs driven between the dry-laid stone of the walls, and gourds and crude boxes.

"Where am I?" she husked, after another drink of the water.

"*Velniai griebtu!*" Jadviga said. "Devil fly away with it if I know! We are near where the *Riga* came down, that is all I know. Among the Neanderthals. Near a cliff, near caves—"

Cynthia felt her stomach heave again. Cold, rancid sweat broke out on her forehead as she clutched at her temples. *Cave. Light. Light that shone* through *me—*

"Try not to think of it," Jadviga said quietly.

Cynthia nodded jerkily and looked at the other woman. Jadviga Binkis didn't look as if she'd been beaten or tortured; she didn't even look gaunt. But there was something in her eyes. . . .

I suspect it's like looking into a mirror.

"How long have I been here?" Cynthia asked.

"Not long. I think they . . . *it* . . . brought you here late last night. Then you were in the caves—no, do not try to recall it! And they brought you here this morning and left you. It is noon now."

Cynthia put her head down between her knees and waited until her head stopped spinning. That took a while; it didn't only feel dizzy, but as if someone had extracted all the contents and then scraped in the inside with a spoon, like a Halloween pumpkin.

"We were at the Cloud Mountain settlement," she said. "The Neanderthals attacked us and we beat them off, and there was a ceremony. Then . . . *something* took over the shamaness, Teesa. Like it did your husband in the fight at the rock."

Jadviga sat down on the bench herself. "Yes," she whispered. Then she made herself look up. "It . . . it is as if he is a prisoner in his own head. Sometimes a little of my husband emerges."

"So he's still there," Cynthia said comfortingly.

Jadviga bit her lip. "Yes. And he is mad. It is almost worse then. He . . . he does not know where we are or what has happened. Then I must try to comfort him; that is why . . . *it* . . . keeps me alive, I think."

Ouch, Cynthia thought. "What do you think is doing all this?"

"That is something I have thought much. I think it is alien . . . not human in its origins. But I do not think it is *an* alien. It is a machine."

Cynthia nodded; that was all too plausible. Whoever or Whatever had turned Venus into a giant terrarium—probably Mars likewise—had left a sentinel.

"We're the prisoner of an omnipotent machine that can take over our minds. Why didn't I stay home? I could have gotten a research position at Princeton; honest I could. . . ."

Jadviga laid a comforting hand on her shoulder for a moment. "I said that I have thought much. There has not been much else to do when . . . when Franziscus is . . . gone. I think that this is a very powerful machine, yes. But I do not think it is very *intelligent*."

"You don't?" Cynthia said.

"If it was, it would communicate better. This *protpisys*, this thing, it just seizes information, but from what it has said . . . I do not think it *understands* what it learns well. It is as if it were a, an automatic alarm."

"That *is* sort of comfortin'," Cynthia said. Then her face fell.

"What is it?" the Lithuanian asked.

"If it's an alarm, could the folks who put it here *get* the alarm and come to see what's wrong?"

Even through her own fear, Cynthia felt a stab of guilt as the other's face fell. Jadviga had been trying to comfort her.

"But Marc and Chris will do *something*," she said. "They're smart dudes and tough, too."

"Yes," Jadviga said. "Would you like food?"

Suddenly Cynthia's stomach cramped with hunger. "Yes!"

One of the sacks held smoked meat, and tart wild comar-fruit. She ate voraciously, as if she'd been working hard for a day with nothing . . .

Which is probably the truth of the matter, she thought. "Well, we can't just sit and wait to be rescued, like some dumb bimbo in those books Marc likes. We've got to be ready, and we've got to find out what we can for our folks when we get back home."

Jadviga winced. "Then there is something I must tell you, about the *Riga*'s cargo. It may get me into a great deal of trouble."

She took a breath . . .

Another burst of arguing broke out among the assembled Cloud Mountain warriors on the hillside. Marc Vitrac sighed. There was a stale smell of ashes and sweat in the air, despite the freshness of the wind from the north. Of course, that had to cross the little dell where the fire had burned and where Teesa had been . . .

Taken. Possessed. Whatever. We'll get her back, and smash whatever did it to her. He had to believe that, or just sit down and wait to die.

"Whatever that powder was, at least it didn't leave a hangover," he said. He had no headache or pains, just a generalized lassitude he could overcome with an effort of will.

Blair started to snap at him, then visibly thought better of it. "I realize you're trying to buck me up and all that, old boy," he said tightly. "But it's wasted effort, I'm afraid."

"I don't have to tell you not to try and live off your nerves, do I, podna?"

Blair shook his head ruefully, then took a long breath and let it out slowly. "Point taken. I *do* wish these chappies would . . . how do you Yanks put it . . . get their asses in gear."

Marc looked out over the fifty or so warriors. *They're scared,* he thought. *Down to the guts and balls.*

They looked rather crapulous, too, still wearing bits and pieces of the finery they'd had on last night for the adoption ceremony, tawdry and ragged in the bright sunlight of afternoon. There was a shrill note to their voices as well. What looked like evil magic seizing their most sacred things had broken something; he didn't doubt that they were brave men, against men or dangerous beasts.

Beasts, Marc thought suddenly. Weh, *let's give it a try.*

"Warriors!" he called out. "Warriors!"

Quiet gradually fell. About half the eyes looking at him were frightened. A fair number were full of hate, Taldi's first and foremost among them. Some were hopeful.

"Whether anyone joins us or not, my comrade and I will go to rescue our women from the beastmen and their wizard," Marc said.

Taldi bristled. *Good*, the Terran thought. *Get his blood flowing.*

"But I do not ask you to carry a spear against magic—even with the thunder-sticks you took in the fight two days ago."

Some of them stirred and murmured at that; it was something to buck them up a bit, against the terror of last night. It must be possible, because . . .

Because if it isn't I don't know what the fuck we're going to do, me, he thought. *Besides, they're here, not just scattering off with their families. Not far from that, though.*

"You know I am a warrior, too. So hear my word, for my word is true. If you help me, I will lead you against the beastmen and their demon. I will do it riding on the back of a thunder-lizard! And if I cannot fulfill my pledge, then you may kill me—I will not resist."

He stood silent then, his arms crossed on his bare chest. Blair stood by his side. Marc thought the other man's eyes had rolled up slightly at the tone, and he'd have liked the flamboyant rhetoric even less if he could have followed the language—as yet he only spoke it haltingly.

But Cloud Mountain custom demanded it . . . and it just seemed appropriate, somehow.

He'd say it was all the books I read as a kid, too. Well, maybe it is, but it fits here.

Marc kept his eyes steady, watching the renewed debate. To his surprise, it was Taldi who shouted the others down.

"You know I am no friend to the black-haired stranger," the man said. "The other is no one's enemy here, but this Ma-rek is my rival and my foe. But he is a brave man. If he can help us reclaim our sacred one, then I will follow him to save Teesa, *until* we save her."

The tribesman's teeth showed in what wasn't even notionally a smile. "And if he fails us . . . I will kill him myself. Whether he resists or not."

The steep ridge where they lay overlooked the floor of the valley, and they were about thirty feet above it. That put them about at the height of the titanosaur herd currently making its way northward. The migration here was much like migrations on the Serengeti, or the American plains in the old days, except that many of the animals concerned could crush a buffalo underfoot and barely notice.

"No," Marc said patiently. "Not those. I need—*enfer*, what's the word for 'ceratopid'—"

He paused and searched his Cloud Mountain vocabulary. Translation was usually automatic, but sometimes you had to hunt when the concepts didn't map onto each other one-to-one.

"—I need a *hornhead thunder-lizard*. One about this size at the shoulder."

He pointed to a place about ten feet high on the tree beside him.

"Ah," Taldi said. "But hornheads charge very well. Will what we have built hold them?"

"We'll find out," Marc said.

There was no point in being quiet or trying to hide. Animals the size of human beings didn't really register on the radar of the biggest 'saurs. Tahyo was lying beside him, trying to cuddle up and with his ears folded right back as he stared.

"Bruhathkayosaurus?" Blair asked, nodding towards the beasts passing by.

"Search me. Cynthia would know," Marc replied, then winced a little at the other man's stoic pain. "Something like that, *weh*."

The fifty or so creatures plodded slowly northward. . . .

No, Marc thought. *They just look slow because they don't move their legs quickly.* Mais, *the legs are fourteen feet long . . . they're traveling faster than a galloping* churr.

They had the classic shape most people associated with dinosaurs, long neck and tail, a head that looked ridiculously small although it was actually longer than a tall man, and a huge, globular body supported by four immense, columnar legs; the upper side was a mottled green-and-brown, the stomach a pale cream. The adults were a hundred and fifty feet long, and fifty at the shoulder—though their haunches were a little higher than that. Sam Feldman had estimated similar beasts closer to Jamestown at two hundred tons on the hoof. Their cries were long, melancholy buzzes, like a huge steam engine with a head cold, and the long necks weaved back and forth as they looked for fodder. The smell was overwhelming, a hard, dry scent leavened with the stink of the gigantic piles of dung they left.

That accounted for the dense grass that covered the whole great valley to the great river westward. They weren't finding much to eat here, except when they dipped to strip up a clump of tall grass or pull a bush out of the cliff, casually masticating something taller than Marc and covered in needle-pointed thorns longer than his thumb and harder than ivory. Elsewhere he'd seen their cousins push mature oaks over by leaning on them and then chew them down to bare logs.

"I can see why there aren't many trees around here," he said, as a six-foot head swept by a little overhead.

It snorted with nostrils on the top of its snout, cocked an eye and looked for vegetation, and then swept on with ponderous majesty. Marc ignored it—as much as you could ignore something four times the weight of a battle tank—and unlimbered his binoculars. Out in the hazy distance between here and the river, other herds moved, creatures huge and still more huge, with long, sinuous necks, and among them squat, armored shapes like monstrous beetles with fringes of foot-long spikes and tails that sported huge clubs of bone. . . . Beside the monsters, 'saurs of merely elephantine or rhino dimensions looked like small game.

"And on the fringes, the predators," he said, handing the glasses to Blair.

"Gigantosaurs."

"More or less," Marc said.

Big yellow-and-brown-striped bipeds, forty feet long, the largest six or seven tons, with substantial three-clawed forelimbs and protruding "eyebrows" of bone. Their heads split wide to reveal teeth like two-foot steak knives, driven by muscle that could shear through bones four inches thick.

Others ranged from there down to the man-sized feathered raptors, packs of greatwolves, saber-tooths, and similar scavengers and minor hangers-on and riffraff. Hundreds of thousands of tons of meat on the hoof were passing through this time of year, and there were plenty of opportunists looking for a share. As Marc watched, four Gigantosaurs caught a titanosaur calf—a three-year-old weighing a mere thirty tons or so—as it bent its head to drink from one of the streams that veined the plain. The great jaws gaped as the six-ton carnivore reared back, its thick, supple neck curved into an S-shape, then slammed forward.

Even at half a mile distance, the scream of the calf was earhurtingly loud, as if God had gotten his toe stuck in a closing door. A stampede went out from the spot like the ripple of a stone thrown into a pond as the plant eaters fled; the armored ones backed into circles, lashing the air with their knobby tail-clubs. The calf and the Gigantosaur went over into the stream in a whipping cloud of spray and flying mud; the others gathered around, dipping their heads to strike like nightmare four-story birds.

After a moment, the flurry of motion died down, and they set their great eagle-claw feet on the calf's carcass as they worried loose chunks the size of Volkswagens and threw their heads upright to unhinge their jaws and bolt the great gobbets down, rammed backward by the peristaltic motion of their thick tongues. Now and then they would stop to make half-completed strikes and hissing roars at their pack-mates, for all the world like newly elected senators divvying up pork.

The Terrans and Cloud Mountain party waited, sipping water and gnawing on strips of dried preserved meat; those tasted like old sandals sweating salt crystals. At last—

"There!" Blair pointed, and handed the field glasses back.

Mark took them, peering and adjusting the focusing screw with his thumb. The beasts in question looked a lot like those used in Jamestown; the main difference was a short thick-based horn on the nose and perhaps a slightly rangier build. He felt a moment's keen nostalgia for that bustling little town.

Wish I'd never left. Then: *No, I don't. I'd go through it all again to meet Teesa.* His mind gibed at him: *Aren't you planning on going back, then, you?*

"Shut up, Marc," he muttered to himself. Then louder, to the tribesmen: "Those will do, if they come close enough."

Taldi took the binoculars; he'd adapted to them with innocent calm after a moment's wonder. Marc wasn't surprised; you *expected* magic to do wonderful things, like giving a man the sight of an eagle or pterosaur.

"They are large," Taldi said. Then he grinned. "I would like to ride on such a thunder-lizard."

From the look in his eyes, he was thinking of what Teesa would say if she saw him on one. Marc smiled himself. *Sorry, podna. I think you're not her type . . . weren't even before we did the mind-meld thing.*

Tension grew as they watched the herd of ceratopids grow closer; they seemed to be edging closer to the cliffs, avoiding the creeks where they got deeper towards the main river . . . which, considering some of the things that lived in the Missouri-sized stream, wasn't surprising. Now and then they'd stop to dig in the dirt with the points of their beaks, crunching contentedly on roots. When some Gigantosaurs came and gave them a once-over, they backed into an oblong with the calves in the center and a ring of belligerent horned snouts pointing out, shaking their bone-sheathed heads like Brobdingnagian rhinos or bison. The huge bone shields were covered in skin, and they flushed with blood as the beasts raged.

OOOOOOONNKKK!

The hoarse bellow sounded across the plain, and a big male with an orange shield flushed reddish put his massive head down and broke into a lumbering trot towards a carnosaur. The meat eater sheered off, easily striding away. The horned 'saur stopped and tossed his head, bellowing again, throwing plumes of dust from under his stamping forefeet. This species tended to have dispositions like rhinos, too, only with less brainpower and more belligerence— their response to anything that seriously pissed them off was a flat-out charge. The big carnosaurs dropped back and followed when the herd resumed its northward passage.

"All right," Mark said. "They're going to come fairly close. Let's get ready."

Taldi gave him a nod, and Blair a thumbs-up. They turned and scrambled down a ravine that split the cliff. Marc went carefully;

the last thing he needed now was to fall and break a leg or dislocate a shoulder. More than his own life was riding on this, more than his friends' lives—more even than Teesa's.

As he dropped the last few feet to the floor of the ravine, a four-inch rodent of some sort stood and chattered defiance at him from only inches away, eyes bulging and long chisel teeth bared, curling its tail and clutching an acorn to its chest. He touched a finger to his brow.

"You can keep it, little podna," he said.

It suddenly fled up a vertical rock wall, and he turned to the pile of torches and clay firepots. A dozen warriors awaited them, mostly younger men—the ones who'd volunteered for this part of the job.

He grinned at them, and they smiled back. If the expressions looked forced for a few, he didn't particularly blame them; his own testicles were trying to crawl up past his navel, and his bladder was doing a balloon imitation as well. The whole operation was mad, but this part was certifiable. He glanced aside at Blair; the Englishman still had the big-game rifle slung across his back.

"You sure you want to take that, podna? We only have half a dozen rounds left and it'll slow you."

"You're taking your bow."

"*Weh*, but that only weighs about two pounds. The rifle's fourteen."

"Still, I think I can bear it."

"Your funeral." *Or your trip down a throat, whole, headfirst.* "Let's go."

The Cloud Mountain warriors had their spears and bows along, too, probably for psychological reasons as much as anything. They trotted out behind Taldi and the two Terrans into the thigh-high grass and among the herds that stretched from one edge of sight to the other. In a way it was worse down here at ground level; there was no perspective, except the one looking up at the creatures that paced by.

"Now I know what it feels like to be a mouse," Marc said, looking out over the plain and its mountains of moving flesh.

Blair laughed with Marc, and the tribesmen looked at them with respect tinged by awe.

It's laugh or scream like a little girl, Marc thought, as they wound their way through a herd of the titanosaurs.

That was more dangerous than you'd think. It was hard to estimate just where the tree trunk legs were going to come down, and close up, the walking walls of flesh gave you a vertiginous sense that they were always toppling over on you. The sound of their footfalls filled the world, like rumbling thunder on a hot summer day or batteries of heavy artillery. Tahyo followed so closely that Marc could feel the cold, wet nose touch his bare calf every other stride.

Taldi threw himself aside with a yell as a foot with hundreds of tons of weight behind it slammed down not four feet from him. That and the miniature earthquake tossed him off his feet and onto his shoulders and neck; half-stunned, he doggedly began to gather the scattered arrows that had spilled from his quiver and snatch up the leather sack of torches. The next time the rear foot came down it would be on top of him. Marc dashed in—you could run under the beast's belly without stooping—and grabbed Taldi by one arm, lugging him through under the vast sagging creamy arch of the belly.

Lice the size of small cats crawled across the massive roof of skin; one dropped, attracted by the humans' body-heat and landed on Taldi's neck, poised with its jaws and sucker parts ready to clamp on his skin. Marc struck at it with a fist and a cry of loathing, but the shell resisted him as well as a lobster's might; it reared up and hissed at him, waving its mandibles. He drew his bowie and smashed it with a blow from the brass cap on the pommel and it dropped away, leaking white ichor. Behind him there was a heavy *clop*-crunch sound as the young greatwolf bit another in half; Marc's skin crawled with the knowledge of what might drop on him at any instant.

Out on the other side he stopped, panting; Taldi shook himself back to alertness, and gave Marc a nod of thanks. Everyone had made it, though some had grazes and bruises and one a bleeding bite from a parasite like the one Marc had killed—the things secreted an anticoagulant to keep the blood of a victim flowing. They stopped for an instant to bandage the wounded man's shoulder and then trotted on.

"We've got to get there before they're too far to turn," Blair said grimly.

"*Weh*. We've also got to get there alive," Marc replied.

The next herd between them and the ceratopids was a larger one of smaller 'saurs—armor-headed things with spikes down their backs and two more sticking out horizontally at the end of each tail and pebbled brown skins; they were the size of large cows, or horses. That made them more dangerous, because they were close enough in scale to see humans and react to them, and vastly more agile than the walking hills. Taldi looked a question at Marc, and he nodded. The Cloud Mountain hunter took a torch out of the bag slung over his back and one of his friends opened a firepot. The hot, scorching smell of glowing oak coals came out of it; when the ball of resin at the top of the torch touched them, it flared into hot orange flame, trailing black smoke.

The nearest of the herd bawled in panic, showing thick purple tongues in their beaklike mouths. He'd counted on that. Animals on Venus were even more afraid of fire than they were on Earth; when it got loose it burned harder and hotter because of the greater concentration of oxygen in the air. Perhaps that was the main reason that humans were able to survive at all in this world of hostile giants.

Taldi shook the torch and waved it through an arc; sparks fell down into the fresh green grass, little flickers of flame springing up and dying where they touched. The whatever-they-were-saurs parted to either side . . . which was fortunate, for at that instant they suddenly shuddered into a gallop, making the earth rumble almost as badly as the titanosaurs had.

When they were past, everyone could see why. A saber-tooth stood with his forepaws on a dead 'saur; the creature was still twitching, and bleeding copiously from a ripped-open throat.

"Circle around him!" Taldi called, holding the torch up between him and the carnivore. "Spread out so he doesn't have anything to charge!"

"*Weh*, that's good advice," Marc said. "*Chat! Chat!*" Which meant *scram, cat!* in the lingo he'd learned at *mawmaw*'s knee.

The grizzly-sized spotted feline opened his mouth and squalled at them, an appalling catamount shriek but bigger; the fangs that gaped back in the killing rictus that let it stab were eighteen inches long and seemed longer beneath the little yellow eyes that blazed out from his dark-brown-and-fawn fur. His heavy shoulders made the hindquarters and the stubby tail that twitched there look nearly as absurd as they were menacing. You couldn't say that about the fangs and the great claws on the plate-broad forepaws.

They circled, keeping faces and weapons towards the saber-tooth.

It's nervous, Marc realized. *Like a cat with a dead mouse when there are wolves around—things that could snap it up like a rabbit, and its kill, too. It wants to bolt as much meat as it can and then get back to where there's cover.*

"Easy does it," he crooned. Then: "*Mais*, wait a minute. Don't sabertooths hunt in—"

Suddenly Tahyo whirled and lunged, *wulfing* furiously. Marc's instincts reacted to that before his mind could; he threw himself flat and rolled.

The other saber-tooth shot through the space Marc had occupied an instant later, paws outstretched to seize him and head back on his massive neck for the killing downward stab. The beast squalled in disappointment as he landed, spinning with impossible speed for something that weighed half a ton. Marc felt like a butterfly pinned to a board as the saber-tooth reared over him; he scrabbled at his belt for his pistol, but even if he got it out in time that would be like poking the animal with a safety pin. Death reared over him with slaver running from fangs that would go in his chest and come out his back. Tahyo bounced forward to throw himself on the huge animal with insane courage—or stupidity. Taldi tried to get between Marc and the animal with his torch, but there wasn't time—

Crack.

The glaring eyes of the saber-tooth bulged and popped as the heavy bullet traversed his skull from side to side, mushrooming as it went and exiting in a pink mist of bone fragments and bits of brain. It dropped flaccid as a flayed skin.

Crack.

Another round broke the right foreleg of the other cat as he braced himself to leap. He spun in place, the thrust of his hind legs turning him on the pivot of his one sound forelimb.

Crack, and a third round punched through his lungs and severed the big veins that ran from the top of the heart. He spasmed and died with blood pouring from his open mouth.

Tahyo's rush stopped. He crouched and peed; Marc sympathized profoundly with the impulse. Instead of following it, he rose and turned to see Blair smiling wryly and working the bolt of the big-game rifle.

"Now we only have three rounds left," he said. "Sorry about that."

"Cost-effective," Marc replied. "I figure I'm worth three bullets at least. Let's get out of here before something smells the blood, Chris."

A couple of the younger Cloud Mountain warriors wanted to stay and dig the fangs out of the saber-tooths; they were coveted ornaments. Taldi solved that problem by knocking one of the enthusiasts down and kicking the other, hard. He dropped the torch, and several of them put it out by the simple expedient of undoing their breechclouts and pissing on it in unison.

Then all sprinted until they were across the front of the herd of ceratopids they'd spotted from the cliff, and on the opposite side of it as it trudged northward.

Tricky, Marc thought.

These beasties were about twelve feet at the shoulder, and weighed in a bit heavier than a big elephant. That made them small enough to notice humans; a couple of the big bulls walking along the edge of the herd were already giving the dozen men the hairy eyeball. The three leaders arranged the Cloud Mountain warriors in a staggered line, trotting tirelessly to keep up with the long stride of the 'saurs. The females inside with the calves would be even more chancy.

"Drop back a little?" Blair suggested, and Marc nodded.

"The wind's from the south—that'll be perfect."

They all did drop behind the herd—though that meant avoiding knee-high heaps of ceratopid dung and the insects swarming over it. One or two of the rearguard beasts swung their heads to keep an eye on the humans, and a raptor pack—these had sleek black feathers with blue crests on their heads—came dancing by to check them out, but decided to move on. Marc watched the cliff-face for the feature they'd picked out—

"We're coming up on the fissure," he said. "Get ready!"

Everyone reached over their shoulders and pulled out torches. The men with the firepots set them down and pulled off the covers.

Marc took a deep breath, looked at Blair and Taldi. Both nodded slightly.

"Go for it!" he cried, and thrust his torch into the firepot.

Flame leaped up, resin burning with an orange flare and a crackling hiss. The 'saurs reacted instantly, halting and milling for an instant, tossing their great heads and bellowing as they took the scent of flame.

"Eeeee-ha!" Marc screamed, and the whole group joined in with a chorus of screeches.

The 'saurs probably didn't pay much attention to the noise, which the men themselves could barely hear under the bellowing and the growing thunder of massive feet pounding the hard-packed dirt. It seemed to fly by under Marc's feet as they fell behind the 'saurs, until . . .

"They did it!" Blair shouted, as pillars of smoke rose up ahead and to their left.

Marc gave another whoop of relief as he lit a fresh torch from his first and threw the stub away. He hadn't been altogether sure the rest of the Cloud Mountain men would rush out to light the piles of brushwood and dried dung that would funnel the herd towards the cliffs, but they had. They were a gutsy bunch, faced with something they understood.

"Cloud Mountain forever!" he shouted.

The ceratopids slowed as they saw the fires ahead and to their flank. Squeezed between the vertical edge of the cliff and flame on two sides, they hesitated; a few turned straight left and charged between the fires, bellowing piteously and holding their great headshields high. One turned back and thundered towards the line of humans. A man threw himself aside just in time to avoid a vicious sideways stroke of the nose horn before the beast disappeared southward, back along the route of the migration.

The rest went straight ahead. "Next question," Marc gasped.

He'd run the better part of three miles now, nearly flat-out; even lungs evolved for thinner air than this were beginning to feel the strain. The tribesmen were panting and blowing, but keeping up, their long legs eating up the distance. Ahead the 'saurs were slowing, despite their *oooonnks* of panic; they weren't meant for long-distance running. They tried to edge away from the line of fires, but that pushed their crowded ranks against the cliff proper; one big male's flank brushed it as he trotted, bringing down a rush and rattle of rocks and small boulders. The ceratopid *ooooonked* again fretfully as they bounced from his armored head and massive back, then grunted with a surprised *oof* as a two-hundred-pounder hit his flank. He swerved away from the cliff, broadsided into an only slightly smaller specimen, and then swerved back towards the rock.

"I want that one!" Marc yelled, pointing. "Drive him! Drive him!"

Ahead of them was a prow-shaped obstacle of rocks and timbers. On the right, it led to a narrow ravine framed by a slab of rock leaning away from the main cliff and leaving a path visible to open country ahead; the side to the left gave onto the prairie. Marc put on a further burst of speed as the beast hesitated and swung his head left, looking after his herd-mates. Blair was near him, face contorted as he called up his last reserve. They came closer to the 'saur, which looked more and more like some great creature of animated stone as you got closer. The wheezing bellows sound of his lungs working grew overpoweringly loud, and Marc was close enough to see scars and blotches on the tough pebbled hide. The animal was twice his height at the shoulder but was covering the ground in a ponderous gallop nearly as fast as a running man could sprint.

"Through there, you *couyon*!" Marc shouted, and threw his torch.

It bounced off the beast's left shoulder. Blair followed suit, and Taldi, and half a dozen of the pursuers. The ceratopid bawled in panic and veered right, brushing the cliff wall again and bringing down a shower of stones. One fist-sized one thumped Marc painfully on the arm; another knocked a Cloud Mountain warrior down and left him shouting with pain as he clutched a broken shin.

"Now!" Marc shouted, as the beast thundered into the narrow cleft of rocks.

He slowed down perforce; there was just enough room for him to squeeze by and not an inch more, and even a 'saur didn't relish leaving half his skin on edges of rock. Marc's cry had been involuntary, and useless; either the tribesmen waiting would react in time, or they wouldn't.

They did. The framework of oak logs they'd spent so long cutting and hauling and pegging together crashed downward as the stayropes were cut with frenzied axe blows, burying the sharpened lower points of the uprights three feet deep in the trench of softened earth that had been cut for them.

The thick, oxygen-rich air of Venus seemed to burn like a thin, hot haze of smoke in his straining lungs, and every movement of his legs was torment. Marc still leaped like a panther to snatch at the running knot on the cliff side of the ravine. Blair swung his machete on the other.

Whick-whang-thunk.

The other frame slid down, each side rattling between a pair of trunks set to guide the edges of the massive gate. The points slammed into the ground, missing the end of the ceratopid's tail by inches; they had themselves a *big* one here. The frame was two-foot oak trunks slotted together in a grid, but Marc didn't think it would hold the ceratopid for long.

"Quick! Quick!" he screamed.

Everyone sprang to grasp the thick poles stacked leaning against the rock on either side of the narrow cleft in the rock, four men to each balk of timber. They slammed the upper points into notches pre-cut in the framework, then heaved to set them as braces. Twice as many men would be doing the same on the other side, up where the head and business end of the creature was.

OOOOOOOHNNNNK!

A massive rattling *thunk* followed, and unhappy shouts from the men up there. The 'saur wasn't happy to be trapped, but he didn't have room to back up and take a run against the obstacle in front of him as the men scrambled to reinforce it. As someone handed Marc a waterskin, he saw the rest of the herd off in the distance, gradually slowing as the scent of fire died down. A ripple ran through the other creatures about, off to the edge of sight, and then they resumed the long, slow trek northward.

The captive 'saur's hindquarters bunched. He even managed to rear slightly before he slammed his bone-covered head into the framework ahead of him again. An ominous *crunch* followed. The water tasted as sweet as any Marc had ever drunk, despite the taste of leather and heat; he drank more, and splashed some across his face for the glorious coolness, then sighed. Taldi sprang daringly up on the frame itself and climbed to the top, peering over the animal's back.

"The wood won't hold him for long," Taldi said, as he dropped back.

If nothing else, this species *ate* oak trees, their parrotlike beaks shearing the tough wood like a hydraulic press.

"Better you than me, old boy," Blair said.

They'd stashed the steel box with the Ice kit in a depression on top of a boulder. The surface had been battered and scorched by the explosion back at their camp, but the contents of the suitcase-sized container had survived a trajectory through the air and a landing on soft earth. Marc opened it with a scream of abused hinges and took one of the loads for the trank gun . . . which had *not* survived the plastique and secondary brew-up of the ammunition. It looked like a giant steel hypodermic, six inches from point to rear; a plunger could be fitted there for manual application.

That was mostly done as a booster shot on a beast already tranked. Just then this one tried to back out of the trap, and the thick oak timbers creaked and groaned and bent. Then he slammed forward again, and there were more crunches and shouts of alarm. Seven tones of muscle and bone . . .

Marc finished screwing the plunger home on the tubular dart and took a deep breath. Then he wrapped it in a scrap of soft, thin leather, put it between his teeth, and swarmed up the framework like a Caribbean pirate boarding a ship in the old days. Tahyo *oooorfed* dismally behind him but submitted as someone grabbed his collar. Marc reached the top of the frame, wound legs and arms around the wood, and held on, with his teeth grinding on the smooth metallic taste of the hypo; the oak logs shook and groaned again, battering him against the hard, rough surfaces, and somewhere one of the thick pegs they'd used to hold the structure together broke with a gunshot crack. Then the 'saur took a step forward and slammed his great battering ram of a head into the frame there . . .

OOOOOONNKKK!

The bellow was enough to make Marc wince, but the screams of fright and the *crunch* of a timber breaking across showed him how little time was left. He swung his legs across the last horizontal timber and sprang.

"Ooof!"

It was five feet down onto the heaving back. His feet shot out from under him on the slick pebbled surface of the 'saur's hide; it felt more like plastic or rubber against Marc's skin than a living creature's skin. He turned quickly, scrabbling with widespread fingers and toes, then sliding forward as the creature rammed his seven tons into the wood confining him once more. If Marc went over the side into the narrow space between the 'saur and the rock, he'd pop like a grape under a boot.

The heated reptile stink of the 'saur was gagging strong, with an iron undertang of blood from the gashes and scrapes along his side.

Gotta get closer to the neck, Marc thought. *Hide's too thick here on the back.*

The huge bony shield covered the neck and part of the shoulders of the beast when it was laid back; it reared upright when the nose was lowered for attack, as it was . . . now!

Marc let the acceleration take him, sliding back a little as the 'saur lunged forward, and then sharply forward himself as the animal crashed into the ravaged framework barring the northern exit of the ravine. His left hand went up and braced against the inside of the shield, shockingly resilient and warm with the covering of flesh and blood vessels. He dropped the hypo into his right hand and raised it high, then slammed the long needle down onto the thinner hide of the side of the 'saur's neck.

OooooOOOOONNK! he roared in protest, starting and shaking himself the way a man might if a horsefly bit him on the neck.

The 'saur also tried to crush whatever had bitten him, by slapping the shield on his neck. With a yell Marc pushed himself back, slewing around and kicking his legs out as he started to fall; the bony mantle clapped to the skin inches from his hands. By sheer luck, his feet struck the wall of the ravine and pushed him back across the 'saur's shoulders as he rammed forward one more time.

The third effort made up for the others. This time two of the main horizontal braces of the framework barring the exit to the ravine gave way; the splintered end of one nearly swept Marc off his perch again, giving him a painful, bleeding scratch down his left arm.

Ooooonnhk?

This time the bellow was much softer, almost plaintive. He could feel the ceratopid hesitate under him, waver, then buckle forward into stillness with an enormous sleepy sigh.

Marc let himself slide free when the monster moved no more. His legs nearly buckled as he touched the ground; he supported himself on the 'saur and the broken remains of the heavy timber framework as he moved forward, gradually gaining strength as his breathing slowed. Lying propped just off the ground, the 'saur's head was as tall as Marc was, and longer. The leathery skin around the fist-sized nostrils was the only unarmored spot on the front ten feet, except for the eyes, and the nose horn was as long as Marc's forearm. One lethargic brown-yellow eye tracked him as he moved forward.

Sam Feldman had explained that the trank didn't knock the beast out, not with only one dose. The animal just stopped giving a damn.

Taldi and Blair came up, panting from having sprinted around the slab of rock that formed the outer wall of the ravine. They looked up at the beast in awe, where he lay with his great head smashed through the framework of two-foot-thick logs. The body stretched twenty feet behind that.

"Good God," Blair said, watching Marc leaning against the animal's sount.

"You are a warrior indeed!" Taldi said grudgingly.

Blair held out the capture kit. Marc took a second hypo and injected the contents into the soft flesh of the beast's inner nostril; it twitched slightly, and the watching Cloud Mountain warriors all jumped.

Mais, *I would myself, but I'm too tired*, Marc thought.

"Now that we've got it . . . ," Blair said.

"*Weh*," Marc replied. "Now for the brain surgery."

"What happens if it doesn't work?" the Englishman asked.

That was a fair question; only about half the operations were successful in Jamestown, and that was with a lot better facilities and more skilled personnel.

"Catch another one?" Marc asked. "Only this time *you* go in with the hypo."

Blair shuddered. Marc nodded and laughed. He slapped the unconscious animal on his massive, stubby nose horn, and poured a little of the water bag's contents over it.

"I christen thee . . . *Steed Noble*!"

CHAPTER THIRTEEN

Encyclopedia Britannica, 16th Edition
University of Chicago Press, 1988

NEW FRONTIER

Phrase often used by the American president John Fitzgerald Kennedy (q.v.) in speeches and policy statements during the 1960s. While first used in 1960 and applied to domestic issues, by 1962 the primary reference was to the space program, the prospective exploration of Mars and Venus, and secondarily to the associated technological developments. The term reached its maximum importance as a political slogan in the late 1960s, when it was also the title of the most popular television program of the period (see Popular Culture, American; Roddenbery, Gene). Some Republican critics assailed it as a disguise for allegedly weak positions on foreign policy, particularly the withdrawal of support for anti-Communist forces in Indo-China, though this became less common after the successful international initiatives of Kennedy's second term (see Indochinese War; Thailand Border Crisis, 1966–7; Six-Day War).

Teesa brushed aside the hide covering the door, and entered the hut, standing motionless by the door as the leather slowly settled back into place.

Cynthia looked up warily; she hadn't seen the Cloud Mountain shamaness in the three days since she'd been released from the data mining in the Cave of the Mysteries. Her mind still skittered away from that. Teesa looked disheveled in addition to the eerie *absence* in her face, like someone who'd been working hard for days and hadn't had the time or inclination to look after herself.

The blank blue eyes looked through the gloom of the hut at her, and Teesa said in English, "Information-gathering is complete. This unit will maintain efficiency more readily in detached mode. You will supply maintenance to the unit. Terminal-mode operation is suspended."

Then her eyes rolled up into her head and she collapsed like a puppet whose strings had met a razor. Jadviga darted forward, catching her before her head thumped on the hut's floor, and the two women lifted her onto a section of the bench that ran around the hut. Jadviga peeled back an eyelid.

"Shock," she said. "Put some of the furs over her."

"I'll get a clay pot of embers," Cynthia said, and snatched up a small shovel of hardened wood to scoop the remains of the fire on the hearth into a water jug.

"That is all we can do," Jadviga replied.

"Do you think . . . ," Cynthia said, as they rolled the unconscious woman on her side, tucked the pot of embers against her stomach, and pulled the glossy pelts around her.

"That she is put here as a spy?" Jadviga said. The Lithuanian woman's rather horselike face was charming as she smiled. "No. *It* can take over our minds whenever *it* pleases. What need of a spy? The KGB would love *it*."

Well, that's bold, Cynthia thought, and raised an eyebrow. "Ahh . . ."

Jadviga shrugged. "I doubt that the security services will be involved much more in my life," she said. "And if only I were not faced with death or worse . . ."

They both laughed. Cynthia checked on the tribeswoman's pulse and temperature; both were low, but slowly rising back to normal. At last her eyes fluttered open.

"Where am I?" she murmured—in English.

"In the village below the caves," Cynthia replied.

To her surprise, Teesa began to laugh. To Cynthia's shock, the laughter grew until it was on the verge of a scream; Jadviga's hand moved sharply, and the water in the bowl she had been holding ready splashed into Teesa's face. That cut off the building hysteria. The Cloud Mountain woman rubbed her hands over her face, and swung her feet down to the floor.

"I am sorry," she said. "But . . . all my life I have wanted to come here and see for the first time the Cave of the Mysteries, the long duty of my mothers before me. And now—"

Cynthia nodded in sympathy. *Sort of like a Christian getting to Heaven and finding the devil running things*, she thought. *Ouch.*

"What happened?" Jadviga asked.

"I am not sure," Teesa said. "Could I have some water?"

"Here," Jadviga said, refilling the bowl from a skin on the wall. "It's all we have, but there is plenty of it." She shuddered a little. "They make a drink, but I wouldn't feed it to pigs."

Cynthia winced; the Neanderthal women brewed it by chewing roots and spitting them into big gourds, then leaving the resulting pulp in the sun to ferment. Even in this place, the stink was unforgettable. So was the reaction of the subhumans to guzzling the stuff. She suspected there were psychotropics in the mash.

"Our stories tell of how sweet and cool the springs of this place are," Teesa said bitterly, but she drank the water and ate the dried meat and nutcakes.

"I can remember a little now and then," she said. "I sat in the Cave . . . there were lights and shapes, like nothing I have seen before. All my life came to me again, as if I were born and lived it over and over, but also stood aside and watched, as you might watch a game of catch-ball. And through me, the . . . I will not call it the

Master. The *thing* that dwells there saw all that I am. And I could feel its thoughts, and those meant nothing to it. It has no more self-hood than an ant."

"Yeah," Cynthia said. "Well, that's something *we* ought to think about."

Jadviga looked up, her eyes narrowing. After a moment Teesa did, too.

"What do you mean?"

"I'm not sure . . . except that *it* isn't a person. And we *are* people. We should be able to make something of that."

"Still looks good," Marc said, holding on to the rope ladder with his toes. "Steed looks healthy."

The ladder was strung from the middle of the beast's neck shield to the nose horn, a good eleven feet, more than a third of his total length. One big, yellow eye blinked at Marc under his brow shield of bone as he examined the gray plastic hemisphere that covered the Ice unit. The tissue around it looked clean and unin-flamed, and it had already begun to heal into a ring of scar; the lower edge was under the sheath of skin and muscle that covered the bony armor just above the 'saur's eyes.

"No infection," Marc said, sniffing to make sure.

Sure enough, nothing but the giant-iguana-and-stable smell of big herbivorous 'saur. Then Marc reached out and flicked open the top of the dome, took up the connector cable, and plugged it into the port.

"How does that read?"

Blair looked at the control box. "Green and go, Marc. All vital signs normal and connectors functioning. But why not use the wire-less system? We don't *need* a hard link."

"Humor me," Marc said. "Issues of *control* now make me nervous."

"You *do* have a point."

Marc scrambled back up to the 'saur's neck; he blinked again as the man passed the eyes. There was a moment's flicker of pity for the majestic animal turned into a giant meat machine, but Marc suppressed it; needs must, and anyway a 'saur like this had no more in the way of brains than a gecko, and considerably less than an ox. He walked and ate and crapped and made little 'saurs, and that was about it. And he wasn't in any pain—if anything, the trickle to his pleasure center that kept him calm and docile made this the happiest time of his life.

"Let's get it done," Marc said, and Blair hit the *release* button for a moment, waiting with thumb poised over the bliss-out control. The 'saur merely bent his head and started to snack on the fodder piled up under his nose; Marc let him eat as he slid down to the ground.

"Here, boy! Here, Tahyo!" he called.

The greatwolf's spotted nose showed from around a rock. He came into view half-crouched to the ground, tail held between his legs and twitching back and forth.

"Here, boy!"

The piteous rolling-eyed look translated roughly as: *Are you crazy, boss? Can't you smell how big and mean that thing is?* Nevertheless, Tahyo *did* come.

"See, it's harmless," Marc said, when the greatwolf was within arm's reach.

The 'saur shifted his weight from one foot to another and sighed as he ate. Tahyo skittered back half a dozen paces, then came reluctantly forward again. He whined as Marc picked him up—with a grunt; the young animal was gaining weight and size every day—and climbed a stepladder to hand him up to the howdah. Tahyo wriggled a little as he was handed over, then retreated to a corner of the enclosure and curled up, probably trying to pretend it wasn't happening from the way he put his tail over his eyes.

The 'saur ate on, unconcerned. The big ones didn't need to feed all the time despite their size, since their metabolism was less active than a mammal's, but it would be a good idea to stock up while they could. Crunching and cracking sounds came as he chomped through two-inch branches and then ate them like candy canes, leaves and needles and all.

Marc stood with arms akimbo and looked at the assembled warriors of the Cloud Mountain People, crouching or standing with their blanket rolls over their shoulders and their weapons in their hands. Taldi stood in front of them.

"Is my word good, or not, Taldi of the Badger totem?"

"Your word is good. You have done what you said you would do," Taldi replied. "Now let us rescue Teesa!"

"And get your holy place back," Marc added. "And rescue Teesa, yes."

Rescue her from more than physical danger. Having your mind taken over like that . . . that really is *a fate worse than death.* Marc looked at Blair's tight-held face. *Rescue Cynthia, too, of course.*

A cheer went up at Marc's words, from the warriors in the howdah and from the two hundred more grouped around the great ceratopid. The meadow where they'd gathered was nearly full; beyond was a long stretch of tree-speckled savannah, with a mixed herd of several thousand antelope a couple of miles away, a smaller one of *tharg*, the big bisonlike beasts flowing up a slope like a shaggy moon-horned tide, some *churr* lying under the shade of a steep hillside, and a bipedal 'saur mottled in green and orange, a plant eater with a face like a giant sheep, grazing off the top of a tree.

And about forty miles thataway, southeast, was the Cave of the Mysteries.

They're still nervous, Marc decided. *They've seen too many things from outside their world. And they're scared about the non-combatants. Time to get loud and flamboyant.*

"I promised you that I would lead you to your ancient homes riding on a hornhead thunder-lizard," he shouted. "And I will. I will lead you to victory!"

There were more cheers. When they'd died down, he climbed the stepladder to the howdah, pulling it up after him so it could be lashed to the side. It had solid plank and boiled-leather protection along the sides, probably enough to stop an AK-47 bullet, particularly since the enemy didn't have more than a couple of them left. The howdah would hold Blair with his scope-sighted game rifle, and the three remaining bullets, plus half a dozen of the best archers among the Cloud Mountain folk and a half-ton of supplies, which would spare them the need to forage as they went. And there was a nice padded seat for the driver.

"Gee-up, Steed Noble!" Marc called, and eased the joystick forward a notch.

The beast raised his head, splinters and fragments dropping

from his mouth, and gave a grumbling moan. Then he turned his head slightly from side to side. The impulses trickling into his head made him want to go in a certain direction, but his own programs for picking the details of a route still operated unless you threw the control farther forward.

He took a step, and then another, in the swaying left-front-leg-right-hind-leg pace that something this big had to use. The Cloud Mountain warriors cheered again, looking with envy at the ones riding in the howdah, then began walking, spreading out to either side.

"Now we find out," Blair said.

"Find out what?" Marc asked.

"What can go wrong next."

"Who would leave such a thing?" Teesa asked, rubbing at the red mark around her brow where the Diadem of the Eye had lain. "A blind monster with such power?"

Jadviga smiled bitterly. "Think what my people . . . well, my people in a way . . . have sent here," she said. "I like to think they would not use it—but they *did* send it."

Cynthia nodded soberly. They were sitting in the sunlight in the courtyard of the hut. That got them out into the fresh air, but it also exposed them to the flies and stink of the Wergu encampment. There was a bleak bitterness in the way Teesa cast an occasional glance around. There was a hate that went back generations here, and it made the fiercest ethnic squabbles back on Earth look tame—people back there might pretend that their enemies weren't human, but they knew better deep down. Here, the contending parties really *weren't* of the same species, any more than cows and horses were.

"Even without the Diadem of the Eye, I can *feel* it," Teesa said, looking east over the valley, the river and lake, to the yellow and black rock of the cliffs and the caves there. "At the back of my head, like a . . . a what is your word, a *machine* talking to itself inside me."

Cynthia nodded again. "There seems to be some sort of distance effect here," she said thoughtfully.

"Franziskus was taken to the cave," Jadviga added. "*It* can control him several miles away . . . but the control fades sometimes, and I do not think it could hold him much further than that."

"But through the Diadem, it could control *me*," Teesa said. "Thirty miles or more away. And through me, Cynthia."

Cynthia felt the skin crawl on her stomach and back. The memory of that icy violation, like spikes of ice driven into her head . . .

"So there are limits on what it can do," she said. "It can't control all the Wergu like waldos. I think the more people it . . . *interfaces* with . . . the less it can do with each."

"As if it were using up its bandwidth," Jadviga said thoughtfully.

The ground grew narrower as they neared the mountain spur where the Cloud Mountain People had once dwelt and where the Wergu now laired. The rolling hills grew steeper, with less grassland and more forest. The narrowing valleys were often swampy; Marc had to hit the *calm* button twice when Steed Noble began to sink a little in a swamp. His species' instincts made them very sensitive about falling over or getting bogged, and he held his head high and complained as they crossed the soft, wet ground and came out in a lush meadow on the other side.

"This is pretty country," Marc remarked to Blair.

The Englishman grunted, the big-game rifle ready in his hands. Still, it was true. Flamingos burst upward from the little lake to their east, living crimson streaks against the still-dark eastern horizon. The air was cool and crisp, full of the smells of water and green-musky-sweet crushed grass and herbs. Wisps of mist clung to the tops of the trees and drifted between them, also tinged with pink by the sunrise. And among them stirred . . .

"The beastmen!" someone shouted. "The Wergu come!"

Marc swallowed through a throat suddenly gone dry, and he heard Tahyo growling thunder-deep in his chest behind him. They'd picked a pretty good spot, too—there was only a couple of hundred yards from here to the forest.

"And a bloody great *lot* of the Wergu come," Blair said dryly.

"*Weh*."

Something like six or seven hundred of them, painted and screaming. The Cloud Mountain warriors were painted, too, but not screaming right now—murmuring, rather.

Marc unlimbered his binoculars; Tahyo put his forepaws on the forward edge of the howdah beside him, growling low in his chest and peeling back his lips over teeth that somehow looked much longer and sharper than they appeared normally. The man's thumb turned the focusing screw.

Hairy faces split to show tombstone teeth, stamping and hooting and waving their hardwood clubs, the black, fire-hardened points of their spears thrusting at the sky or booming the shafts on their hide shields. Bones through noses, human femurs crossed through topknots, here and there a shaman with the skull of a bear or saber-tooth or carnivore 'saur in one hand and a *baton de commandment*—a thick wand—in the other, dancing the cursing dance at the aliens.

"You see Binkis?" Marc said, passing his binoculars to the Englishman.

"No," Blair replied. "But I think I see who's leading them . . . the older one, the one-eyed?"

Marc took the glasses back. *So that's what an old Neanderthal looks like*, he thought. He hadn't seen many, but then, all the ones he'd met so far had been trying to kill him, which was young man's work.

The old Wergu was certainly hooting and gesturing hard. When a younger male darted forward, the older one clubbed him smartly on the back of the head, and then hit him in the face a couple of times for measure. The noise the others were making hid the sound, but Marc winced slightly inwardly at the thought of the solid hard *tock!* sound the knobkerrie would make.

"I'd say he's trying to keep them at the edge of the forest," Marc said. "Not such a *couyon*, him. He's their tactical control."

"Which is precisely what we don't want," Blair replied, taking a loop of the sling around his left forearm.

"Well, they're brave at least," Marc said. "They're not running away at the sight of the 'saur."

"Perhaps they're too stupid to be afraid," Blair said.

"Or they're fighting with their backs to their homes and children," Marc said, but quietly.

Aloud, to Taldi: "If they charge, shoot as many as you can with arrows. Then keep close to Steed Noble."

The Cloud Mountain man dipped his head slightly in a taut acknowledgment.

"And . . . ," Blair whispered, resting the rifle on the edge of the howdah.

Crack.

Through the binoculars Marc saw the ancient Wergu jerk backward and then spin, clutching at his left arm and then looking incredulously as it came loose in his hand. He shrieked once, sank to his knees, and then forward onto his face to lie twitching for a few seconds as his powerful heart pumped diminishing jets out through the stump.

"*Here they come!*" Marc snapped. "Save the ammo, Chris."

"Bloody right," Blair replied. "Use our steed."

Marc ducked down, until only his eyes showed over the edge of the howdah; and he pushed the joystick forward, thumbing off the calming circuit at the same time.

OOOOOOOONNNNKKKK!

He could feel the quiver that went through Steed Noble as the electronic tether was removed, up through the boards and leather padding of the floor. The suddenness of the charge that followed put Marc's teeth together with a snap, and made his eyeballs feel as if they were going to pop out through sheer inertia; Tahyo pitched backward against the feet of the bowmen, yelping.

The massive feet came down, *thud . . . thud . . . thud . . .* then *thudthudthud*, as the ceratopid burst into an elephantine gallop. The Cloud Mountain men behind him yelled and clutched at the grab-bars of the howdah; one nearly toppled over the side as it swayed and tossed.

Ahead was a knot of Wergu with AK-47s. The assault rifles gave them confidence, or maybe it was natural fearlessness; they stood and shot, and bullets began to snap by. A few struck the great bone shield over Steed Noble's head, and Marc could hear the hard rapping sound, like high-velocity hail hitting concrete.

Trickles of blood ran down from the tiny wounds in the thin sheath of flesh over the bone, but they had no chance of seriously hurting the 'saur, unless a golden BB hit an eye. But they could kill *Marc* quite effectively and finally. And they were getting closer; the 'saur was doing better than twenty-five miles an hour now. Marc ducked down farther.

Suddenly the knot of Wergu riflemen seemed to realize that they were facing something twelve feet high and thirty long, and that he was *pissed*.

They burst apart like a ball of dandelion fluff struck by a puff of breath. Steed Noble ducked his head and tossed one overhead with a jab of his horn, so high that a trail of blood droplets fell neatly along the length of his spine and tail. Tahyo's head tracked that one like a radar set, with a pitch of his ears that said: *Wow, I didn't know they could fly!*

Marc spat in disgust to get the blood out of his mouth; wrenching his focus back, he turned the joystick to steer the 'saur toward the largest clump. Steed Noble needed little encouragement. He gave a whistle like a ruptured boiler and crashed into the midst of them, goring right and left with his horn, stamping with yard-wide feet. The Cloud Mountain archers in the howdah had recovered enough to shoot; the platform was violently unstable, but the range was short. Marc turned left down the line of Neanderthals just outside the forest edge. Branches scraped along the top of the howdah, and men ducked with yells, but the Wergu broke to either side like foam before a ship's prow, or dirt to either side of a plow.

Except that dirt doesn't scream or bleed, Marc thought grimly. *Or go* squish *like a* peunez *when it gets stepped on by something that weighs seven tons.*

He glanced back out into the meadow, blinking eyes watering after a branch had lashed him across the face. With half the Wergu gone, the Cloud Mountain warriors were coming forward with a will, shooting as they ran. The remaining Neanderthals wavered, then broke in a hooting mass as he turned Steed Noble in a wide circle and headed towards them.

"They flee!" Taldi shouted exultantly, freeing his spear from a Wergu's back.

"That they do," Blair said. "And those that don't very much wish they could."

He said it in English. Marc nodded, as the warriors finished off any Wergu still moving with spear-thrusts. He tried not to let it bother him; they played for keeps around here.

"Let's get going," he said. "Once they're running I want to keep them on the run."

"Now is the time," Teesa said firmly. "Their males have all gone to fight."

"Yeah, but I don't much like the look of the womenfolk, either, you know?" Cynthia said ruefully. *Guess this is it, sister,* she thought. *Talked the talk, now you better walk the walk.*

"Teesa is right," Jadviga said firmly. "We must act now, or never."

Cynthia nodded soberly. The three of them pulled back the furs along a section of the bench around the interior of the hut. Beneath lay the weapons they'd made: three crude chipped-stone daggers, and clubs made from sections of wood taken from the rafters.

"I will lead," Teesa said.

Cynthia's brows went up. "You remember the way to the Cave? I thought you were pretty well out of it. I sure as hell was."

Teesa nodded, and smiled grimly. "I was, yes, out of it. But all my life, I have repeated to myself the things my mother and the other elders said about this place. Even though I have never been there in my waking life, I know it as one hand knows the other."

They pushed the daggers through their belts and took up the clubs, and slipped out from the dim interior into the bright fly-buzzing haze of the courtyard. The sound of chanting and hollow-log drums came from the south end of the village, near the lake, where the Neanderthal women held a ceremony to aid their menfolk. The usual drifts of wood smoke were about, and the usual stinks, but less of the common noise—the screeching and hooting and grunts.

Plenty of children and girl-adolescents were left. They watched the humans, some scowling and hissing, one turning and scratching her feet in the dirt at them. Younger children simply stared; one of about two watched Cynthia while clutching a crude wooden figure to her chest, a thumb in her mouth. Cynthia grimaced slightly; the Wergu children looked a *lot* more human than the adults. It was hard to wish them ill.

And at the end of the row of huts . . .

"That is where the old one lairs," Teesa said. "The Diadem will be there."

I hope, Cynthia thought.

An old Wergu woman was. She hooted at them as they approached, clutching arthritis-gnarled hands and making pushing gestures, white hair swinging on either side of her jut-browed bristly face. After an irresolute moment Cynthia pushed past her.

A hand shot out and clamped on her shoulder, shockingly hard. By reflex she twisted and grabbed, a self-defense move designed to rip against the thumb of an attacker. The fingers stayed clamped on her, like a mechanical grab inside a glove of rough leather, and bone began to creak under the grip; the Neanderthals were *strong,* ape-strong compared to humans. Cynthia hissed in pain and reached for her knife.

Jadviga clamped her lips and swung her club. The wood went *crack* on the Wergu woman's elbow, and the oldster screeched and let go. Teesa was behind her; she planted a knee in the other's back, hooked her left arm around her chin, and swept the sharp stone knife with her right. The Wergu ululated and flopped and was still, with a spreading pool of crimson spreading beneath her bent form and swatch of white hair.

"Okay," Cynthia said with a slight wince. "Let's look."

The interior of the hut was crowded, but not as disorderly or dirty as you might have expected from the Wergu settlement as a whole. Bags hung from the walls, and weird collections of bones and herbs and sticks; there was a heavy sharp smell, almost medicinal. Gourd bowls were heaped with unidentifiable substances, or colored pebbles; one brimmed with gold nuggets. A stone lamp with a crude wick burning in fat stood before a niche that held a small Wergu skull . . . a sacrifice? Sacred relic? Remembrance of a loved one? There was no way to tell.

And one stone that jutted from the hut's wall, the Diadem of the Eye. Teesa darted towards it, then hesitated, her hand slowing as she reached towards it. Cynthia felt her own skin crawl in sympathy; it had been the center of the tribeswoman's life, the most holy relic of her people . . . and it had betrayed her. Now it stood for the dreadful violation of the self that Cynthia had shared.

"I will do it," Jadviga snapped.

"No!" Teesa said.

She reached out and took it. They all held their breath, but it was nothing but an inert piece of metal as she dropped it in the pouch at her side.

"Now to the Cave! *Quickly!*"

Steed Noble paced down the narrow path, his head weaving in a ceratopid equivalent of nervousness, as the forest way wound downward towards the lake and river where the holy village of the Cloud Mountain People had been. Great trees crowded close on either side, types of oak and beech, others he couldn't identify, with odd spiky branches and long drooping leaves mottled in dark green and pale white, towering a hundred feet and more overhead in a tangled mass of branches.

Lianas dipped from branch and trunk, and flowering vines climbed in a profusion of blue and purple and trembling sheets of gold. Insects buzzed through the olive-colored gloom beneath the great trees amid a languorous musty scent of blossom and decay, but only a few scampering monkeys could be seen, and a few three-foot-high feathered 'saurs scampered across their path in a scatter of dead leaves.

"Me think it maybe *too* quiet," Marc said.

Blair made a peculiarly English *mmmph?* sound, and then Marc saw how the branches above were stirring, more and faster than the slow wind could account for. Tahyo had been looking upward, flicking his ears; now he growled and then *wulfed* again and again, his call for alarm and danger.

"Watch out!" Marc shouted, and "*Beware!*" in the Cloud Mountain tongue.

He drew his pistol and shot, a long tongue of red flame in the dimness. The first of the Wergu dropping from the branches above folded in midair with an *urrggg* as the flat elastic snap of the 10 mm round sounded. He bounced off the 'saur's shield and fell under the steady pile-driver beat of the enormous hoof-toed feet. A thrown club struck the pistol out of Marc's hand a second later. The weapon fell under Steed Noble's left rear foot and was ground out of shape against a rock. Marc shook his hand for a second, cursing at the pain.

More of the subhumans were dropping, their limbs outstretched like giant hairy spiders. One landed in the howdah and grabbed a Cloud Mountain tribesman by the front of his face and the rear of his skull and *lifted* the head off with a dreadful wet tearing-ripping-snapping sound, and blood fountained into the air for an instant. Then the others were on the subhuman, their flint-headed toma-hawks rising and falling with thudding crunches as the hominid roared and tried to grapple. A second landed on the 'saur's tail and started to climb into the howdah. He had time for just one hooting scream as Tahyo rose and set his jaws on the beastman's face and squeezed.

Another came down on the 'saur's nose, just above the horn, and began to scramble up towards Marc with inhuman agility, his knobkerrie in one hand. Blair's arm came past Marc's shoulder; the Cajun winced away in anticipation, and slitted his eyes against the muzzle-flash.

Crack. Crack.

Two deliberate shots, and the beastman toppled backward. More were falling all around them, and there was a confused scram-bling scrimmage amid the boles of the trees, screams and bellows and shrieks of sudden pain, the whirling chaos of any sudden fight with no way to tell what was happening. Marc stabbed at the button that would halt the 'saur and reached for his machete, although his right hand was still a little numb.

Mais, our guns, they don't seem to last, eh? I'll be down to a stone hatchet myself, pretty soon. The thought made him want to laugh, which would be a bad idea right then.

"Stand fast!" Marc heard Taldi shout. "Stand fast, Cloud Moun-tain men! The beasts are few! Kill them. *Kill!*"

After a dazed moment Marc realized that was true; only a couple of dozen had taken part in the ambush, probably the only ones left with the heart for it. Outnumbered scores to one, they quickly went down, but they took more than a few of their enemies with them, plucked apart or clubbed into splinters of bone and flesh. The tribesmen stood panting and glaring about them, blood running from hatchet blade and spear point and knife.

"Forward!" Taldi said, and suited words to action, loping down the trail.

Marc pushed the joystick forward again, and the rolling motion of the ceratopid increased as the muffled drumbeat of his feet beat faster. It seemed like only a few moments later when they burst through into bright sunlight: not open country, more in the nature of scrubby second growth, but without the overarching canopy. A dozen strides later and they passed an odd-looking falcon-faced totem pole, old and moss-grown and leaning out of plumb, with a rude stone altar before it. Then they were out on an open slope, and below them was a river and a lake and a village, and across the water a cliff pierced by the mouths of many caves.

The Cloud Mountain men raised a long exultant cheer. Blair nodded towards the village. Scores of figures were scuttling out of the buildings, down the stream towards the lake and the forests and swamps there. Most of them seemed to be women carrying children, or youngsters on foot, with a guard of males.

"The lost homeland of the Cloud Mountain People, currently occupied by the Wergu. It looks very much as if that ambush was a last stand and suicide mission to let the females and young escape."

"*Weh*," Marc replied. "I think our Cloud Mountain friends are a bit prejudiced, them."

"Understandable, but there you are. By all means, let us proceed with our organic tank, shall we?"

Marc turned the joystick, and Steed Noble began a cautious descent of the rough trace. "To the village, or the caves?"

The two men were tensely silent for a moment. Teesa and Cynthia—and Jadviga Binkis, for that matter—would be in either one or the other. A wrong guess might be the difference between rescuing a living person and finding a gutted corpse . . . if they were alive at all, which was impossible to tell.

Can't think like that, you, Marc told himself. *Not if you want to function—and you need one hundred percent right now.*

"Caves," he said. "Some of the Cloud Mountain Texians will be going into the village, and they'll find the women if they're there."

They would indeed; they were trotting alongside Steed Noble and baying like wolves as the straggling line of stone huts came closer. A knot of Wergu fighters held the street, behind an improvised barrier, their shields up. The Cloud Mountain men put shafts to the strings of their new bows and loped towards them. The ones in the howdah complained as Marc turned the beast aside and towards the river.

Taldi silenced them. "The holy one is there!" he barked. "Watch out—there may be more of them hidden among the rocks."

"This is the holy *place*," one of the bowmen replied. "Is it not cursed for un-sanctified men to come here?"

A shadow passed over Taldi's face; then he shrugged. "If it is cursed, let the curse rest on me!"

"My eye," Marc murmured to himself. "He's determined, that one!"

A score or so of Cloud Mountain fighters accompanying Steed Noble hesitated at the edge of the water; it was cold and fairly rough here. Marc waited while Taldi waded over, holding his bow over his head; the water came about to his waist, no more than thigh deep on the 'saur. Marc pushed the joystick forward, and the big beast took a first step in.

Oooonnkk, he said plaintively. Then: *Ooon! Ooon!* Which probably meant *cold, cold*. He advanced tentatively, making sure of his footing each time; the water never reached more than halfway up his columnar legs, but he had to hold his great low-slung head up, and he complained again when his tail dipped into the rushing mountain stream.

Marc was more concerned about what waited on the other side. The semicircle of cliffs was a thousand feet high, dark rock below, crimson sandstone above. The noon sun leached shadow and contrast from it, but the cave-mouths were still black eyes into nothing. A flight of pterosaurs took off from the higher reaches as they came close, medium-sized ones with twenty-foot wingspans and long fin-like crests at the back of their heads. Their shrill hissing cries echoed from the rocks; amid rock and water and crushed herbs, the ammonia scent of their rookery was strong.

The Cloud Mountain men fell silent, the looming cliff weighing on their spirits. So did the carvings along the winding path that led upward through patches of rock and shrub, totem poles ancient and decayed, uncared-for since their grandfathers' day.

"Which one is the Cave of the Mysteries, Taldi?" Marc called.

"There," the tribesman said, pointing with his spear. "Along the well-worn path, between those piles of rocks." Then he dashed ahead a dozen feet. "Look! Look!"

It was a long 'saur feather. Blair leaned down recklessly from the howdah. "It's one of the ones Cyn was wearing!" he said, suddenly grinning like a wolf. "We're on the right track!"

"And this one is from Teesa's garb!" Taldi said.

"If it was dropped today," Marc said.

"Here," Taldi said. "More! Lying light on the grass. These were dropped of a purpose, as a sign."

Marc slid to the ground and whistled. Tahyo came down from the howdah in a scrambling rush, panting up at him. He showed Tahyo the feather and watched the wet black nose wrinkle as the greatwolf took the scent.

"Follow!" Marc said. "Follow, boy! Come on, *boug*!"

Tahyo cast around, then put his nose to the ground, looked up, whined, and trotted away. The path he followed was a rising one, heading for the mouth of the largest cave.

"That settles it," Marc said grimly.

Blair extended a hand. Marc leaped, caught it by the wrist, braced a foot on the 'saur's knee, and leaped again, hauled upward by his own spring and the Englishman's strong arm. Tahyo paused and looked over his shoulder with a *follow me!* expression.

"The very Cave of the Mysteries," Taldi whispered.

"Where else?" Marc said, and pushed the joystick forward again.

Teesa shuddered. The approach to the Cave of the Mysteries was bad enough, but now she felt . . . like something was touching each bone in her spine with a cold finger that slid inside her flesh to touch the cord there.

"*It* is awake," she said. "I can feel it. And it seeks to know what passes."

The three women looked over their shoulders, crouched against the boulder that had fallen from the cliff side long ago and half-buried itself in the dirt. Back on the other slope the Wergu were streaming out of the forest and down towards the village.

"Our people must have the victory," she said. "Now we must protect them!"

The three looked at one another, nodded, and walked forward. The last of her folk's spirit-poles lay on the ground nearby; she bent and touched it for an instant, taking comfort from the rough feel of the wood under her fingertips, and the connection with her blood. Then she looked up grimly at the ragged, irregular hole of the entrance. Generations of her people had shaped and polished it, but it still looked to her now like some misshapen mouth gaping to devour her once again, twenty paces across and as many high. Few memories remained of her first passage through there under the control of *it*, but those would make her wake sweating from evil dreams for the rest of her life.

If I live, she thought mordantly, and smiled.

"Let us go."

The three of them approached, useless clubs clutched tightly in their hands for comfort. The shadow fell chill on them as they entered, the rock of the floor like a single slab beneath their feet. Ten yards farther in, something moved, moved with a creak and rattle of metal.

It was Binkis, his features terribly calm. The rifle was slung over his back, and he dragged a *thing* on a wheeled dolly behind him, a thing like a blowgun dart . . . *no, more like a bullet*, she thought. That was a thing of Jadviga's clan of the Sky People, and so was the cart beneath it. Some inconsequential part of her mind dredged up an English word: "dolly."

Binkis looked at them. "Units will return to the holding area," he said. "Contamination of the observational sphere has reached out-of-parameter levels. This locus is endangered. Readjustment is necessary to reestablish unimpeded interactions. Resistance is futile."

Teesa heard Cynthia mutter something under her breath, something like, "Oh, lordy, now he's quoting from a *New Frontier* episode." Then Cynthia said more clearly, "That thing there . . . the biobomb . . . won't that contaminate your observational sphere anyway?"

Binkis nodded in two motions, one up, one down. "That is unavoidable. The premature intrusion of source-globe sapiens has already introduced it. In this region it will reestablish parameters for some time."

"Franziskus!" Jadviga said earnestly. "They may not have planned to actually *use* it!"

"Probability too low to calculate," the *thing* that spoke through her husband's face said. Then the man showed for a flicker: "You know them, darling! The *Yanki* have the ear of the only city on Venus. They will destroy it to isolate the Americans, and then blame them for the plague. Here far fewer will die."

Teesa's hand moved. She took a deep breath, reached into the pouch, and brought out the Diadem. Then she dropped it around her brow and reached out with either hand, clamping them tight on the back of the other women's skulls, and *pushed*.

The world vanished.

"This is as far as he can go!" Marc said.

Oooooonnnnkkk! Onnng! Onnng! Steed Noble chimed in.

He waved his great head back and forth, setting a foot on the steep path up and pulling it back as rock shifted and clattered under the great disk of gristle and bone. It would take the full power of the Ice unit to make the beast venture farther onto steep, uncertain footing. All his instincts must be screaming at him. It was a matter of size. If you dropped a mouse off a mountain, it would land unharmed. A cat might be injured, or possibly killed. A man would certainly die. Something the size of a seven-ton ceratopid would *splash*, even from a fall that a man could survive.

"Then let's get going," Blair said grimly.

Marc pressed the *stay-put* button, and Steed Noble's head drooped until his beak touched the ground. A line of drool dropped to the ground, and the beast's yellow reptile eyes half-closed as he sighed in ecstasy. Until the switch was turned off or the batteries ran out, not even being dismembered would distract the 'saur much.

They all slid to the surface. "Wait here," Marc said to the Cloud Mountain warriors.

Most of them were glad enough to do so; Tahyo was, too, flattening himself to the rock and laying his ears back, rolling his eyes in a pleading expression. Taldi simply shook his head and followed the two Terrans, though his face turned a sickly shade under its natural amber and his lips were peeled back in a fixed rictus of determination.

The rocks rattled under their moccasins as they took the last few yards, throwing up a little dust. The papery smell of it contrasted with the cold stone breath of the cave. Marc's mouth was dry and his heart thuttered under his breastbone, but he felt steady and alert for all that. Blair brought the heavy rifle down from across his back and worked the bolt, a long *chick-chack!* as he put the second-from-last bullet into the chamber. They paused for an instant to let their eyes adjust to the gloom, and then they saw the tableau of motionless figures. They scarcely seemed to breathe. The sudden outward flutter of hundreds of tiny hand-sized pterosaurs with long rudder-tipped tails was a jarring contrast; then silence settled back over their fading cheeps and twitters.

Teesa stood with her back to them, and her hands on the backs of the heads of Cynthia and Jadviga. The Diadem of the Eye was on Teesa's head, and even from the rear Marc could see how the jewel on her forehead was shedding a crawling pattern of green light. That glittered in Binkis' unmoving eyes.

"Teesa!" Taldi shouted.

None of the figures moved. Marc put out a hand to restrain the Cloud Mountain warrior, but he brushed past.

"The wizard has enchanted you, but I will set you free!" he called, and dashed forward.

His knife was in his hand as he drove for Binkis, but the Lithuanian still didn't move—or perhaps that which used him as a puppet of flesh didn't let him. Instead Taldi suddenly pitched forward onto the rock-slab floor of the cave. He gave one scream as every muscle in his body convulsed, and then there was a crackle of bone and he was limp, with blood running from nose and mouth, eyes and ears.

"That's a weapon on the dolly," Marc said tightly.

"Yes, old boy, it is," Blair replied. "And an EastBloc one. Cyrillic lettering. Offhand I'd say it was meant to be delivered by a medium-sized missile."

"*Weh*, I think Teesa is trying something. And I don't think we should upset it."

"But we must do *something*."

Marc took a deep breath. "Whether or not it works—," he began.

"—one has to finish," Blair finished.

Marc took a step to the left of Cynthia. Blair moved to the right of Jadviga, raising the rifle.

The universe vanished.

Where am I? Marc thought.

What it *felt* like was standing on an infinite gray plain under a gray sky. Looking down, he could see that the gray surface under his feet was somehow crawling—like a mass of tiny ants, or perhaps of even tinier machines, blinking on and off without color or light. The air felt . . . neutral, without scent or heat or cold. When he took a step, nothing changed, but he could sense an almost infinite motion, and suddenly he was standing next to the others.

Cocain! he thought.

The space around him did feel *big*, without having any dimensions that he could put a name to.

The others were looking around themselves as well. All except Binkis, who stood and stared at them as he had in the cave . . .

And perhaps he still is, him, Marc thought.

. . . except that his eyes were blank surfaces of the gray seething whatever-it-was.

"Bandwidth is insufficient," he said in the same flat voice.

It had no more affect to it than before, but now Marc could hear . . . or sense . . . a vast irritation in it. Something of the feeling a man might have when he was interrupted in important work.

"You have betrayed the Cloud Mountain People," Teesa said. "We who served and guarded you so long!"

The terrible eyes moved to her. "Memetic framework is insufficient," Binkis said. Then he paused for an instant. "There were others before you. After you there will be more. The study program continues."

"You're an observer?" Marc broke in. "You're a . . . a computer left to observe the experiment here on Venus?"

"This is congruent with those aspects your memetic framework can access," Binkis said. "You are an incompatible element. The time frame is incorrect and inconsistent with parametric projections."

Blair cut in. "We're unpredictable, eh? But what's the point of a study program if it only tells you what you expected to find out?"

A longer pause. "This is in congruence with the primary code," Binkis said. "Consulting decision tree."

Silence stretched. The subliminal flicker of movement from the not-ground and not-air increased.

"I think this is a projection," Cynthia said tightly. "An analogue we can interface with. We've been trying to talk it out of using the EastBloc weapon, the biobomb—"

"Biobomb?" Marc said sharply.

"Mutated smallpox. They were going to use it on Kartahown and then blame us for contamination—get us in Dutch back on Earth and wipe out our advantage, then go back to their original plan of building up Cosmograd until Venus was theirs."

"Sons of bitches!" Marc said, and shot a venomous look at Jadviga. "And now we know about the sabotage on the *Vepeja*!"

"No," Blair said suddenly, and seemed to draw a deep breath. "That was me."

"*What!*"

That came from several voices at once, Cynthia's loudest and most outraged.

"I'm an agent. Not theirs! I'm a *French* agent. Deuxième Bureau. I *am* French . . . well, my mother was, and she raised me. But only the first fiddle with the valves, on my honor!"

"On your honor as a *spy*?" Cynthia said bitterly.

"On my honor as a human being. Yes, we—they—wanted to slow you down while the Union got its space program going. But not vileness, not a plague!"

"Sister," Teesa said. "He speaks the truth."

Suddenly Binkis turned his head to look at Blair. "Your code and mine are congruent. A temporary reduction of contamination within the sphere of observation."

"No," Blair said sharply.

"Analysis of memetic framework is insufficient," Binkis replied;

there was a tinge of . . . regret? "Observations are beyond my paradigm. Consultation with the primary species becomes imperative."

The universe returned.

Blair raised the rifle to his shoulder. The echoing *crack* boomed back and forth in the great chamber, but the bullet went wild as Jadviga Binkis launched herself into his shoulder. She dashed forward as he staggered.

"Franziskus!" she gasped. "Fight that thing! Fight it now!"

For a moment his face writhed, and then he turned and strode away, the dolly rattling behind him. The Lithuanian woman ran after him, her voice fading as they turned a corner in the narrowing cave.

Blair lowered the rifle, his bare chest heaving and covered in sweat despite the coolness of the air. Marc felt the same uncertainty . . . just what *had* happened? A light was shining from beyond the curve in the passageway. Or not a light, but something that shone through the very rock itself, until the fabric of the world rippled about him, and he saw once again the crawling lights beneath the surface of things that he had experienced in that *other* place.

Teesa's hands tore the Diadem from her head. *"Run!"* she shouted. *"Run now!"*

They did, a confused scramble out into the air. The waiting Cloud Mountain warriors took one look at their faces, and then over their shoulders, and turned and sprinted down the pathway towards the river. All over the cliff, every bird and pterosaur took flight at once, thousands lifting from the crimson stone in a screeching, shrieking tide.

"Take the 'saur; it'll be faster!" Marc shouted.

He had to grab Teesa by the arm and nearly throw her up into the howdah. The rest followed in a scrambling rush, Tahyo virtually climbing over his back in a blunt-clawed, wild-eyed scrabble. He twisted at the joystick just as Blair dropped the heavy rifle and made a flying leap for the harness that held the howdah on Steed Noble's back. The giant creature turned in his own length, starting a miniature avalanche from the ground around them. The real article was starting higher up, and a sheet of rock slid free of the cliff-face and earthquaked to the ground, sending four-foot boulders rolling nearly to the 'saur's feet like cosmic dice.

Then they were moving. Teesa screamed and screamed again, her hands beating at her temples; the light of the Diadem's jewel flared. The non-light leaked out of the cave-mouth behind them as they reached the water; this time the 'saur took the ford without hesitation, spray flying twenty feet into the air on either side, and they were through and up the slope on the other side, passing some of the fleeing warriors.

The world twisted.

For a moment Marc felt weightless, and then there was a roar that went on and on, filling the universe with its white noise. That died to merely a cataclysmically loud rumble, as Steed Noble paced on at his best freeway-ramp speed, slowing only a little as the slope steepened again. The whole Cloud Mountain war party was running, too, as the village that had been theirs and then the Wergu's and then so briefly theirs again shook itself into mounds of rock. Trees toppled in the forest all about, under a sky full of wings; a crocodile three times the length of a man thrashed its way out of the sacred lake below and ran staggering across the heaving land. Dust billowed past them, choking-thick, and Marc coughed until his eyes ran.

When Marc halted the 'saur and turned him, they all sat and stared, frozen. Where a thousand feet of cliff had reared on the other side of the water, a tumbled fall of scree stretched across from bank to bank. Dust still screened it, and boulders still shifted and bounced, but Marc could see where the water would pond back to fill the valley and make another, deeper lake. Dribs and drabs of Cloud Mountain folk still staggered and crept up towards the 'saur; surprisingly few of them were missing, but many were injured.

Smack!

Marc came to himself with a start. Blair was sitting and looking shocked, with a handprint across his face; Cynthia slipped down to the ground and strode away to stand with her back to the faux Englishman, her arms crossed.

Blair started to follow, then nodded at Marc's shake of the head.

Teesa was weeping, quietly and hopelessly. When Marc put his arm around her shoulders she accepted it without hope.

"The Cave of the Mysteries is gone forever, and it was never ours," she said, as the tears trickled down through the dust below her turquoise-colored eyes. "And the Diadem will never speak to me again, and my people's long home is gone, and now you will leave me and return to your Jamestown, and there is nothing left in all the world for me."

He took her in his arms, smiling down into her face. "Now, *ma negresse*, I've been thinking about that, eh?"

CHAPTER FOURTEEN

Venus, Gagarin Continent—eastern border of the Jamestown
Extraterritorial Zone
1990

"You've taken a lot on yourself, Lieutenant Vitrac," General Clarke
said grimly.

He made a gesture behind himself to keep the others quiet, es-
pecially Sam Feldman, who was quivering with a mixture of scientific eagerness and genuine emotion.

"Yes, sir, I have," Marc said.

Apparently he wasn't in the least discommoded by the fact that
he was appearing before a superior officer in breechclout and moccasins. He inclined his head slightly and gestured:

"But first may I present my wife, Teesa Vitrac, and my son,
Marc Junior."

The General's hard-clenched aquiline face relaxed a little as he
looked at the young woman. She smiled, and the exotic beauty of
her amber-skinned, slant-eyed face blossomed into loveliness; the
year-old child in her arms had something of that look, but his eyes

were a darker blue and his hair was ash-blond rather than his mother's bright yellow. The barbaric finery of feathers and worked leather seemed to suit her, and so did the AK-47 slung over her back beside the quiver full of arrows.

"I'm pleased to meet you, General," she said easily, juggling the baby and extending a hand in the manner of Western civilization. "Marc has told me so much about you."

He blinked. *Evidently there was some truth to that report,* he thought. *Nobody could learn quite that Cajun accent without alien hyper-tech. Or gotten complete fluency so fast.*

The rest of the . . . traveling circus, he thought, *has come just inside the boundary of the Extraterritorial Zone.*

Though it wouldn't matter much, since east of here is nothing but wandering tribes for hundreds of miles, for all the claims of Kartahown's kings.

He ran a quick expert's eye over the neat rows of leather tents, noting the lack of dirt and disorder, and estimated that there were three or four hundred men, women, and children. All looking enough like Mrs. Vitrac to be her close kin.

Which they are, of course.

A girl of about ten Earth-years ran by, white-blond hair trailing, her arm around the neck of a greatwolf nearly as high as she was, its panting tongue dangling over the monstrous sawteeth. There were two or three other greatwolves in sight, all closer to the puppy stage; he thought he knew where the Cloud Mountain People had picked up *that* idea.

And not only that one. A fair-sized herd of tame *churr* was just crossing the stream that marked the border, under the guidance of whooping mounted warriors equipped with bows and lances and lariats. Dozens of sturdy two-wheeled carts were parked around the encampment, and gear was being unloaded. There was a pleasant scent of wood smoke and cooking already. Others piled wild shamboo before the beak of a 'saur of unfamiliar species. Cynthia Whitlock and Christopher Blair came from there, hand in hand and also in native dress; she wasn't carrying a child in her arms, but from the look of things was six months or so along.

"Wing Commander, and . . . Mrs. Blair," the General said, correcting himself in midsentence. "Good to see you alive."

"The two who disposed of the EastBloc biobomb," Marc said.

"Ah, yes, that," Clarke said. "I'd like to hear more details. We'll have to keep it quiet."

At Marc's raised eyebrow, he went on: "Give us some credit, Lieutenant. That trick would only work if we didn't know they were doing it. Now we know and they won't try it again. Other things, but not that."

Marc nodded, then began to wind up for his speech. Clarke made a chopping gesture.

"Save it, Lieutenant Vitrac. Yes, you're right. These people will be a valuable addition to the Extraterritorial Zone. And yes, we'll confirm the treaty you—with your damned impudence!—drew up with them. Full internal autonomy, commercial ties, educational access . . . they're the first people we've met who *want* that."

"Thank you very much, General Clarke," Teesa Vitrac said. "My people have been looking for a new home. And we've made a good start on . . . how do you say . . . our *relationship* with the Sky People."

The baby looked at him and solemnly sucked his thumb. Clarke laughed.

"You'll have to fight to keep that tyke out of Dr. Feldman's hands," he said.

"Sorry, Sam. Looks like there's definite proof that Venusians are *H. sap. sap.*," Marc said, grinning at the older man.

Teesa joined in the chuckle; then she sobered and produced a slivery diadem. "This was our pride and glory, but it is nothing now," she said, and handed it to the scientist.

Feldman's pleasantly ugly face lit up, transformed. "And this is proof there were people here who *weren't* our kind," he said.

"Yes." Marc Vitrac's nod matched Clarke's.

The General shook his head. "And what happened to Binkis and his wife, if they weren't crushed under the rock? That seems a little . . . prosaic."

"I doubt we'll ever know," Marc said. He looked at his wife and shrugged expressively. "And who cares, eh?"

EPILOGUE

"I can fly!" Franziskus Binkis said, laughing. "I can fly! Jadviga; I can fly!"

She crouched weeping and pulling out strands of her hair. He leaped, bounding half his own height in the air, and came down laughing even as he fell. His chest heaved as it tried to drag in enough of the air; it was dry and thin, with an acrid papery scent of stone, dust, and ancient incense. For a moment there was the same feeling of twisting dislocation behind him, and then there was only the ruddy sandstone. His mind felt as light as his body, freed of the intolerable weight that had filled it. Strips of softly glowing yellow light on the high arched ceiling cast a complex pattern of brightness and shadows across the walls, illuminating faded frescoes and bas-reliefs blurred with unimaginable time.

If Franziskus Binkis had stopped to study their subject matter, he might have found them disturbing. Instead he pulled himself erect and danced across the great room like a gangling cricket, ex-ulting in a gravity only one-third of Earth's. At last he came to a stop before a throne. It stood on a plinth of polished jade, drilled and worked into a fretwork of vines and tiny flowers made from chips of ruby and emerald, diamond and tourmaline. The spindly arms and back were of some silvery metal, wrought in the shape of elongated human forms.

The figure seated on it might have been their model, inhumanly tall and thin, clothed in robes of dull scarlet, the skin stretched over his slender scimitar features a deep russet brown, with a great crimson jewel above his yellow eyes, and black hair falling to his shoulders. Behind him stood a globe twice the throne's height, the lines of barren continent and shrunken sea, canal and polar ice caps, picked out in delicate glass and metal. Some fragment of Binkis' ruined mind noted the differences from the Mars whose photographs he'd studied, with more of life and less of desert.

The seated figure was utterly motionless; it took a moment for Binkis to notice that it neither breathed nor blinked, and that there was the faintest film of dust on the open eyes.

"You've been here awhile, eh, *Velnio Ishpera*, eh?" he said, staggering and laughing. "Quite awhile, you old devil's spawn!"

The whisper of soft shoes on the glass tile of the throne room brought Binkis around. The man approaching had something of the same look of mantis elegance as the figure on the throne, but he was very much alive . . . or was it a he? The muliebrous features could have been man or woman or creature from the stories his grandmother had told, supple as a snake in close-fitting black. The long blade it held in one hand shimmered black as well, but its edge caught the faint light with a lethal glitter. Yellow eyes regarded Binkis, and long silky-white hair tossed in a gesture.

"You are right, vas-Terranan," the stranger said, in good Russian with a lilting, purring accent. "He has kept vigil here for long and long. Very long, even as we of the First People keep count of time."

"Well, who is he, then?" Binkis said, brushing the back of one hand over his mouth with a rasp of bristles.

"Timrud Sa-Rogol. Last Emperor of the Crimson Dynasty. The Kings Beneath the Mountain, they who ruled a world for ten thousand years, and fell from power before your mayfly race did more than live as beasts among beasts."

The long head went to one side, and the half-human ears cocked forward. "But now let me question you, man of the Wet World. How do you come here, to disturb his rest?"

The blade rose. "And why do you think you can do so, and live?"